The Erenwine Agenda

Paul,

thank you for joining in the creative flow!

Maia

The Erenwine Agenda

a novel

Maia Kumari Gilman

ASEI Arts, a division of Light Vibe LLC
New York

For information, contact:
ASEI Arts, a division of Light Vibe LLC, 112 West 27th Street, Suite 500
New York NY 10001 | email: admin@aseiarts.com

Published by:
ASEI Arts, a division of Light Vibe LLC
New York NY | Distributed by Ingram

Name: Gilman, Maia Kumari, author
Title: *The Erenwine Agenda: a novel* | Maia Kumari Gilman
Description: Second US edition
New York NY: ASEI Arts, a division of Light Vibe LLC, 2017

Identifiers: ISBN 978-0-9988421-3-4 Print
ISBN 978-0-9988421-2-7 Ebook

Design Advisor: Lori Dalvi
www.aseiarts.com

Praise for The Erenwine Agenda

"*The Erenwine Agenda* is a modern work of fiction that addresses many of the issues that face our generations today. In the story of Amalia and Mark we move through many layers and perspectives of innocence, science, lifestyle, idealism, environmentalism, romance and realities in being conscious humans living now, and doing business with corporate interests. Fracking and natural gas are the major focus in how they affect us, as other concerns are addressed. Their story has a surprise ending and thought provoking situations and solutions. This book is a journey of awakening and finding positive ways of taking action to assist a world in environmental distress."

—Janet StraightArrow, Shaman/Owner of Be The Medicine

Praise for The Erenwine Agenda

"A timely and contemporary novel about love and care for the world—*The Erenwine Agenda* helps us understand how we might navigate from a place of non-communication to a place of resolution. The primary characters, who are both of mixed ethnicity but of different cultural backgrounds, live a clashing breakdown of the polarities within themselves and in the environment around them. The story skillfully takes the reader from one event to another until Superstorm Sandy shocks the characters into redefining a new position in the world. The story feels very real as it puts us head on in conversation with ourselves, with the corporate structures that govern our lives, and by extension, with our idealism. *The Erenwine Agenda* crosses disciplines, crosses cultures, and crosses opposing viewpoints to arrive at a more compassionate and empathetic place."

—Raya Ani, Architect/Founder RAW-NYC Architects, 2017 President of American Institute of Architects (AIA) Middle East

Dedication

To the Mountain

A Note about the Novel

In preparation for writing *The Erenwine Agenda*—set in the fall of 2012—I used a wide range of sources published between 2011 and 2013. Current information is available in print and online, made public by corporations, governments, newspapers, non-profits, scientific research institutes, and university publications.

While *The Erenwine Agenda* is a work of fiction, and all energy, architecture, construction and consulting companies mentioned are my own fabrication, both climate change and hydraulic fracturing are real processes that merit observation. This novel does not support one particular organization over another, and the reader will find many perspectives in this work. I encourage the reader to come to an independent conclusion about the issues, and to stay informed about present-day trends and leading-edge advances in energy development and procurement.

It is my vision that readers will be inspired to find a mindful, informed, and solutions-based approach to energy issues in the world.

—Maia Kumari Gilman, Spring 2017

Chapter 1

Thursday, October 18

Amalia Sengupta Erenwine stood in the middle of the gravel lot in Binghamton's Aqua-Terra County Park, and eyed the mud puddles ahead on the trail. Lace-ups were a good start, but she needed something more heavy-duty on her feet. Betsy stood on the far side of the clearing, head bowed over a printed set of Polson Grohman's architectural drawings, in a quiet huddle with the environmental center partners and the gas executives from Atlantia Actuaris.

With Betsy across the clearing and a moment to herself, Amalia could breathe it all in and enjoy it for what it was: a spectacular natural environment. The park gave her a boost of energy; just to be in it was enough. She put the camera in her bag opposite her packed lunch, rested the bag on a tipped-up stone slab at the trailhead, and glanced ahead to see dark clouds gather on the horizon beyond the fall colors of upstate New York.

Trying to let go of her inner conflict with the gas company's investment had drawn it closer, and she found herself facing the reality that her internship in architecture was underwritten by the natural gas industry. Fracking supported her growth as an architect. Her environmentalism turned so awry, so quickly, on her move to New York City.

She turned her face to the sky above and opened her eyes to the autumn trees, their branches uplifted. The ground was soft beneath her feet and the coming breeze felt gentle on her face, warm on her back. She shifted her gaze beyond the trees and looked above them. Looked again. A shimmer expanded above and beyond the trees, a good thirty or forty feet into the sky. Maybe it was the air. Maybe she'd leaned back too far, made herself dizzy. She closed her eyes. Tried to recalibrate. In the background, she heard the hum of an all-terrain vehicle.

The assembled group moved closer—client partners, Betsy, the gas executives—and Amalia returned her focus to the work she'd come to do. To get through her internship she would have to sharpen up. Intern Development Program requirements were strict for architects-in-training, and Day One hadn't gone so well.

Day Two was evolving into a brighter prospect: a visit on site, upstate, and a chance to redeem herself. She stepped forward to shake a hand with the nearest member of the party, one of the gas execs, and her back foot slid beneath her on the muddy terrain. Ground squelched under her and she went down, hard, her fall broken by the yield of wet land. The gas exec reached for her hand and pulled her to her feet. "Thank you." She looked up into his eyes, but couldn't read his expression. Amused? She bristled inside as she tried to brush off the mud, an ineffective act at best. At least she wasn't hurt.

Betsy spoke into Amalia's ear, "All I want you to do is to listen." To the group, she said, "May I suggest we move through our work quickly as the weather is turning gray and we don't want to be stuck in a thunderstorm." Her voice was clipped, and the wind whipped her ponytail and Burberry scarf into her face. Betsy led them back to the parked cars.

"Head into town for something to eat?" It was the man who'd pulled Amalia up by the hand . He winked at her. She'd seen him in the meeting yesterday—Simon? He walked closer, held her arm, opened his car door.

She nodded and got into the low-to-the-ground red Mustang.

She'd driven over from the airport in Betsy's rental, and welcomed the opportunity to be away from Boss Lady for a few minutes. Betsy gave her a look of warning. Amalia pulled the seatbelt around her.

"Last car available on short notice." He turned the key in the ignition and the engine roared to life.

"It's a real babe magnet." Oh god, did she say that? She felt a familiar flush that she commanded to stop but it continued to march up her face.

"Emily, is it? Emily Erenwine, that's a tongue twister. Where you come from?" They still hadn't left the lot.

Amalia fiddled with the stiff edge of her seatbelt. Betsy had pulled out and was around the bend of the access road, now beyond sight and on her way into town. "Amalia. It's my name."

"And where you from, Amalia?"

She knew it wasn't what he meant. "I'm half Asian and half European. Indian and English." Anything to end the conversation and get him to catch up with her boss.

"So you're a half-breed." He smiled and looked at her, then back out at the gravel expanse. "I'm Simon." He revved the engine and peeled out of the parking lot.

She let out a breath she hadn't realized was held inside. "We met in the meeting yesterday."

"The fated meeting. You really know how to pick a fight, don't you? Taking on the gas industry? Come on. What were you thinking?"

Amalia looked out the window to the side of the two-lane country road toward the wildflowers strung out along the side. They passed so fast, the flowers looked like banners. Why engage the creep? The soft sky had turned and rain began to pound Binghamton while an electrical storm hammered in the far distance. She didn't have to answer.

A few minutes down the road, Simon turned left into a parking lot next to a bagel shop with an unpronounceable-looking name. "*Nēzüntōz*," she said, spacing out the sounds. Not so unpronounceable. Simon had fallen silent—had he intuited her creep comment? She got out of the car and trotted to catch up with him, hand over her eyes to shield from the rain.

The six of them squeezed around a café table: Betsy Polson and Amalia; the gas executives—Simon and his colleague, a woman who'd been at the meeting the day before—Samantha, Amalia thought; and the clients behind the environmental center project—a married couple, Jeffrey and Susan. Amalia's throat itched with something she wanted to say. She coughed it down.

"Betsy," Simon said. "Back at the site you said you were confident—but what your office released yesterday triggered us to very nearly pull our funding for the project. Have we got you on board or not?"

"That was not intended for public consumption. Or anyone's consumption. An intern flexing muscle is all it was." Amalia felt a kick to the shin. Betsy did not make eye contact. "And yes, Simon, we are on board with Atlantia's investment. The clients would be nowhere without it," Betsy said.

Susan spoke up. "You should know, Betsy, that we're not certain of your support of natural gas. That could undermine the environmental center. We're looking for you to advise us on this. We need your technical expertise."

"I assure you, we are prepared to do whatever it takes to make this project go ahead smoothly."

Amalia looked down at the tabletop and traced a pattern with a fingertip. Would Polson Grohman Architects and Engineers lose its clients' funding? She'd been selfish to slip her pros and cons spreadsheet into the presentation material. Or had she been just surreptitious, and well-intended? Who was she kidding. She was a one-woman tornado with no clear path, a renegade without an organization to back her cause. Sabotaging her career before she'd barely begun.

Amalia looked up from the tabletop to see Betsy gaze straight at Susan and Jeffrey. "This is how I advise you. Go with gas. It's as green as we're going get on a large-scale, cost-effective basis for the moment. Atlantia's offer to fund you is generous. It's an opportunity to showcase—"

"Betsy," Amalia said, no longer able to keep it in, "if they don't want to use gas, could they go back to the geothermal and solar options? They'd be more sustainable." She tried to hold her attention on Betsy but felt Simon put a hand on her arm. Touchy, he was. Maybe it was ok. He was the one she needed to listen.

"Tell us what you're suggesting, Emily," he said.

"It's Amalia." She'd speak. "If we're not tied to natural gas, then we can avoid the fracking issue. It's killing the earth—"

"This is your problem here, Betsy." It was the woman who'd come with Simon—Amalia was sure now it was Samantha. Simon looked at Samantha and gave a slight head shake. Was he taking a side?

"Amalia spoke out of turn," Betsy said. Amalia felt another sharp jab to the shin and suppressed a wince. "And she does not speak for PGAE."

Amalia put her hands on the table. "Excuse me for a moment? I'm going to use the bathroom." Amalia walked to the back. What was she doing? Sitting with some greasy people and a Boss Lady who kicked her. But, if she could get Simon to listen, then—

She washed up in the restroom and looked up at the light fixture. She'd gone to grad school for green design, an idealistic venture at best, it now seemed. She let her eyes go blurry in an out-of-focus moment, and looked down to see a brown patch on her black suit jacket. Mud.

She couldn't go back to the table, not until she'd figured out what to say. She unlocked the door and stepped back out into the café where they couldn't see her. Amalia's eyes scanned a bulletin board pinned with community notices. She heard Samantha say, "You put a clamp on her, Betsy, and we're good to go," then in Simon's voice, "No, she's an asset."

Amalia focused on the posters in front of her and her hand rifled through the edges of those that overlapped. One stuck out from beneath the others: it had a gold-printed edge, and was on the kind of printer paper one could buy to look fancy, without spending a lot. She tugged at it until it came loose from its push-pin hold.

"Fracking and You: Community Meeting, All Encouraged to Attend."

She whispered the words to herself. The event would be held at a church the next weekend. She folded it small and put it into the tiny breast pocket of her suit jacket. If she couldn't figure out what to say, then at least she could connect with others who knew.

Amalia returned to the table emboldened and stood opposite Simon. "What do the locals think of your investment?"

"Amalia." A warning tone from Betsy.

"No, no, it's a fair question." He smiled at Amalia and stood, came around to her, pulled a chair out for her to sit down. "I like this girl."

"Woman," Samantha said. She straightened in her seat.

"Yes, indeed," he said, and Amalia didn't know whether to laugh or to cringe. She tucked her hair behind one ear and accepted the gesture from him. She sat down. He might know no bounds, but he'd kept the door open to the conversation, unlike Boss Lady.

"I was just wondering what the locals make of their county park being turned into a fracking site."

"Amalia. That. Is. Enough."

"Betsy," Samantha said. "Simon considers her a warm-up for public process." She coughed. "Not that we all agree."

"We're not fracking at the site," Simon said.

"Easy to say, no one's fracking anywhere in New York State right now," Amalia said. "But do you want to? And what about the fact you're fracking in Pennsylvania, right across the border?

You think their New York neighbors won't mind seeing your logo all over their park?"

"Mind? I'd think they'd love it. We'd boost the economy!"

Betsy sat forward. "Your investment could come as a pass-through income source from us. From PGAE."

"Yes," Simon said. "So Polson Grohman appears to be the investor." Thunder clamored for attention on the horizon and Simon looked out. "If that storm lets loose, they won't be running flights from Binghamton this afternoon." He looked back at Betsy. "If you can give us your word you're on board with Atlantia's investment in the project, and you'll give natural gas your architectural 'green endorsement,' then we're good to go." Simon motioned air quotes around the words.

Amalia and Betsy drove through the early darkness in the rental car to Betsy's home in New Jersey, their flight canceled due to bad weather. Amalia agreed the safest course in the current situation was to get to the nearest home, in this case, Betsy's.

Betsy's hands gripped the wheel the whole way—for many hours, her knuckles tight and white. The car illuminated from within every time a lightning flash cracked through the hail, and the glassy light blocked out the orienting view of outside.

"Why didn't you fire me after that yesterday? Or today?" So much respect already lost, she had little to lose by asking.

"Simon spoke up in your defense after you left the office yesterday. But don't push it. I might still fire you."

Curiosity tugged her gut. "What did he say?"

"He said your opinions were not unique, and if we let you vent steam, you might be an asset to the process."

Was that a good thing, or patronizing? Her mind twisted around with it. She was sure she was being manipulated, but she couldn't see or say how.

"Actions, Amalia. Actions speak louder than words. We hired you because you have a certain spark, and training—and I don't believe we have seen the best of you yet."

Amalia looked back from the hailstorm to Betsy's storm-lit face. "Thank you?"

"You remind me of me at your age." Betsy laughed and her hands loosened on the wheel.

Little branches blew down on the roof of the Honda Civic rental as they drove into Betsy's town. "Lots of trees here. Always like this after a big storm."

"Any old growth near you out here?" Amalia strained to see into the darkness beyond the glass of the passenger side window.

"There would have been, in the reservations—but now, I think it's only one area near a private school. And it's getting cut down, or most of it is anyway." The sky was clear but the storm had left its mark on the residential neighborhood—not only did the percussive release of wind-driven branches continue on the car roof, but larger limbs poked out into the dark roadway, making the two-way street a one-lane obstacle course. "You're very quiet."

"I'm stunned. They're cutting down the last stand of old growth forest?"

"For the school to build a parking lot or something, when they extend their building facilities."

"You're kidding."

"It's private property. The Sierra Club's been lobbying to have it protected, and they've been trying to work with the school to come up with some other options."

"Surely the architects would say something?" Her voice squeaked.

"You are so idealistic, Amalia."

"Excuse me?" Her ears prickled with heat.

"Your idealism is marvelous, but you don't have all the answers, so please don't act like you do."

She didn't want to quit but it was beginning to seem like the best path. Better to call it sooner than later. "Am I supposed to talk to Sharon in HR, first? Or should I give you notice tonight?"

"Amalia. There's another way. We're not trying to boot you

out. We want you to stay. Otherwise we'd have fired you after yesterday instead of putting you on probation."

Her eyes stung. She didn't want to quit, but what other way was there? If she quit, she'd be back to square one in her search for a hard-to-find internship, saddled with a wall of student loans she couldn't breach, and unable to get ahead in the career she'd dreamed of since childhood. Not to mention the issue of her grandfather's hospice bills, and her inability to help out—

"We have aggressive environmental and energy goals for all of our projects. We assert those to the clients. We help bring operational costs down. And I think we're doing the best thing for the environment, given the constraints of the projects. I think you should see it through."

"What, my probation?"

"Look. You can jump off the boat and go swim over to some environmentalist raft, or you can stay in it and make a change from inside. I don't care which you do, it's up to you. From where I sit, I see you're going to have a bigger impact if you stay."

"And you're open to my ideas?"

"I am open to reading your report, which you will write at the end of your probation."

Betsy stripped off her jacket and tossed her keys down on the kitchen table, poured herself a helping of—no, a very big helping of—red wine. "Want some?"

"I'll pass. I'm good."

"Really? Your call." Betsy hovered at the counter. Her hands shook around the stem of the glass.

"You okay, Betsy? That was quite some drive."

"I just need to unwind from it all." She took a sip, then a swig, and put the glass down. "Kids are asleep. They're five. Ben's asleep. Don't want to wake him. You okay on the couch?"

"Sure, Betsy, whatever's easiest. I don't need much."

"You sure you don't want a drink?" Betsy sat down with the bottle at the long slab of a kitchen table.

"I'll pour for myself." She reached for the glass Betsy had left for her on the counter. Amalia took a sip. Pretty good. A California red, cheap, one Amalia had taken to housewarming parties when she was a grad student back in Canada. She'd let herself unwind a bit; Betsy seemed more open to talking.

"Glad we made it back," Betsy said. "Took twice as long—should have been three or four hours tops. Quite a day." Her hands had stopped shaking and some color returned to her cheeks.

Amalia smiled. She'd try to be gentle. "I thought you did a great job—handling—the car in the weather."

"And do you think I did a good job of handling the client and investor in our little crisis?"

"I—I'm sorry, Betsy." She took a deep breath and let it out slowly. "I'm happy to be learning from you. I didn't mean for it all to come apart like this."

"And what did you mean?"

"I just meant—wanted—I wanted somebody to state the obvious."

Betsy took a sip and put her glass down hard on the stone. "Which is?"

Amalia inhaled. "Gas isn't green."

Betsy feigned a laugh. She stood up and put the empty wine glass in the sink.

Chapter 2

Mark Stone stood tall at the podium at the Javits Center on Manhattan's West Side and assessed the crowd: a lunchtime group. "I'm Mark Stone and I am a geologist with Atlantia Actuaris. I'd like to welcome you all here to this morning's sessions at the Energy Symposium at the Javits Center. We've had two days of listening to speakers talk about some very vital issues surrounding energy delivery, ranging from solar power to wind turbines, and now I'm going to take you back in time. I'm going to take you back millions of years to the time of the formation of the great shale beds that lie below much of our land." He clicked the remote through to the first slide.

"This is an ESRI image of sedimentary layering in the Atlantic Ocean. How many of you know that the sedimentary layers of the Atlantic came from earlier deposits from what we now call Gondwanaland?" He looked out; the audience was attentive but only a few people nodded their heads.

"Okay." He took a deep breath. "Think back to the first time you played in a sandbox as a kid. Think back. Imagine all the sifting and packing you did with the sand, and imagine this was going to have a transformative effect on the world of the future. It's a pretty amazing thought. At the time, it might've seemed what you were doing was random, but there was some order to it. You had a plan. You had a goal to create a sand castle or a tunnel or at least a pile. You did it by design, a playful design." He continued in spite of a couple of departures from the audience. He knew his words weren't for everyone.

"Think back millions of years to the seabed you see here. Imagine a great force mounding the layers. That's order. It's not the order of a Creationist God or an Evolutionist paradigm. It's an ordering of geologic structure, perhaps with a purpose, perhaps not." He gathered strength.

"There is order here, and it precedes our human scale and sensibilities. It might not have had an interior intention of creating a sand castle or a tunnel, but by its inherent ordering structure, something was set up for the future." He continued through the next set of slides and explained in further detail the formation of the beds and the process of gas extraction as a gentle and benign, worthwhile pursuit. He wove in the statistics he'd practiced the day before, to murmurs from the audience. No challengers. Not that he expected any, from this crowd—many of the audience members were from competing energy companies, also presenting at the forum.

"I believe this inherent order was set up for the future use of humanity. Maybe not intentionally, that's debatable, but it's there and it's of value. We have a tremendous resource base available to us in this time of need, when the earth's population is surpassing expectations for growth. At Atlantia Actuaris, we believe everyone has a right to the same goods and services. Everyone has a right to a warm home in winter, to the ability to get to work on time, whether by car, boat, plane, train, you name it. And as we see it, it's the underlying geologic structure of these shale beds that allows this to happen." There was silence from the audience. He took another deep breath.

"If you ride a bike. You're not only using human power. Think how the bike was made. If you walk or run. How do you think the shoes you're wearing were made? You can even rollerblade to work if you want. I've seen people doing that since I arrived in the city. They go up and down the Hudson River walkways like nobody's business. They're not going on leg power, at least not alone. How did those inline skates get made?" He was on a roll.

"I ask you to consider this: our world at present is linked to this structure beneath our feet. We do have a symbiotic relationship with the earth, which is true; we can only take so much at once. We have to be cognizant. All of you here working for these companies, and all of you, the visiting public, New Yorkers who've chosen to attend today, I ask all of you this: can we imagine a world in which we can walk to work, drive to soccer practice, fly to grandma's house, and in which we can live in coexistence with this natural world around us? I think we can. I believe we can do it together." He stopped, nodded his head. That was it, all he'd prepared. There was light applause. He tapped his index cards on the podium, pocketed them, held up a hand to the audience, mouthed "thank you." He began to back up from the stage.

"What's your stance on the escaping methane gas causing explosions on your sites?" A faceless voice called out.

Mark scanned to see who had spoken, but he could not find the source. He stepped back to the podium and the crowd shifted. His Public Relations department had said he should "respond with a positive take, and not undermine the seriousness of the issues." Make it comfortable; soothe the energy in the room. "Thank you. We do understand there was an impact from some of our work in a discrete area. Atlantia is working with the homeowners to rectify the situation. Because our work is proprietary, as many of my competitors here today know, we cannot divulge specific details." He heard a few murmurs. Not enough to shift the focus.

"That's a whole load of horse shit, if you'll excuse my language." The man stood up. "Part of my dad's house exploded. Do you know what happened?" A camera flashed on him. The man looked like he'd come from an office on his lunch break, clean cut—suit and tie. The man continued and looked straight at Mark. "There was an explosion in his house, while he was home. The insurance company wrote the house off. At least he had insurance. He suffered burns, treatable. He's okay; angry, but okay. He had to move, obviously. And the claim is still up in the air. Insurance says it doesn't cover damage from unregulated industries. Gas company says it's protected under law. That it's protected from releasing specific information about the claim. He did have help from county government. He knew some people."

Mark tried to take a deep breath. "I hear what you're saying, sir, and I'm sorry your father suffered an inconvenience, but there's no connection to horizontal drilling." He stood taller at the podium. An inconvenience? Could he not find a more compassionate word?

"There is a connection." The man pulled out papers from his bag. "This. It explains the connection between my dad's house explosion and an increase in natural gas concentrations due to extraction in the area. Tells how the gas channeling through the concrete borehole casings on the frack site led to the explosion."

He recalled the incident. "That was ages ago. And not related to our company's work, I might add." Mark stood taller. He tried again for a deep inhalation but it came in jagged. "I do understand your family had a circumstance that caused difficulty and I wish you all the best in your recovery."

A woman called out, "What about the cancer clusters in Texas around the wellhead sites? They're saying gas emissions around the frack sites are harming people more than they thought."

Mark knew of the study—it purported a carbon dome over emission sites. The woman didn't have a clue; her generalizations gave her away as a non-specialist. He could move on. He was not prepared to go further, and PR had not prepared him for more.

"We welcome your comments on our Twitter page," he said. "I'm afraid that's all the time we have today, folks. Thank you for your rapt attention." He backed away from the podium, then remembered the free pens he was supposed to give out. It seemed trivial, but this was what he was paid to do. He pulled a company pen from his pocket, held it up to the crowd in a final wave.

Mark stood behind the curtain and accepted a glass of water from a young event organizer. That was all right. Went ok, could have been worse. Pulled out his cell phone, checked his messages. His breathing began to feel normal.

George's voice came through—"we've got trouble with a sub." It was not something Mark got involved with, not unless it shifted across his desk in PR. A subcontractor was not his concern.

He hoped this voice mail message would not translate into a PR issue for him to spin—something George in Engineering would hope Mark could explain away. He felt some envy for George, back of house where Mark had been posted as geologist for the company, until Mark filled in for Simon on a talk, and it went so well they created a new position for him.

He moved onto the next voice mail message. An older woman's voice, a Reverend Mildred, from a church in upstate New York; something about a panel discussion on fracking. Would he do it? Appear on stage, in church?

Curious. Mark saved her message and smiled to himself, amused by the thought of what might come to pass as a result of saying Yes to the invitation.

Chapter 3

Friday, October 19

Amalia awoke on Betsy's sofa, with four wide eyes upon her. The twins. She squinted and came into morning focus. "You must be Betsy's boys. I'm Amalia." She tried to read the identical, stony faces.

One of the boys crossed his arms and glared at her. They burst into laughter. "We know! Our Mom and Dad told us upstairs. They said to wake you up." The boys piled onto the couch next to her. "Can we make a fort with your bed?"

"Maybe you should ask your parents?" she said, and looked around for a distraction. She picked up the nearest book: *Ook and Gluk.*

"It has lots of fart jokes!"

Oh dear. "What are your names?" She put it down.

"I'm Jonathan and he's Jacob. Can we have breakfast now? Are you taking us to school today?" This was a more jubilant start to the day than she'd expected.

"Jonathan! Be nice!" A deep voice came from upstairs. She heard the shower and footsteps between the rooms, morning patter. It sounded melodic, with the staccato of voices in the foreground. "Enough, boys." The gruff voice came around the corner.

"Hi, I'm Ben." He extended a hand. "Welcome. I see you've been greeted by our reception committee."

"You have a lovely family," Amalia said. "Thank you."

"It's no trouble." Betsy came in behind him, dressed and with wet hair. "You need to get moving if we're going to make the train. Shower and clean towels are at the top of the stairs." Betsy herded the twins into the kitchen.

Amalia left for upstairs and found bath towels, shower and solitude. She stepped out of her mud-streaked clothes and turned to look at herself in the mirror of the medicine cabinet over the sink. She didn't need the house in the suburbs, but the partner and babies who would grow up to be hilarious young men? She took a deep breath, undid her bra and slipped out of her underwear. Tested the shower stream with her toes and stepped into the warm flow of water. Solitude spread out in the enveloping steam. The day would be okay.

She stepped out of the shower, dried herself, picked up her shirt. Tried to brush off the dirt but the dried mud caked deeper into the fibers. She remembered the mud on the rock where she'd put down her bag at Aqua-Terra the day before. Wait—her bag—where was her bag? Had she seen it since they got back to Betsy's? Maybe she'd left it in the car. She dressed in her old clothes and headed back downstairs, clean yet unkempt.

Betsy handed Amalia a small plate of scrambled eggs. "Jacob says he wants to take you to see the truck that's outside.

Amalia took the plate and fork and followed Jacob to the front porch. She sat barefoot on the chipped paint of the steps and Jacob sat next to her, close. A truck driver waved from where he stood on the lawn, next to an intake pipe that protruded a few inches from the ground.

"That's the tank truck," Jacob said. "That's where the oil is."

"Oil!" she said, through a mouthful of eggs. "To heat the house?"

"And see the hose? The oil comes from there."

"I see." So Betsy's house was on oil.

"And the pipe? That's what the oil goes into. And then it goes into the ground!" Jacob said.

"Into a tank? Into an underground oil tank?"

"I don't know. Let's go back," he said, and hopped up.

"Ready to go?" Betsy spoke through the bathroom door. "We need to get walking down to the train."

"I don't have my bag. Do you think it could be in the rental car?"

"I didn't see it when we came in last night, but it was dark. Ben, would you mind taking a look outside in the rental car while I say goodbye to the boys?"

Amalia took a long last look at her face in the mirror. Somber. She opened the medicine cabinet: hair elastics, nail snips, mascara. Bug spray. Sunscreen. Baby soap, shampoo and a rubbery bath toy–looking thing. Not much else. What was she looking for? Some clue about how to get into family life, but without the oil tank. It was bad enough the environmental center was sponsored by a natural gas company, but to have Boss Lady's house running on oil? She unlocked the bathroom door and returned to the kitchen.

"No bag." Ben was back from a quick search of the car.

"It might be at the restaurant we were at yesterday. Let's get going or we'll miss the train," Betsy said, and leaned over to kiss her boys whose mouths were full of food. "Bye boys, I love you. Have a great day. I'll see you at aftercare. Love you," she said, and kissed Ben.

"Bye, everyone, nice to meet you. Thank you for having me," she said, even though they'd never invited her. She followed Betsy. Out on the street, Amalia looked back at the house, the first time she'd seen a day-lit view of it.

"It's a 1920s house," Betsy said. "Needs some work, but it's home."

"It's lovely," Amalia said.

"Yes, it is lovely. And it needs a paint job. All in good time."

"You're not planning to paint?"

"We are planning to paint, and to reroof, to reinsulate, and to work on the drainage, and rebuild the chimney. We're also going to replace a large part of the cladding. And that's just on the outside."

"And you have an underground oil tank?"

"We made the mistake of not insisting it be removed before we bought the house. And now we're stuck with it." Betsy pursed her lips at the old home.

"But why not get it out?"

"You know, Amalia, you make a very good point, and I'm thinking about the spreadsheet you snuck into the presentation package the other day." Betsy crossed the street. "The one row of information you were missing there was *Cost*."

Amalia was quiet for the rest of the walk down to the old suburban train station, where high ceilings and stone steps graced the interior. She looked up into the expanse of the building, old and worn, yet still clean and efficient.

"Got your wallet? We can reimburse this." Betsy fiddled with a pendant at her neck.

"In my bag, but I have some cash here," Amalia patted the breast pocket of her suit jacket, full with the flyer she'd folded small up in Binghamton. Amalia bypassed the line up at the wicket in favor of the ticket machine, and when it was her turn, she punched the touch-screen buttons, looked at the selections. *One-way to New York Penn.* Her eyes scanned the list. *Monthly Pass.* What would a monthly pass cost? She pressed the button. Almost a quarter of her month's rent. She went back to the *One-way* ticket option and chose it.

They both looked up when they heard the train approach and ran to join a group of dark-clad people in long trousers and trench coats who gathered at the train doors.

"PATH is cross-honoring your tickets. We are stopping at

Hoboken," the conductor announced over the train speakers. "No trains will be stopping in New York."

"We'll be late to meet the engineer," Betsy said. They climbed the steep stairs up into the belly of the train. "It's close. We might make it."

Betsy pointed out the window. "This is downtown Newark we're coming into now."

The old layers of buildings stepped back from the rail line. The train rumbled over a bridge across a river tributary and the water looked glassy and still. Betsy looked out the window to the right. Amalia noticed their heads angled together, momentarily in sync.

They passed over another bridge, water and rushes on both sides of the train. A solar panel field took up much of the foreground view to one side, and she could make out the new World Trade tower on the horizon in the other direction. "This is a beautiful area, I had no idea it was like this outside the city," Amalia said. "It's idyllic."

"The Meadowlands. The great processing center of industry in the Hudson River Delta. It's tidal all the way up to Poughkeepsie. The river has its own unique ecosystem—the ocean flushes out the delta."

"Is that what they say? That's happening?"

"It's what I feel," Betsy said.

"You have feelings about water?" Amalia looked out at the marshland around them and up to a low ridge. "I do, too," she said, through the glass and to no one in particular.

"Too crowded. Follow me." Passengers queued for the PATH train in Hoboken so Betsy led them out of the fray, to New York Waterways.

"Wall Street or World Financial, ma'am," the clerk said.

"Didn't you used to go uptown? Oh, never mind. World Financial it is." The boat sat in dock, empty of passengers. Amalia looked around the terminal at the curved glulam beams that formed the structure of the ramps, and at the dark concrete and steel of the building above. She peered into the water at the massive footings: no barnacles. She looked again. There were remnant oyster shells embedded in the piers.

A small group of passengers shuffled onto the boat and each person greeted the crew with smiles. Amalia followed Betsy to the top deck and sat outside on a storage container, where the wind whipped her hair into her face and the sun bore down on the water, making her squint. Hoboken looked blurry, and in the other direction, Manhattan slid across the horizon like a silhouette. They took off and the boat bounced hard in spite of the calm day.

Amalia looked up at the new Freedom Tower—the new World Trade. The structure was up; the cladding almost complete. The guts of the building still showed at the top. But it seemed whole, which she thought was good. The building's taper made it seem more elegant than its neighboring counterparts, although it still loomed above. It was the closest she'd been to the WTC site.

They exited the ferry with the other passengers and walked left. In front of them, a surprisingly clamshell-like concrete structure rose from the ground. Grasses edged the solid fringe and beckoned them.

"The Irish Hunger Memorial. We can take a minute. We gained time on the ferry." Betsy moved ahead to the structure and Amalia followed, walked inside. On the left, text on the wall framed the path where they wound through:

and breaking stones...the bits of lighted turf.

On the right, more text:

a brooding stillness.

The memorial wove around them like a blanket.

On the left:

We all live in each other's shadow.

A recorded voice spoke into the dark tunnel: "three hundred million years old, Irish limestone from Kilkenny...the weight of history bearing down...two miles of text, none carved, all appearing in shadow." They stepped into a little shelter and through an arch, and Amalia felt a collapse in her chest. She struggled for air. To her right, a bare hearth. They continued.

On the left, and up: cranes on the new Freedom Tower reflected light off dark glass. And up still: the last pale pink wildflowers of the late-October season. She followed Betsy and came eye to eye with a sparrow, its feathers fluffed in the wind. Children's voices drifted up from the playground across the street. A purple wildflower sprung from the rock in front of her. On her left stood a cairn. Amalia meandered further up the concrete path, afraid to touch the stones, but they invited her.

At the top, she looked at the ferry dock below, and she rested her weight on the rock before her. She had a chill and her hands wrinkled against the dry fall air. New Jersey spread to her left and right across the Hudson. She turned and saw Betsy had gone back, so she did too, and stood before the cottage on the way down. She stopped in the little house, went to the hearth and laid her hands in the space. Felt what might have been the heat of generations before her. Amalia passed through the corridor and felt the weight of words and stone upon her.

At her left:

the roof of the house, falling in and the thatch catching fire.

At her left again:

the potato murrain has unequivocally declared itself in Ireland.

And at her right:

Fever.

The potato famine had been an environmental tragedy. But wasn't it made so much worse than it could have been, by politicians' responses at the time, and by what they thought was the correct thing to do? She wondered what her English ancestors had made of it at the time as she stepped out into the Manhattan day and into the shock of the city.

Betsy had hailed a cab. "So beautiful and so tragic at the same time," Betsy said. Amalia got in. "157th Street exit on the West Side please," Betsy said to the driver. She pulled out a report from her bag and handed it to Amalia, who buckled in for the ride. "Have a look at this while we head uptown," she said. "It'll give you an idea of the project. It's an existing conditions survey of the building with the proposed aspects of the new work."

Amalia scanned the headings and photos as she sat back, her mind still on the impact of the potato famine. Could something have been done differently? A word caught her attention in the report and she sat forward. She read in quick chunks down the page, eyes following her finger where it traced down the lines. "You're putting in geothermal?"

"We're looking into it. That's one of the things we need to talk to Sunil about today when we meet. The surveyors will be there again, too. We need the cellar depth above sea level. And the geotech is going to weigh in later about any underground water. The mechanical engineer will be there this afternoon, but I have to get downtown for a meeting at Landmarks." She paused. "I wonder if you could stay on your own there and finish up."

"I could, yes." For geothermal, she would stay. She'd make this work.

"Write down everyone's questions and bring them back to the office. Don't tell them 'yes' to anything." Betsy pulled out her phone and scrolled through messages, tapped her responses.

Amalia leafed through the document, aware of the Hudson River on her left, the city on her right, and a feeling of ancestors pressing her on. She dug into the report.

Amalia lurched forward into a soft stop when the cab pulled up at a residential street corner. Betsy pulled out her purse to pay. "I still need to find my bag," Amalia said.

"And I still need to deal with the car rental. Call the café we were at." Betsy lost no time in getting out of the cab and slammed the door behind her. Amalia followed down into the old brick building.

"There's a little bit of water on the rock here," Sunil said, "and some cracking along the foundation wall above it. Where this schist ends." He indicated with his flashlight.

"Yes, I saw it last week," Betsy said. "Settling, do you think?"

The air in the cellar was musty and it made Amalia cough. The strong light of the engineer's torch against the stone wall cast long shadows, offset by the dim light of a fluorescent bulb in a socket in the center of the high ceiling. Tall columns punctuated the space; sidewalls of bedrock loomed. And, it turned out, the engineer was—a good looking fellow. The shadows in the space only magnified his sculptured profile.

"How close are we to the subway tunnel?" Sunil pulled a map from his backpack. "There could be some vibration from the train." He traced his finger from south to north on the map. "We'll have to look at the survey to know for sure what the alignment is." He put his hand on the cool rock and stood for several moments without breath. He inhaled. "I feel slight movement."

"Are we going to be ok with the geothermal? If there's already vibration here—is there a risk of seismic activity? We can't have that," Betsy said.

"We can erect a vibration monitor," Sunil said. "We know there's seismic activity. Bear in mind, any drilling at all could trigger a micro-quake. It even happened with water wells, hundreds of years ago."

"And is all that going to be ok with the subway so close?"

"These ones here would be pretty small holes, if we go straight down," Sunil said. They might be six inches in diameter. We don't have the rear yard area for a horizontal geothermal well. It's when the holes are opened with water pressure, to access more heat energy, that the micro-quakes happen. It's a good question for the mechanical engineer, and for the geotech, and for the geothermal installer."

"All right. Let me know what you find in general, and keep the geothermal in mind in particular. I'm going to see if the lift is ready." Betsy extended a hand to Sunil.

Sunil reached out and shook Amalia's hand next. "Nice to meet you. Are you staying around today?"

"I'm going out front with Betsy now. I'd love the opportunity to talk more about geothermal with you. Maybe later?" She turned away, aware of the flush on her cheeks, and hurried to catch up to Betsy, who was already halfway up the stairs. Good project. She might get to talk to a cute guy about bedrock and earthquakes.

"Amalia, when we're up there it's important you stay within the area the lift operator says is safe. Stay focused. We're here for the building, not the guys."

"I know." So transparent, she was. And, glad for the dim light of the staircase.

Betsy waved to the lift operator out on the street. A bright orange lift sat in the middle of the sidewalk. Must have arrived while they'd been in the cellar, Amalia realized.

"Hello, I'm Gracious," said the man with a gentle lilt in his voice. He shook their hands in turn.

"You are indeed Gracious," Betsy said. "Are the surveyors here?"

"I'm the surveyor, ma'am," Gracious said.

"And the lift operator?"

"The lift operator left," he said. "But I know how to operate the lift."

"Are you sure?"

"Yes ma'am, I am a licensed lift operator." He smiled at Amalia. "And, mining engineer, back home."

"I suppose we are in very good hands, then, Gracious," Betsy said. "Take us on up."

They stepped onto the open metal grate of the bucket floor, strapped on, and took the battered hardhats offered by Gracious. One had a *Local 7* sticker on the back and the other had a 9-11 *We Remember* sticker on the front. Amalia put on the 9-11 hardhat and it slid down over her eyes.

"It needs to be adjusted for you." Gracious took the hat from her and slid the headband inside to secure it. She put it on, but it was tight. Betsy fitted her own, and put the hardhat on over her long hair. Pearl earrings glowed on her earlobes below the brim.

Amalia's stomach lurched when the lift jerked up from its base. Gracious guided the lift through the control panel and looked back and forth between the telescoping arm and the building face. Sidewalk and cars slipped farther out of view, and the building passed before them like a mountain cliff. "This is beautiful, look at this brickwork. And what's this?" Amalia pointed to the weave of decorative vines and flowers on the façade.

"Terracotta, architectural glazed terracotta. There's more of it up at the top. That's what we are here to see," Betsy said. "There's water getting into the building and one of the areas we suspect it's coming in is around the old terracotta below the parapet. We need to come up with a cleaning and paint-stripping scheme for it, too. Somebody painted over parts of it. This is good," she said, once they had reached the top. She pulled out a rubber mallet from her bag. "We're going to sound the terracotta. Watch and listen." She tapped the mallet on the surface of the first yellow tile and it gave a dull thump sound. Betsy pulled a sheet out of her bag and marked the elevation drawing with a check mark over the tile drawn in the same location as the one she tapped, and added a *Y* over the square. "For Yellow," she said. "And the check mark is to indicate the tile is sound, and is securely attached."

She tapped the next tile, and marked the sheet with a check mark and G. "For Green," she said. The third tile gave a clear ringing sound when she hit it.

"Sounds like a bell," Amalia said. "It's quite a nice sound."

"Another reason it's called sounding." She marked the sheet with an *X* and a *Y*. "*X* for unsound, and *Y* for Yellow again, as you know." Betsy looked across and down. "We've got seventy feet of tile across the top, and five stories of horizontal brick details and mortar joints, unflashed, still to be surveyed. This could take a while," she said. "How do you feel about doing this on your own after I leave?" She paused. "No, my mistake. Too many open joints and unique conditions here. You don't have enough experience for this," she said. "It's a building survey. You have to know how to do this. We have professional liability at stake here."

"I know."

"We're doing a Local Law 11 survey today, as well as confirming our exterior survey from this lift. If this building fails inspection, the owner will have to put up a sidewalk shed to catch parts if they happen to fall. It's a City ordinance. The City's very proactive about buildings and building safety." Betsy continued the survey for as far as the lift would allow. "Gracious, could you please move us over a few feet?"

"You got it," he said.

They continued to work their way across the front of the building for another hour. "This is more like archeology than architecture," Amalia said.

"In some ways, yes, except we are building new as well, with the renovation on the inside."

"Digging into the bones of the building," Amalia said. She smiled at Gracious, then looked out behind her. The lift had taken them high above the street. Down the hill and out to the west she could see the Hudson River. "Hello, Hudson River," she said.

"Those are the Palisades," Gracious said, and pointed out beyond the Hudson. "Good strong rock there."

"I guess you know about rock," Amalia said. "You do, if you're a mining engineer. What kind of mining were you engineering back home?"

"Petroleum engineering, natural gas engineering. In Nigeria."

"I'm going to have to get back," Betsy said. "We'll finish this later. Gracious, would you take us down?"

On the ground, they untethered and took off their hardhats. Betsy stacked the two together and gave them back to Gracious. Amalia's head hurt where the headband had pressed in, and hurt more after she took off the hardhat. She pulled the elastic from her hair and loosened her ponytail into a fan of hair over her shoulders. Gracious locked the lift and Amalia followed Betsy into the building where back in the cellar they found Sunil.

"I don't know about the system you're going to spec, but I can go over any structural issues when the mechanical engineer gets here. I've got the column grid down." He waved his notepad.

"Here's Suky now," Betsy said. Amalia turned at the sound of footsteps on the cellar stairs. A woman with long black hair and a bright purple anorak walked into the large space. Suky radiated health from inside.

Betsy walked Amalia and Suky to the area below the fluorescent lightbulb, and outlined the goals for the heating and cooling of the project. "We've got a good existing wall assembly here, but we might need to beef it up in some of the rooms, which will affect the equipment," Betsy said. Suky nodded and unzipped her purple backpack, took out a spiral-bound notepad and began to write notes. "Please connect with Sunil before you go to find out the borehole possibilities. You still don't have your bag. Take some money. Make sure you take a break for lunch, Amalia." She fished out a wad of twenties from her wallet. "The 1/9 is at 157th and Broadway; just make sure you get on the downtown side of the tracks."

"Thank you." Amalia put the round wad of money in her outside breast pocket, lips tight.

"I'll see you back at the office after my Landmarks meeting." Betsy waved goodbye to the group and walked out up the cellar stairs.

Amalia looked over toward Sunil. She'd hoped to grab a coffee with him, but it would have to wait.

She followed Suky. The women worked their way down inside the building, roof to cellar, and considered its heating, cooling and powering. The door to the roof was unlocked, stuck; with a double thrust of both of their bodies against the door, they were able to force it open. Amalia stumbled and caught her balance.

"This restoration is going to be featured in a book. We can't allow for any media slip-ups on the job." Suky stopped and watched Amalia's face before she continued. "We're still figuring out some of the viability of the geothermal system, and of the solar on the roof. It's something of a demonstration project. We can't have any leaks on the job."

"Building leaks or media leaks?"

"Amalia, I heard about your spreadsheet. It's not the kind of thing we want to get out. It could damage the success of this project."

"But that was about the environmental center." She scratched her shoulder.

"I know, that's what I told Betsy. I'm letting you know," Suky said. "Little actions go a long way in this business. New York's a small town, if you know what I mean."

After the walkthrough and with a quick nod goodbye to Suky, Amalia descended to the cellar to look for Sunil. He was gone, had finished his work. She walked up to 157th as instructed, and took the 1/9 train downtown. Where did the energy come from to make the trains? And run them? For how long? Where were they going, as a society? She let her eyes drift down the interior of the train car.

A woman, very pregnant, walked down the aisle. She clutched a cardboard sign. The train rocked and the woman swayed from one pole to the next. Amalia looked at her face. She was trying to maintain her balance, her inner gyroscope knocked out by the train's movement. She walked in front of Amalia and stood, held onto the pole. Amalia looked at her sign.

MONEY OR MORAL SUPPORT APPRECIATED

The train jerked to the side and the woman lost her balance, fell toward Amalia. Amalia reached out and grabbed the woman's hand in her own. "Won't you please sit down? It's not good for the baby." Amalia's hands remained in the woman's, clutched.

The woman nodded and looked relieved to be off her feet. She sat next to Amalia and smiled, then bowed her head. "Thank you."

"Of course," Amalia said. "How far along are you?"

"Seven months," the woman said. "The baby moves over and over, he doesn't stop," she said. "I'm worried. I'm on the train all day and night."

"You've got to get off the train; it can't be good for the baby." Amalia felt panic rise in her throat, sour and unwanted. She looked around to see that no one was paying them any attention at all.

"I'm scared to go back to the shelter." The woman lowered her voice. "I got slashed up there." She showed Amalia the scar.

"Don't you have any family?"

"They—we are Catholic. I cannot tell them. I am all alone here."

Amalia shivered. She couldn't leave the woman like this, on the train. "What's your name? I'm Amalia."

"Rose. I'm Rose."

She couldn't bring someone home from the train. Amalia put a finger into her little breast pocket and pulled out some money. She gave Rose twenty dollars, kissed her on the cheek, and got up and walked away and off the train as the doors pulled open at 110th Street, almost fifty blocks before her stop.

Amalia ran up the broken subway station steps into the brightness of the day, grayed over with imminent rain. Why run? Her heart felt cobwebby and unclear. She walked fast and turned a corner, looked up at the stony visage of the Cathedral of St. John the Divine. Couldn't handle it, not after what the church had done to Rose. Driven her underground.

She walked right and saw an awning cantilevered out from a storefront wall. *Hungarian Pastry Shop*. That would do. She looked in; it had a safe, warm glow. Thank goodness. It had begun to rain, and hard. With a yank on the door she entered and stepped up to the counter. Asked the woman with long liquid eyeliner for a macchiato coffee. She looked around at the scene: colored tables, old lights and beaten chairs, well worn by the butts of many. A student hangout. She turned to watch the rain hit the old awning; the door opened beneath it and a tall, thin man walked in, his jacket collar pulled high over his head in an attempt to simulate an umbrella.

He looked like a wet puppy. No, maybe a wet otter. Wet, and animal, to be sure. She smiled. He pulled the jacket down and straightened it and his hair before he came up to the counter. He broke out into a grin when he saw her looking. The Wet Otter. Something familiar about his look, but she couldn't place it. Wait. Yes. He'd been standing outside her office, her first day on the job.

He waved to the liquid eyeliner lady who was busy at the other end. "I'll have an espresso." He turned to Amalia. She stared back at him, then looked away. Didn't know anything about him, had no context for him. One had to play it safe in Manhattan. Right?

He took his coffee from the counter in front of them.

She turned to Liquid Eyes and asked for a paper take-out cup. Her gut twisted with a No! when she poured the coffee into the new cup, but she ignored it, and drained the mug. "I don't know what to do. I'm in knots."

"Are you ok? Sit with me." He looked over his shoulder at the now heavy rain outside.

Amalia leaned on the counter and let out a loud sigh. "If you must know. I almost lost my new internship for standing up for what I believe, I had to shadow my boss, who's intense, I haven't slept in my own bed in two days, haven't changed my clothes. I held hands with a destitute pregnant woman in the subway, and I'm mad at the Catholic Church."

"Sit?" It was no longer a command.

She sat. "Can I borrow your phone?" He obliged, slid it across the table between them. She searched the number for Nēzüntōz and called to ask if they had found her bag. No. Anger turned to overwhelm. She stood and pushed the phone back to him. "Thank you." She walked around the table toward the door, felt his eyes on her back. She waved without a look.

Outside on the street, the rain had eased and pattered down on the awnings and sidewalk. She was closer to home than to work. Could she ask the building superintendent to let her into her apartment? He had a spare set of keys in his basement hang-out.

She walked the thirty blocks back home, in the drizzle. She was already wet. Maybe that was why Rose lived on the train. At least she could stay dry. Amalia turned around. She should go back to Rose. No. She'd walked away. No going back.

She pushed on and found Jerry's space, called out to him. Another voice answered over loud classical music. "Not here!"

"I need to get into my apartment," she said. "There should be a spare key. I'm Amalia Erenwine? My name won't be there."

"No name, no key. No ID, no key." Strains of violin rose in the background.

"I don't have my ID, it's lost, and the apartment isn't in my name, it's in someone else's name. I'm subletting." This had never been a problem with Jerry before.

"Sorry, miss. Jerry's coming back tomorrow. If I could give you the key I would, but if I do, I could get into a lot of trouble."

Amalia's eyes welled up. She nodded. A tear fell, and then a few more. The man gave her a tissue and she wiped her eyes, blew her nose. "It's not your fault. You're just doing your job." She listened as the music changed its pace. "This is nice. It's sad, though."

"It's Bach. You know Bach?"

"Of course I know Bach," she said, but this was unlike any Bach she had ever heard before. He handed her an old record cover. "*Jascha Heifetz: Partita No. 2 in D Minor.* This Bach, this made me cry."

"Maybe the Bach didn't make you cry. Maybe life made you cry."

"Maybe." She turned to exit the basement stairwell for the light of day. Twenty-two more blocks to the office.

Once there, Amalia wove through the cubicles to her desk and sat down, flicked her computer's mouse to turn on the screen. She waited while the machine fired up, cast a glance at her new colleagues across the office. Jen worked on a computer drawing. Betsy's business partner Max Grohman was in his office in an open-door meeting with Sharon. Betsy was still out at Landmarks. Amalia clicked through after the computer lit up, and saw an email sent from Betsy's phone.

Need you to start looking at paint-stripping and terracotta cleaning for the condo. Pull up the MSDS research and we'll go over it Monday.—Betsy

P.S. For the probation report, I want you to make it more than a list of what you observed this week, I want you to tell me how you would manifest your ideals. Make it real. Give me some examples. Due Monday.

Fine. There was an email from Simon to the team. It summarized the meeting upstate.

Endorsed

caught her attention. There was an email from Suky with details of the geothermal system to be specified on the condo conversion. Nothing from Sunil.

She looked again at Simon's email. Was her bag in his car? He would have written to her about it, wouldn't he? His cell phone number was appended to the email signature. "Simon? It's Amalia Erenwine, from PGAE. From the environmental center meetings." She spoke to his voice mail. "Just wondering if you have my bag." Where was Simon—still in town, in a hotel? Gone back to Atlantia's headquarters in Philadelphia? Maybe she could stay with him. It was a possibility. What would everyone say if they knew she'd crashed with Simon?

She looked again at Betsy's email. There were challenges to get specific about information and to clarify her thoughts. Could she do it? She sat upright and stretched out her arms to the side.

She spent the rest of the day on terracotta research online, and pulled together file after file of cleaning specifications and product data sheets. Some of the best cleaning came through the use of methylene chloride, and the more she read, the more ill she felt. Looked up at Jen, who had her head ducked down into her own work.

The building and its terracotta were so beautiful and delicate. Needed a careful facial cleanse, not to be defaced or defiled by this methylene chloride. She read it would work. It would remove the paint spots. It would remove traces of graffiti, but what else would it do? When she looked at the data sheet for information, she read a long list of possible causes for concern.

Cancer. Respiratory problems. Fatality.

She searched online for more information, read the Environmental Protection Agency's pages, and the Occupation Safety and Health Administration's—OSHA's. Methylene chloride, it turned out, was an endocrine disruptor in animals and humans. It messed up reproduction. The chemical name rang a bell but she couldn't place it.

Methylene chloride.

There was so much back and forth in the disputes about the accuracy of the information she'd read about fracking, she couldn't be sure. Was it one of the thousands of ingredients injected into the earth, and spewed back up with waste water, then reinjected back into the ground in a new location for disposal?

She made some notes on the pad next to her. Jotted:

Find another way, away from this. Swim in the other direction.

She'd heard someone say, "What you resist, persists." Wasn't sure it was true. Was she not beholden, as an environmentalist, to pay attention to the wrongs, to define them, to shine a light on them for others to see?

Whatever. No time for analysis. Just needed to get the information together. She dug further online and found there were alternatives to paint stripping. It didn't have to be all methylene chloride. There were less toxic options. Did they work as well? She printed out those sheets and saved the PDFs in a folder on the server, ready for her Monday morning meeting with Betsy.

Amalia went home with Jen to Brooklyn, a short ride on the

F train to Boerum Hill. "You can sleep here." Jen pointed to the couch.

"Your roommate's ok with it?"

"Paige is away."

"This is great, thanks so much." Amalia took off her suit jacket and laid it on the edge of the couch. "Where are your rooms?"

"Down the hall. It's a one bedroom."

"You share a room? How does that work?"

"Pretty well. She's my girlfriend."

"Oh! I didn't know. It's—will Paige mind me being here?"

"No, not unless you hit on me." Jen laughed, fracturing her serious tone. "Turn off the light in the hall before you turn in? I'm a light sleeper." Jen waved goodnight, pulled her dark hair down from its workday ponytail, and went down the bright hall to her room.

So this was a Friday evening in Brooklyn. Amalia kicked off her shoes, turned off the hallway light, and lay down for what she hoped would be a solid night's sleep.

Chapter 4

She took something of him with her when she walked out of the restaurant. Mark sat for more espressos and drew in his sketchbook; drew her face from memory. It seemed the thing to do in this place, so he did it, not because he was inspired, but to occupy his hands, and to doodle. Okay, inspired.

Her eyes. Gold-flecked, dark-brown and wide. He looked up at the rain.

Why had she said she was mad at the Catholic Church? How could one be mad at something so large and grand? It didn't make sense. To be mad at the Church was akin to being mad at geology. It was there. It developed over a long time. It wasn't perfect, but it held them up.

Chapter 5

Saturday, October 20

Amalia looked up from the couch in Jen's apartment at the cozy clutter mounded in the shadows, a bag of folded laundry. Three shirts hung ready on an ironing board.

She rolled over to face the kitchen peninsula next to where she'd slept. It loomed high above her, cliff-like. She felt underwater. The dream she'd been in now interwove with the abruptness of her waking.

Amalia glanced at the dim streetlight through red curtains.

A blue whale loomed in her mind's eye, a relic of the night's dream.

The whale was sick, as were others. What made them sick? Sonar testing could damage their systems, but this dream was about something else—it was about something in the water. She felt a surge behind her. One of the blue whales nudged her.

She rolled over onto the floor, then pushed herself up to stand. She had to go.

Should she wake up Jen? It was so early, the sun still hidden behind the Brooklyn horizon. Amalia opened the laptop that sat on the peninsula and woke it from its hibernation. She typed in bus company information to get to upstate New York and saw that if she left right then, she could get to the community meeting. She looked awful in her muddy, many-days-old outfit. Jen wouldn't mind if she borrowed some clothes.

She eyed the bag of laundry. Yes. Slid the toggle over the string. The first garment on top was a dark t-shirt. That would do. She shoved her hand down the side and felt around. Cords. Fine. She stripped down to bare and put on the t-shirt and cords. Threw her suit jacket on top, and buttoned it once. She rolled up her dirty clothes into a ball and put them at the end of the peninsula. Wrote a quick note to Jen at the bottom of a receipt she found on the counter. Once at the door, she put bare feet into her sensible shoes, and slipped out. She left the door unlocked.

Amalia hustled up the stairs of Jen's garden apartment to the sidewalk, and shivered in the fall morning air. With a glance back at the nineteenth-century brownstone row house, she ran. No time for exploration.

She caught the F train at Bergen over the bridge from Brooklyn and up to the Port Authority in time to catch the bus.

Chapter 6

"Shale gas in North Korea."

Mark looked down and his eyes scanned across the centerfold of *The Economist* magazine. So there was shale gas in North Korea. He wondered what his geologist counterparts were up to there. They wouldn't have to answer to the public.

He looked up at the line of passengers that filtered onto the bus. Squinted, made out a woman's silhouette in the sodium lights of the Port Authority bus lanes. It was her again. He stood and moved the roses he'd brought, waved to the empty seat next to him, but she hesitated. Long black hair spread across her shoulders, over a little black suit jacket.

"You're—" she said, and moved down the aisle to a spare seat halfway down on the right.

Fine. He sat back down, his legs bent at the knees like a grasshopper's. She had some problem. Not his problem. He opened the magazine and went back to read about shale gas in North Korea. After Manhattan, beyond the Lincoln Tunnel, the bus groaned into highway speed.

He stirred when the bus shifted gears. They pulled off the highway to the county road that led upstate. Mark's thoughts wandered outside and his eyes shifted from near focus to far. A

Deer Crossing sign. He shuddered and closed his eyes, sent a word of prayer up for his parents.

He felt the bus slow and heard the driver mutter, so he looked up. A small red light lay on the ground ahead. The bus advanced and Mark saw the light was a road flare. A fire truck came into view around the mountain bend. Deep below, the Marcellus Shale.

The bus slowed and Mark got a look past the fire truck. An ambulance. He couldn't see what else. A passenger stood up behind him. "Oh my god!" He looked over his shoulder, and saw the woman stand up and look out the window as the bus pulled to a stop. She covered her mouth with her hands. Mark stood up and looked out the front windshield but didn't want to look to the side.

"Do they need help? I'm a doctor." A man stood up at the back. The bus driver had gone and returned and was back with an eye-witness account.

"Be my guest. There's one volunteer firefighter out there on the road—and a couple of paramedics with the ambulance." The bus driver let the man off. "I'm going to radio headquarters and see what we're supposed to do. I can't get around."

Mark couldn't see; didn't want to. He sat down. He wasn't a doctor or a paramedic. Just a shale-gas geologist with no accident skills.

"Stay back behind the flares." The doors opened with a hydraulic gasp and the passengers filtered off the bus. Mark stayed where he was and the woman came up, put a hand on the back of his seat.

"You ok?" She leaned over him when another passenger squeezed behind her, and her purple shirt—the writing on her chest—peeked out from underneath her suit jacket.

"I'm fine. You shouldn't go out there." He inhaled and caught her scent, but he hadn't meant to. Baby powder. Maybe he had meant to. She walked past and down the bus steps. He steeled himself and stood up, followed her and her baby powder–scented purple t-shirt out to the two-lane county road. Past the fire truck, beyond the flares, before the ambulance—he smelled it before he saw it—charred car parts and animal hair—a mid-sized car, once beige, flipped upside down, the front half crumpled into black. Something white stuck out the window of the car. Air bags. Something rounded at the front, beneath—the remains of the deer.

The woman in the purple shirt stood next to him, her hand over her mouth. "The driver lived? He must have crawled out the window before the fire." She looked at Mark. "You ok?"

He didn't feel the attraction to her anymore, even though she stood close enough to touch. Felt only the sad pit in his midsection and he tried to keep it closed. He knew he had to face it, and he turned to her. "My parents—died in a car accident."

"Here, come with me. Away from this." She pulled him by the sleeve toward the mountain side of the road, away from the car, by the side of the bus. "Do you want to sit inside?"

"No, but I want to get something from inside." He waved to the driver to let him back on and grabbed his pack along with the magazine and roses from the front where he'd sat. The woman in the purple shirt waited for him between the mountain cliff side and the bus, out of view of the accident.

He turned to look at her, took a breath. It felt right, so he took a chance. "They died three years ago. Coming up four this winter. Kancamagus Highway. It's in the White Mountains. New Hampshire."

She nodded. "And the flowers?"

A siren came up around the bend and passed the bus, stopped in front of the fire truck. "Police are here now." He put the backpack on the ground, held onto the flowers. "What are you doing on the bus?"

"I have a meeting." She squatted on the gravel road shoulder. "Sit? We're going to be here for a while." She unbuttoned her jacket and nodded to the flowers. "So who are the roses for?"

"I'm single," he said, then wished he had not. He held the roses to his chest, and the magazine slipped out from his armpit to the ground. He squatted next to her, balanced on four fingers and his feet, solid on the side of the road. *Shale gas in North Korea* splayed across the gravel. "What does your shirt mean?"

She looked down at *Free Pussy Riot!* written in large letters across her chest. "Hah!" She'd ignored the I'm Single comment.

"What, did you get dressed with your eyes closed?"

"Something like that." She stood up again and crossed her arms, towered over him where he perched. "Chilly, now, this time of year."

"You an activist or something?" He tried to conceal his interest in her. She'd already rejected him twice. No, three times. Didn't want to screw it up. "How come you're out here?" When she didn't clarify, he said, "I have a thing," and put the roses on the magazine, on the ground.

Chapter 7

Amalia squatted down, sat cross-legged in the gravel and looked up at the underbelly of the bus; her eyes went fuzzy on *Coach USA* written on the side of it. Thought of the whales in her dream. Funny this fellow had shown up again. But, Suky had said yesterday that New York was a small town; maybe this was what she'd meant.

Amalia regarded the man next to her and could see he was eager to continue their conversation. He was in a new context now. She should ask where he was from. No, she shouldn't—she hated when people asked her that. "Where are you from?" She winced at her own lack of verbal discipline.

"New Hampshire, but I live in the Philadelphia area. You?"

"Pennsylvania. I'm from Canada before." She waited for the usual retort of No, Where Are You Really From? But the retort didn't come.

The man kicked a heel into the gravel and his arms encircled bent knees. "I'm mixed. My parents are Indian and English."

"No way, me too!" she said. "I thought there was something familiar about you. I'm half Bengali."

"Ah, I see," he said. "And I'm half Abenaki."

"What part of India?"

"Not India. New Hampshire. Native."

She wished she could brush away the heat from within her cheeks. "You still look familiar," she said. "Like me. One of your parents was English?"

"English and French. They're with me every day."

"Really? In spirit?" She turned to look at him.

After the driver of the bus reoriented the vehicle in a three-point turn, the assembled group of passengers shuffled back on board. The seats, unclaimed, offered a new canvas for arrangement, and the man sat down first, Amalia next to him.

Chapter 8

Mark spotted his ride waving, an older woman who stood in front of the Greyhound Bus Station in Binghamton, New York. She had one hand on the door of an aqua-green Oldsmobile. "You said I should wear a red rose so you'd know me, but they didn't have just one." He handed her the bouquet.

"Surely, for the young lady, not for me," she said, and waved the roses toward the Pussy Riot woman from the bus. "It's nice to meet you both. I'm Mildred."

"I'm Amalia."

"Nice to meet you," Mark said. He looked at Amalia. "I'm Mark."

Mildred looked at him. "You two don't know each other?"

"Can we drop off Amalia at a local address? She said it's near the bus station."

"I have it, I have it here." Amalia pulled a worn flyer from her jacket pocket and read, "Mercy Church. On the map it looked close. Across the river?"

"That's where we're going," Mildred said. "Mercy Church. Hop in. That's where the discussion is." She started the car and pulled out into the main street of the old town.

Amalia swatted Mark on the shoulder from the back seat. "I

guess we're going to the same meeting, then. Why didn't you say your thing was a meeting? It's the meeting about fracking."

"We have an Alcoholics Anonymous meeting at the same time, but we hope they'll join us when they are done," Mildred said.

"Are you going to the AA meeting?" Amalia shifted in the back seat.

"No, it's the fracking meeting," he said. Why would she think he was going to the AA meeting? He popped a breath mint.

"Very nice of Mildred to pick you up. How come you got a ride? Not that I'm questioning it, I'm very happy to have a ride, too."

"He's the guest speaker," Mildred said.

"One of the guest speakers."

"No, you're the guest speaker, my dear. The others backed out."

"You're the guest speaker at the fracking meeting? About what, exactly?"

"I'm speaking based on my experience as a geologist in the Northeast. I'm not speaking with any affiliated group," he said. "I'm the only speaker, Mildred? I thought this was going to be a panel discussion." His sights changed from that of an easy afternoon to one of heightened focus.

Mildred looked at him then out the window at the river where they'd crossed. "We thought so, too, Mr. Stone, but we had cancellations. One couldn't fly over because of yesterday's thunderstorms. Another was sick. And another said her company wouldn't let her, and she was very sorry about it. That leaves us with you. Unless Amalia would also like to sit on the panel? Do you have something you'd like to say about fracking, dear?"

Amalia sat forward again. "I have something, yes. But I'm not a scientist. I'm an architect. I'm not an architect. I studied architecture and I'm an intern."

"Architect, eh? I like to think I know a thing or two about architecture. Daddy sold kit homes across the continent."

"I'm not an architect. You can't call me that."

"Dear, whatever you are, it sounds like you have something you'd like to say, and I'll take an architect on my panel," Mildred said. "Where do you work? New York City? You came off the bus together."

"New York City, yes, but I'm not an architect. Call me an intern."

"So you'll do it?" Mildred looked up into the rearview mirror.

Mark looked at Amalia over his shoulder. This would be interesting.

"Ok, I'll do it."

And yes, the afternoon had become more interesting. He smiled to himself.

"In the nick of time," Mildred said, and turned off the main drag onto Walnut Street, pulled into the handicapped parking spot that also read, *The Reverend Mildred McCaine.*

"You're the Reverend," Amalia said.

"You're looking at her." Mildred shut off the ignition. "Chief Bottle Washer and The Reverend Mildred here. Come on, kids, we've got no minutes to spare." She flicked the blue handicapped parking tag that hung from her car's rearview mirror. Mark grabbed the roses from the back seat. "Glaucoma—best thing that ever happened to me in getting good parking spots!"

Mildred led them into the old stone church and down into a large meeting room, punctuated with columns and full of seated guests. High windows beamed afternoon light into the space. "Fellowship Hall. I like to call it The Room of Real Life," Mildred said. "Sometimes it seems the work I do in the Main Sanctuary is all for the support of what happens in this room." Mildred waved to a man on the other side. "Frankie, a new chair for our second speaker, please."

Frankie brought over a chair and lined it up next to Mark's. "We thought there was going to be one of you." He handed Mildred a small foil package from his sweatshirt pocket.

"Not now, Frankie, goodness!" She patted her hips as if to

look for a pocket, didn't find one, so passed the package to Mark, who tucked it under his chair. Mildred turned to the group of a hundred or so villagers, and clapped her hands. "I'd like to offer a blessing over this space and all who have come here today, to allow us the grace of heart we desire in seeing each other's views, each other's opinions, and each other's higher purposes in being here as we set forth in our first Meeting on Community Issues." Mildred closed her hands in a moment of prayer. "Welcome. We're gathered here today to hear two experts discuss hydraulic fracturing, or fracking. This is Mark Stone, a geologist, and Amalia—"

"—Erenwine," Amalia said.

"—an architect. Amalia, Mark, tell the audience about yourselves. And then we will take your questions. I have the list." She squinted at a sheet she pulled from her pocket. "I have 32 of you who wish to speak, so far. I will call you in the order written here, which is the order in which you submitted your questions. Anyone else wishing to speak, line up here and wait your turn. Please: be concise, be polite. Let's begin!"

Mark pushed the bunch of roses under his chair next to the foil packet and stood up. "I'm Mark Stone, a geologist with a natural gas producer here in the Northeast. As for myself, I'm from Moultonborough, New Hampshire. I'm here to answer your questions as best as I can based on my experience in geology. I'm not able to answer questions related to my company."

"Why not?" A man called out from the audience.

"Because I'm not authorized by my company to do so. I'm speaking about geology." He sat down.

"And Amalia will introduce herself," Mildred said.

Amalia looked at Mark, and her face reddened. "I thought you said you were a geologist." Amalia appeared to have come unhinged at the jawbone, but he saw her shift, and she collected herself. She took a long breath in, stood up. Looked at Mark, then out again. She wiped her palms down the front of her cords, straightened her suit jacket. "I'm Amalia Erenwine and I am an architectural intern from New York City. Actually, I'm from Canada, but more recently from Philadelphia."

"And what do you have to share about fracking? Tell us," Mildred said.

"I've been researching fracking. And I studied green building." She sat down.

Mark looked out at the audience. A rougher crowd than had been at the Javits; more worried faces, fewer suits. He was more concerned about his cohort on the panel than the audience—at least from the crowd, he had an idea of what to expect.

"Let's take the first question, shall we?" Mildred looked at her index cards. "The first person with a question is Margaret." She motioned for Margaret to stand up.

"Hi there. I'm Margaret. My question is for my sister who lives in Pennsylvania across the border in the Northern Tier. She's been getting headaches since the frack wells went in. She wants to know what you have to say. This question is for Mark Stone." She sat back down in her chair.

"Hi, thanks." Mark began to stand up and then sat back down. "I'm sorry your sister is having headaches. But I'm not a doctor, I'm a geologist. I can't say how that will resolve."

Amalia stood up. "I'm not a doctor either, but I don't have to be to know fracking causes headaches and much worse afflictions too. This whole fracking process is out of control and must be stopped!" She raised a fist in the air, stretched the buttonhole on her suit jacket. She looked around the room. A couple of people applauded. The rest glared. She sat down.

"Margaret, maybe you can tell us how your sister got her headaches, that might help," Mildred said.

Margaret nodded. "After the well bores went in a few years ago, my sister and her children started to notice a funny smell. They saw the laundry was yellowing. At first they didn't think anything of it. They started to get headaches. The smell continued. They contacted the gas company who said it was the water company's fault. They contacted the water company who said it was the gas company's fault. They contacted their doctor, and another doctor, and the health insurance company. And the gas company brought in bottled water for them, but didn't say why. My sister's headaches are still getting worse and worse. And now, they don't know who to turn to."

Amalia leaned forward. "Why don't they ask their neighbors and get together to file a law suit?"

"They don't talk like that. They don't believe in lawsuits." Margaret said.

"But they need to rally!" Amalia said.

Mark raised a hand. "If I may. There is a public process in place at most of the gas companies these days. Your sister can write to the gas company head office and get a response within days."

"You mean a response like this?" Margaret held up a piece of printed paper. "What good is a form letter when you have children to feed and a farm to tend? I'm here as her voice. And Mark Stone, if you don't have an answer for us today, I'm going to—to write your name down in my little black book of officials to report to the media." Margaret sat back down.

Mark opened his mouth to reply but Mildred held up a hand. "Next question! Oliver. Where's Oliver. Did you bring us something good to eat?"

"You can all come down to Oliver's for a good old steak dinner after this. Is this being recorded? Oh good, Frankie's got the video on." He waved to the camera. "Oliver's! On Main Street." He turned back to the panel at the front. "Folks, this is a big deal. From what I understand, hydrofracking can cause water to catch fire, and people have died because of it. Shouldn't we ban fracking within our county boundaries?" This met with a boo from some and applause from others. Amalia stood up.

"Please," she said. "Yes, it does cause water to catch fire, and yes, you should organize a ban in the county. But the state might override your ban, that's the problem."

Mark stood up. "I'm sorry, no, we need to clear this up. Fracking does not cause water to catch fire. That's a myth. What happens is in some limited cases, a small amount of methane gas escapes from a shale bed—and it can build up in the ground or in the water. This is a natural process, by the way. It happens to be augmented by human activity. Methane is flammable, so if you go so far as to light a match near it, it will cause a small fire." He sat back down. "Think of the gag where someone lights a match behind someone passing gas."

Oliver didn't seem to think this was funny. "My customers wouldn't want to drink that water. I serve tap water all day long in my restaurant," he said. "How am I going to assure people it's safe to drink if we know there's fracking going on in the area?"

"A very good question, Oliver," Mildred said. "We wouldn't want to drink your water." She looked at Mark and Amalia.

"The water is getting poisoned not only from the methane," Amalia said. "It's also getting poisoned by the chemicals in the fracking fluid. Did you know there are hundreds of products added to frack fluid by the different companies? Some of them are carcinogenic."

"And some of them are as benign as walnut hulls and instant coffee," Mark said.

"And more attention should be given to the carcinogenic ones," she said, and looked at Mark.

"What are we talking about here? What kind of chemicals?" A man from the audience spoke from his seat, front and center.

"Benzene and toluene are some of the more well-known ones," Amalia said. "I don't know them all, and in fact, they haven't even all been disclosed, but I can tell you about one. It's called methylene chloride. I know about it from my work." She straightened up. "In my work in the city, I research different products that the architects I work for end up specifying for using in building projects. One of the products that came up in my research this week was methylene chloride, which is used in some strong paint strippers. I think it's also been detected on some fracking sites."

"You think—" Mark said.

"No, not you, dear," Mildred said. "Let Amalia finish."

"I don't have the MSDS with me now, the Material Safety Data Sheet, I mean the sheet that explains the safety aspects of the materials, but from what I can remember, and don't quote me on this, but methylene chloride can cause death in some cases? And it can cause cardiac abnormalities in more situations, and it's a potential carcinogen." Amalia sat down.

"Potential," Mark said.

"And headaches? What about headaches," Margaret said.

"I haven't researched it totally, I only read the data sheets," Amalia said.

"Get your facts straight before you come here, then," the front and center man called out from the audience again. "We don't need more of a runaround. We've had enough talkback for now."

"What's the sheet? I'd like it," Margaret said.

Amalia stood up. "You can ask any chemical manufacturer for their MSDS on any product they sell. Most of them are available online. There's also a Technical Data Sheet. Knowledge is power, people."

Margaret stood up. "So why don't we have all the information on all the chemicals the gas companies are using?"

"It's the government's fault," Frankie said from behind the video camera.

"If I may," Mark said. "The chemicals used are proprietary in some cases."

"Proprietary my ass!" Oliver said. "I'll tell you what proprietary is. Proprietary is when someone asks me for a recipe. They're asking for my work. But for real? If I were put under subpoena to give the recipe, would I give it? Of course I would. Why? Because it's the only thing to do. We serve the public, not the other way around."

"You're a restaurant," Mark said, "and we're talking about mega corporations that run the gas industry."

"Yes, speaking of mega corporations," Amalia said, "aren't you with one of them?"

"We do have a government report," Mildred said. "It lists the known chemicals. I have it in my office."

"The problem is some of the gas companies are using third party products in their fluids," Amalia said, "and the third parties won't disclose to the gas companies what's in them."

"But isn't that irresponsible? I would think it's not even legal," Oliver said.

"You're right," Amalia said. "It's irresponsible. And apparently, it is legal. Until proven otherwise. Or until the law changes."

"Next question!" Mildred said. "Frankie."

"Isn't it true the natural gas supply could be got by terrorists?" Frankie shifted from foot to foot where he stood with the video camera.

"I'm not sure what that has to do with hydraulic fracturing," Mark said.

"I'll take this one," Oliver said from the crowd. "Any part of our energy supply could be had, and with the increase in production, it only increases the likelihood of an attack."

"It's not going to come to that," Mark said. "The energy supply of the country is very secure, and by increasing our domestic production, we reduce the instances of overseas interventions."

"Please," Amalia said. "Interventions? Just say wars!"

The three men in red t-shirts came in late and stood at the back of the hall. Mark saw

Jobs!

written across their chests. He looked at the men and saw their statures: proud, defiant, and below it all, strong-shouldered with their feet braced against the floor.

"Welcome, boys, come on in," Mildred said. "I have you on the list, I got the questions you sent, and you're in time, you're next. Everyone, these gentlemen have come from a rally in Albany!"

They looked back and forth at each other and one spoke. "How can we make sure the jobs stay in the community once fracking comes back to New York? We've heard they sometimes hire from out of state, at least for the rig and trucking jobs. I can understand for the mineralogy jobs, but even then, I'm sure we've got lots of qualified folks from around here who've studied engineering. We need the jobs created here, to stay here. To go to local people." He looked at Mildred, who looked at Amalia and Mark.

"If I may," Mark said, "the gas companies do want to hire locally, and it's to their advantage to do so. Local expertise can make a project go more smoothly, whether it's because of knowing the roads, or the subterrain. They've got a package they bring in, and it's honed for efficiency. That allows them to generate the jobs in the first place. The local trucking companies could advertise to the gas companies, to make it known they have the expertise. I think the gas companies are open. Same with colleges. They could pitch to companies to sponsor classes."

"I'm sorry, did you say the gas companies should sponsor classes?" Amalia stood up. "You can't let the gas companies come in and run the institutions! Do you have any idea of how much of a muddle that will create?"

"You might be muddled," Mark said, "but it's a good idea."

"Ma'am," the man said, "I can see this is a shock to you, but are you aware of the number of unemployed in this region?" Crossed his arms so his biceps pushed forward on the sleeves of his red t-shirt. "People have lost touch with the land, and big companies have come in and hired people to push paper all day. If we're going to save ourselves, we need to get back to the land. And if the economy doesn't support farming, we're going to do it through fracking. It's our birthright to work the land. Some of us have been here for generations, and we know this land like nobody does."

"Angel is next," Mildred said.

Angel stood up with her question. "We should organize a ban on fracking." She sat down. "And that woman said the state would override a ban. What about it?" She crossed her legs and swung the top foot back and forth, hard.

"Thank you, Angel," Mildred said. "Very succinct. Do we have a response from each of our panelists?"

"Yes, I believe you should organize a ban," Amalia said. "It's also a very effective way to raise awareness of the issues, and it will prevent homeowners from striking random deals with gas companies that could undermine the whole community. There hasn't been enough research done about the effects on water, for one. But even so, there shouldn't be fracking. It's killing the earth." She took a deep breath. "At least the churches and temples could divest, like universities are doing." She looked at Mildred. "What do you say, Mildred?"

"We're a non-partisan church. We don't take sides."

"But you could," Amalia said. "You're in a position of power." Mark saw her straighten her shoulders. She appeared to gain some steam from the conversation; he wasn't sure which way the discussion would go. Wasn't sure he wanted to see. No, he did. Decided to listen. He'd wait it out.

The man in red spoke up. "Lady, you can't ban fracking. If one neighbor signs and another doesn't, the gas companies are still going to take the gas. They can go underground if more than something like 65% of the area's signed up."

"When a church divests and goes to another form of energy, it's so powerful. It sends a message when individuals can't." Amalia stood up, hands on her hips.

"Is it true fracking can happen even if homeowners don't want it?" Angel posed the question, looked at Mark.

"It may well be true," Mark said. That's the sort of gray area in debate with some of the companies and the local legislatures around the country. Here's the thing. I don't think a ban is a good use of your time. For one, it's ineffective. As Amalia said earlier, the state can override it. Two, it's shortsighted. Why would you put off exploration that's bound to happen? Three, it's mean-fisted. You're cutting off a viable source of income to landowners who want to sell the mineral rights to their land. It's all a waste of time. And divestment is—"

"—the only reasonable response." Amalia cut him off; her voice rose in the silent room. "We've got all number of problems coming from fracking, with water, earthquakes, cancers, you name it. You could ban fracking through a zoning resolution if you don't like the divestment option."

"You need to be more specific," Mark said. "You're making yourself look foolish."

"No, she's got it." Margaret stood up at her chair. "I don't like the way you're talking down to her. We do have cancer clusters in the areas where fracking's been going on. And it is documented. I agree, she should have her facts together, but that doesn't give you an excuse to put her down. The health impacts from fracking are documented. There's lots of nonpartisan groups running studies, and state and federal government agencies, too. Maybe like she said, a ban could be through a local zoning resolution, or maybe it could be through a state-level bill. What we need is the science. I have the current research here," she said, and lifted a large canvas tote bag up off the floor. "This is the tip of the iceberg of what we ought to be collecting."

"Ok, so you have some studies you've printed off from the internet at the library."

"No wait, I agree with her," Amalia said. "You can't go putting people down for lack of science. That's the whole point. We don't have enough science to know what's going on. If we had clear scientific evidence before us that there were no problems, would we even be here today? I don't think so. Take it down a notch, Mark. Get off your high horse."

"Do you feel better now, Amalia? Because getting emotional about this isn't going to solve any conflicts," he said. "I can't see how finger pointing is going to answer anyone's questions."

"All right," Mildred said. "Next question. Manny."

Manny and a little girl stood up, and Manny read from a handwritten page.

"We live in another town. My house is near an injection site, where the chemical water is put back into the rock after it's used." He looked up, then back at the paper. "My wife has had three miscarriages. We do not know how to prove it. We cannot agitate. We must remain quiet because of—because of—" he stroked his young daughter's hair. "We might not be able to stay," he said.

Mildred motioned for Frankie to turn off the video camera.

Amalia looked at the girl, half her father's height. "You are very brave to come here today," she said. "I'm so sorry your mommy lost three babies." She sat back down.

Mark looked at the man, felt a jab inside, and stood up. "If there is a connection between your wife's miscarriages and the frack fluid, then of course something should be done. But without proper toxicology reports on the fetus, there is no way to tell. I'm not a doctor, as I said before, but I speak with enough toxicologists in my work to know what they would say."

Amalia looked at Mark. "How can you be so cold?" She crossed her arms.

The girl spoke to her father, and he whispered back to her. She looked at Amalia and Mark. "We have saved the blood." There was a gasp from the audience. "It is in the freezer," she said.

Amalia looked at Mark. "Surely there is something we can suggest?"

He looked back at her and was silent. Where the jab in his ribs had been, was now a spot of calm. He felt suspended, a momentary lapse of awareness of his position in time and space.

"Why don't we take a short break now," Mildred said. "We could all use a breather. We have many more people on my list, and a lineup along the back wall. I'll write your names and you can sit down." The group of standees broke up and the screech of chairs on the old linoleum floor signaled the end of the first half.

Chapter 9

Amalia stood in the basement kitchen of the church, alone with Mark.

"We have to clear something up," Mark said. "It's not fracking causing all these problems. It's the after-effect of fracking and it's controllable. It's the way the wastewater is being dealt with."

"No," Amalia said. "You have to look at the big picture, you know, Seven Generations and all, Mr. Abenaki."

"You can't throw my ethnicity around. Besides, I'm only half." He didn't look too happy.

"It's fine to be half native and not care about the earth? And it's fine to be a geologist and pretend you're doing something sustainable? I don't think so, Mark." She felt herself heat up inside.

"What does being half anything have to do with anything? That's your problem, not mine. That's the issue. Your issue. And as for being a geologist, it's quite a righteous way to serve the earth."

"Serve the earth? Oh, come on! You can't believe you're serving the earth by working for a chemical company. You sold out."

"Oh, I sold out? Well—it has nothing to do with the color of my skin."

"We're the same color," she said.

"Yet you think you're so much better than me," Mark said.

"You keep saying we're the same, but you know what? We're not. You can stop throwing Seven Generations in my face. I know more about my people than you ever will about yours."

"You don't know anything about me. If you could for a moment step outside the viewpoint of this gas company you work for, you'd see we're more on the same page." She inhaled a lungful of air. "I don't know why we're fighting. It's not like we can figure this all out by ourselves."

"Thank you, Ms. Pussy Riot. That is the first sensible thing you've said all day."

"Excuse me? I've been on this panel all afternoon answering question after question as best I can. I'm not an expert. I don't even know how I ended up doing this." She blinked and stopped for breath. "You know, I forgot my bag up here." She looked up and out the window. "When I came up for work on Thursday."

"Right." He leaned on the wall. "The phone call you made from my cell. What are you working on up here?"

"An environmental center. The one I mentioned on the panel."

"Of course you are."

"And it was supposed to be sponsored by Atlantia Actuaris."

"Oh?"

"And I may have screwed up the deal."

"I see. So you're projecting your guilt on me?"

"No, I'm trying to tell you something. We need this project to go ahead and I don't see how it can be a proper environmental center if it's funded by the gas industry."

"So you did something to screw up this deal? Simon said something about you being in trouble."

"What?"

"The other day. I saw you. Before the coffee shop time. Simon and Samantha were coming out of a meeting, and they said you were in hot water. They even pointed to you when you were up the block."

"Simon and Samantha? You know them?"

"I work with them. They came out of the building after you."

"So—you work for Atlantia Actuaris?"

"Yes. I do."

"And when were you going to tell me?"

"If you'd slow down long enough to give me a chance, you might learn a thing or two."

Amalia felt it in her gut; an inner belly flip let her know she was still in the middle of it, in spite of a strong wish to be away from him, and away from the church.

Mark continued. "So you did something to screw up this deal?"

"Come on. I didn't do it on purpose." Her heart raced. "I was trying to tell the truth, something you don't seem to know a lot about." Told herself to keep at it in spite of the voice tremor that welled up inside, deep in her throat.

"What? I'm telling the truth! Amalia, how do you propose to provide enough power for the millions of people in the Northeast or the millions in the country? Sure, there's other options, but they're not developed. This is the best we can do for our country."

"Two minutes!" Mildred popped her head around the corner into the kitchen. "We're very excited to continue with both of you." She grabbed the kettle from the stove and filled it with tap water. "For the roses," she said, and left with the kettle slung low.

"I'm starving." Amalia looked around the bare kitchen. "Maybe we should go to Oliver's? Escape while we can?"

Mark gave her a look of disapproval.

"I don't know how to answer these questions. How do you do this all day?"

"I don't do this all day. I'm a geologist."

"Who's responsible for this mess, then?"

"It's not a mess," he said. "It's a PR situation."

She looked at him, mouth open. How could he be so blind? Amalia put her hands on her hips and took a step away from the wall, back from Mark. Reminded herself to breathe.

Mildred came back into the kitchen. "Ready to go?"

Amalia took another deep breath. "We need to shift."

"You got that straight," Mark said.

"You two need some Reiki to calm you down." Mildred closed her eyes, paused for a moment, then came forward and put a hand on the top of each of their heads. "I ask that the clear stream of Reiki be passed through me in a blessing for these two in their journey of understanding together, and that they be able to move forward without holding up the rest of us." She snorted a laugh and withdrew her hands. "That ought to work." Mildred brushed her hands to the side as if she could sweep away the discontents of the afternoon.

"Can I try something?" Amalia smoothed her hair where Mildred's hand had laid.

"Be my guest, it can't get any worse," Mark said.

"It's not a matter of worse," Mildred said. "It's unfolding."

"Unraveling, you mean," Mark said. "Let me guess: you want everyone to sit in a circle and hold hands and say what they love about this place."

"How did you know?" How did he know? That was weird. Amalia was surprised he'd guessed.

"I may have a timer in here somewhere. We could give each person three minutes to talk," Mildred said.

"That will take forever," Mark said. "We can't."

"What if we break into groups? We could each take a group. If we split up into three, it'll still take two or three hours, but we have time," Mildred said.

"No, it's too long. No meeting should take more than an hour if it's going to be productive," Amalia said. She was relieved to feel determined about something.

"You have to allow some time for the process." Mildred opened the cupboard over the church kitchen stove. "Here it is." She held up the egg timer.

"Are we going to do this? I don't think this is a very good idea," Mark said.

"Why not?" Mildred turned the egg timer upside down on the

counter. "It might loosen things up. It's a great idea," she said, and nodded to Amalia.

"Thank you, Mildred. I'm glad someone thinks I have some good ideas."

"I still sense some tension here. You two need to get yourselves clear before you speak to the group. No hotheads here. We are a group of peace. Three laps each," she said, and pointed to the stairs. "It's a small lot."

"What?" They both spoke at the same time. Amalia couldn't quite believe it. Wasn't going to budge.

"You heard me. Three laps each of the back parking lot before you begin. That should knock the edges off."

"Fine." Mark walked to the stairs.

Good grief. "If he's fine with it, I'm fine with it," Amalia said. No way was she going to let him take higher moral ground.

Mark walked up the stairs, pushed open the emergency exit and held the door open for Amalia, then took off to the right.

Mildred followed them. Amalia ran left. Such silliness. What had she got into? The two passed in front of the trees at the back of the parking lot, too stunned to snipe at each other. They passed again in front of the church exit doors. Crossed at the trees, and again at the church. Mildred let the door close behind them when they were done. The parking lot was full of cars and Amalia saw a few out-of-state license plates. They distracted her from her irritation, for those moments alone.

They walked back, shorter of breath, into the room. Amalia looked sidelong at Mark, who took his seat. He stripped off his fleece vest to reveal a full chest of graph paper–printed wrinkle-free cotton, rolled up the vest to put it under the chair, and pulled the roses out from underneath it. He jumped up and put the flowers in the kettle of water Mildred had left on the side table.

Mildred put the egg timer on the table and turned it over. "Now sit here in silence for three minutes and consider your duty."

Mark looked at her. "I'm sorry?"

"Your duty. What it means to you. Time is running out," Mildred said, and pointed to the egg timer.

Amalia looked at Mark and opened her mouth to speak.

He put a finger to his lips, then shook his head, pointed to the timer.

Fine. Amalia sat down on the metal chair and took off her jacket in the hot room. She looked down at the text. *Free Pussy Riot!* screamed from her chest. She hung her jacket on the back of the chair.

"*Free Pussy Riot!*" Mildred said. "Do I have a t-shirt for you! My old Greenham Common t-shirt."

Amalia shrugged.

What was her duty?

She had to speak up for the earth, for the water. But why? Because of the dream she'd had about blue whales? It was her grandfather's mesothelioma. She had a need for his life to be redeemed, to be held up, to be made an example. Didn't want it to happen to others, not again.

She'd felt a warm charge from Mildred's hand that alarmed her but had felt familiar, too, so she'd stood with it, in silence, and had breathed it in. She recalled the feeling as she sat there in the chair, heartbeat still fast from the parking lot run.

That feeling. Familiar. Her mind scanned back to a visit with Grandfather in Calcutta, when it was Calcutta, and not Kolkata. Kali Temple. Priest smudged sandalwood on her third eye. Seemed to see through her. But there was warmth. And allowing.

She took a deep breath. She could allow it.

She wasn't so good at speaking. Researching was easier. If she hid behind facts and books and articles, how would anyone ever hear her voice? She'd tried to write the spreadsheet and it had not gone well. Why not? Maybe because she was trying to fit into someone else's vision, someone else's message.

What was her duty? To clarify her own message so she could speak more on behalf of people like her grandfather, and for the land, and the waters and the earth. She could do it. She could clarify. She could speak and she could write.

She didn't only want to write about fracking. Wasn't that the whole point of being at the meeting, and of writing the spreadsheet? Was there more than fracking in her line of sight?

Chapter 10

Mark couldn't focus on the task at hand. Instead, he was seized by anger at Mildred's co-opting of the church for her own political means. And to think she'd influenced so many innocent people in the process. Amalia, too.

He kicked back his heels beneath the seat and hit Mildred's foil-wrapped lunch remains and they skidded out from beneath the chair; he rose to grab the package, looked across the room to the trash bin and aimed. Still got it, got the touch. He smiled and went back to his seat.

What was his duty? Was it a construct of ego? And if it was, what did it mean for his time here? His time anywhere?

He was off duty, so he wasn't representing the company. He thought back to his employment contract. Was there anything in it that said he wasn't supposed to speak outside of the company's limits? He was not there to represent the company's interests.

Or was he? He'd slid into PR speak. Of course, he had to defend the industry; it was being attacked, and so by extension was his job. His livelihood. But what was his duty? It was his duty to defend the company, but there was the bigger duty of being brother and mother and father to Timmy and there was duty to his church.

He mulled it over. Didn't have a church anymore. He wasn't a

Catholic with a Capital C, only with a little c. And what was left? He felt abandoned by the church. Abandoned by the Pope. He'd never even met the Pope. How could he feel abandoned by him? There was a deep hole in his chest that felt liquid and hot. His heart. He tried to calm down, to not panic.

He'd felt something akin to his mother's touch when Mildred put her hand on him, a vague and distant sensation in his memory. He recalled the sweat lodges they'd attended in his teens, on family vacations, across the country. The thought roused him to attention. Felt the hot, sweet air of the sweat lodge enter his mouth, throat, windpipe. Swallowed it into his lungs.

Chapter 11

Amalia took steps to maintain her dignity in front of Mark. Breathed in, felt herself planted and grounded. Tried to both shield herself from him and also welcome the opportunity for dialogue. This mix left her more confused, so she sat down and tried to do nothing.

She watched the assembled group settle into three circles of companionship and newness; took her place in one of the circles, while Mark and Mildred did the same. The door from the main sanctuary opened and a small group of people walked in. Amalia looked up and watched them assess the crowd.

"Come on in!" Mildred welcomed them with a wave from where she sat. "Pick a spot and have a seat on the floor in one of the groups."

Some of them filtered through to Amalia's group. "Hi. I'm Bob." The man sat down cross-legged on the floor, inside the circle of chairs set up around Amalia's circle.

"What do you love about this place, Bob? We're doing an exercise," Amalia said.

"I love that it supported me even when the rest of my life was torn to shreds."

"And you?" Amalia turned to the woman who'd come in with him.

"I'm Hailey."

"And what do you love about the land here?"

"I love. I love that it provides the vegetables and plants I use to dye my wool. And that it grows my beautiful sheep, which provide my wool. And I love that I have a new chance every day to do this over again, better and better." She looked at another man who'd come in with them.

"I'm Hank," he said, "and I'm an alcoholic. Are we supposed to say that here?"

"It's ok," Amalia said.

"It's important. Isn't this the fracking meeting? It's bloody important," he said. "I think the oil and gas industry's abusing the earth like I used to abuse alcohol. I think we're addicted."

"So it's not the industry that's the problem," Hailey said. "The industry is the enabler. We're the ones causing the problem. We're the users."

"The industry is enabling our addiction to oil and gas," Hank said.

"Yes! Well said." Hailey clapped.

"Maybe we're in a codependent relationship with the petroleum industry," Bob said.

"Or maybe we're in a codependent relationship with the earth," Hailey said.

"You make it sound like a bad thing," Hank said. "Our relationship to the earth is a good thing, necessary. It's life-giving."

"Ok, so we're in a dependent relationship with the earth, and a codependent relationship with the petroleum industry," Hailey said, "and fracking is an inciting incident that triggers a bad string of events within the enabling relationship. I also want to say," she said across the hall, "that I love you, Mildred, for holding this circle."

"It's not me," Mildred said, "it's Amalia over there, and Mark. They're the ones who had the idea. I brought the egg timer. Oh! I forgot about the egg timer," Mildred said, and swept it off the floor with her palm.

"I'm Sunny. This is Amreeta, my mom. We've come from Virginia." Amreeta and Sunny sat next to each other, their knees touched, older woman pressed into younger son.

"You've come from Virginia? For this meeting," Amalia said.

"Yes. My mom prayed for what to do for a long time. And then I found this meeting online when I was surfing one night, and I showed it to her. She said this is it. So we came." He turned and whispered something to his mom in a language that to Amalia's half-trained ear sounded like Bengali. Amreeta patted Sunny on the knee and brought her palms together before her face in a gesture of prayer. "My mom wants me to say this. My father worked as a petroleum engineer in Iraq, in Northern Iraq. He loved the land there so much, as much as he loved the land in West Bengal, in India, where he and my mom lived." He stopped.

"What happened to your father, Sunny?" Amalia thought it was okay to probe. He'd brought it up, after all.

"He was sent by the Iraqi army to fight in Kuwait. My mom says he loved that land as much as the land in Iraq, even though he was fighting there. He defected to the other side, to the Kuwaiti side." He looked at Amreeta, who nodded. "He was killed in the war. And he is honored in the Kuwaiti Martyr's Gallery." Sunny looked down and fiddled with his backpack. "I was very little then."

Amreeta spoke. "He would have loved this land in America all the same. The lands are not divided. The land and sea are one."

"Ma, there are the tectonic plates," he said.

"It's people who divide the lands," his mother said. "It's not what the land wants to do."

"I understand." Amalia nodded. "And what do you think, Sunny?"

"I love the US. But we lived in Sweden for a while too, and I loved it, as much. But war? I don't know what it feels like." He looked down and fingered the buckle that hung from his backpack. "I try to feel it."

"You try to feel war?"

"I try to feel how my father felt. I try to feel how he felt about his home in India, and how he felt about being sent to work in Iraq. I try to feel how he felt when he worked in the oilfields near Basra. And I try to feel how he felt when he was forced by the Iraqi army to fight in Kuwait." He took a deep breath. "I try to feel how it felt to die away from home. I try to feel how it felt to die on soil he loved." He stopped and turned to look at his mother, and then unzipped his backpack.

"What do you have there?" Amalia pointed to the folded contraption Sunny pulled from his bag. The folds, unfolded. The fabric, the straps, so old and used she could hear them crunch.

"Oh my god, he's got a bomb!" Hailey pushed herself up to stand. "Call 911!"

"I'm sorry! I'm sorry! I didn't mean to scare you! Please don't call the police. It's fine." The whole room stopped its dialogue and the three groups disassembled.

Some people stood, some sat on chairs turned around. Two people pulled out cell phones and dialed, spoke into them. Most stared at Sunny without comment.

Amreeta looked at the old, faded object in Sunny's hands and slapped him on the face. "What did you bring that for?" She stood up with her hands on her hips and shook a finger at the men who stood over Sunny. She grabbed Sunny's hair in her fist. "This boy is very silly!"

Mildred walked over to Amreeta. "What's going on?" Frankie followed, hand in his sweatshirt pocket.

"Tell them, son." Amreeta held tight to Sunny's hair.

Sunny cowered in his mother's grip. "I saved this gas mask from Kuwait. It's the one my father used. It's the only thing I have to help me make any sense of things." He shifted. "This is kind of why we're here, actually. It's what my mother was praying about."

"Your mother was praying about gas masks?" Mildred looked at Amreeta, who stood planted with her son's hair still in her fist.

Sunny looked up at his mother and winced when he angled his head. "Please, Ma?"

She let go and exhaled, stood over him, arms crossed. "Stand up and address this crowd," she said.

He stood. "I'm so sorry. My mother was praying for me to get a good job." He smoothed his hair. "I graduated from engineering and I'm going for the petroleum jobs in the Northeast. There's a lot of work for someone like me. I could help take care of the family." He looked at Amreeta. "She's very concerned about me getting a safe job. And what we're reading doesn't sound so safe."

"Depends what you're reading," Mark said. "What are you reading?"

"OSHA reports. From the Occupational Safety and Health Administration," he said. "Workplace safety—that's what she's concerned about."

A siren wail drifted from blocks away.

"And the reports—" Mildred said.

"It looks like the jobs in natural gas are a bit sketchy, but the engineering side is more or less safe," he said.

"What did the reports say, Sunny? More specifically?" Amalia repeated Mildred's question. The siren wail grew louder with proximity.

"They said because of unregulated chemical use, workers are exposed to toxins and they can't protect worker safety as they should because there are too many unknowns."

"That doesn't sound too good, son," Oliver said. "I'd listen to your mom."

The siren approached the parking lot and the sheriff's car pulled up to Mercy Church. A radio crackled outside the door and Amalia saw the sheriff look sidelong through a corner of the window. "We've got people in the church." His voice could be heard through the glass. "I don't see the assailant." The emergency exit doors swung out. He took long steps down the stairs into the hall, drew his gun at the crowd and panned from side to side. "Hands up!"

"Oh my god, he's got a gun!"

All hands went up. Sunny's backpack fell to the floor, and the gas mask slid from his lap. "It's a misunderstanding," Sunny said.

Amalia and Mark followed Mildred and Officer Barnes through Mercy Church. Officer Barnes took out his notebook and pen and straightened his back, hat forward on his bald head. "So you're not going to press charges?"

"Goodness no, of course not," Mildred said.

"Do you have some ID on you? Operating Permit?"

"In the office, yes, but do you need it?" Mildred stood a little closer to Amalia, who wondered if there was anything she could say or do to help. She'd felt more connected to Mildred since the Reiki. Wished she could return the favor.

"I do, ma'am. A complaint like this requires it."

"But it's not a complaint, it was a misunderstanding," Amalia said.

"It's gone down in the system as a complaint, and the 911 transcript will have it recorded as a bomb threat. We need ID. And your Operating Permit for a place of assembly of more than a hundred. You had well over a hundred today. Good turnout, by the way."

"All right, Officer. Officer Barnes, is it?" She peered at the tag on his chest. "Follow me," Mildred said, and left the hall to go up to the sanctuary.

"A small congregation meets here." She waved her hand over the old wooden pews. "We hold community meetings. AA and that sort of thing." She indicated the small panels of stained glass up high.

"It's beautiful," Amalia said. She glanced at Mark who seemed more focused on Officer Barnes.

"I was married here," Officer Barnes said.

"Must have been before my time." Mildred exited the sanctuary on the other side and flipped on the ceiling light in her office.

She took her purse out from below her desk where she'd left it. "Here's my New York driver's license."

"And I'll need to see your Operating Permit."

"What?" Amalia noticed Mildred's cheeks flush red. Mark coughed.

"Your permit from the Binghamton Fire Department. The one that says you're allowed to run this place, Ma'am."

"I have my certificate." She went to a filing cabinet and poked around. "Think like a librarian, my sister Muriel always says." Mildred put a large manila envelope with Canadian stamps down on the desk.

"Are you going to open it?" Officer Barnes looked down at the envelope.

"It's from Canada."

"Your Operating Permit is from Canada?"

"No, I'm a licensed reverend in Canada. In BC. I just keep it in the original envelope." Amalia took note; Mildred was from British Columbia, too? They had that in common. She'd have to ask—

"And where is your local Operating Permit?"

"Mildred?" Mark's tone was gentle and Amalia wondered what he could say to make it better. "You don't have a local permit." It was a statement more than a question.

"Please don't tell anyone." Mildred looked at Mark, eyes wide, cheeks bright.

"Don't tell anyone? You're running an illegal operation here, and there's been a bomb threat," Officer Barnes said. "And you don't want me to tell anyone? Are you asking me to lie on your behalf?"

"No, officer, of course not. It's just—it's just—we're doing good work here. People are opening up. It means something." She sat down. "Are you going to arrest me?" She looked up at him with wide eyes.

"Do you have anyone you can call? Your husband?"

"My husband passed away," she said. "Last year. We moved here for his dialysis."

"They don't have dialysis in Canada?" The officer looked up out the window.

"Of course they do, it was just too long a wait. So we came here."

"Ma'am, do you have legal residency in this country?"

She nodded. "We were citizens in both countries. My husband taught here at Binghamton University before we moved back to Canada."

"Thank goodness. Otherwise we'd be deporting you."

"So you're not going to arrest me?"

"If you report yourself to the Fire Department and get an Operating Permit, that should be fine. I'll give you thirty days. In the meantime, you can't hold any more meetings here, or run any more services, not until you get straightened out."

"Ok." She exhaled, and Mark put an arm around her shoulders.

Amalia stood next to Mark, who considered the odd still life arrangement on the table before them: egg timer, roses, gas mask. He took a picture with his phone.

"You need Jesus in there too." Amalia pointed to the crucifix on the wall behind the table.

Mark looked up. "I don't know. I'm not sure he would approve. We're not being very brotherly or peaceful about any of this."

"You mean in Kuwait, like Sunny was talking about? And in Iraq?"

"Sure, in war, but here too. I mean the fracking companies are clawing at the earth like they're tearing at their own clothes. And the fracking protesters are erecting signs and barriers with the same panicky motions."

"You're with a gas company," Amalia said.

"I am. And we're so misrepresented."

"Look, you're the job guys and you're the power guys. You hold all the cards here."

"We don't hold the cards at all. Nobody owns any of the land like it's theirs for all time."

"You mean the leases? You have the land leases for a short time?"

"No, I mean any of us," Mark said. "All of us. We're here on borrowed time, on a planet we need to sustain. There are plenty of people in these companies who want to do good. Look, the rock can handle it. It's the people I'm not so sure of."

"What are we talking about?" Mildred came up to the table. "You know Officer Barnes said we all have to go."

"Mark was—"

"Nothing." Mark straightened up and looked at Amalia. "I was saying nothing."

Amalia pulled Mildred into a big embrace at the Greyhound station. "This was quite the day."

Mark stepped closer behind her and joined in the embrace. "Thank you, Mildred. Good luck with the church."

Mildred handed Amalia a bag of take-out from Oliver's. "You two are tremendous together. Don't screw it up." She passed Mark a plastic bag of red roses. "You keep half, I don't need this many," she said. Mark put them in the top of his backpack; Amalia carried the gas mask under her arm like a football, tucked into the fold of her suit jacket. A gift from Sunny, who said he no longer wanted it, his need for it passed in the release of the meeting. "Wait!" Mildred ran back to the church and returned with the egg timer. "You'll need this." She gave it to Amalia.

Amalia and Mark got on the Coach USA bus together, and sat side by side. "Should be enough light left to see the trees in fall color," she said. They settled into their seats in silence. He closed his eyes and pushed his head back into the headrest. She sighed.

"Sleepy? Do you have a magazine or something I could read? I didn't bring anything."

"Sure." He pulled out a couple of trade journals and a copy of *The Economist*. "How about *ArcNews?* Exciting details about mapping."

"Actually, that sounds good." She opened it in front of her; it was so big it blocked the entire view out the front window of the bus. The headline at the centerfold was positioned over a texturized map dotted with colorful blobs. "This isn't like any map I've ever seen."

"They spatialize data using GIS. You know GIS? This one's an ESRI map. It's software I use at work."

"I know GIS. Geographic Information Systems." She gave him the magazine and twisted out of her black jacket, folded it and put it overhead. "Ok," she said, hands extended. "May I have the magazine back, please?"

"I thought you were offering me a hug." He handed it to her. "So, are you going to tell me what's up with your t-shirt?"

"Oh, you know Pussy Riot. They're the Riot Grrrl band from Russia? You know? They got arrested for freedom of speech."

"How does one get arrested for freedom of speech?"

The bus pulled out from the curb into the street. "It's not even my shirt." She pulled out the bag of take-out from near his feet and opened it on the tableau of *ArcNews* magazine. "So how do you frack? I mean, how does it happen?"

"An easier topic for us, for sure." She wanted to know; she'd wait until he spoke. He looked uncomfortable and then said, "Ok. You've seen the diagrams?"

"Yes, cross-sections of the earth. They freak me out, so close to the water table."

"No—they're careful when they do it."

"Honestly, Mark? How can they be? How can they know for sure? And this 'they'—it's 'you'!"

"It's George in the engineering department, it's his group, it's not me." He twisted in his seat to look right at her.

The bus pulled into the Port Authority after the sun had set and Manhattan continued to shine with electric light. They went out onto the street. "Shall we see if Jerry's there? At your apartment?" Mark had made an attempt to be gracious.

"Bus. Uptown." Amalia led him over to Tenth Avenue where they caught the M11 and he followed her to seats at the back. She looked out the window. "How did you end up at the Hungarian Pastry Shop that day? I forgot to ask you."

He pulled out a little rectangle of paper from his bag and handed it to her.

Holy Name Church
St. Mary of the Angels Chapel
Celebrate Water, Celebrat Life!
Presentation on Fracking

She first noticed the typo. And then fracking. She looked up. Holy Name? "Is this near where we met?"

"I was on my way there. I was skipping out of the rest of the conference."

"And you never made it to this presentation at Holy Name."

"At the last minute I decided to go to St. John the Divine. Just for the church. But it started to rain, hard, so I ducked into the coffee shop. And saw you."

The bus pulled up near her place and they got off, walked over to Amalia's apartment. She tried the front street door, which was locked. They went to the side and down the cellar steps and knocked on Jerry's door. The window was dark, and neither Jerry nor his friend answered.

"I never thought for a moment I'd be in this situation. Shut out. I don't have the lease on this apartment." She looked up at the brick façade. "This is an illegal sublet. Jerry happens to have overlooked that detail."

"So, Plan B, then?"

"Yup, Plan B it is." They walked to another bus stop and took a bus back down to West 28th. Mark's hotel rose before them in the middle of the shuttered street.

"This is the Flower District," he said.

"Obviously." She stood in front of the modern hotel, arms crossed, and looked up and down at the bare street of roll-down gates.

"In the morning it comes alive. They set out flowers and potted trees and the whole block is transformed."

"I will have to take your word," she said.

"That will be a first." They went inside and stood in the lobby. "I'll get you an extra pillow and a blanket." He spoke to the concierge and came back. "Or would you rather stay at your friend Jen's?"

"I could call her again."

Mark handed over his phone and Amalia dialed Jen's number from the little slip of paper Jen had handed her in the office before they'd slept over together, tucked safely all this time in her suit jacket's breast pocket. "Jen? It's me, Amalia."

"You left so fast this morning."

"I'm in the city." She felt herself blush. "I still can't get into my apartment."

"I'm out—with Suky. Or I'd offer for you to stay."

"Oh, really! Have a good time. Say hi to Suky." She hung up.

"Why did you hang up so fast?" Mark took the phone back. "So she's out with Suky?"

"Maybe they're on a date." Weirder things had happened. "I guess I'll take the pillow," she said, and went to the desk to claim the pillow and blanket the concierge had left on the counter for her. Amalia hugged the bedding to her chest for the whole elevator ride. "So this is kind of like home?"

"No, not so much," he said, and unlocked the door, held it open for her. They went into the room. "The company sets me up with a suite. Kind of like a home office. They're sending me to Wales next week." He waved a hand over the couch. "Be my guest."

"This will be fine," she said. "Thank you very much." She kicked off her shoes and propped the pillow in the corner of the couch. Loosened her hair from its scrunchie, took off her earrings. She lay her head down.

Mark unfolded the blanket and sat at the end of the couch with it draped on his lap. He looked over at her. "Are you going to sleep now?"

"I'm going to sleep now. Thank you." She pulled the corner of the blanket over her bare ankles. He was kind. She shut her eyes and refused to watch him, although the thought that she might look made her curious.

Chapter 12

Sunday, October 21

Mark sat up in bed and blinked at the sight of the beautiful woman in his hotel room, who appeared to hate him. No, he corrected. She appeared to be asleep. He thought to try something, and shifted out of bed, opened the curtains. "Great day for a city tour," he said, and turned to see her stir, wake, and shield her eyes from the brightness of the West 28th Street morning light.

She went to the window, pulled the curtains back. "Let's get out. I don't care where. I need to try my apartment again."

"Is that a yes?"

"Yes. Why not. But we're not going to talk about fracking."

They assembled themselves for the day and left the hotel; stopped at Bryant Park on the way uptown and settled down at the café tables and chairs. He bought her something to eat, and something else for himself; soon enough they were done, and on their way. They walked in front of the library and past the intersection. "Grand Central is there," Amalia said. She waved her hand down toward the terminal building. "You don't want to see it, do you? I'm agitated. I feel like walking. I need to be in motion." They walked uptown and strode in time with each other's paces until they stood in front of the Metropolitan Museum of Art.

Amalia pulled him up the stairs of the museum; they went inside and showed his bag to the security guard. The guard asked Mark to unroll Amalia's Pussy Riot t-shirt, and he did. He held it up and the guard laughed. "Put that away."

They turned right and wound their way around the stone wall into the coat check area, back out into the grand lobby. She looked up at the vaulted ceiling, then down at the floor. "Chunky terrazzo," she said. "I've never seen such chunky terrazzo. What's it made of, can you tell?"

"Marble and granite, probably." Mark bobbed down and swiped a finger over it. "Lots of quartz." They walked up to the ticket line and looked at the suggested donation price posted behind the desk. "I'll pay," Mark said. "Since you're wallet-free."

"But it's not a date." She kicked at the floor.

"Agreed. Not a date. We're still going in together?"

Mark followed Amalia through a gallery of Baroque paintings, past a tour on the left. Amalia looked over her shoulder, drawn in by the commentary. He stood behind her.

Amalia watched the museum docent, a small woman who spoke to the large group. "She puts herself in this very interesting ball gown which you would never do in a painting; her skirt is described incredibly well in light and shadow." It was an image of a woman painter with two young women behind her. "She shows you the lining of this panel. It says, 'I am very wealthy, I can afford to have a lining of silk.'"

Amalia turned to look at him. "Something about this gets me, the fluidity." He saw her cheeks soften. The group moved left to cluster around another painting and Amalia and Mark walked back out to where they'd begun. "You lead," she said.

They moved through a dim hallway of sketches and into a bright gallery of glass display cases. "I see the hidden hand of Camille Claudel in these," he said. "These are by Rodin. Claudel was his inspiration. He looked at the sculpture and then back at

Amalia. "I took a Women and Gender Studies class at Dartmouth and wrote a paper about them."

"I never took you for a..." her voice trailed off. "For a person who would take a Women and Gender Studies class."

"I was in grad school, stuck on details. My advisor suggested I take a class in something different. I've always seen sculpture as an extension of geology, but there weren't any courses I could take about it then. The Fine Arts Department secretary suggested it. She was right, it was great." They stopped in front of a muscular Rodin bronze. "I met my girlfriend there, too. Ex-girlfriend." He looked up at the limbs of the model. They continued through the galleries until one painting stopped him. "Mother of god," Mark said.

"What?" Amalia caught up and stood before the painting. "Wow, that's a face. *Gertrude Stein, by Pablo Picasso*."

"I'm done. I can't look at these paintings anymore."

"You'll love this," she said, "look out the window here." She waved him over to the interior window that looked over and down into the Egyptian gallery. Mullions cast a grid of light and shadow from the far side of the space onto a pool of shallow water below. "First, I have to introduce you to my Durga." They walked through a gallery of Buddhas and up an intimate stair to a third floor room. "Here she is," Amalia extended an arm and looked into the case. "Mark, meet Durga. Durga, meet Mark. Durga: Earth Mother."

"I wasn't expecting—so many arms." He peered at the tag. "'*Durga the Buffalo Demon Slayer*.'" He stood back. "Buffalo are sacred in my culture."

"In Abenaki culture?"

"You call Durga yours, but she's not yours, and you said as much when you said others come here to pray. She's not even Indian. She's Nepali. It says so here."

"Durga existed before those boundaries." she said. "She could be Indian, she could be Nepali. Isn't religion like that? Different umbrellas covering different parts of the earth? The color is different, the light and shade are different, but it's all still an umbrella."

"I'd like you to see the Egyptian gallery. Very geologic."

"My parents went to Egypt."

Amalia looked at him and opened her mouth to say something.

"It's ok, you know. It's ok to talk about them," he said.

"What? Nothing. I wasn't," she said.

"Amalia, it would be better for me if we did. Otherwise I'm going to keep feeling like I have to tiptoe around. And for your sake, not mine." He sat down on the floor opposite Durga. "It's not contagious, you know."

"What, death?"

"No, grief." He looked at her. "Why don't we leave this gallery and go somewhere more cheery?"

"Somewhere outside."

They walked out of the South Asia gallery and back down into the main hall, noisy with the weekend tourist crowd.

"Can we leave? And come back?"

"You have your little pin thing." She touched the metal Met Museum circle clipped to his shirt collar. "Shows you paid."

They went out the building and stood at the top of the steps. Amalia sat down and looked up at Mark. "I don't think I want to sit here," he said. "I had this feeling. Like I'm walking through a doorway."

"You don't look ok."

"I'm ok." He blinked. "I'm ok. I felt something big shift inside."

"Do you need to go to the bathroom?"

"No!" He jogged down the steps to join her and they walked left around the museum and into Central Park. "They died in a car accident." Mark walked at her side along a gentle uphill path. "It was in New Hampshire. A snowy day. They slid." He looked up at the clear sky. She reached out for his hand, and he let her, but he didn't make an effort to grip in return. "Are you crying? They're my parents," he said. "They died four years ago this winter. I was 23."

"So you're 27? You seem older. I'm 27," she said.

"Parenthood aged me. I mean, I'm a guardian to Timmy now."

"I thought you said he doesn't live with you anymore."

"He still comes home." He took a deep breath. "I'm ready to go back inside." Amalia followed him; he pulled open the museum doors with two hands, walked in, and bore left.

They stood in the Oceania gallery in front of tribal masks and carvings. "There was a landslide." Mark looked at the statues, backlit by the hazy filtered light that came in through the museum's archival blinds. "There. In Papua New Guinea. A lot of people died."

"What happened?"

"The soil was unstable. The f-word might have caused it."

"Fracking."

"I said 'f-word' because you said we shouldn't talk about it today."

"You always do as you're told?" She sat down at the foot of a totem and looked up at it. "We should pray," she said. "Because the people there can't get to their ancestors here. We have them. We should pay respects, is what I mean. Like they do upstairs."

"Do what upstairs?"

"People pray upstairs in the South Asia gallery. This is a temple."

"So I'm beginning to see."

"They're displaced. They need to be honored."

"Who's displaced?"

"The statues. The figurines. The icons. All of them are out of context."

"Out of context."

Later, they walked across the park, 81st to 81st, she mused, although he didn't get the geographic joke until she explained it.

East to West. She'd wavered between distance and intimacy in their conversations all afternoon; for his part, he just wanted to stand closer. Didn't really matter what she said. They went to her apartment and followed in a woman with an armload of grocery bags. Upstairs, a sign hung taped to Amalia's apartment door:

"By order of management, this suite must be vacated,"

she read. It was signed with a scrawl.

"There's no date on it," Mark said. "And it's not on letterhead. It doesn't look very official."

"How can I contest it? I know I'm not supposed to be here. If I talk to the management company they'll kick me out, and Joan'll get in trouble." She slid her back down the wall and squatted on the floor opposite the apartment door. "My friend Sandra's Great Aunt Joan. Kind of a distant connection."

He slid his phone across the floor. She dialed. "Jen's not answering, it's going to voice mail." She gave the phone back. "I haven't exactly had time to make friends since I moved here, not outside of work."

"You can come back to my hotel," Mark said.

"But this day is not a date." She stood up. "Ok. Let's do it." He followed her into the elevator and they emerged out onto the street.

"Do you ever date anyone?" Mark walked at her side across the street.

"You're very conservative."

"Ok. So you're a Democrat. But I'm not a Republican."

"I might vote Green next month."

"And I'm going to vote Libertarian."

She waved her hand out to the bus as it approached and it slowed down in the middle of the street. They rode down to Mark's hotel and walked across. "I still haven't seen this the way you say it is with all the flowers."

At dinner, they sat on the roof deck level of the hotel. Amalia ducked out to use the Ladies' Room. Mark looked up at the old walls on either side of the modern open-air deck, the brick pitted and shadowy in the evening light. He picked up his phone and scrolled through messages while she was gone, and was interrupted by a call from an unfamiliar number.

"I got a call from Amalia Erenwine."

"This is Mark. You must be Jen. How was your date with Suky last night?"

"Uh—"

"Ok, sorry, kind of creepy."

"That's ok. I'll return the favor. Are you hooking up with Amalia?"

"Sadly, Jen, she said she's not interested in me because I'm a Libertarian."

"Craziness."

"I know!" He looked up. "Here she comes. Good luck with Suky." He handed the phone to Amalia. "Jen for you."

She took the phone. "Thanks. Jen! ... Yes ... Can I stay with you tonight? ... When is she getting in from her trip? ... Could someone else let me in? ... I don't know. I'll think about it ... So it sounds like you're having fun, then? ... Ok, say hi to Suky ..." She hung up and put the phone on the table between them. "I don't feel like raining on Jen's parade."

"Are you two done here?" The waiter put the bill on the table.

"This one's on me," Mark said. "Stay with me, or you could get another room here."

"I can't afford a room," she said. She reached across and squeezed his forearm.

"I'll lend you the money."

"I can't afford to pay you back."

"Then stay with me like we'd planned."

"Nothing's going to happen."

"I promise. I will keep my politics in the closet."

Chapter 13

Monday, October 22

Amalia stood at reception with her backpack, now impregnated with clayish soil from the site, and damp with mildew. It smelled of days-old chicken tikka masala. Betsy had found the backpack on site when she returned the rental car on the weekend. Jacob had found it on a rock, which he'd climbed and then fallen off. Betsy had put the whole thing into a garbage bag and handed it over. Amalia put her wallet in one back pocket of the borrowed cords, cell phone in another. Walked down the four flights, strode out across the street, and caught a bus uptown. Betsy had—with discretion—asked her to go home and to shower and change.

She leaned her head on the thick, cool glass, and watched buildings peel off out of sight behind her. Her eyes closed for a moment and she thought of Mark. Her chest felt warm. Was she getting the flu? She hoped not. The warmth spread around her back; it was not a bad feeling. She rang the bell for her stop and got off, walked over to Amsterdam and 81st, and with keys at the ready, approached her front door. Jerry stood outside and hosed down the sidewalk.

"Jerry! I missed you on the weekend. I was locked out."

"Miss Amalia." He held the hose to the side. "I am so sorry."

He shook his head, which made his gray curls bob from side to side. "It's the management company. Did you get the letter on your door?"

"No, not yet." Amalia ducked her head in a half-nod and opened the front door of the building with her key, skated across the terrazzo floor, slick with a sheen of water and mop strand streaks. She went up in the elevator and counted each floor. A whole city of people accustomed to vertical transportation. She wondered if humans would evolve to use fewer muscles because of it. Fiddled with the key at her apartment.

The note was still taped to the door. She put down the plastic bag, and with one hand on the doorknob and another on the key, twisted and pushed the door hard. It still stuck, even after the humidity of summer had past. She fell forward into the apartment, over an envelope that lay at the threshold. She picked it up, grabbed the plastic bag from the door, and went inside. Slipped her sensible shoes from her blistered feet, and pressed *Play* on the apartment's answering machine.

"Amalia, it's Jen. Call me. Why aren't you picking up? It's Saturday 10 AM. Did you lose your cell?" Amalia deleted the message.

"Amalia, this is your father. We can't reach you on your cell phone either. You're probably away for the weekend. We're not so worried we'd call the police." Didn't delete. Was she not worthy of a police call?

"Hi, Amalia, this is Sandra. My Great Aunt got an email from the management company. Is there a problem there? I hope everything is ok. Skype me as soon as you get this message." Deleted.

Amalia went to the kitchen counter and held the envelope from the management company, weighed it like a heavy lump, then put it back down. She lifted the lid of the worm bin. "Ok in there, guys?" She ran some water into her cupped hands, and sprinkled it on the top of the soil. Replaced the lid with wet hands and wiped her fingers dry on the thighs of her borrowed teal cords.

She went back into the single room studio space and took off her jacket, emptied all the pockets of all the clothes onto the little desk, and switched on the computer. She took off Mark's belt and hung it on the back of the desk chair. Ran her finger over the smooth leather and stopped at the nubby bump where he had used the same belt hole over and over again.

She took off the cords and stood like that in Mark's shirt. She'd left her underwear at Jen's house in the bundle of clothes, with her socks and red t-shirt and suit pants. What an odd few days for her wardrobe. What an odd few days for her, for that matter. She felt upside down.

She bent at the waist and looked at the apartment, upside down. She unfolded and stood, serenaded by Norah Jones, and slipped out of Mark's shirt with the buttons done up. She put on bra and panties and knee socks and chose dress-down suit pants. Put her hand on Mark's shirt on the closet shelf. It felt warm from her body heat, and she put it back on, tucked in the hem and arranged the extra fabric in a bubble around her waist.

She pulled out a silk kurta top from the closet and held it up, took it off its hanger, and put it on over the suit pants and men's shirt. The middle was bulky. She untucked the shirt and let it lie loose beneath the kurta. Not a bad look, kind of odd, but it felt good. Oceanic. She went back to the closet and pulled out a thin wool scarf with a blue and green patterned weave. Opened the folds lengthwise and wrapped it around her shoulders.

What else did she need? Her cell phone seemed to be dead. She popped open the back of the phone and dug the battery out with a fingernail. Sure enough, the battery was suctioned in by a tiny pool of water inside the phone. She found a bowl, scooped some dry rice from the cloth basmati bag on the counter, and dropped in the battery. Nothing to lose in trying. She had already planned to get a new phone.

Amalia picked up the envelope she'd left on the counter and ripped it open with her finger. The letter was on gold-stamped letterhead from the management company, and signed with a flourish. No surprises.

Chapter 14

TROPICAL DEPRESSION 18
FORECAST/ADVISORY NUMBER 1
NWS NATIONAL HURRICANE CENTER MIAMI FL
AL18 1500 UTC MON OCT 22
CHANGES IN WATCHES AND WARNINGS WITH THIS ADVISORY...
THE GOVERNMENT OF JAMAICA HAS ISSUED A TROPICAL STORM WATCH FOR JAMAICA.

UTC 1500.

Eleven AM New York time. Mark read the message on his phone; he got way too many email updates from the National Weather Service. He'd have to change his subscription preferences. There was the clearest of fall weather with him there in New York, and he planned to take advantage of it all until he had to catch his flight to Wales. Hiked himself back up to Central Park to traipse the Ramble, and did that with gusto until he sat down to eat take-out lunch in the park, and thought back to his weekend with Amalia.

Maybe it wasn't that his Libertarianism was in question. Maybe it was his Catholicism. He shuddered. Pulled out the British Geological Survey data to review for work. Needed to get Wales on his mind; but first, he pulled out his phone to see if

Amalia had written. She had not, but there was another update from the National Weather Service:

TROPICAL DEPRESSION 18 INTERMEDIATE ADVISORY NUMBER 1A
NWS NATIONAL HURRICANE CENTER MIAMI FL
AL18 200 PM EDT MON OCT 22
...AIR FORCE HURRICANE HUNTER PLANE EN ROUTE TO INVESTIGATE THE DEPRESSION...

Air Force hurricane hunter pilot—a job he was glad he did not have. He needed two feet on stable ground. He was more useful to the world that way. He looked again to see if there was an email from Amalia, but there was not. Still not.

Chapter 15

Back in the office that afternoon, Amalia sat in a meeting with Sunil and Suky about the environmental center. Betsy was out with a family emergency—Jacob, they'd said. Max Grohman sat at the helm. Amalia fiddled with Mildred's egg timer in front of her, and took a big breath.

"I don't think we should be using natural gas on this project. I think the way it's extracted is too risky. Its emissions are not particularly green. I think the responsible thing to do is to present other alternatives. And we have other alternatives."

"She has a point," Max said.

"The prudent thing to do is to compare the options," Suky said.

"I started a spreadsheet," Amalia said.

"No way," Max said. "We're not going there."

"The risks of fracking are not being well-managed," Amalia said. "I believe it's our responsibility as designers and as community leaders to offer people another way. I'm not saying that natural gas is bad."

"You're not? I thought that's what you were all about," Jen said.

"It's a transition fuel," Suky said.

"Natural gas and oil are being sought from greater and greater depths," Amalia said. "If the supply runs out, don't you think the industry's going to find another source or another way in? That's what scares me. It's not being handled like a transition fuel. I think we're afraid of living without it. If we let go of our fear, we might be able to relax into seeing there are other alternatives, and we might also see the risks of the alternatives we were thinking were viable, healthy choices."

"You make it sound like a diet," Max said.

"It's totally different," Suky said. "With all due respect, I don't think you can come in here and wave a wand and expect us all to change overnight in the face of what are complicated engineering systems."

"I'm an intern," Jen said. "Amalia's an intern. We're not supposed to know how to structure a project. We're supposed to be learning from all of you. So why did you give Amalia the assignment to research the fuel sources in the first place?"

"Would you have done anything differently? Betsy could have given you the assignment, Jen," Max said.

"If she'd given me the assignment instead of Amalia last week, I would've handled it differently. For one thing, I would've made the question much narrower than Amalia did. She took the basic assignment and blew it way out of proportion. Now look where we are."

"I can't believe you'd say that," Amalia said.

"It's true. I'm sorry, that's how I see it. If everybody's truth telling here, well, that's my truth. I would have simplified it."

"And you might've missed something."

"You missed a lot yourself, Amalia, like how this was all going to unravel by your questions."

"I didn't plan for the project to get so challenged. But I did make everybody think. And you know what? It was the church meeting last weekend that opened my eyes, not the research I did here. Meeting Mark."

"Who's Mark?" Sunil spoke up for the first time in the meeting.

"He's a petroleum geologist."

"Mark is a petroleum geologist? You never told me," Jen said. "I thought he was just a Libertarian."

"What's wrong with being a Libertarian? Pass me that egg timer of yours down here, Amalia," Max said.

"You want the gas mask too?"

"I do not." Max took the egg timer and looked at it. "Okay fine, I'll take the gas mask, too."

"That's a great conversation piece," Sunil said. "For the environmental center?"

"I thought the same thing," Amalia said.

"Gas mask's a meeting dissolver," Max said. He put the mask on the floor next to him and stood up. He turned the egg timer over and spoke. "We all want this project to go ahead. That's why we're here. If Betsy was with us, she'd say the same thing. It's been a difficult few days. The clients are on the verge of losing their second set of funding options and emotions have become quite raw. We need to get past this. I understand it's important to vent, but, we have a job to do. We are here in service of the project. Our clients Susan and Jeffrey have entrusted us with the architectural component of the job.

"We may have some historic property options, if we can recreate a structure that was there before the land became a county park. That would mean a redesign. The big question is not how to power the project, but is the project viable? I think it is. We'll need the client and the county to weigh in. It's their partnership. I think we have enough to pursue the project." Max looked at the engineers. "Sunil and Suky, can we agree to look into the options we discussed, and reconvene next week? We have some puzzle pieces to put together, and it's going to take us some time. We have a direction. Let's call it the end of the meeting for now. I will follow-up with everyone in the morning by email. Betsy will be back in touch when she's returned to the office. Thank you." Max picked up the gas mask.

"Sunil's right, we should give it to Susan and Jeffrey," Amalia said. "It would be so great for the center. It's kind of cool. The environmental center gets the gas mask. Very appropriate." She stood up and straightened her spine. "I feel better."

Sunil walked around the table and stood next to Amalia. "Hey. How about dinner tonight?" He spoke in a quiet voice, not for the group, but just for her.

Her heart raced, a sudden departure from the calm she'd found in the meeting. "That'd be great. Let me wrap up here."

"I can pick you up at home. Or we can meet near here."

"Meet me at my apartment at seven." She tore off a piece of paper from her notepad and wrote her address on it.

"See you then," he said.

See you then, she echoed inside, to the butterflies that tickled.

Chapter 16

Mark pulled his knees up onto the back of the seat in front of him in the Yellow Cab and took his sketchbook from his bag. He tried to draw the driver ahead of him, but thought of Amalia. He hadn't been able to concentrate since they'd said goodbye. The more he thought of her, the dizzier he felt. The less he thought of her, the more he wanted to.

He'd try to read instead. He pulled out his book and put the sketchbook away; he needed to get through some reading before the election. Not that he needed to read in order to change his mind: he would vote Libertarian as long as the party was on the ballot. He'd kept the Republicans in his back pocket as an "in case" for the past couple of months, if the Libertarian Party ended up getting knocked off the list. The party had won the right to stay on the ballot. So why was he stuck on reading about Catholic Libertarians? They were a paradoxical bunch. The Republican vice presidential candidate was one of them. And yet he, Mark, was one of them, too—one who didn't find much in the Republicans' social views to agree with. His stomach growled.

He was irritated she hadn't spent the day with him. Why hadn't she? She was at work. In New York City. How did she spend her days? Did she think about him at all? He was impressed with her rigor at keeping their boundaries tight when she slept overnight. Impressed, and irritated.

She'd already said she wasn't interested. Said that, but didn't act it. Maybe she was gay. Could he ask her? No. It wasn't his business, didn't matter. But to him, with his mind tied up in Amalia, it mattered very much. Could it all be stuck in the works because he was planning to vote Libertarian? It didn't seem possible.

Maybe he and Amalia could meet in the middle. Somewhere in New Jersey, between Manhattan and Quakertown, Pennsylvania—at a train station halfway across the state? He shuffled his knees down the back of the seat in front and planted his feet on the floor of the taxi, put his book in his bag, and got out at JFK International Airport.

Chapter 17

At the end of the workday, Amalia sat down to write the email she'd composed in her head. Betsy hadn't mentioned the report; just as well, Amalia thought, since there was no report. She opened a new document on the screen and began to type:

Dear Betsy,

At the restaurant on Friday, I found a pamphlet for a community meeting on fracking. I went to that meeting this past weekend. I believe fracking—hydraulic fracturing—is causing irreparable environmental damage. I met people this weekend who are experiencing reproductive issues from it, who are getting headaches from it, and who are worried about serving poisoned water in their restaurants because of it.

I met people who are in need of solid jobs, and who see the natural gas industry as their only hope. I met a young engineer whose father died fighting in the oil fields of Kuwait. This young man carried his father's gas mask around while he tried to find a safe way to work in the fossil fuel industry.

I don't think it needs to be this way. I think our office has a role to play in offering solutions. I don't know what all of those solutions are, but I would like to be a part of creating them.

I will continue to work on the report, and the spreadsheet, with your permission. If you would prefer I do it outside of office hours, that's fine.

I'm sorry I'm not able to offer a clearer conclusion. I need to do more research.

Sincerely,

Amalia Sengupta Erenwine

Associate NCARB, B.A., M.Arch.

She looked at the letter. She crossed out *Sengupta* and wrote S. She'd never called herself by her mother's maiden name before. She deleted the S. and typed again: *S-e-n-g-u-p-t-a.* Amalia attached the letter to an email that she entitled *Letter* and sent it to Betsy with no text in the body of the message. She pushed off from her desk and walked to the lunchroom at the back of the empty office. She sat down and looked out at the dark courtyard filled with air conditioning compressors below, then turned around to leave for her date with Sunil.

Amalia pulled two bottles of beer from the cupboard and put them in the freezer. Quarter to seven. She hoped Sunil would be late, late enough at least that she could spruce up the apartment. She put her fingers in the bowl of dry rice and fished out her cell phone battery. Popped it in the phone, turned it on, and jumped with a clap when it reengaged, alight. She scrolled through messages and saw an email from Mark. She decided not to write back—she'd call instead.

He answered on the first ring. "I wondered if that was you."

"I found my phone! My whole bag."

"Hey listen, I'm at the airport but I'm on standby for an emergency management session—I might have to go and take that call. We got a report this afternoon, there's a big storm coming through the Caribbean."

"Why are you doing emergency management for the Caribbean? I thought you were going to Wales."

"Storm's tracking up this way. And I'm still on for the trip. They have to secure the sites in Pennsylvania. Are you watching the presidential debate tonight?"

"Sorry, why are you securing the sites? You mean the frack sites?"

"They might be in the path of the storm. They're going to fly over tonight. They're being proactive. It's a Tropical Depression over the Atlantic."

"And you're going to fly over it—is that why you're going to Wales?" She looked around the apartment. Sunil would be there soon.

"No. George and the others are flying over the Pennsylvania sites. I'm going to Wales for business meetings." His voice disappeared for a moment when the line cut out. "Hey. Can you talk later? The call's come in on the other line. You want to watch the presidential debate over the phone together before I fly out? I'm sure it'll be on at the airport."

"I have plans. Going out for dinner. With a colleague."

"Is it a date?"

"Are you jealous?"

She jumped when the buzzer rang. Darn, he was early. She let him up and grabbed her phone, logged onto Facebook, and typed, *Date!* She spun once around the apartment and moved a pile of books, which made little difference to the spartan look of the room. She pulled the plug in the bathtub to drain the water where her tikka backpack had soaked in shampoo, and hung the pack from the showerhead. She pulled the curtain and dried her hands at the same time he knocked on the apartment door.

Amalia opened the door with a smile and her phone buzzed in her back pocket.

"Hi!" She stepped back and Sunil came in, while she pulled her phone out to take a look. She waved the phone with one hand. "Sorry," she said.

"No, take it. I'm early."

It was Mark, and he'd texted her a smiley. She looked up from her phone.

"Why are you blushing?"

"I don't know. It happens a lot." Amalia put the phone in the back pocket of the jeans she'd changed into, and closed the door behind Sunil.

"Maybe you're allergic to something. Maybe that's why you blush so much," he said.

"Are you up for pizza?"

"I'm game," he said. "Let's do it."

She grabbed her oceanic scarf from the hall table and put it on around her head and shoulders to keep the warmth in, and the cold out. Put on her gray wool jacket and put her stocking feet into tall boots. She adjusted her scarf around her ears and tucked a piece of hair in. They walked to the front of the apartment and stopped to pick up her string bag before they went out to the elevator. She locked the door behind them and her phone buzzed in her pocket.

Amalia and Sunil took the subway to the restaurant and settled in with a pizza that filled the space between them. He fiddled with a napkin. "I didn't think you'd say yes to dinner. With me. You're so—aloof."

"Me? I'm not aloof."

"You are. You project this air of 'I'm busy and I have better things to do than to talk with the structural engineer,'" he said. "The other day. Uptown."

"Then? My boss was there. I was on probation. I had in mind you and I could go to this little taqueria around the corner for lunch."

"I know that place. I live up there." He pressed forward into the table. "You're on probation?"

"Not anymore. I was that week. I let some ideas out too quickly."

"Intriguing." He sat back. "Amalia Erenwine, International Woman of Mystery." He took a bite of his pizza.

Amalia nodded with a mouth full, then jumped. "My phone

buzzed." She stood up and pulled it out of her pocket, set it on the table.

"Are you going to check it? You keep looking at it."

"I'll put it away." She ran a finger around the edge of the plastic case. "I'll check first in case it's important." It was from Mark:

Storm warnings for Jamaica upgraded as of 8pm...

Her phone buzzed again.

We're in the path—no worries, though, very broad swath.

She typed,

Call me later!

and put the phone back into her string bag. "Done," she said. "Tell me." She leaned forward. "What do you think of geothermal power?"

"Really? We're on a date and you want to talk about work?"

"No, I don't want to talk about work—but I want to know. You said the other day it can cause earthquakes."

"It has, in deeper installations. Larger ones. There was a case in Europe and another in California."

"How does that compare to the risk of earthquakes from fracking—from the injection of frack fluid waste back into the rock?"

"This is what you want to do on our date?" He looked up at the restaurant patrons who came in the front door. "I feel like you're interviewing me."

"I am, kind of."

"For what, engineer or boyfriend?"

"I'm sorry. I'm tense about this stuff." She sat back in her seat and brushed her forehead with the back of her hand.

"Amalia—I like you—but you're right, you are tense about this stuff.

"I'm sorry, I don't mean to be such a pain," she said.

"I'd like to be able to have a relaxed conversation without it becoming tense over work or you checking your phone every few minutes." He drummed on the table, caught up in something. "If this isn't clicking, isn't it better to say so now?" He looked over her shoulder and waved the waiter back over. "Could we get this to go?"

Amalia felt all her energy drop out and pool around her ankles. It was over. Never started, but it was over. The waiter approached.

"Two packages or one?"

Sunil and Amalia looked at each other. "Two," they said in unison.

They were silent on the cab ride they shared uptown. The cab pulled up to the corner of 81st and Amsterdam, she gave Sunil a wad of bills she did not count and she got out, the conversation unfinished between them. Jerry stood on the street side, with a lit cigar. "Something to celebrate, Jerry?" She closed the cab door behind her and didn't turn to wave.

"My niece had a baby!" He offered her a cigar and broke off a tip, lit one for her. She coughed while she pulled on it. "You only live once," he said, and brandished his cigar, torch-like, to the sky.

"I don't know, but tonight, I'm up for a cigar." She took a couple of puffs. So many babies in one week. Rose having a baby, Jerry's niece having a baby. Didn't surprising things come in threes? She must be forgetting another baby. Oh, Betsy's kids. Not babies, but still. And more than three kids that week. Now that she'd disproven her Theory of Threes, she—

"...and so the building management made that change," Jerry said. "Okay?"

"Sure." What? "Thanks, Jerry." She butted out on the curb and kept the cigar in one hand while she went in and took the elevator up to the apartment.

Once inside, she put the cigar on the counter next to her worm bin, dropped the pizza leftovers in the fridge. Caught a whiff of cigar smoke on her oceanic scarf. She took it to the bathroom and hung it on the shower rail. The room smelled of shampoo, diluted tikka masala and Cuban cigar. A sweet and spicy combination that both stimulated and comforted. She sat on the futon and called Jen. "How did you get so sure of yourself? I have the impression everyone thinks I'm a rabid environmentalist."

"This came up with Mark?"

"Sunil. We went out tonight."

"On a date? How did it go?"

"Not so well. I'm a bit overwhelmed," Amalia said. "And I have to move. I might need to stay with you for a while."

"You can. The couch is yours. But Paige wants her Pussy Riot shirt back."

"That was hers? So I was wearing her cords too? Oops." She laughed. Amalia got up from the couch and went into the bathroom, poked at the backpack, opened the bathroom window.

"How did it feel to try on the Pussy Riot identity?"

"Pretty righteous, actually." Amalia took the scarf down from the shower rail and sniffed at it, rehung it out in the living room on the back of her desk chair. Great Aunt Joan's desk chair, not her desk chair.

"Maybe that's your clue to your not knowing who you want to be. Try on some different t-shirts for a while and see how they fit. If you think people are treating you like a rabid environmentalist, try on a different t-shirt for a while and see how they respond."

"I only have solid colors."

"I don't mean literally, Amalia! I mean in terms of how you see yourself, what you project. What do you want to project?"

"I don't want men to find me off-putting."

"You're hot, Amalia; there is no way they find you off-putting. But—maybe you're a little—desperate."

"Maybe a little." She took a deep breath. The phone buzzed in her hand. "I have another call." Mark.

"Remember who you are. Don't be who people think you are. Be who you really are. And call me back!" Amalia dropped one call for the other.

"How was your date?" Mark sounded like he was with her in the room.

"Not a date."

"Flight's at ten. Debate's at nine."

"You were serious? You want to watch the presidential debate over the phone?"

"You know my guy's going to win."

"Who, your Libertarian? Gary Johnson?"

"No, I'm thinking Republican."

"Don't. You're not going to vote for Mitt Romney. I'd rather you split the vote, and vote for Johnson!"

There was background disturbance on the line. "I need to get back to this other call. Can we speak later?" The line went dead.

Amalia sat back on the couch with her laptop to watch the last presidential debate before the federal election. Such a tragedy it was only the Democrats and Republicans on stage. It wasn't a real debate without the other voices.

Her phone rang and she saw Mark's name on the screen. "Listen, they're talking about energy sectors." She put the laptop down and went to the fridge to get a yogurt, and settled back down on the couch with it and the laptop next to her. "Oh! Obama said we need to control our own energy. Here we go." She and Mark listened in silence. "No! Dick Cheney does not show good judgment! Oh! I spilled my yogurt on my shirt." She tried to scrape it off with her spoon. "So how does the energy sector tie into all of this? They haven't really said—they keep skipping back to national security."

"Same thing," Mark said. "Work's calling on the other line—talk later?"

Amalia moved off the couch and folded herself at the hips into a deep bend. She let her arms hang down while she listened to the debate. Her phone buzzed a few minutes later with a text message from Mark.

Calling you now.

And he was. She answered on the first ring.

"Where are they?"

"Pakistan," she said. Hey, what if instead of discussing war, they had to give a state of the union report for every country on earth?"

"That would take forever," Mark said. "They'd never do it."

"What if they had to give equal attention to the US's position in relation to all the other regions?"

"Isn't that what the Secretary of State does?"

"No, really. If you focus on war, you get—more war," she said. "Maybe the Secretary of State should be president. I'd vote for Hillary Clinton."

"I have no doubt you would."

"Hey, my laptop froze up," Amalia said. "I'm going to have to restart."

"Can you listen on a radio?"

"Yes, hang on." She went to the kitchen and turned on Joan's radio over the fridge.

"I should get some food," he said.

"Ok." Her hand lingered on the radio. "Are we done for the night?"

"I think so," he said.

"I'm tired."

"First time sleeping in your own bed in a while?"

"Actually, since—last Thursday. Almost a week."

"Any word on moving?"

"Yes, I need to. I was thinking about Hamilton Heights over by this condo we've been working on but now I'm not so sure. There's this guy—"

"A guy you're dating? The guy you went out with tonight?"

"We're not dating," she said. "Mark, I told you—I like you, but—"

She turned off the radio, closed her laptop, plugged in her phone and went to bed. When she awoke in the middle of the night, she did not know where she was, and looked for Mark across the room.

Chapter 18

Tuesday, October 23

Mark arrived in the town of Brecon, South Wales, the next morning. He got out of the taxi on the left and looked across to the Guildhall. Hundreds of years old, by the looks of it. What a face; he could climb that stone wall. Spectacular. He walked up to the façade and felt the grooves in the hand-worked stone.

Inside, in the Council Chambers, the Atlantia Actuaris team wrapped up its presentation to the group of local business leaders. Mark caught the tail end of it. "We've chosen the town of Brecon as our base for its centrality and popularity; explorations will be in more remote sites across a much broader area, north and south. As we move forward, we'll be pleased to include the neighboring towns in our efforts. And yes, Mr. Williams, there will be jobs. We'll make sure they go to local people." Applause followed. Simon approached Mark at the back of the room.

"Hey buddy, glad you could make it. This is great. We've got a real foothold in here. We need you to smooth it over with the resisters."

"I can do smooth." Mark pushed his hand across the air in a swoosh. "Give me a minute, and you can introduce me around." Mark powered his phone on—picked up a signal, and a pile of roaming charges too, no doubt. A message in his email caught his eye.

I will take you to court over this.

The anonymous letter caused him to choke back a deep cough. Must've been a mistake. He deleted it.

Chapter 19

Amalia held the phone in the crook of her shoulder and listened to Betsy list off a set of tasks. "We're in redesign mode," Betsy said. "I need you to do a one-day charrette and push through this. I'll work on the financials from home today. You and Jen work on developing the ideas and sketches."

"Ok, Betsy."

"Max is coming back after his ten o'clock meeting. You can show him what you have then. I don't think any of the tenants have booked the conference room, so you can work there. Get some more of those roses, too."

"Roses?"

"Yes, for the conference room. I liked those old ones you brought yesterday. Some fresh ones would be nice. Make it an office reimbursable."

"How's Jacob? We were so worried."

"He'll be fine. They're checking him. Running tests. Ben and I are taking turns at the hospital and with Jonathan at home."

Amalia frowned at the phone. "Please tell him I say 'hi'."

Amalia walked down to Columbus Circle and passed the spot where she and Mark had first bumped into each other; he'd seemed lost in a trance. She pulled open the heavy doors of the

Time Warner building and went down the escalator to Whole Foods. Picked a dozen deep-peach roses and took them to the register. The total was double the cost of a movie ticket, half of what she had left for groceries for the month. A reimbursable office expense, for sure.

Back at the office, she brought the flowers to the lunchroom, unwrapped them and trimmed their bottoms. She looked at the Saturday roses lying on the counter next to her. She wrapped the old ones in the plastic from the new ones and stood them up in the trash bin next to the door. Rinsed out the water jug and wiped a smear of plant goo from its rim, poured in the florists' powder and turned the faucet on to add a light wash of water onto the plant food. Stood the new roses up in the glass and as she arranged them, she inhaled. They had a light smell, not potent, but fresh. She went into the conference area and put them in the center of the table.

Betsy's scanned sketches lay in a spread. Max must have printed them. Amalia sat down and wiped some water drops from her hands onto her work trousers, and pulled the sketches toward her. How to go about it? Max would be back in a couple of hours. What did Betsy want them to do? And why had she left Jen and her in charge? She spread out the sketches and put her hands together in front of her.

"Are you praying? That bad, huh?" Jen walked in with a rolled up map.

"No," Amalia said, "I'm preparing."

"Looks like praying to me."

"So what." Amalia pulled the sketches toward her. "How shall we start this?"

Jen rolled out the large topographical map of the site area and laid the roll of trace over it at one end, gave it a nudge, and it unrolled in Amalia's direction. Amalia got up to slide the roses to the end of the table, and she and Jen adjusted the topo and trace in the middle. "I got this out of Betsy's office."

"You went into Betsy's office?"

"She did ask us to work on this." She smoothed out the sheets in front of her. "This is the location of the center as we've had it up to now," Jen said. She ran her finger over the tracing paper and marked the outline of the proposed building footprint with a black pen.

"And this is the site boundary." Amalia ticked it off with a pencil around the perimeter of the site. "Trees here. You remember the grove?"

"I haven't been there," Jen said.

Amalia stood up. "How can we design for a place we haven't been to yet?"

"You do it then," Jen said. "You design. I'll draw where you tell me."

"Ok. The grove of trees is over here." Amalia indicated an area on the map. Jen followed the line Amalia's finger outlined and bubbled circles on the trace. "And the old foundations of the building are here." She took her pencil and drew in a rough footprint. Jen traced it in pen.

"Do we have to build the new farmhouse in the exact same place as it was before?"

"Depends what Atlantia Actuaris wants—isn't it to showcase their investment?"

"Would it be drawn somewhere?"

"What, the structure? Maybe on a survey. Or on a demo plan."

"I don't think we have demo plans for the site. They were going to raze whatever's left. It was handled as a note on the title sheet," Jen said.

"What about the survey?"

Amalia leafed through Betsy's sketches while Jen went to find the survey. Betsy's professional hand was apparent—creative and steady—but her sense of connection to the land seemed to miss something Amalia had been aware of when they visited the site.

There was no sense of direction to the sketches, no sense of north, south, west or east. Amalia had felt depth, too, when she was on the site. She'd felt planted, with roots below ground and branches above. These sketches didn't capture that.

She picked up a pen and ripped off the trace Jen had started, and unrolled a new section to work on in front of her. It rolled to her right, and off the table. She let it go. Her hand hovered over the page for a moment and then she began to sketch. What came out was not a plan, or an elevation, but a vivid three-dimensional drawing of a farmhouse porch that wrapped around, with deep sunlight and shade pocketed in window recesses and punctuated by balcony railings. She added steps that led up, with broad slash lines and quick hatches that brought depth to the overall image. No north, south, west or east on the sketch, but a sense of it carried through in the shading. She took a deep breath and tore off the tracing paper from the roll.

"I found this," Jen said. She unfolded a large plot and laid the survey out over the topo map. She turned Amalia's sketch ninety degrees to face her. "Gorgeous," she said.

"But should I show it to Betsy and Max?"

"Why not? She asked us to get started on the concepts."

"I know. I—I got in a lot of hot water the last time I let something out too early," Amalia said.

"The spreadsheet. Yes. We haven't had a chance to talk about it, have we? You know they have a nickname for it. They're calling it *The Erenwine Agenda*."

"Good grief. That sounds much more dramatic than it was."

"It put the office in a real tailspin for a few days there."

"I know. Maybe we can spin it around this time?"

"You mean today? With the sketches?"

"With the charrette as a whole. Let's see what we can pull together," Amalia said.

"Her notes here say to look up the historic photos. Do you know where those are?"

"I've never seen any," Jen said.

"I could look online for some. Betsy's notes also say something about *Sec of Int*. What do you think that is?"

"I don't know. You could look it up. The more we get through before she and Max get back, the better."

Jen went back to her desk and Amalia stood over the strewn sketches. She picked up the black pen she'd used and chewed on its cap. Amalia turned to follow Jen to her desk.

"I typed in *sec of int* and a list of all the past Secretaries of the Interior popped up."

"Keep looking." Amalia came to the computer.

"They're all men. No, wait, there was one woman. Did you know the Secretary of the Interior is eighth in line for the presidency?"

"That would have to be one heck of a plague to get there," Amalia said. "Go back to the search results. There, scroll down." She watched the search results roll out on the screen. "Oh! That's it. *Archeology and Historic Restoration*. It's the *Secretary of the Interior's Standards and Guidelines*." They scanned the sections of text. "I don't think this is going to help us. It's a summary. We need a manual. What's that?" Amalia pointed to a line of text. "*Ken Salazar, Secretary of Interior, Talks Climate Change, Fracking*. It's from April 2012. Go there."

Jen pulled up the page and they read,

Ken Salazar, Secretary of Interior, Talks Climate Change, Fracking, Energy Issues At Colorado College State of The Rockies Conference.

"There's a video link, can you turn on your volume and we'll watch?" Amalia pulled up her desk chair next to Jen's.

"We're not supposed to have volume in the office," Jen said.

"And when did you get all, 'we're not supposed to'? Turn it on low."

They listened to the soft computer audio and watched a Colorado landscape and a soundtrack roll out in an old advertisement for the 2012 State of the Rockies Conference. "This isn't helpful," Jen said.

"It might be," Amalia said. She grabbed a pen and paper from her desk and wrote the name of the conference down.

"This is a wild goose chase," Jen said. "We don't know what we're looking for."

"Scroll down, there's an article below the video," Amalia said. She read out loud,

"A couple weeks ago in North Dakota you said you hoped fracking wouldn't become the 'Achilles' Heel' of the oil and gas industry. Could you expound on that?

Secretary Salazar: There are three complements of the rule we have under consideration to the [fracking regulation] rule we hope to be able to move forward with. First, part of the rule will be disclosure. The second will be well-bore integrity, and the third will be the monitoring of water that's used in hydraulic fracking."

"There it is. The feds are on it." She sat back. "There's something else, though." A thought, a flash that niggled in her periphery. She slid Jen's keyboard closer and typed, sat back when she saw the search results. Leaned forward and read, "*An Exploratory Study of Air Quality near Natural Gas Operations, 2012.*"

"Exploratory? Amalia, you've got to let this go."

Amalia shook her head, and her hand flew to her mouth. "Holy shit. I was right. Listen." She read aloud, hand on her belly,

"Methylene chloride, a toxic solvent not reported in products used in drilling or hydraulic fracturing, was detected 73% of the time; several times in high concentrations. A literature search of the health effects of the NMHCs revealed that many had multiple health effects, including 30 that affect the endocrine system, which is susceptible to chemical impacts at very low concentrations, far less than government safety standards."

"Seriously? This is getting in the way of your professional growth," Jen said.

"I can't believe you!" Amalia stood up and pushed her chair back to her desk. Her hands shook, but she didn't know what to do about it. The familiar hot flush landed on her chest and face. "Fine, let's get back to the drawings."

They spent an hour on the topographic map, the survey, and Betsy's sketches, and traced together the old environmental center design with the new farmhouse onto one sheet of paper. Amalia continued to sketch perspectives of the farmhouse, soothed by the repetition of strokes over tracing paper. When Max returned, Amalia explained their work. "We thought we should keep to trace for now. But we couldn't find the photos."

"I know where they are," Max said. "The building was pretty well documented in the 1950s before the fire took it out." He looked at the stack of Amalia's hand sketches of the building. "How did you get the feel of this? You haven't even seen the pictures."

"I looked at Betsy's sketches, the ones she emailed. I got a sense from those. And from the site."

"Well done. We can use this for today's work. It'll give Susan and Jeffrey a good idea."

"I need to spend some time apartment hunting," Amalia said. They'd spent an another hour with the drawings and historic photos, while Max moved on to follow up with the new hotel project. "I was hoping to go out at lunch today."

"So make your calls at lunch. I'll stay, you go and do that."

"Really? You're a pal."

Outside on the street, Amalia considered her options. She didn't like the idea of making apartment calls from so close to the office when she was supposed to be up there working, so she took the bus uptown and went to her apartment to search from there.

Her apartment had that cigar smell. She sat down at Joan's desk, fired up the laptop and pulled up *The New York Times,* Craigslist, and some random real estate websites, read them aloud to the room. The last ad caught her eye, because it was the least expensive. Maybe it would be ok. Maybe she'd never run into Sunil up there. She dialed the broker's number and asked about the listing.

"It's going to go within the hour, I guarantee it. You'd better get here fast if you want to have a chance to see it. It's a beauty.

And the price! It can't be beat. It's my hottest listing." The woman sounded breathless.

"I'll be there," Amalia said. She looked around for anything she might need—ID, check book—Social Security card? Pay stubs? It all went in her string bag.

She dashed out and got the bus uptown to meet the woman, both of them now breathless, at the foot of the building at 140th Street. Amalia was both disoriented and exhilarated.

The broker took her into the first floor apartment and touted all of its features: new paint, refreshed floors, new cabinet door-knobs, plus! a stainless steel fridge! plus! a faux-granite countertop! The apartment smelled of a combination of primer and insecticide and it gave Amalia a headache. She stood in the middle of the space and felt the blankness of the walls around her on all sides, close and unyielding.

"Two thousand dollars now and it's all yours, given the credit check passes, and you're employed, and you have an in-state guarantor to co-sign your lease," the woman said with a flash of very bright teeth. She pulled out a copy of the lease to be signed. "You'll get half back when you move out—it's security. Assuming you don't do any damage, change anything, paint anything, or pretty much ask the landlord for anything," she said. "You'd better move fast, I had a couple from Wall Street here not five minutes before you and they've gone to the bank to get cash for their payment. I'll give it to you if you can sign and pay now."

"It's lovely," Amalia said. "I'm sure I could make it very homey. But it's a lot of money. I'm not sure."

"This is the best deal around, I tell you. And next to the train. You go to Columbia? There's a group of Columbia University students upstairs in a three bedroom. Very nice people. Like you."

"I don't know. Maybe you should give it to the couple." Amalia thanked the broker and said goodbye. She walked out the front door and looked up at the building. It was handsome, but it wasn't for her. She walked farther uptown to the area closer to the condo project, to see if she could feel anymore connected to a building nearer to an area she already knew—if only from a half day's site visit.

A big park up ahead on her left: she approached and realized it was a grand cemetery perched on the side of a hill. It all looked quite dignified. Not spooky. Quiet.

Amalia walked next to the low stone wall and looked up at the trees that branched out over the wrought iron railing and over the street. She imagined it as somewhere one might sit with a picnic lunch.

She looked up and across the street and saw a young woman with a baby come out of a corner bodega with a bag of groceries. Maybe she could get something to eat there. A coffee at least. "You've got to eat better, Amalia," she heard her mother say. She walked up to the corner at 154th and crossed when there was a break in traffic. Not many yellow cabs. She'd heard there were other cab services in the city that drove around in long black cars, looking for hires on street corners. She'd heard their ads on the radio.

Walked back down Amsterdam on the other side of the street. On her left was a funeral parlor and a Church of God. She looked down the street at the two-way traffic. The wall of building mass on her left felt softer and more porous. Was it because of the cemetery? She looked up. The apartments looked like they'd seen better days. There was a red *No Trespassing* sign on the wall, over a row of tidy trash bins, lined up and emptied.

Amalia went down into the bodega and looked around the crowded store. Women chatted, men stood at the counter with coffee, deliveries were unloaded onto shelves at the back. Labels leapt out off the shelves into her sight line, most of them familiar, some not. In the ten minutes she was in the store, she heard a mix of Spanish, English, French, Arabic.

The man behind the counter rattled off something in Spanish, then, "What do you need, honey?"

"A coffee. But what I need is an apartment. Do you know of any?"

"Hey, the super next door has an apartment. I know it. Go ask him," he said.

"She doesn't want to go ask him," said a woman in the aisle. "You call him yourself. Do the girl a favor."

He picked up the phone. "Hey, Titian. You have that apartment up there? I have a lovely lady here who wants to see it." He held the phone to his chest. "What's your name?"

"Amalia," she said.

"Beautiful," the woman said. She smoothed a lock of loose hair from Amalia's face. "You married? Got kids?"

"No, not yet."

"Why not? You're getting old, you know."

The man behind the counter hung up. "Can you wait five minutes? Titian's coming down to show you the apartment. If you like."

"Sure, that would be great."

"Cuban?"

"I'm from—well, my parents are from England and India."

"Oh." The woman nodded. "I see." She called to the back of the store. "She's from India. Come and see."

A woman came from the back of the store. "Ah I see, very pretty. She looks Cuban."

"Maybe I should pretend to be when he gets here."

"Be yourself. You don't need to worry about Titian," the woman said.

Titian the Super arrived within minutes and took Amalia up to see the one-bedroom apartment. They walked up four flights of narrow stairs and lit hallways. A waft of cilantro came out of one apartment, a mix of turpentine and vanilla soap came out of another. Latin music drifted from the top floor down the stairwell. He opened the door with a key attached to a carabiner with about a hundred other keys on it, clipped to his belt.

"It's been empty for a month," he said. "We had a leak from a radiator upstairs and it took a while to get it fixed down here. New sheetrock walls," he said, and banged on one with a fist to show her.

Amalia looked around at the apartment. 'This is a one bedroom? It looks like a studio."

"This is the bedroom." He showed her in the back toward two tall windows that looked out onto a dim areaway below.

"I thought this was a closet," she said. She looked out of the bedroom into the main space. From the living room, a narrow little window looked onto another wing of a building up an air shaft outside. She went to the window and disturbed a pigeon when she opened it.

"Works great," Titian said. "New windows."

They didn't look so new to Amalia, but they were not original. Double paned. The room felt solid. There was a funny angle to the door wall she hadn't noticed at first. Was the hallway outside a diamond shape? They must have entered on an angle. The kitchen looked like a hotel bar kitchen: tiny and squeezed onto a portion of one of the living room walls. The bathroom had—

"—all new tile, new toilet, new lights," said Titian.

The apartment was clean. It felt open. "Can I paint?"

"Oh Miss, the painter's mother got sick. I can paint for you. Anything light. You tell me. You show me. I'll do it for you. When do you need the apartment?'

"You haven't got other people waiting?"

"Waiting? Yes, always people waiting. But I haven't shown this one yet because it's not ready. People like to see it finished, you know? But you? For a lovely Latina like you, I'll show you."

"I'm not Latina. They thought I was, downstairs."

"But you should be!" He laughed. "Catholic?"

She smiled, uncertain of how to respond. She supposed that technically she was half Catholic. Half Hindu, half Catholic, and truly, neither. Too hard to for her to explain in a moment, and she didn't want to lie. "How much is the apartment?"

His laughter slowed. "The landlord wants seven hundred fifty dollars. Half a month's rent for the security."

"Credit check?"

"They said downstairs you're ok." He nodded his head toward the door. "We don't have a credit check here. It's ok. It's ok! You can pay this week?"

"I can pay this week. When can I move in?"

"How about next week? I will paint it first. You tell me the color. Can you give me the security deposit now? To make it official."

"Sure, sure," she said. She pulled out her checkbook and the bank teller's face from Monday morning flashed in her mind's eye. She wrote him a check and said a silent prayer he wouldn't deposit it before she'd figured out how to get the money in her account.

"What color do you like? If you show me now I can buy the paint this week and paint on the weekend. Then it can dry out before you move in next week."

"Do you have paint chips?"

"No, you show me a color you like." He pointed to her scarf. "Like, you show me by pointing, and I find it."

"Oh, I see." She fished out her phone from her bag and pulled up her most recent photos from the week before. She scrolled through. It was all pictures of Central Park, from her lunchtime walks. "How about like this?' She held up the phone. "You see the tree bark color and the fall leaf color?"

"You want it like a painting. I can do that. You text me the picture." He took out his phone. "You move in October 31st."

"I'm so grateful," she said. "I never expected to find an apartment this way."

"It's best way," he said. "Otherwise you pay broker fees, you line up. You have headaches. And you don't get to choose your color." He smiled. "Call me next week. We'll take care of it. Nice to meet you." He went into the bathroom to move tiling supplies and rags, and Amalia left, door open behind her. She went downstairs and out to Amsterdam. "Thank you, bodega," she said.

Back in the office after a quiet ride down, Amalia stood with

Max and Jen around the conference table, Betsy on speakerphone. "We've got it sorted out," Betsy said. "Where have you been?"

"I went out for lunch," she said. "I went to see an apartment. I'm sorry. I didn't see the time."

"Sunil is going to be there any minute for the condo structural review," Betsy said.

Max stood at the table. "Amalia. You join Sunil in Meeting Room One."

"Ok, Max." She walked out and into what she hoped would not be one of the more awkward meetings of her life.

She settled in to Meeting Room One and awaited the arrival of Sunil. Her cell phone rang. It looked like a long distance call—maybe Sandra or Great Aunt Joan. "Hello?"

"Amalia, it's Mark. I'm in Wales. I'm standing in a flat the company wants to rent out for me." He spoke to someone in the background.

"What was that, are you with someone?"

"It's the estate agent. She said it's already rented to the company, she was showing it to me. It's a work apartment." He spoke to Amalia. "The company keeps apartments all over. I need to talk to you about this storm coming. You need to get things ready."

"What could there be to get ready? Groceries, I guess. I have a flashlight."

"Have you checked your zone map?"

Amalia heard a woman's giggle in the background. "Ok. I'm sensing this isn't the best time for you to talk about this," she said.

"No, it's fine, the agent is standing next to me twiddling her keys. She's taking me out for dinner."

The line screeched to a close before they'd said goodbye, she supposed in a long distance jaunt between Wales, a satellite or two, and home.

Sunil arrived and was a gentleman, and very professional. Amalia smiled. They could do this, work side by side. It would be fine. They smoothed out the kinks in the project and by the end of the workday, they'd reconciled to be friends. Not that they ever talked about it, Amalia realized; it just evolved that way.

Jen and Amalia left together at 6:30. "There is so much you have to tell me. What happened with Sunil and Mark? And the apartment? And why are you clutching a grocery shopping bag to your chest? Give me the five-minute run down. I've got to get to yoga," Jen said.

"Nothing happened with Sunil. And nothing happened with Mark. But you were right—I do need to be more open. I went uptown. I found an apartment. Or it found me, I'm not sure which."

"So when do you hear? If you got it?"

"I have it, it's mine—I wrote a check but now I have to figure out how to cover it before payday." She paused. "I was thinking of asking you, actually."

"I wish, but I don't have that kind of cash. Your parents?"

"Maybe. I don't think they'd be thrilled. They're paying my grandfather's medical. They'd tell me to move back in with them."

"What about Mark?"

"I only just met Mark!"

"Ok, what about Sandra?"

"She's in Europe. She'd have to wire transfer it. I'm not sure it would work out in time. Plus, I don't think she has that kind of money."

"But her great aunt does."

"I need to get off her great aunt's rent rolls. You know how weird it is to live in the apartment of someone you've never met? Her perfume is still in the medicine cabinet."

"Ew. Listen I have to go." She picked up her tote bag and yoga mat. "Totally forgot to give you this." Jen opened her bag and pulled out a roll of Amalia's muddy clothes. "Class starts in ten minutes. Call me later if you like. And congrats!" Jen took off with her yoga mat rolled and slung in its bag over her shoulder like a bayonet.

Amalia waited for the bus and pulled out her phone. There was one new text from Mark: *a smiley*.

She wondered how Mark's company was doing with the storm prep. She hadn't heard anything more about it so it must be fine. The bus came and she sat at the back, looked out at the darkened city. He always texted her if there was something critical. In how long? They'd met on Saturday. And she'd only had her phone since yesterday. Ok, so 'always' was an exaggeration in her mind. But it made her smile.

Back at her apartment, she sat down at the computer and checked her email. There was a message from The Reverend Mildred who had forwarded her a link to a *Defend our Coast* protest rally in Canada, something about a gathering to protest tar sands development. It seemed far away, but Mildred had written,

The voices of many carry across the winds and the waters.

Amalia wrote back,

Divest from fossil fuels!

Mildred didn't have to go to Canada to take a stand. She could do so within her own church, didn't she see?

Sandra had written,

Any luck finding a new apartment? I'm so sorry about this. Please let me know how it's going. I feel terrible you weren't given much notice.

She'd write back later.

First, she had to figure out how to fund a New York kind of lifestyle. She took out her phone and called her parents. "I have a problem."

"You have my full attention," her mother said. She heard her walk into the kitchen and open the fridge. "I'm getting a soda, so I can listen to you better," she said. Amalia heard the fizz of the drink over the phone.

"I have to move out of Sandra's great aunt's apartment. I need money to pay for the next month of rent and deposit, and I don't get paid until next week. And the landlord wants the money now." She waited to let this sink in.

"You'd like me to wave a magic wand and make it happen for you."

"No, I didn't say that. I'm telling you what's going on in my life."

"Amalia, let me be clear about something. When you decided to move to New York, it was our understanding you would be funding the adventure on your own. We're not in a position to support that lifestyle. I wish we could, but we can't. Not now with your grandfather's hospice bills."

"I know, and I feel terrible for asking. How is he? I don't know who else to turn to."

"He's taking it day by day over there. The nurses at the hospice have set him up with a webcam. They're very high tech, you know? It's not that we don't want to support you. We do. We don't have the actual cash to send you. You always have a home here. I can clear out the sewing stuff from your bedroom."

"There's sewing stuff in my bedroom?"

"I'm working on a quilt."

"That's cool, mom, you can use it—I mean, I'm not there, so you should." Amalia felt her eyes sting. "I want to stay in the city, Mom, I want to see you and Dad, but I'm not done here."

"Ok. How's work, Amalia? Maybe you could ask your boss for an advance."

"Work's been interesting. It's fine. But I couldn't ask them. They're too cash strapped."

"You are welcome here anytime. All the time. This is your home. Know you can always come home when your city adventure is done."

They hung up and Amalia sat back in the chair and poked through loan shark websites online. After a few minutes she stood up. Maybe she could sell something. She imagined this was what drove women to prostitution: the need to sell something fast without having to go to a loan shark. She wasn't going there.

She could make something to sell. She could sell her sketches. She pulled up Etsy online and looked around. How hard could it be to start an Etsy shop? But in time to make the rent? She could at least try. She pulled out her portfolio box and rifled through her drawings. Maybe she could sell some of those? She laid out the work on the Persian rug, and spread it over the couch and desk. There was enough. She could keep some to show potential employers, and unload the rest.

She looked at Joan's combination scanner/printer/fax machine and wondered if it was up to the task. She tried to fit the images on the glass but some of them hung over the edge. She could crop the edges but then she'd lose some detail. Maybe take the drawings to a copy shop for scanning? She couldn't spend money to take a chance she might make money. In theory, sure. She didn't have it to give. In the end, she resorted to pictures of the art taken on her cell phone, emailed to herself. They looked nothing like the original images. She couldn't sell them.

She wondered what Mark was doing. Why hadn't he texted her? She went to her phone. The last message from him was vague. And she hadn't written back to him. But what was there to say after a smiley? Another smiley? It was an unsatisfying language, the language of emoticons. It didn't show you what to do next.

She pulled up his number and called. It went to voice mail without a ring. His phone must be off, out of range. What was he doing over there? She went back to the computer and moved some drawings out of the way. Sat back and picked up a sketch from the computer table. It was of a scene from Vancouver. Everything about the sketch tugged at her: the weather, the context, the company. She picked up her phone and dialed by memory.

"Hi, Nadel? It's me, Amalia. Have I caught you at a bad time?"

"No, it's fine. It's good to hear from you." He sounded far—was it the distance, or him?

"I have to get out of my apartment," she said. "I was subletting and—the sublet is over. I have to be out this week."

"I'm sorry to hear that."

"You know Sandra? From architecture school? Her Great Aunt Joan's apartment, the one I moved into?"

"The lucky break that allowed you to land in New York."

"Not so much of a lucky break anymore. I need a new lucky break."

"There have got to be a million apartments in New York."

"I found one. I can't afford it."

"The princess comes down to earth," he said.

"Not nice. You're not being fair." She went into the bathroom and took the backpack off the shower rail and put it on the floor next to the sink.

"Make a list of your actual costs. Figure out what you need. And call me back."

"Why?" She looked at herself in Great Aunt Joan's mirror, opened the medicine cabinet, and held Joan's lavender oil in one hand.

"I'm going to lend you the money."

"What? No. I didn't even ask you."

"I can't believe you, Amalia. You're so passive aggressive. You totally asked me for the money."

"No, I never did. And don't call me passive aggressive."

"I don't mind, just be honest about it. I'm happy to lend you the money. It's not a lot. I can wire-transfer it to you."

She listed everything she could think of and needed to pay for before the end of the month. She even splurged on a taxi ride. And a pizza and beer for Sunil and Jen, whom she hoped she could rope in. Company would make it bearable, even if there was not a lot of stuff to move. Could she ask Sunil to help? She could, but it would be weird. Jen would help. She'd bring friends and turn it into an Obama campaign meeting. She tallied the costs and called Nadel back.

"Not so bad," he said.

"I miss you," she said. "You always were way more understanding of me than I ever was of you," she said.

"You've got to look out for yourself. If you don't, who will?"

Later, when she lay in bed beneath Great Aunt Joan's patchwork quilt, she felt the memory of Nadel within her. But when she awoke in the middle of the night, her eye caught Mark's shirt on the back of the desk chair, and it was he who she had in her mind's eye when she went back to sleep.

Chapter 20

Mark sat with his estate agent Anwen in front of the fire in the hearth at the White Hart Inn, his back turned sideways to the door. She'd suggested a drink on the way to his new flat, rented by Atlantia for the duration. He didn't see the men come in, her men, she said when she stood up to greet them with a wave and a jiggle of her hips. "My men, this is Mark. He's arrived from New York." Mark took in the three: the dark bearded faces, the receding hairlines, the gruff moustaches—all three men bore a resemblance to one another, and to Anwen. "My brothers," she said.

He'd finished his pub meal, and was on his second pint—more than he went for at home, but Anwen had insisted. And as he'd said to her, it was a business expense. No reason not to. Now, on seeing Anwen's brothers' silhouettes emerge in the low doorframe of the old stone pub, he wished for a moment he'd allowed himself to keep a clear head. Protective, were they? One man sat down next to him and put an arm, heavy, across Mark's back, gripped his shoulder.

"What you want with our Anwen?"

"No, now, boys, never you mind. This Mr. Stone, he's in the mining business."

"Oh, is he, now." One of the Moustaches grabbed Mark's beer

mug. "Another for the gentleman from New York," he said, and swung the mug in the air to get the barmaid's attention.

Mark eased out of the grip of the brother. The beer continued to flow and he became the center of stories, laughter, and backslaps that pitched him forward into the table. Still, it came back to mining. What were they after? He felt he ought not to ask, didn't trust their loose lips, his alcohol-softened tongue.

There was a slow descent into haze, Anwen's long red hair brushed across his cheek when she leaned forward across the table, and—he asked for a glass of water in an attempt to salvage his sobriety. The last clear thought of the brothers was of the three on their feet, arms shoulder-to-shoulder, in a sideways body wave that moved in time with an old Welsh miner's song. Half the bar patrons looked on, joined in; half ignored, caught up in conversation, until updates of a football match came on the television, Cardiff versus Watford they said, and all eyes turned to the big screen.

She pushed off from her brothers at nine in the evening, with a wink, and wrapped herself into Mark. "Take me home. Take me to your home."

"We've had so much to drink," he said. "You shouldn't drive." He wobbled when he pushed off the table to stand, and she giggled. Jet lag and beer had him cornered.

"I'll leave my car," she said. "We'll walk. Your flat's near enough." She curled into the crook of his arm, strolled out into the gray of the Welsh night. "That's a waxing gibbous moon," she said, and pointed up to the half moon in the dark sky. "The half ellipse. Growing bigger, swelling."

Was she so transparent? Or was he drunk? He only wanted to be with one woman now, and that woman had said no thank you, she was not interested. It wasn't this Anwen he wanted. Didn't want, but was drawn in nonetheless.

When they arrived at his flat, she unlocked the door for him—she still held the keys—and went in first, kicked off her shoes and led him upstairs to the bedroom as if it were her own.

"I've got that coal miners' music in my head," he said.

"Not what I had in mind," Anwen said, and turned on the radio in the living room. "This," she said, "might be a wee bit more lively." Top Ten pop songs blared, and she led him in a drunken striptease up the stairs to the bedroom.

In the end, he couldn't bring himself to go through with it, and went into the bathroom alone, and when he returned to the bedroom, she was asleep.

Chapter 21

Wednesday, October 24

Mark rolled over on the double bed and into limbs—not his own. He looked up to see Anwen's long red hair spread out on the pillow and sheets; tried to remember how they had come to be like this. Ah, yes. The pints. And the additional pints.

"Good morning, handsome," Anwen said. She rolled back to him, and half sat up in his bed.

He stood up and pulled a shirt from the back of the couch, went to the bathroom and splashed cold water on his face. A single towel hung on the wall and he used it. Had it been put there for him? "Good morning." He squinted at his reflection in the mirror. He'd looked better.

"Quite a time last night," she said.

"But nothing happened. I mean, you stayed over, but nothing happened." His recollection was bleary but he was confident he hadn't done anything he'd regret. He hoped. This hangover, though, was the more pressing concern to be addressed. Mark went back into the bedroom.

She pouted. "Nothing happened? Not what I remember."

Mark ran a hand through his hair. He'd better get moving or this was going to drag on. "Do you have coffee in this town, or only tea?"

"My word, only tea? Who do you think we are? We've the best coffee in Wales here in Brecon." She threw off the bedcovers. She'd taken off her trousers and left them next to the bed; she pulled them on as he spoke, and he turned his back to look away.

"We should go," he said. "Come on, I'm going to need something strong to shake this transatlantic jet fuzz in my head. Not to mention the beer, courtesy of your brothers."

"What time do you have to be there?" She'd murmured something in Welsh he couldn't comprehend. "Time to get you to The Hours."

"I need to get an adapter for my cell phone charger before I do anything else," he said.

"You know that's going to cost you a pretty penny, using that over here," she said. "You ought to switch over to a local mobile company."

"Sure, but I don't know how long I'm going to be here."

"I thought you said you were staying." She sat down on the settee, half-clothed, cross-legged.

He tried to look away but found her magnetic, so he—kept his gaze on her. "I'm here for a few days this time, but I don't know when they're having me come back. It's a public relations thing. PR. You know?"

She ran a hand through her long hair and scratched her head. "I'll bet you're married. You're married, aren't you?"

"What? No. I thought we had a great time last night."

"Ah yes, mister, so did I." She stood up and looked for her bag. "You'll need these," she said, and tossed him the keys to the flat, pulled her shirt over her head, fast.

He caught the keys and put them on the dresser. "Anwen."

"The gas on the hob must be lit with a match. You can't park in the disabled spots. And you know? I'm not even going to tell you how to get to The Hours." She flounced out the flat.

"Wait!" He dashed out after her and ran down to street level but was stopped at the threshold by the damp morning that came up to meet his socks. He couldn't see which way she'd gone. She'd parked her car at the pub around the corner last night, and he could see neither it, nor her. He tiptoed from the house to the street then decided against a search. Wet socks.

Dammit. He stood at the door and looked up at the little church across the narrow street. A neighbor's garden sprung fall colors. The town curled around him like an autumn leaf, old and warm-toned.

He turned and looked up at the long frontage of row houses, white, similar in age and appearance, all with new windows hung over dark stone sills. He went back inside and looked around. The two-story flat was furnished, small and tidy, ample for one person. He'd call Timmy later, but he'd still be fast asleep now, middle of the night over there.

And Amalia. He needed to call her too. He hoped she was up to speed on the storm track. He wasn't worried about Timmy, who had a home full of ample provisions and a large network of friends, neighbors and coworkers to look out for him. His cell phone buzzed: Amalia. "You must have known I was thinking of you."

"I woke up from a bad dream." She cleared her throat, sounded tired. "More alarming than bad. It was about Easter Island," she said. "It was at the center of the earth."

"You mean at the molten center? Land masses can't get sucked into the core of the earth. I suppose if there was a planetary—"

"Mark! That wasn't my dream. Listen. Can you talk now or not? No one in the background?"

"She left."

"She left—when?" Her voice held a singsong of tired amusement.

"Amalia, you're calling for a reason. Isn't it the middle of the night there? This dream of Easter Island. Rapa Nui."

"What?"

"Rapa Nui. Easter Island."

"Rapa Nui. It was the largest on the map. There was a map of the earth, and it was the largest."

"The largest what?"

"Land mass. Continent. It looked kind of like Australia but more huge, and it took up the whole view of the map."

"What kind of projection was it? Because the masses near the equator would appear to be—"

"Mark. Really? Listen."

"Sorry." He sat on the settee. Anwen had left a hair elastic there and he picked it up and stretched it open with five fingers on one hand.

"Easter Island, Rapa Nui, it was on this map projection that looked kind of like Google Earth. I don't know what kind of projection that is. Google Projection. The image was kind of luminescent too, kind of how a computer screen lights up an image from inside. So the map was glowing, Rapa Nui was glowing. It wasn't spinning around like Google Earth, but it had the potential. It felt kind of—kinetic. Like you could search it more closely if you wanted. But this was a stepping back view, you know? Like we were standing a couple of feet away from the computer screen. Are you with me?"

"I'm listening."

"Rapa Nui was the earth. It was the whole earth. There weren't other land masses, at least not on the side of the globe that was showing. I'm not talking geologic shift. It's not like all the masses had swarmed together to make a big new continent."

"Or big old continent," he said.

"Or big old continent. Neither new nor old. Simply present."

"It sounds like a computer screen capture. What was your sense?"

"I don't know. It was a message. It was like, 'Look at me. I am one and the same: Rapa Nui, Earth.' There was no difference. What happens in Rapa Nui happens in the earth. For all of the earth. I didn't understand it."

"But it felt important enough for you to get up and call me to tell me about it."

She was silent. Then, "I miss you Mark."

"I miss you too." He fiddled with Anwen's hair elastic, thought of Amalia's dark brown eyes.

"What happened in Rapa Nui?" She sounded sleepy.

"I read a report that puts the stone used to create the sculptures as coming from below sea level," Mark said.

"As in, underwater quarrying?"

"No, as in, land that used to be above sea level is now below sea level."

"Ah." Her voice was distant.

"And from the stone's weathering, the sculptures, the stone heads, might be older than they thought." They were silent on the phone for a moment. "You should consider getting out of town. This storm's getting bigger."

"I'm not getting out of town," Amalia said. "People did that last year during Hurricane Irene and they got it worse upstate than they did in the city. And besides, this is a tropical storm."

"So was Irene, when it got to New York City," he said.

"You're being reactionary."

"I'm being cautionary. There's a difference. Look, you'll need to check the SLOSH data. I don't have it in front of me. I can fire up my laptop and send it to you."

"The what?"

"The flood zone data. The SLOSH data. Architects don't look at it?"

"I have no idea what you're talking about." She'd moved on from sleepy to irritated.

"Storm surge modeling. This is important, Amalia. I need you to check with the City to see if they have an evacuation plan in place."

"You're kidding me. Look, don't worry so much. I'm on high ground. And my new apartment is, too. Did I tell you? I found a new apartment. And I called my ex-boyfriend tonight. Nadel. He's loaning me the money for it."

"Nice of him. You could have asked me, you know."

"Would it have been any less complicated asking you?"

"Maybe. He's your ex. That sounds messy."

"And you?"

"Amalia, I should tell you something. About Anwen. The estate agent you heard on the phone last night."

"You know what? You don't have to tell me anything. I don't need to know. I don't want to know. You don't owe me any explanations."

"See, it's all about what we think we owe one another. You owe your ex money. I owe you explanations."

"I said you don't owe me explanations."

Mark heard a car engine turn off outside. Footsteps tapped up the stone walk. A light rap on the door, tentative.

"Amalia? Hang on. There's someone downstairs."

"Oh, you want to get off the phone."

"No, I do hear someone. Stay on the phone while I check, if you don't believe me."

"Sounds like fun. I'll meet the Welsh postman."

He walked out the sitting room and down the stairs. "Opening the door now, let's see who it is." He opened the door. "Anwen!" Anwen stood in front of the house. Her boxy, olive car was parked in the driveway of the church opposite Mark's flat.

"Anwen as in the estate agent?"

"I'm to take you to the meeting," Anwen said. "I forgot."

"Oh. Anwen. Please come in." He stood back. "Amalia, I need to go. Anwen is here to take me to a meeting."

"Thank goodness. I thought she might have stayed overnight."

Mark ended the strange call and faced Anwen, who looked flushed.

"I'm sorry," she said. "I ran out so fast. This has happened before. I've been left in the lurch, you see."

"We had a lot to drink last night," he said. She put her hand on his chest and he covered it with his palm. Took her hand off and held it, walked her into the flat. "Wait here." He fiddled with his phone.

"Who were you talking to?"

"A friend from back home," he said. "Give me five minutes? I'll be quick."

"We haven't eaten," she said. "Do you have time to come for breakfast?"

"I have no idea what time it is. In New York it was—six. But with Daylight Savings? I'm—"

"Take your bath?" Her hand slid down his side, and he pushed it off, without anger, he hoped.

This was so unlike him. He ran up the stairs to the bathroom. Grabbed his toilet bag from his suitcase and ran hot water in the tub. He looked up. There was no shower head. He was tempted to call out to her and ask her about this annoyance but didn't want her in there with him. He needed to get his head clear.

The water ran into the bathtub and he went back to the bedroom to lay out his clothes. Unzipped the suit bag that hung on the back of the bedroom door and took out the navy single-breasted jacket. It had fared well enough on the journey. Was this a tie sort of a meeting, or could he get away with a sports jacket? Would he be overdressed? He had no idea.

He went into the bathroom, closed the door, and stripped down to bare. He put a foot in; hotter than he'd expected. He lowered himself into the tub and submerged his shoulders and head so his folded legs bent up at the far end. Not sized for him, to be sure. There wasn't any soap. A towel hung on the coils on the wall.

Without soap, and without a showerhead, there was not much to do except to soak. He shifted up and down, stretched his legs and shot his torso up out of the water. Bent at the knees, he sunk his chest under the water. Did more tub calisthenics until he felt clearer of the previous night. The only thing he couldn't shake was Amalia's voice on the phone, sleepy and in search of clarity.

"How are you coming along?" Anwen's voice floated up the stairs.

He sat up and ran his hands over his head to squeeze water out of his hair, then emptied the bath and climbed out. The floor was quite warm. He toweled off. Fact was, he admitted to himself in the mirror, he remembered every detail of the night. He wrapped the towel around his waist and grabbed the clothes from the floor so as to add an extra layer between him and Anwen, should she interrupt on his way to the bedroom. She did not.

He moved everything off the bed and pulled up the sheets and blankets. He hated to leave with the rumpled reminder of last night like this for a whole day in his absence, didn't want to come home to it later. He tried to make it look normal. It didn't feel normal, and neither did he.

"How long does it take to get there?" He held onto the rail down the stairs to the living room.

"I'll take you."

"Thanks. I'm sure I could have found it myself."

"No, it's fine, no trouble, really. When are you coming back?"

"Late," he said. "They're taking me to a few different sites."

"I'll fetch you," she said.

"No, it's ok. I'm sure they'll drop me off here." He had his briefcase in one hand and the plastic bag with his hardhat and boots in the other. "The keys."

"I gave them to you. Upstairs? I'll get them," she said. She ran up the stairs and grabbed them from the bedroom. "You're very tidy," she said when she came back down. "You made the bed."

Anwen drove them in her boxy car and parked in the old town, led him across the way to a little café up Ship Street. "Welcome to The Hours," she said, and opened her arms in a gesture of pride.

"Looks lovely. Books and stuff," he said.

"Ah, so you're not the bookish type."

"More arty than bookish. I mean, I draw."

"You do! Draw me!" She took a seat in the cafe-bookstore, warm and crowded. Anwen took off her jacket and plumped up her breasts, her hair.

She's putting it on, he thought; going for some goal, beyond getting him back in bed. "I don't know about that." Mark took a menu, looked down, tried to hide his face.

"Oh, now, embarrassed, are we? No need. I pose nude. I mean, I've done it. And there's no need to be ashamed of the flesh. You certainly were not last night!"

"I'm—not." He looked down at the menu. "Not interested. In the food. On the menu."

"Oh?" She pulled his menu toward her and ran a fingernail down the items. "Try this." She tapped at one dish. "It's a must-have. And I must have—"

"I like you, Anwen—"

"No buts. I will hear none of it. Toffee pudding it will be." Anwen waved down a server who took their orders. "Two coffees, two toffee puddings."

"Settled? Like that?"

"I act fast." She whipped out a lipstick and touched up. "Where are they taking you today? Or should I ask you after I've buttered you up with the toffee pudding?

"I don't know, actually. Some sites south of here, and across the water, too." He looked around the café at the book-lined walls.

"Over in England?"

"I—I'm not supposed to say."

"Over the water and yonder is more England."

"I can't."

"Even for a friend? For an overnight friend who took you out on the town? And got you a little toffee pudding in the morning?" She pouted, crossed her arms.

"Don't. Please." The server brought two coffees to the table and Mark doctored his heavily with cream until it cooled; he drank it all in one go. Needed. To. Get. Clear. Fast. "What's your interest in—my work?"

"Little me? No interest. No interest at all." Her legs, crossed, uncrossed, crossed, and she pushed her coffee to the side, hands clasped on the table. "We were coal miners, see." Anwen sat erect, forward, eyes on him.

"Aha."

"Deep pit miners, my men were." Eyes didn't blink, even when the server approached, brought their breakfast to the table. "My men's work was shut out. Closed off." She dug into her toffee pudding and served a spoonful to Mark, which he ate with reluctance. "Worked the colliery, they did, until Thatcher shut them down."

"What've they been doing since then?" They'd looked older than her, older than him, to be sure, and much larger. Big hands rose up in his mind's eye, memory recall still bright from the night before, in spite of beer and a desire to feign amnesia.

"Odd jobs." She fed him another bite of her pudding even though his own sat before him on the table. "If there's a chance you can help, sir, you owe it to them. To us. To me."

Sir? When did he become sir? And jobs? So that was it. She wasn't a fracking protester—but the opposite. But—did he owe her? "I'm sorry, Anwen. I can't—I'm not able to, not authorized to—" He could, though. He could help connect her and her men to the jobs that would result from Atlantia's growth in the region.

She pushed back, picked up the coffee cup and swigged it like a mug of beer, regarded him from over its rim. Cup down. She put her hand over her heart, took a deep breath, and dug into her toffee pudding with a flourish of the spoon. "Let's think about that nude portrait, shall we?"

He ate in silence, uncertain of the best words, the safe move. Watched her while she ate, and looked up and out at old Brecon, silver-gray with the glisten of a morning rain shower. "Thanks for taking me out on the town," he said when they'd finished their meal. "This place is amazing. And I can now say I have had toffee pudding for breakfast."

"You mean, thanks for last night?" She put a hand over his, and he pulled away. "Come, then." She stood up. "Let's get you to your meeting." They returned to the car a block back; the slow pace of the old town grounded him. She drove him a long way, it seemed to him, and when they were near the Guildhall she double parked and pointed the way down a narrow street, blocked with delivery vehicles and walled in by old storefronts. He leaned over to kiss her on the cheek and she turned to kiss him on the lips, but he pulled back.

"So where are they taking us today?" Mark stood with Simon in front of the Guildhall.

"It's you and me. I'm going to drive us to a couple of sites, show you what you'll be speaking about, and then I thought we could hit a pub or two on the way back. How was your flight?"

"Busy. I was prepping material."

"You don't need to prep material. You need to open your mouth and talk."

"I need to know about the places we're working. I need to know who the people are. What their state of mind is."

"The state of mind is kind of grim around here, now, I have to tell you. All I've heard about these last two weeks is about this little girl who went missing. I was even asked to volunteer to look for her."

"Was she found?"

"No." His face was solemn. "The whole countryside is—sad."

"I'm sorry, I hadn't heard." He would have to ask Anwen later.

The two stood in silence and looked at the assembled business group break up from the morning meeting, and reassemble into pods of interest and congeniality. "Let's go. There's nothing and no one waiting for us," Simon said. They walked out to the main hallway.

Mark stopped to look at the framed images on the wall. "Love this old building," he said.

"The Guildhall. The history of the guilds—and of the trades here—that's ancient." Simon nodded to the door. "My car's down the street." He pointed Mark around the corner. "How's your flat?"

"Nice, cozy. No shower head. But strangely, it has radiant heating in the bathroom."

"Probably hot water pipes underneath. The older buildings

leak energy all over. There's an energy rating system, you know. You can look up your building. My flat has it."

"Where's your flat?"

Simon indicated down the road. "About a five minute walk. By your place."

"My place is five minutes from here? Walking? Anwen said she needed to drive me last night. And then she took me on a long drive to a place for breakfast this morning. And then to here."

"I'd say you were getting the runaround. Who's Anwen? You getting busy already? You just landed! Dude!" He punched Mark on the arm.

"She's the estate agent. Didn't you meet her when you arrived?"

"I met an older guy. He took me to a pub and I met his wife. I'll introduce you. Thing is, he didn't seem very happy about Atlantia Actuaris being here. He and his wife had that going on."

"More protesters here than back home?"

"Ok fine, so don't tell me about Anwen."

"And I'm not, because there's nothing to tell. Where are we going today? What's the state of things here?"

"Three other companies are working in the area. It's a public relations thing at this point. The permits are where they are. We're exploring. Nothing happening on the extraction side. It's up to you, buddy. Calm the masses. Promise of jobs."

"About that," Mark said. "My job is about more than calming masses of people from random hysteria based on unscientific anecdotal evidence. I'm a geologist. I work with the earth."

"And that's why they love you. They trust you. You're—earthy."

They walked down the street to Simon's car.

"You're renting this?" Mark looked at the old metal shell of a car.

"Bought it from the estate agent. Wanted something of my own. He said it was his old company car."

"Vauxhall Cavalier," Mark read.

"1984."

"Old car," Mark said. "A year older than me." He went to the American passenger side. "Left hand drive. I keep forgetting." Walked around the front of the car. "You bought a car from a fracking protester?"

"Mark. You're over-thinking. When you talk, it's golden. You'll turn them all around."

They pulled out and drove down High Street. "I kind of—look at my notes, close my eyes, see the ground—the land I mean—feel it, and then I talk."

"So you get in touch with the material. Cool. Do that. I'll get you in a good place to get in touch with the ground here. That's what today's all about. So we're good."

Mark sat back. "I guess."

"This Anwen. You know—I know when things get—opened up, so to speak—it's easy to talk. Let words slip. But you can't share the site locations. We're not authorized yet."

"It is not going to be a problem. There's no opening, Simon, I told you." They drove out on the A40, past farmland and the River Usk. Past expansive sheep farms that looked centuries old. The river wound near and far, and they continued to travel through villages along it. "That ever flood?"

"Nah. Maybe. I don't know. Probably." Simon switched on the radio. "No CD player."

"I'll do it, you drive." Mark tweaked the knob to hold it stable on BBC Wales. The news was grim, as Simon had said. The news shifted to music. "I recognize this." Synth and drums. "It's that Korean song."

Simon drummed on the steering wheel, music loud over the landscape that rolled away. "Hey, sexy lady," Simon sang. The land shifted from green to gray, farmland to former coal mine. Simon pulled over on the right before a town, parked the car. Mark got out and followed Simon down and around the site.

They stood at the edge of the old coal pit, now covered and out of use. "So they want to drill down the shaft? That can work."

"Minimize the impact. Work with what is already here. They've been mining here since Roman times. Bloody brilliant, if you ask me."

"You sound like a Brit already," Mark said.

"You—you've already hooked up with this Anwen."

"Would you let it go, already? Nothing happened with Anwen."

"Fine, fine. Don't get in a huff when I mention a woman."

"I'm not in a huff."

"You're huffing," Simon said. "You're sending up puffs of dust beneath your feet."

Mark kicked into the old site, his dress shoes covered in gray, textured grit. "I am not huffing." He looked down at his shoes. "Shit. Should've changed into the work boots." He bobbed down and swiped the grit with his fingertips, rubbed it between his fingers, sniffed it, tasted it. "Ok. Fine. Something happened with Anwen." They walked around the old mine in a clockwise direction along the old road that surrounded it. "She took me out for drinks. Last night. Some pub I can't remember. And that's it. End of story."

"You know, the women here, they're very—I don't know how to say—I wouldn't mess with them, Mark. Or their brothers."

"Brothers."

"There's a lot of loyalty. We're outsiders, Mark." Simon sped his walking pace toward the car. "Come on, I have another site to show you."

"An old mine?"

"No. Glamorgan. They call it the crucible of the Industrial Revolution—the coal mining. Mostly farmland now. We've set up a trailer on site."

"I'm going to take a leak over there," Simon said. "Meet you at the site trailer."

Mark sat at the edge of the passenger seat, switched his dress shoes to work boots, looked around. So this was Glamorgan. In this valley, nestled between rounded hills—mountains, here—he felt as comfortable as he ever did in the Notches of his native New Hampshire. Mark went up the trailer steps and opened the door Simon left unlocked for him. Gangnam Style rhythm bounced in his head. There was a computer and a light on a desk, old. He turned on the power, jiggled the mouse.

He had a few minutes. He went online, logged onto his personal email. There was something from Timmy, a joke, and something from Amalia. He scanned the joke and replied with a

Ha!

and settled back in the chair to read Amalia's message. It was brief. It said,

Are you doing something over there I'm not going to want to know about? Tell me now. I need details. A.

She'd already asked him about Anwen, and she'd said she didn't want details. Did she mean about his job?

The second odd message in two days, but this one he could source. He didn't have to tell her anything. And she'd said they didn't owe each other anything. Or had he said that to her? The words twisted in his mind, and he felt fuzziness descend again. He'd send her something brief.

Nothing fixed. There's a lot of competition for sites, jockeying for position. I'm on a site now—you'd like it, it's beautiful. Looked at an old coal mine earlier today. You'd have had something to say, I'm sure.

He heard Simon outside and another man's voice that carried the intonation of a question. "Papers are all in here, sir," Simon said. The door opened. Mark turned off the screen and pushed the folding chair back on the floor. "This is Mr.—"

"Mr. Welles," the man said. He carried a shotgun.

"A local farmer."

"I want to know what you're doing on my land." He shifted.

"Ah, sir. Please come in." Mark stood.

"No. Thank you."

"This is private property," Mark said.

"I know, it's my private property," Mr. Welles said.

"All right. I'm sure we can find someone who can help you," Mark said. "We're not the right people for you to speak with."

"You're here. You're here on my land. You have set up a camper van on my land. You're in the middle of my property."

"Maybe we should have come with the guys," Simon said to Mark.

"Maybe you should not have come at all," Mr. Welles said. He gripped his gun.

"Look, we don't need to be here now," Mark said to Simon. "We can come back. Maybe the visit was premature."

"Mr. Welles. There is nothing happening on this land at present. This trailer is part of a scientific expedition. We are visitors. I can give you the phone number of the company headquarters."

"I have the phone number of the company headquarters. What I want is someone to answer the phone. I have you here. Come on now, lads." He motioned with the shotgun for the two of them to follow him outside. Mark picked up his bag and turned off the desk lamp. Simon closed the padlock on the door behind them after they'd all exited and stood down on the soft ground. "Come with."

"I'm not sure this is a good idea," Simon said.

"My cell phone's on—we can always call for help," Mark said. "Let's see."

They followed Mr. Welles along one side of the perimeter of the property for almost a mile. He said little, but pointed out the features one by one with the barrel of his gun. "Catnip. Mint," he said of the hedgerow outcrops. "Sorrel. Thyme," he said of the patches in the meadow. "My Holsteins," he said, and waved the shotgun across the field toward a herd of cows that grazed on the hillside. They climbed over a broken stone wall. "Harebells." He swatted the tall green stalks with the tip of his gun. At the end of the next stone wall, Mr. Welles made a sharp turn for home and left them alone in the field. He tipped his hat when he walked away, back turned.

"So we're standing in the middle of a Welsh field, abandoned by a pissed off local farmer, armed with a shotgun. Great," Simon said.

"No, listen. It's all about connecting to the local color. Here we have it." Mark bobbed down and dug four fingers into the earth.

"You don't seem very concerned about the gun."

"I grew up with guns. Use with respect. Treat with care." He raised a fistful of soil. "You have a bag?"

"I don't know what you're doing. But I have a chip packet. Empty."

"Turn it inside out. That'll do." Their four hands turned the metalized plastic inside out and got the soil into the bag.

Mark looked up at the figure of Mr. Welles disappear down the slope. Harebell stalks brushed up against his boots, which made him appear to float down the hill. Simon's eyes followed. "I hadn't realized what a slope we'd climbed," Simon said. "I'm about done with this. And Mr. Welles may be back with his shotgun, if we don't get going soon."

"I don't think so." Mark rolled the top of the chip packet down and put it in his vest pocket. "Assume it will go well. Don't assume you're hated before you've even started up. Like on the Pennsylvania site."

"Nah. That'll be fine," Simon said. "That was just the curing time on the concrete. The project manager was under the gun."

"One of the subcontractors."

"Yeah." Simon looked around.

"You're too jumpy."

"Fine, have it your way. Stay. Wander. I'm heading back to the trailer." Simon followed off on the path trod in the grasses by Mr. Welles.

Mark looked away and farther up the hill. They'd hiked up a fair distance. He continued up for a while, along the edge of a stacked stone wall. The sky was clear blue, not a cloud in the sky, and the wind was slow. The air was sweet, warm on his face, but chilled his back. A perfect combination. He turned back after a few minutes, thoughts blank. He went back down the hill. Simon came up toward him. "Hey, man."

"Where have you been? We need to get going." Simon was out of breath.

"You said look around, so I did."

"I said, Mr. Welles is going to come back with his shotgun, if I recall correctly." They went back down the hill, faster than on the way up. "I'll close up, don't think I shut off the computer."

"Already done," Simon said. He checked the trailer door was locked before they got into the old Vauxhall Cavalier and headed out. "If you want local color, check out a pub. Fit it into your speech. Make it regional. People love that. And see if they have any coffee while you're at it. You look like hell." Simon's tone had changed, and Mark wondered if he'd read the correspondence with Amalia.

They drove back through farmland and stopped at a pub off the road, a small stone structure with slate roof tiles and a large Welsh lion flag draped out front. It was busy with tourists and locals. Mark wasn't sure where the people had come from; the roads were quiet. The pub was noisy, and he heard a blend of English and Welsh languages meld across the room.

Mark closed his eyes and tapped his fingers together, his elbows on the edge of the wooden table. "I have a sense of something as we've driven through. And it's something I spoke about at the energy symposium last week. The geologic connection between Wales—the UK—and America."

"Sure, the land was connected at one point. Gondwanaland."

"Exactly. You see the slate roofs here? And you know the ones on the flats in Brecon."

"Yes. They're like the slate roofs back home. Different, but same general idea."

"Yes. There's a difference between American slates and Welsh slates. But they're also more similar than different. And that's because they're related."

"Ok."

"Have you heard of the Avalonian Arc?" He looked up at the server who approached and put down a pint and a coffee on the table. Mark took the coffee.

"No. Avalonian what?"

"Arc. It's a theory that explains the geologic connections between the UK and America, through a description of the evolution of the sea bed. The sea bed, Simon; untapped potential." Mark pulled out his wallet to pay.

"Feeling rich on your untapped potential?" Simon waved for the check and pointed to Mark.

"It's a business expense," Mark said. He sat back and checked his phone.

"Miss anything good? Anwen?"

"Would you stop about Anwen?"

"Why, is there someone else?"

"Give me a minute." Mark scrolled down through the messages. "Looks like I missed a lot. Did you get the alerts about Sandy?"

"Ah, there is someone else."

"No, dufus, the tropical storm. It's picking up. Supposedly around Jamaica now." He stood up. "I'm going to step outside and make a couple of calls."

"Be my guest. I'll use the little boys' room and meet you at the car."

"Little boy you are." Mark ducked through the low doorframe and out into the parking lot. The sun had set, and left behind a luminous and eerie sky, from which drizzle fell through fog. Wales. He liked it.

He spoke in turn to Timmy, Amalia and Anwen. To Timmy, he spoke of batteries and food. To Amalia, he spoke of flood levels in New York City. She chided him for his over-preparedness. To Anwen, he said goodbye.

"On the phone? You dumped a girl on the phone? Even I wouldn't do that," Simon said, back in the pub.

"We weren't dating. I didn't want it to become a thing."

"From the look on your face, it was already a thing."

"It was a mistake," Mark said.

"A mistake is a thing—and it can turn into something bigger. We need to fit in. Think about what we're doing here."

"I know perfectly well what we're doing here." Mark said. "Exploring. Permitting."

"Semantics," Mark said.

Chapter 22

Thursday, October 25

Amalia rolled out of bed and knelt on the floor, arms back alongside her hips and thighs. She bent forward and rested her forehead on the floor. Wasn't ready for the day.

Her sleep had been disturbed by the dream of Rapa Nui, and the conversation with Mark. She wondered if he was with Anwen. What time was it there? She looked at the clock. Uh-oh, she was late. How come her neighbor's alarm hadn't gone off? She jumped up and ran into the bathroom. The tikka backpack and cigar scarf still lay on the floor. When had she last showered? She couldn't remember. She lifted the backpack and scarf; neither seemed to have a bad smell. She turned on the shower and slipped out of her kurta and leggings and stepped into the hot stream. She rolled her neck from side to side, loosened the night's tightness away.

She soaped her collarbone and neck and chest with Great Aunt Joan's Lily of the Valley soap and left her hair long and damp, hands down her body in a rushed attempt to catch up on time lost to sleep. The water ran over and down her body to her toes, out the drain. She hummed when she stepped out of the shower.

She'd have to eat out. She ran to the bathroom, aware of the clock hands' march toward 9 AM. She hung up the towels, brushed her teeth, swiped a smear of moisturizer over her face. Would have to do. She grabbed the tote bag and at the last moment decided on the tall boots instead of the sensible shoes. She looked around and saw Mark's belt on the back of the desk chair. Mark. She wrapped the belt around her hips, to the nubby hole he used for himself. She looked outside.

Checked her phone on the way down in the elevator. Mark had nudged her about storm updates. She ran a quick search.

Ofel intensifies into storm; 17 areas under new storm signals.

Ofel, she thought, then read aloud:

"Residents living in low-lying and mountainous areas under public storm warning signal No. 2 and 1..."

And what were storm warning signals No. 2 and 1? She clicked the link. Ah, a storm in the Philippines. Far from her. No impact. She could relax; yet, she did not.

Amalia and Jen stood over their desks and held the ends of the topographic survey between them. "We're going to need somewhere large and flat to work on this," Amalia said.

"Maybe we could work on it in Meeting 2," at least until Betsy gets back, Jen said. "I had a meeting in there yesterday with Suky, it looked fine."

"Yeah! Suky." Let it go—not her place to pry.

Jen took her end of the topo map, began to fold it back up, and walked it toward Amalia. They cut contours from chipboard, layered and sliced and glued the parts to make a three-dimensional view of the environmental center site. "This would be way faster digitally," Jen said. She rubbed her hands. "I'm getting blisters."

"Betsy likes physical models. If we're going to surprise her, we might as well do it with something she'll like."

"True. Maybe we could do a cutaway section to show the geothermal wells," Jen said.

"If we do geothermal," Amalia said.

"We have to do something. Natural gas is still on the table."

She thought for a moment. "How could a project get so off track? Oh, wait, I remember. Sorry, Amalia."

"Look, the project was off track before I ever said anything about the natural gas part of it. It's not my fault."

"How can you say it's not your fault? We had a clear path when the natural gas industry was underwriting the center. We had a job, we had a project, and the office was getting funded."

"Are you mad at me? Seriously?"

"You kind of jeopardized the whole office, you know. All our jobs."

"Atlantia Actuaris is still funding the center, as far as I know. Mark—" She hadn't told Jen he worked for Atlantia. Choked on the words. Amalia sat back and waved the X-ACTO knife in the air. "I can't imagine cutting in layers deep enough to show it realistically. The glue is already hardening."

"Maybe I could do a quick terrain model of the section. We could print it out and show it next to this site model."

"That sounds quick!"

"Even a wire frame would be fine. We don't have to render it."

"I bet Mark has good terrain modeling software."

"The gas guy?"

"He's a geologist." Her heart pounded. She'd better tell Jen soon or she'd end up a fraud. "He put this magazine in my hands the other day that had some pretty cool mapping software. Maybe the models already exist. I could ask him."

"Could we look online?"

Amalia went back to her desk and searched for ESRI geothermal well section online. She clicked Images and looked across and down the page. "I got it!" She clicked on a colorful, cross-sectional image that looked like undersea worms. "Jen? I've hit on something."

"Good," Jen came out from Meeting 2. "My hands need a rest. What is that?" She pulled up her own desk chair next to Amalia's and peered at the screen.

"This is pretty crazy looking. I don't think this is geothermal."

"Who's this?" Jen pointed to the screen.

"I'll search them." She pulled up the company's website. And sat back. "I feel like I'm behind the curtain."

"Which curtain?"

"I don't know. To see the Wizard of Oz." She clicked through a few links on the page of the company that came up. "They have an app for tracking rigs." She looked in and squinted at the screen-captured image on the page. "Tracking for oil, gas and thermal."

"Thermal is geothermal, presumably," said Jen. "You're against gas, but you're for geothermal? And it's the same companies doing the work, or at least, supplying the technology to do the work?"

"Sunil said something last week. He said geothermal can cause earthquakes," Amalia said.

"We're way at sea here," Jen said. "We need Betsy."

"What could Betsy do? She's a proponent of natural gas. And her house is on oil."

"How do you know?"

"Jacob told me. We watched the oil tank fill up outside their house last week."

"Wow, talk about being behind the curtain!"

They worked in silence for a while until Sharon poked her head in. "You ladies working through lunch? It's after two."

"We got caught up in this." Amalia stood up and stretched tall.

"It looks great," Sharon said. "Betsy will be in soon, can you clean up before then?"

"Betsy's coming in? How is Jacob?" Jen looked up.

"He's fine, she's coming in."

"Ok." Sharon went back to her office.

"She's got a kid straight out of emergency and she's coming in."

Amalia sat back down and looked at the model. "Let's put in the foundations of the old farmhouse. We could make it so it's removable. So it rests on top of the model."

"This is when a computer model is just so much better," said Jen.

"I know, I agree, but the point is to get something tactile the clients can get hold of. Trying to think about it from Betsy's perspective." They wiped up the white glue and closed up the X-ACTO knives, put the unfinished model on the side table next to the calculators and pens.

"Lunch?"

"Yes. We can plan our new firm."

"We're starting a new firm?"

"We might need to, depending on how this all turns out," Jen said.

Chapter 23

Mark approached his flat alone after dark, back now after a day of meetings with Atlantia and local business reps at the Guildhall. The front light was out. Had he left it on? He unlocked the door and stepped inside.

Someone was there, he could feel it. Anwen? Simon? Either might have a key through the leasing agency. Why would either of them be there?

"Hello?" It caught in his throat. He looked for something to brace himself with, to embolden his step into the apartment. A stick? He took off his shoes and tiptoed up the carpeted stairs, aware of his breath, shoes in one hand.

A shriek beneath his feet and a swoosh. A tail. A cat?

He flicked on the light switch.

A cat. A large, scared, tabby cat. "What are you doing here?" Caught his breath. Put his hand on his heart but didn't slow it down any.

Looked across to the kitchen. There was a note on the table.

The cat is Matilda, she's mine, and I'm leaving her here in your flat as an incentive to stay.

Anwen had let herself in while he'd been out.

Good god. Was she serious? He couldn't take on the responsibility of a cat when he'd be away and back and gone and—and—who knew what was next. He sure didn't. He stroked the tabby who was by now on the kitchen table. "You're a sweet thing. But I can't be here for you." He petted her fur smooth and the motion soothed him closer to stillness.

Tea. That's what the Brits did, had tea, yes, to solve all problems? Mark struck a match and lit the gas. The hiss and whiff of the stove was familiar, yet different from back home. He put on the kettle and waited for it to boil.

He fondled the chip packet of soil while he waited, poured a little of the earth into his palm, closed his eyes. Watched Matilda—the cat's name, Anwen wrote—watched the cat sniff the corners of the room, then the stove. He wondered about the source of his flat's Welsh gas. Maybe he could tell a story about making tea the next time he gave a speech.

The water boiled on the stove. He stood up, turned off the gas, and made a cup of tea, then emptied the soil from the chip packet onto the center of the table. Matilda jumped back up on the table and sniffed her nose at it. Mark sat down to draft a speech to the business communities and residents of Brecon and beyond, one hand on Matilda's fur.

Chapter 24

Friday, October 26

Mark took in the passengers around him in First Class. Had a flash of a thought to check if Anwen had secured a seat. Stupid. No way would she go that far. Nor would her brothers. But—maybe he'd take a stroll down through coach later.

He settled down with a glass of wine and a print-out from the British Geological Survey. Tilted back the seat, began to relax into it. A flight was always a good transition between one continent of responsibility and another. On second thought, he ditched the BGS print in favor of a nap.

Eyes flashed open when he felt a touch on his sleeve. Jolted up. Flight Attendant. Not Anwen. "Sir, we received a message for you in the cockpit. You're to call your headquarters in Philadelphia and speak to a Samantha."

"How?" Mark unbuckled and started to stand up at his seat.

"You can make the call from your cell phone, Mr. Stone. It was announced at the beginning of the flight." The attendant smiled. "Another glass of wine for you, sir?"

He pulled out his phone and powered it on. It seemed too quiet on the plane for a phone call. He didn't want anyone to overhear. "Sam. Mark Stone. What's up?"

"We need you in Pennsylvania. A car is going to pick you up at the airport in New York. They need you to help them activate the hurricane management plan."

"We did that already. On Monday."

"This is different. If we don't get this nailed down, it will be your job to clean it up in PR."

Mark scrolled through the last day's worth of messages. He came upon Amalia's, the one that had gone unanswered back at the trailer in Wales. Had he closed out of it? He must have, but he couldn't remember if he'd sent her a reply.

He took out a pad of paper from his briefcase and his pen hovered for a moment, interrupted by the attendant who brought him a glass of wine. He sipped it and wrote:

What do we need to convey BEFORE the storm comes?

Story of how we came to be working here in the region, powering the land.

Serving the people. How many people?

Technology assists us regardless of weather events.

He turned to a fresh sheet of paper.

What do we need to convey DURING a storm?

We are on top of energy supply, and the mechanisms for drawing power are safe.

Reassure. Use reassuring words. Tones.

Present some facts, but not too many.

He turned to a third piece of paper.

What do we need to convey AFTER a storm?

We are there for the people.

We have checked on all sites, supplies, delivery systems, etc. Give a few more facts.

Be ready with the 1-800 number.

Link to media articles about how others have fared. Not so bad.

Prepare for next time; we were prepared after the last times (Hurricane Irene/Tropical Storm Lee).

He sat back and sipped. That would do for a basic framework. His thoughts turned to other natural disasters. He'd had to prepare words after Hurricane Irene—his first foray into PR. And he'd done well, well enough they'd asked him to do it again, and again. Funny, he'd never seen himself as a publicity guy. A rock and science guy. The one event that nagged at him, though, was the one he was relieved he hadn't had to speak about: Papua New Guinea.

Amalia had touched on it at the Met. Or he had; he wasn't sure who'd brought it up. But why would she? He must have started it. Why would he have shared those doubts with her then? Defenses must have been down. He sipped his wine.

Maybe there was a lesson to be learned there. If he turned away from the Papua New Guinea disaster, was he turning away from an opportunity to build a stronger base, create a stronger company? He pulled up a fresh piece of paper, a fourth. He wrote *PAPUA NEW GUINEA* at the top and sat back and closed his eyes.

He made a note as it popped into his head:

Research the facts, get an eyewitness. Speak of the learning from the event. Tie it into the weather events and disasters of the past; make it specific to the need to supply energy to the population. Make international protocol development part of the mission.

He tapped his pen on the pad, and rewrote

International Protocol Development.

He circled the phrase and rewrote it at the top of a fifth piece of paper. He caught the words and bits of phrases as they floated up in his mind.

water, geology, anthropology, animism

What did he know about animism? He thought back to anthropology class at Dartmouth. It preceded Christianity. And was still practiced in a lot of countries. He assumed also in Papua New Guinea.

Next to animism, he wrote,

Papua New Guinea?

He put his head back on the seat. What did this have to do with writing his speech for Hurricane Sandy? And it was now categorized as a hurricane. Why was it called Sandy? Why not Sally, or Serena, Sarah?

Call hurricanes by some other name. They're just storms. Get this in the International Protocol. Make these storms less iconographic. Less personified. Stop giving them so much power.

He looked up at the cabin ceiling to the nozzles and lights that pointed down. Writing an international protocol for energy development. How the hell did he get into that? He didn't know, but he felt—affected. By one person who'd had a subtle influence all week long.

He doodled on the page.

IPEDS. International Protocol for Energy Development and Security.

Maybe he could buy the domain name. But why? What did he think he was doing? He wished he could call Amalia. Oh wait—he could. He dialed and she answered before it rang. "How'd you do that?"

"I have radar for you, apparently," she said.

"Things going well there?"

"Yes, better. I've been running meetings. But the boss' little boy is in the hospital. So that's not so good. Where are you?"

"In the air. Amalia. About this storm coming. I need to talk to you."

"About the storm?"

"No. Yes. But not now. I need to talk to you about Papua New Guinea."

"Sorry, did you say you want to go to Papua New Guinea?"

"No! Listen. I'm flying into New York and driving out west. I'm not sure I'll have time to see you but I'll call you when I land, ok? Or maybe I'll come back through the city after my meeting."

"I'm confused. So you don't want to talk about the storm?"

"I'll call you back. The connection's bad." He sat back, sipped his wine, and doodled on his notepad.

Circles. Think in circles. He drew concentric rings around the words on the page.

"Like a top-up?" The flight attendant came back with the bottle of wine.

"No, I'm good. I'll have some herbal tea if you have some," he said. Time to detox. He closed his eyes and tilted the seat back as far as it would go.

"We'll be landing in twenty minutes," said the voice over the sound system. Please straighten your seat backs and trays into an upright position and prepare for landing."

Mark stirred. He saw the flight attendant had left him a cup of tea—now cold. He looked around. There had been a dream—vague and connected to Anwen.

He needed to find freedom in this situation, but given it was not a situation of his own making, how could he do it? And was it in fact not of his creation? Had he wished it upon himself, back there in the Reverend Mildred's church?

If that was the case, he'd make a new wish. To be free of the fear that followed him from room to room, and to be open to a broader flow of information that would take him down a different stream. He slipped the notepad in his briefcase and tilted his seat upright. Held the cold tea in one hand and secured the tray with the other. "Landing," he said to himself.

Mark left through the JFK passenger exit and out into the area filled with limo drivers and cabbies who held car service signs. He found his name in the sea of signs and faces and waved to the driver.

"Good flight, sir? That's all you have?" The driver pointed to Mark's briefcase and travel bag.

"That, and a big sleep deficit." They walked across to the car. "How's the city doing with the storm preparations?"

"Storm? It's in Cuba. I don't think it's going to come here. All the hype last year and it missed us."

They drove in silence most of the way. Mark dozed and woke, and dozed again, jostled along the highways of New York and

New Jersey. He woke up when the driver pulled into a Travel AA rest stop for gas, and sat up, pulled out his phone and checked for messages. There was one from headquarters.

Storm bigger than being reported by NOAA, please check in when you arrive.

He was a fan of the National Oceanic and Atmospheric Administration. He'd need a coffee to clear the head, to help put it all into perspective.

He dialed Timmy and left a message. "I'm back, landed. They're sending me on site, then I'll be back home. Call you after work tonight. Love you, buddy." He wondered how Timmy would get along with Amalia. And how had it gone with Helene? The two had never connected for a significant period of time; Timmy had been living with Mom and Dad, and Mark and Helene had been busy snuggling in the mountains of New Hampshire.

Dialed headquarters next. "Sam—Mark, here. What's up?"

"NOAA is moving slowly. We're getting conflicting reports."

"What can I do?'

"Put your hydrogeology hat on when you get there and see if the contractors are missing anything," she said. "There's a rumor the neighbors are filing reports. Be open, Mark, use your senses. You're a sensitive New Age guy."

"Must be someone else you're thinking of," he said.

"We'd all like to know."

Whatever. "Goodbye, Samantha."

The driver took Mark all the way to the hydraulic fracturing site area of Atlantia Actuaris in the Northern Tier. They passed a large *Atlantia Actuaris Yard 03* sign at the side of the road.

"Take me to the site trailers. I'll get to the wellheads later." They drove up the hill past groomed, flat clearings, gravel-topped and functional, where small green wellhead pipes emerged low from the ground, hard to see by an untrained eye.

"Don't see so many rigs up, these days," the driver said.

"Less drilling, more filling."

"I like that. You in marketing?"

Mark assessed the terrain. The site was clean, a few trailers lined up next to each other. Water tanks—painted green—edged the parking lot. A shuttle bus sat parked on the gravel driveway with its driver asleep behind wheel. The site secretary sat behind her desk, with a Sudoku puzzle atop a pile of manila folders before her. "Hi. Mark Stone."

"I know, Mark." Mary sat up straighter and put the Sudoku on the shelf beneath her desk, and began to type at her computer. "Sign in?"

"Need a coffee. Came straight from JFK. Off a flight. From the UK.

"Coffee's old but you're welcome." Mary pointed to a coffee pot on top of a filing cabinet, its orange-red light lit up.

"I'll take the coffee." He signed into the site register, grabbed a Styrofoam cup.

"You're supposed to meet George from Engineering at Wellhead 2. He's there now. The others are outside waiting for you."

"Is there a problem? I thought we completed that repair."

"No problem, just checking."

"How's the solar transmitter working?"

"Love it," Mary said. "Sends the data back to the Philadelphia office. No need to keep the print-outs on site here. Less paperwork for me."

Mark headed back outside, coffee cup in hand. He looked out along the sandy-colored sedge row while the trucking subcontractor and site foreman spoke at length about storm preparations on the site. Something drew him to the edge of the field and he pulled away from the conversation for a moment. What more was there to see? He closed his eyes and in his tired state, wobbled.

"Hey, are you ok?" the foreman said.

"Tired from the flight. I'll take a walk, clear my head,"

"No problem. We'll be going down the road to the next property so catch up when you're ready. Meet us with George at Wellhead 2."

"Good." Mark stepped away from the meeting. Samantha had said to look for the cohesiveness of preparations in light of the coming storm. Hadn't they been on it while he was in Wales? They seemed to have everything under control here. He'd have extra time, and would be able to check on Timmy before the hurricane, and stay with him if need be. He could touch base with Amalia, too.

Amalia. There she was again in his thoughts. He wondered what she'd make of this place. She had a harshness to her critique that was not balanced—even if endearing, at times. Endearing and annoying.

He felt with his feet along the row of sedge and stopped, bent down to touch the soil. He picked up some of the gritty, light-textured earth between his fingers and rubbed it, then smelled his fingers. It had a sharp, pungent smell. He stood up and looked down away from the site and toward the slope below. A small stream ran parallel. It was low at present, but with the expected water level rise of the coming storm, it could breach its banks. He looked across to the site and estimated the rise in elevation from stream to work site. A two-foot rise over fifty feet, he guessed.

He looked back at the foreman and saw him indicate height with his hands; perhaps water level rise was on their minds. Wind would be another factor. Security of the water trailers in high wind would be key. He knew they'd already started that—in fact, they'd discussed it in their flyover trip on Monday. He didn't see anything to alarm Samantha, or himself. He could suggest they beef up the rip rap along the shore, but it wouldn't have any impact on runoff from the trailers if one should shift in the wind and spill.

And it wasn't only water. He didn't know how the chemicals would interact with each other in a groundwater event. They could line the stone rip rap with oil spill barriers. The ones with human hair might work. He imagined a weave of boulders and barriers along the stream, at the top of its banks. But it wouldn't take into account fluid seepage into the earth. Maybe a mat of spill barriers around each container. Elevate the containers over spill barriers? No, too heavy. Not at all feasible. That would be a major feat of dunnage engineering, and not one accomplished before the storm. And then there would be the wind loads.

He looked up. The foreman turned a corner and was soon out of sight. Mark pulled out his phone to call Samantha, but found he had no signal. He did see there was already a new text message. Phone must have synched on the drive over. It was from Amalia.

Where are you now? What are you doing over there? Nervous about Frankenstorm. Call me!

Something moved in his peripheral vision. "Hello?" He heard something rustle, but no voice came in response to his. He stopped. Maybe a bear? He looked around as he moved. The nearest edge of the woods was a stone's throw away from where he stood. He looked deep into the thicket and let his eyes relax into the multihued tones of brown and gold, deep forest and chameleon green. A deer moved. He saw its tawny coat against the tree bark backdrop. And another deer. It was a family of four. Mark bent down to have a look from a lower angle. The family moved in unison, and then apart, in unison, apart.

They seemed at peace and unaware of his presence. He lowered himself to the ground from his crouched position and crossed his legs to sit on the dry earth. He pulled a stalk of grass and drew in the soil in front of him. First a circle, and then a dot at the center. Where was he now, at the center, or on the edge? In his career, he felt he was at the center. But in his personal life, he felt at the edge. There was no alignment.

Without warning, over his head, the hiss of a bullet whizzed past, and before him the deer bolted out into a splayed movement through the trees. Another hiss over his head and the deer were gone, and the forest edge, quiet.

"Who's there?" He looked in toward the trailers but saw no one. He called out to the foreman but heard no reply. He looked around. Saw no one; felt a taste of bile rise from his lower belly up into his chest, throat.

He couldn't go back to the trailers now. He felt quite undone. He walked around the ring of water containers—trailer-sized themselves—to the parking area, and found the employee shuttle bus. The driver sat at the wheel behind a local newspaper. Mark rapped on the glass door.

"There was a shot. I was walking. Shots fired. I'm with the company."

"There's no hunting here. It's posted. But there was a bear all week. Maybe someone decided to get rid of it."

"Someone from the company?"

"There's supposed to be no firearms on site. But you know how it goes. Could have been anyone."

"There was no bear," Mark said.

The driver slid the paper onto his lap and put up his feet on the dashboard. Mark looked at the cover story.

Frankenstorm.

He waved goodbye to the driver and headed back to Mary in the site trailer.

He walked up to the first trailer next to the parking area. Before he went in, he pulled out his phone again. He had a signal; was back in the land of the connected. He sat on the metal step and leaned on the handrail post to call Amalia.

It went to voice mail. "Hi, this is Amalia, please leave a message." Felt the sweetness of her voice, singsong even in a recording.

"I'm back in the States. I had a weird experience. Give me a call." He hung up. What more was there to say?

He didn't want to continue the meeting over at Wellhead 2. He had come off thirty-six hours of no sleep and a traumatic experience with a hidden sharpshooter. Maybe on a better day.

But this was a fine day. The weather was calm, he was well, and he was at work. His body was at work. His mind was not on it. He pulled himself up and opened the door to the office trailer.

"Mary?" She turned from a file cabinet to look at him. He

squinted to adjust to the dimmer interior compartment. "Shots outside. Shots fired outside."

"Really?" She walked to the window. "Did you get it? That thing has been menacing me all week," she said. I assume you shot it good? Dead? Don't want an angry bear wandering around."

He stood at the window and stared outside, blank.

"It wasn't me. Someone with a gun. Bus driver said there are no firearms on site."

"The bus driver? What does he know, he's a subcontractor."

"Aren't you all subcontractors?" Mark's phone rang. "Excuse me." He looked at it and saw it was Amalia. He waved a hand in the direction of east. "It was that way, at the edge the woods."

Mary nodded and Mark stepped outside and answered the phone. "Shots were fired." He sat back down on the step. "Might have been a bear."

"Mark? Where are you?"

He rubbed his head and scrunched his eyes while he held the phone. "Something happened with the estate agent in Wales."

"I figured."

"It's ok, I broke up with her. I mean, I wasn't with her."

"Too much information, Mark. I told you, I don't want to know."

"But I want to tell you." He looked out at the site. "I'm getting spun out of the company," he said, low. "They have everything all locked down here, there was no reason for me to come." He looked over his shoulder. Mary moved around in the office, on her cell phone.

"You're paranoid," Amalia said. "Are you back home? Come to the city for the weekend. You need a break. I'll take you to the Museum of Modern Art. Anywhere you want. You're freaking me out."

"I'm in Pennsylvania. On one of the sites."

"No wonder you're freaked out. You're in a freaky place. Get out of there."

"This is my job, Amalia. You're putting me down when you say that."

"I'm not putting you down, Mark. But I do think—what you're feeling is—you're realizing your work isn't in alignment with what the earth wants."

"Come on. The earth does not have wants."

"Ok. What is deserves," Amalia said. "Look. You need a break. I need to pack my stuff up this weekend. There'll be beer and pizza. Come over. We'll hang out, watch the weather forecast online, all that fun Frankenstorm stuff."

Mark pressed into the headrest of the subcontractor's shuttle bus seat and closed his eyes. Twenty minutes' catnap until they reached his motel. The day was a blur; it had begun in loosely urbanized Wales, taken him through airports in London and New York, and ended up in rural Pennsylvania. And somewhere in there, shots were fired. He was so tired he could have daydreamed the whole thing.

"Motel stop," the driver called out, and Mark jerked forward, surrounded by subcontractors who grabbed sports bags off the overhead rack and filed out the bus aisle to the motel at the end of sunset.

He pulled his carry-on suitcase from the rack above and wheeled it out and off the bus, nodded thanks to the driver, and followed the others into the lobby of the motel. Most filtered out to rooms already booked, one stopped at the desk next to him to pick up a message. Mark gave his name to the clerk who passed him his key, his room pre-booked by Mary only an hour earlier.

Mark's attention drifted to voices beyond the reception desk, in the closed-off breakfast area. George from Engineering stood with the subcontractor that Mark had been warned about. The hotel lobby was an unexpected place for a revelation, but when Mark saw them there, he knew. Knew it must have been him who'd sent the strange email threat. George had set him up.

He'd decide in the morning how to handle it. For the time

being though, he had only one thought, which was to fall into a deep sleep.

Chapter 25

Amalia sat at her office desk and opened the day's email messages. Simon's name caught her eye. What did Simon want?

What's the nature of your association with Mark Stone?

She hesitated, decided she would not reply. She hoped Mark knew what he was doing. And what was that about shooting a bear? He was out on a new American frontier.

She typed in *hydrofracturing site safety* and came up with Citizens Advisory Committee reports from 2011, but nothing that gave her a window into what Mark was up to. Maybe the feds? She went to the EPA's website and typed in the same search criteria. Still nothing useful. There was a link on the sidebar for site-specific health safety information, which when clicked, elicited a Health and Safety Planner online. She bookmarked the link and wondered if Mark was aware of it.

What was she concerned about? It was all those chemicals. What would happen to all those chemicals if they were hit by a hurricane force wind? Would they go into the ground, fly around? Mix up? Maybe it was a flood issue.

She searched for natural gas flood zone preparation online and came up with a lot of flood information from different governments around the country, but nothing specific to the gas industry. She went to the NY Department of Environmental Conservation website. She entered hydrofracturing and this elicited a long list of opinions and studies conducted within the department. At the very bottom of the list was one that caught her eye:

Chapter Six, Potential Environmental Impacts,

written in 2009. Maybe in there? She clicked through the first pages and saw it was based on research from 1988 and 1992. The data was over twenty years old. Policy built on such old data? She sent the PDF link to her personal email to read on the weekend. In the meantime, she could always call Mark back and ask him. Not that he'd tell her anything.

And what about that? To call Mark back seemed fraught with trouble. He'd gotten into some tryst in Wales, and was freaked out about work. What on earth was up with him?

She wrapped up the computer work and spent the rest of the afternoon in a huddle with Jen over the site model. Max went home early to Long Island, Sharon to Westchester, Betsy to New Jersey, all to hit their local grocery stores and search for batteries before the weekend storm preparation crowds gathered. The tenants swung by Meeting 2 to check out the progress, and they, too, left a little earlier than usual. "To get a head start on things," they said.

"Everyone's overreacting!" Jen said.

"They all live outside of the city, maybe it's different there," Amalia said. "We can get what we need here. We'll be fine. Do you want to stay over? My place is higher than yours. You're welcome to."

"I do not believe it will come to that. But I'll be happy to keep the offer in mind."

"I'll be packing. It's no trouble. I owe you a night of couch surfing."

"Is Mark coming over?"

"What! Stop looking at me like that. What about you and Suky?"

"Paige is cool with it. And Suky is out of town this weekend—family thing in L.A."

"All right. So you're free. Come on over. I could use the company."

"If I don't you'll be breathing down my neck about it. How about if the storm looks close on Sunday, I'll come over. Maybe."

"Fine," Amalia said.

"All right. Let's get back to work here, shall we? What about getting those 3D well sections incorporated into a report?"

"I'll call Mark about it; he might have something more specific he can point us to. What you and I were looking at before was sales stuff for the software."

"When we start our own firm, Mark should join us. As a consultant."

"Mark is a petroleum geologist. He is, at this very moment, on a hydrofracturing site, freaking out about some NRA gun nut. I can't think of a less balanced person."

"Mmm hmm."

"Oh my god, you are so annoying! You can come and stay if you're not going to be annoying. I'm going to call him about the geothermal sections. Maybe he at least knows of some geology atlas." Amalia stepped out of Meeting 2 and went back to her desk to call Mark from the office landline. The office was quiet around her, 5 PM on a Friday before a weekend of storm anticipation. It went to his voice mail. " I have a question about geothermal for you. And seriously, think about coming into the city this weekend. I'll be packing. And storm watching. It'll be fun!" She hung up and sat back in her office chair, tapped the phone and slid it into her bag. She turned off the computer screen and gathered her hair scrunchies and put them on her wrist, grabbed her coat from the back of the chair and went back to Meeting 2. "I'm about done. I couldn't reach him."

"Ok, I'll finish up here."

"You're going to stay on a Friday when everyone else has left?"

"I'm kind of enjoying this." Jen looked across the conference table at the model and map. "I'll finish the edges off at least."

"Don't stay too late. And come over! Come over. I don't want to be alone huddling over Facebook looking at hurricane status updates by myself all weekend."

"If you put it that way, I could spare you the pain."

Back at home, Amalia's cell buzzed with a new message. Simon. She took out the battery and set the pieces of the phone down on the counter.

Mark might call. She reassembled the phone and laid it next to the worm bin and watched the device for signs of activity.

Chapter 26

Saturday, October 27

On the bus uptown, Amalia checked her phone for messages in hopes Mark had written something of clarity.

You free Sat night?

A text.

Yes!

She wrote from the back doors of the bus.

Coming in on bus arriving 5ish. Dinner?

The bus braked and she leaned hard into the pole when it came to a full stop. She pushed the back doors of the bus open and stepped out onto the curb and she sent a message back to Mark. She looked up; the sky, gray, was bright, yellowish. It gave her a ticklish sense inside, or maybe it was the text messages. She couldn't tell the difference.

She didn't want to know what had happened in Wales. Or on the frack site. She wanted to slow down and take a good long look at it all. Dinner this evening. She'd have to save money—but she had Nadel's loan now. Nadel! She had to get Nadel out of her head; didn't need his approval.

She walked up to the new apartment, buzzed for Titian, found him in her new apartment with three cans of gallon-sized paint, radio set to a Latin ballad in the background. All the paint cans were open: white, pumpkin, olive gray. Her eyes watered and music swelled into a round sound that drew her in. "Oh, great colors, like the photo." She squinted. "Is this low VOC?"

"What's that?"

"The smell—I'm not going to be able to stay here long."

"Don't worry, miss, I have onions."

"Onions?"

"After I paint, I put cut onions in the apartment to collect up the smell."

"Ah. You know, with the low VOC you might not need onions. It's less stinky paint." They looked at the colors, and decided which would go where. Amalia dipped a foam brush into the first can and painted a heart on the wall and then painted over it. She opened all three of the windows—four, including the tiny one in the bathroom—and the breeze from outside carried a good portion of the smell away. Titian cut up onions and laid them on the floor around the edge of the apartment. "My eyes stopped watering from the paint," she said. "Now they're watering from the onions!"

"You cut onions for a living, you stop crying. Put a piece of bread in your mouth, you stop crying."

"Really." She wiped the brush on the edge of the can and rested it on the lid. "Do you have family in the hurricane path?"

"I have family all over."

"In Cuba?"

"Yes, Cuba, Florida, Maryland, New York, you name it, we're there." He stopped the chatter and turned back to the wall.

She stayed to help Titian paint most of the apartment, for the fun of seeing the autumn park colors come to life on the walls: wet pumpkin, offset by soft gray and crisp white.

"We'll leave the onions here overnight," Titian said. He rolled up the drop cloths, turned off his radio and took the buckets and brushes out to clean in the basement. "You stay if you like." He gave her a set of keys. "Like this," he said, showed her a quirk of the door lock, and left.

Amalia stood alone in the oniony, wet apartment, windows open to the wind. She felt like she was in the center of an art studio, and she was the focus of the painting, a live painting, in motion, and the colors wrapped her like clothing. She pulled out her phone to take a picture and saw it flash with a message.

Mexican? Tonight? Or Indian? I'm up for spicy. Mark.

Indian! I'll take you to a fun place. Meet @ Port Authority? Or hotel?

Port Authority.

Corner of 42nd closest to Times Square?

She left the windows open and locked the door behind her, whispered "thank you" to the walls, and left. She took the train downtown and decided it was a friendly line, not so crowded, and not worthy of the worry she'd been inclined to project onto subway travel. It was the same station and line she'd gone through from the condo site when she'd come up with Betsy and met Sunil. Familiarity made her feel at home.

She didn't see Rose this time, pregnant and homeless. But she did get off at 110th again and looked for the café. Down a tree-lined street of townhouses, onto a view of a grand cathedral, then a right turn. And there was the café, with its little red Columbia University 'Safe Haven' sign in the window. It did feel safe. She stepped back and read the words on the old awning: *Hungarian Pastry Shop*.

She bought a coffee and a piece of flourless hazelnut cake to go; lunch.

Later, after stretching it out along the length of Amsterdam Avenue back to Great Aunt Joan's apartment—it no longer felt like her own—she stopped for a proper meal in a diner and called her parents to let her know she was fine. She didn't expect the hurricane would track so far west as Scranton, but she knew they'd be concerned for her.

Her father got on the phone. "Have you got batteries? Water? You know you should fill the bath with water for toilet flushing."

Her mother piped up in the background. "Tell her to have an emergency contact. We need an emergency contact in the city."

"I'm fine, Dad, my apartment is very high up. I'm not in a flood zone. And I might have company, my friend Jen might come if the hurricane tracks this way."

"Tell her to get canned food, and don't forget a can opener."

"I can't hear between the two of you!" Her father gave the phone to her mom.

"Hi, sweetheart. You know, you can always come home. We're not expecting it to get this far west."

They signed off with a promise to touch base with updates. She sat in the diner and looked out to the bright gray sky. A steady wind skimmed the building tops with no indication of breeze below, save the occasional discarded plastic shopping bag caught in an updraft.

She spent the rest of the afternoon on a hunt to collect liquor-store boxes which she flattened and carried home, then reassembled with packing tape in the old apartment while she listened to Anoushka Shankar. She had to give them turns, Norah and Anoushka; she felt it was fair to give them equal air time. Not having a sister of her own, she guessed this was how it should go. She folded the cigar scarf into the tikka backpack and put them aside. The worm bin had never left the apartment, since it had been assembled there after she moved to New York. She hoped her worms would survive the trip.

Amalia looked at the bathtub. She didn't want to fill it with water, it seemed like overkill. A shroud of discomfort came over her head and settled on her shoulders, cloak-like. The wind picked up outside and the glass rattled in the frame. She went to the window to look outside, but when she glanced up at the sky, it looked as it had all day, even-toned, bright, yellow-gray.

And about that. Why were they having this storm in the first place? She hadn't heard anyone connect it to global warming—not yet—but it was worth a look. She wondered what Mark thought. For all their differences, she could not imagine he was a global warming cynic. She hoped not. His choice of profession could be overlooked, or at least understood, in a broader context.

Views on global warming—now, they could get nutty. He could be a gun nut.

It was dinner. They were friends. It would be fine. And she needed to ask him about geology atlases, and about the geothermal well sections for the environmental center project. As long as they stuck to discussions of sculpture, it seemed, they were fine. Not in agreement, but at least in a state of mutual parallel enjoyment. Better than she'd had in a long time.

She taped up the last of the book boxes, six in total. How had she accumulated six boxes of books in a few months, when she hadn't even had the intention to stay there for the long term? She had another dozen or so in her parents' garage in Pennsylvania. She pulled all of her clothes out of the closet and piled them up into her two suitcases. Her boots fit on top. She brought the worm box to the front hall and set it on the floor below the tall mirror.

She looked at herself in her jeans and gray t-shirt. She'd have to return Mark's clothes—and what did she have of his? She went back to the closet and rifled through the laundry in the pile on the floor. His dress shirt, his gray t-shirt. His belt hung on the back of the desk chair. She wrapped up the clothes and secured them with the belt, put the pile on top of the worm bin. She looked at herself in the mirror again. She'd grown speckles, pumpkin and heathery gray spots, paint spray. There were spots of white in her hair, too. She looked at her hands; all three colors were underneath her fingernails.

Portable décor. A walking showcase of portable décor. She smiled, slipped on her shoes and pulled her wool coat back on over her jeans, flipped her hair up into the scrunchie that sat on the hall table, and left the apartment.

She gave Mark a fifty-fifty chance of showing, given his odd mood the day before; still she went down to meet him at the Port Authority. It was quick to get down there and she waited, perched on a metal bollard by the taxi dispatch. A pocket of calm on a busy corner. She felt him come up behind her before she saw him, and turned. He walked out from the Port Authority bus terminal and gave her a grin and a wave. Looked up and down the street, dodged a line of pedestrians, ran across the sidewalk to her. He dropped his backpack at her feet, and embraced her in a tight hug.

"I missed you."

"You too." She buried her face in his cotton jacket and looked up. He kissed her, fast, on the lips. His warmth startled her and she pulled back, grabbed his hand.

"Welcome back to the city!" She looked down the block. "See that there? That's the New York Times building by Renzo Piano." She waved toward it with her free hand, didn't look at him, didn't want to look back. "That with the red zig zag stairs."

"The ladders up the side—it looks so climbable."

"It is—people have climbed it." She indicated its height with one hand, and Mark squeezed her other hand. Amalia flagged down the next taxi and held the door open for him. "St. Marks Place, please." She buckled up and leaned back, but he didn't. He sat close to her and draped his arm across the back of the seat. He stroked the top of her head and twisted a lock of her hair in his fingers.

Across town, they hopped out onto the street and stood in front of a tiny restaurant storefront strung with red chili pepper lights inside. Panna II. She led him in by the hand.

They sat for an hour and ate spicy food, made jokes about the chili peppers. The waiter brought them ice cream on top of the large meal; by the end of it, they were so stuffed they had to walk up and down the block to work their bodies back into a comfortable form.

It was early; six o'clock, and the Saturday evening crowds had begun to gather while the sky darkened. Amalia dragged Mark into a t-shirt shop and held up a rasta shirt against her frame. "Like it? On me?"

He picked up a paper lantern, folded flat, and bought it for her as a housewarming for her new apartment. "I'll hang it for you if you like. Take advantage of my height," he said.

"I can't take advantage of you." They held hands for the walk up St. Marks Place. "I wanted to ask you about something, about geothermal, actually. It's something we're looking at for work and I wondered if you're familiar with it."

"Somewhat, yes. What did you want to ask?" He stopped to look at a table of glass bongs on the sidewalk, poked at them.

"I found a website today that tracks oil, gas and geothermal installations, all together. I never saw them as 'all together'—only as non-renewable versus renewable."

He looked up from the glass bongs. "I had a thought on the way over. On the flight. If we had some kind of international protocol, we could define energy systems in new ways that make sense for the technologies we need to develop. I don't think renewable and non-renewable are the only ways to look at them. But this protocol could help to open up the research."

"Protocol for what?"

"For how countries develop energy."

"Like the Kyoto Protocol? Or Davos?"

"Those are there. But they're very—sided. They come from an environmentalistic way of thinking, and industry and governments are dragging their heels."

"Our government is."

"Here's the thing. There might be another way of going about this. If industry led the charge to take technology transfer as far as it could across international lines, with environmental goals worked in, we might find there are other governing principles we can work by aside from renewable versus non-renewable. I'd like to see more collaboration—not confrontation."

"And how is that different from the other protocols?"

"It's what's next."

Chapter 27

Sunday, October 28

Amalia met Mark the next morning on the corner in front of Andrews Coffee Shop; they touched each other's arms, kissed a soft kiss, pulled away. They went inside and sat in a window booth, jackets and bags cast off to the side, Mark looked around the bright space toward the old oven.

"I would love a brick oven pizza."

"You're crazy. Coffee for me," she said to the waitress.

He ordered a hot tea. "You know, it's almost lunchtime in Wales."

"What is your company doing over there?" She pressed forward.

"I told you, it's exploratory. We analyze the area for possible pockets of gas, or for extractable gas that's embedded."

"In shale." She sat back. "You know the day we met, I mean the day we met for real, Mildred's meeting day? I had a dream that night, I mean, the night before. The morning of the meeting. The dream woke me up and prompted me to run to the Port Authority to catch the bus we were on."

"A Rapa Nui–like dream?" He sat back with his tea.

"Kind of. I was under water and there were these huge blue whales, or something like blue whales. There was a mother and a baby, and a conservation biologist swam with them. She told me while we were underwater that the whales were getting sicker and were at risk because of some human activity and then she said architects should be charging their clients a conservation fee. Actually, it was more like a conservation tax, a governmental thing, on all development projects. And then this mama whale nudged me, kind of rolled me out of my dream, and into Jen's apartment."

"You were at Jen's?"

"Locked out of my apartment. That's why I had the borrowed clothes on."

"Got it."

"What do you think?"

"I don't like the tax idea."

"Ok, beyond that. What do you think?" She put her hand over his and rested it on the table. "Do you think we can get messages that way?"

"I don't know."

"I want to know what you think. Taxes aside. Politics aside."

"I—I think we have a great ability to tap into a stream of creative thought that's bigger than we realize. I don't know how dreams play into it. I—I would pray to your Durga."

"Is that what you do?"

"I pray all the time but I'm not sure what good it does me. It's when I'm not thinking about it that the ideas bubble up," he said. "I had a dream on the airplane," he said. "Kind of a half-awake, half-asleep dream."

"Tell me."

"Ok. It had the woman from Wales in it. And nothing happened with her by the way. She slept over one night after we had been out late at the pub, that first night."

Amalia squeezed his hand. "Tell me about the dream."

"I was in the airport in Papua New Guinea, which I've never seen in real life. In my waking life. Anwen, that's her name, was standing on this thing like a music box, and she was turning, drawing attention. And I went outside, and it was dry outside, like from desertification, more than it would be there. More like an American desert. Then I went with a driver through this spaghetti of roads, and there were green highway signs directing us all over, and we followed one, but I had no control of where we were going."

He stopped.

"And then you woke up and prayed?"

"No. We landed."

Chapter 28

Mark tipped his head up to look at the digital news strip around the building's edge in New York City's Times Square. They'd walked up after breakfast, and wandered without a goal. Hurricane Sandy dominated the newsreels, and the sky grayed behind the mass of buildings and TV screens.

"What do you think of staying in the city? Or do you need to be back home with Timmy?"

"Timmy's in East Stroudsberg, Pennsylvania, and the college has them covered. The mayor here in New York has done a pretty good job of convincing me this is an excellent place to ride out the storm."

"You came in to ride out the storm?"

"That, and you said you need help with moving." He looked up at the screens. "If you'll let me."

"I need to buy a bed."

"I have never in my life bought a bed," he said. They walked from 42nd Street back down and into Macy's Department Store, busy with pre-storm bustle, shoppers with bags of blankets.

She looked at the directory overhead. "Upstairs."

"After you," he said, and opened his arm to let her up first. They were alone on the escalator and she turned to face him, eye level with him, one step up. He held onto the handrail with one hand and put the other hand on her hip.

"I should call Jen." She rested her head on his shoulder and he pulled her to the start of the next escalator to ride up to the ninth floor, side by side.

The clerk came over, a woman in a tight black suit and heels, bright red lipstick.

Amalia shook her head at Mark and sat down on the edge of the bed, then lay down on her back, with her boots pointed toward the fluorescent lights overhead.

"Try it out," the clerk said. "You'll both need to lie down on it to see how it feels, how you move on it when you roll over."

"It's for me," Amalia said.

"Ok." The clerk's voice trailed off. "I'll give you two a few minutes." She smiled and turned, walked out of sight into the back.

Amalia sat up and looked at him, extended a hand to him. She looked over for the clerk. She pulled him onto another mattress and lay down and patted the space between them. He gave her a kiss on the lips and she put her leg over his and pulled him toward her.

"We're having a sale," the clerk said, back on the floor showroom.

"Great!" Amalia jumped up. "I need one today."

They struggled to get the demonstration model mattress out the freight elevator to the street, and between the two of them managed to manhandle the queen sized beast to the sidewalk, then to the subway entrance—the clerk's suggestion; a passerby helped them navigate down the stairs and the toll clerk let them through the emergency exit to the platform.

"How are we going to get it into your elevator? And back out? Should we take it up to your new place?"

"I don't know if we'll make it there and back. The subway's shutting down for good, later," she said. "Silly. Shutting down the subway a day early when no one even knows if the storm is going to come here for sure."

"It's preventive. It's a good idea. I think you think it's an inconvenience because you want to move your mattress to your new apartment."

"I'd rather be stuck at Great Aunt Joan's than at the new place. Her place has everything I need."

"Even if it doesn't hit here, there's still going to be a storm surge. Could affect the subway."

"I remember. You mentioned the modeling—on the phone?"

"SLOSH data. Sea, Lake and Overland Surges from Hurricanes—SLOSH."

She rested her forearms on the top of the mattress where she stood, and rocked with the movement of the subway. "No, it's a good idea. Better to be safe than sorry."

"You should go," Amalia put her hands on Mark's chest. "Go back to your hotel. Don't look so glum. We'll see each other tomorrow."

"The buses aren't running. I'm going to be walking back to the hotel as it is, now."

"Some of them still are." She lifted the lid of the worm bin and poked at the soil.

"What's that?"

"It's a compost. My worms."

"Where do you put the soil?"

"I haven't yet—I guess in Central Park?"

He smiled. "See you tomorrow? For an early breakfast?"

"I got a text from work that we're going to be closed tomorrow. It's more because of transit than anything else. And the boss' kids' school is closed."

He nodded. "My office in Philly is closing tomorrow too. And I wouldn't be able to get back, even if I wanted to. So we could spend the day together."

"And hurricane watch."

"This would be a good place. Better than my hotel."

"You're not in Zone A, though."

"No, but my hotel's low. This is better."

"Ok, so come here tomorrow. Jen was supposed to come too, but I haven't heard from her." She kissed him.

"Thank you, Hurricane Sandy," he said.

"About that. Why do you think we're having this hurricane?"

"Because it's hurricane season, and we're in a hurricane-prone area."

"But not really. And why has it got so large?"

"Air masses over the Atlantic. Humidity. Currents."

"Spoken like a true expert." She poked him. "No, really. What do you think?"

"I think. I think I am looking forward to storm watching with you tomorrow, here in Great Aunt Joan's apartment, and I think we will be fine." He took off his jacket.

"You need to go," she said. Put the jacket onto his arm.

Mark bundled her into a warm hug. "I'm staying."

Chapter 29

Monday, October 29

"What do you think they're after?" Amalia looked out to the built edge of the Amsterdam Avenue horizon, on the phone with Mark. In the end, he'd gone. It was her wish, although perhaps not her desire. The sky, heavy and gray, moved fast.

"Simon is after the good life. And you, it would seem."

"He's not. He just sends me weird emails," she said.

"George, he's after truth in engineering, truth in statistics. I work with Simon and George. We're a team."

"They don't seem so team-like to me, leaving you those messages."

"I don't think it's them. Why would they?"

"Samantha then? Maybe she's got the hots for you. Or it's that woman in Wales."

"Or her brothers."

"You need to do something."

"I know I need to make a change, I just can't see how to do it."

"Come up here. Forget the work stuff. Last night this storm didn't seem so serious. Now I don't want to be alone in it." She looked around the apartment—it felt so spare with her stuff in boxes. She moved the bundle of Mark's clothes and shifted the worm compost box into her arms, back onto the kitchen table.

Pulled the quilt from Great Aunt Joan's bed and folded it on the back of the couch. Her Tibetan prayer flags remained strung along the Amsterdam Avenue side of the living room windows. Colorful enough.

He arrived in good time, kissed her quick when he stepped through the door, and she put her arms around his waist. "I got a cab," he said. "The weather's not so bad yet. And it's speedy—no traffic."

"Are taxis even supposed to be out?"

"I have no idea. Maybe I got lucky. People are walking, checking it out." He slipped off his shoes at the door. "Got any food here?"

"Be my guest." She led the way into the kitchen, glad she'd put the worm box back on the counter. "There's some bread, and some cheese."

Mark padded into Great Aunt Joan's kitchen in his socks and rummaged in the fridge.

"My dad says I should fill the bathtub with water."

"I brought a flashlight and batteries. I have an emergency blanket in my backpack. And the bathtub's a good idea." He opened the freezer. "You know you have exploded beer bottles in here."

"Oh. Sunil was going to come by and help me move this weekend. He wanted to help his parents in Queens instead." She looked into the freezer. The beer bottle caps had popped off and a frozen waterfall of beer flowed from each. "They're pretty."

The wind blew a cluster of leaves onto the window that faced 81st Street and the leaves stuck on the glass, suctioned by the pressure. Mark walked over to the other window toward the view of the library across Amsterdam. "How was Jen going to get here?"

"I don't know, taxi, maybe? I'm going to try calling her again." She dialed and watched Mark remove the beer bottles and her packages of vegetables, held together by frozen liquid. "You don't have to."

"I'm helping. You don't want to leave it like this, do you?"

"You're sweet." She shrugged. "Voice mail. I'll text her."

Ok? Come over!

Jen wrote back,

I'm at neighbors upstairs, up high. No worries. You?

With Mark at home. Aunt Joan's.

Go girl!

No way!

What are you afraid of?

Freaked out by wind.

I meant with Mark!

"You found her?" Mark wiped out the freezer with a dishtowel he found in the drawer next to the sink.

"I found her. She said she's with neighbors." She sat down on the kitchen floor and leaned on the doorjamb. She watched Mark wipe down the interior of the fridge.

"You don't have to do that, you know." The apartment lights flickered. "Could get a power outage. We should close the freezer. Keep it cold."

"What about the tree out there?"

"It's far enough below from the glass, but the branches could fly around."

The metal replacement window frames rattled and Mark went to look out the window.

"Come back, don't stand so close. Last year some windows blew out. During Hurricane Irene. In other buildings."

"I don't think we need to worry about that," Mark stepped back. "Maybe we could push your new mattress against the window?"

"What about the other two windows?"

"We could push the mattress up against the window near the tree. We can avoid being near the other two windows." He helped her to shift the plastic wrapped mattress into the bedroom and up against the window on 81st Street.

Sirens wailed up the street beyond where Amalia stood pressed against her kitchen window. She felt silent inside; not much to say, and her senses were attuned to the weather outside.

"Come away from the window." He was back at the computer; they watched the water rise online while the wind whipped at the building and sucked the glass in and out of Great Aunt Joan's window frames. "The storm's so much stronger with the full moon, the spring tides."

Amalia looked up at the library across the street and wished she could see the Hudson, and yet was relieved she could not. She looked down at Amsterdam Avenue and put her hand up and held it a few inches from the frame. "The water's coming in." Mark stood behind her with his hands on her shoulders. "It's spraying in around the frame."

"Stand back. We should stay away from the windows." He steered her back into the room.

"I should call Jen." She dialed, but it didn't connect. Banged her phone down a little too hard on the counter. "Do you think the cell phone signal is down?"

"Maybe busy," Mark said. "Could be lots of 911 calls."

She's not texting back."

"Give her a few minutes, she might be tied up."

The phone rang in her hand.

"Amalia!" Jen sounded high.

"Jen, are you ok?"

"The water's rising. We can see the Gowanus Canal coming up the end of Bond Street."

"Oh my god." Amalia covered the phone. "Her apartment might flood."

"I went out to have a look with everyone else, but I'm inside now."

"What floor are you on? Don't tell me you're still downstairs."

"Third, now, at our upstairs neighbors'. Paige is here too. Neal and Steve are on the roof."

"Your neighbors are on the roof? What the hell are they doing up there?"

"Getting video footage."

"Oh my god. Get them inside. The windows are sucking in and out here, Jen!"

"The Gowanus Canal is getting close, so I'd say the East River is not far behind, here."

"Jen—"

"I need to go. The gusts are crazy."

"Don't go up to the roof, ok? Make those crazy roommates of yours come down!"

"I barely know them. I'll try."

"Be safe, Jen." The line had already gone dead.

"Amalia, you should see this," Mark said. She came over to the desk where he sat and looked at the computer over his shoulder.

"Oh my god, is that a shark swimming in the floodwaters in front of that house?"

"There's no way this is real."

"No, it looks real. If it was doctored they would have tried harder to make it look dramatic. This looks like a poor little shark got lost in the floodwaters. Where is that?"

"I swear this isn't real." He looked at the text. "New Jersey. Know anyone in New Jersey?"

"Betsy. My boss. And her family. She emailed us all last night to say the office would be closed today but that if we needed to we could go there to use the space."

"Nice."

"She's pretty nice. Kind of tightly wound. Her kids are cute."

A gust of wind brought another lash to the building. "More book?"

Amalia pulled the quilt off the back of the couch. They sat with the blanket over their legs and Mark read aloud. "Where were we." She put her hand on the book. "Rose," she said. "I met a pregnant homeless woman who lives in the subway."

"Wasn't that the day we ran into each other at the coffee shop? I'm sure she's inside somewhere. The city must have provisions for someone like her."

"But she didn't want to go to a shelter. She'd been there. She got slashed up, she showed me the scar." She looked at Mark.

"Look, what could you do? I'm sure she's fine." He put the book in his lap.

"I should have brought her back home with me."

"Amalia. You can't bring the homeless of New York back with you."

"Why not? I mean, what are we all about here? We all live in this big city and pretend we don't care about each other." She went into the kitchen with her cell phone and tried to dial Jen again, with no response. She tried to log onto Facebook on her phone but it wouldn't connect, so she sent a text message instead.

You okay there? xo

She peeked out through the curtains to the library and up and down along Amsterdam. It seemed the power was still on out there, but since it was still daytime and bright, it was hard to tell. Her phone buzzed with a message.

Ok here, you? How's it going with Mark?

I was worried about you.

I'm fine. Go back to Mark!

Ok fine!

She went back into the living room to find Mark at her laptop with the comforter around him, settled in at Joan's desk. "Come back here, Amalia." He reached a hand out of the quilt to pull her in, and she sat perched on his lap at the desk.

"This looks terrible, Mark." She scrolled up and down the website he'd pulled up. "The water level's rising. I hope everybody down on the shore is ok."

"There's nothing we can do." He turned her by the hips to face him and reached up to brush her hair out of her face, and the blanket fell back as he did. She leaned forward to kiss him, and with a sudden crack, they lost balance when the desk chair tipped backwards and crashed to the floor, which landed them both on the chair, on the blanket, and on the floor.

"Sorry. It's been a while."

"Me too." She nuzzled into his neck and pulled herself up next to him so she lay sideways.

"Let's not talk," he said.

"No, we should." She pushed his finger from her lips.

He lay an arm across her waist and they faced each other where they lay on the blanket.

"It's hard for me to relax into this."

"Because you're worried."

"Yes."

"About Jen."

"Jen, and the millions of other people out there."

He pulled himself up on the couch. "Come with me." Mark stood to get up and extended a hand to her, and grabbed the quilt from the floor with the other hand.

She followed him into the kitchen and he opened the curtains to look out at Amsterdam Avenue. He stood, quilt wrapped around himself, then wrapped it around the two of them while they watched an emergency vehicle drive southward, its lights on and siren off. A metal construction sign rattled up the road in the wind, and to her, it seemed the rain was moving in all directions at once.

"Look, there's nothing we can do now. We're safe. We're high up, we're together, and we have power." He turned her around to look at him and the curtain fell closed behind her. "Do you want to call Jen back?"

"No. I can't do anything, and she wouldn't be able to get here. Not today. Maybe tomorrow." She put her arms around his waist and pulled him in tight. "I don't want to be alone," she said.

"You're not, I'm here."

She rested her head on his chest and felt him breathe. Heartbeat oscillated with wind outside. The blanket fell to the floor and he lifted her up onto the kitchen counter and she wrapped her legs around his waist and they kissed again.

His cell phone rang in the other room. "You want to get that?"

"No." He moved down her neck.

"Could be important."

"This is important."

"It could be your brother." She rested her head on his chest and listened to the wind, his heartbeat. "I'm sorry. I'm too stressed to be romantic."

"Volume expressed in a gaseous state, experienced through sound."

"What?" She lifted her head.

"Volume as sound. That's wind. What we're hearing."

She put her head back on his chest. His heart was steady. "Can I call Jen?"

"You can call Jen if I can go online to check the storm updates."

She smiled. "Deal." He lifted her to the floor.

"I don't want you to be uncomfortable." He hugged her in tight.

"I'm ok." She looked up at him. "I like you a lot."

He pulled her in closer. "I love you, Amalia." She looked at him, loosened herself from his arms, opened her mouth then froze, lips open. "You don't have to say anything."

Amalia backed away, arms wrapped around herself in a hug.

What was there to say? Jen had sent several texts that arrived all at once, and there was one from Betsy, too. She went back into the living room and perched on Mark's knee as he checked the weather and news websites.

"It's bad out there," he said. "It sounds windy, here. Insanely windy." He wrapped one arm around her waist while the other hand clicked through web links. "It looks like we're in it, now," Mark said. "Worse than before."

"What is that?" Her hand flew to cover her mouth.

"Transformer fires."

"Oh jeez."

"And this." He clicked over to a story about Queens. "Didn't you say the date guy, the beer guy, was in Queens with his parents today?"

"Queens is big. I'm sure he's nowhere near that. This is ocean-front. But how awful." She dropped her hand. "I feel foolish, doing what we're doing, being the way we're being, when all of this is going on." She turned toward him to block the computer screen, and he ran fingers through her hair.

"Stay. Stay here. I could make us something to eat." She went back to the kitchen, opened the cupboards and found some rice, and put it on to boil. She had some eggs in the fridge too, and put those in a pot to cook.

Kedgeree. Was kedgeree romantic? She couldn't think of what else to make. As the pots boiled, she chopped the few vegetables she had left in the fridge and added them to the rice while it cooked. He loved her. She opened Great Aunt Joan's spice cupboard and rooted around.

Turmeric. Bright.

She found a third pot and fried a knob of butter in it, added the turmeric before the butter turned brown. They were fluid together. She found some salt and red chilies at the back. Once the eggs boiled, she turned the pan off, and also let the rice down on a simmer. They'd met over an egg timer. Where was that egg timer? She went to her backpack and pulled it out of the main pocket. Funny. It felt like Mildred was with them.

Mildred. She peeked out the window at Amsterdam Avenue, wet, windy, dark and bare. Flashing lights in the distance sped downtown on Broadway. Hoped everyone was ok out there. She put her hands up against the window frame. Cold. Had she imagined the spray before?

She turned back to the stove and flipped the egg timer again, then went back to the living room. Mark had the laptop open again.

"Why don't I take a turn online. You watch the stove."

"Okay, I'm getting too sucked into all this. What do I do?"

"You can mix it up together when the rice is ready. The eggs need six more minutes. Then we shell them and slice them over the kedgeree."

"The what?"

"The kedgeree. I don't have any salmon; it's good with salmon too."

"I've never heard of it."

"Kichari?"

"Nope."

"It's Anglo-Indian."

"Like you."

"I'm not Anglo-Indian. I hate that phrase. I'm just me."

"I know. That's one of the many things I love about you." He stood in the doorway and she walked over to him with the egg timer and put it in his hand.

"Remember this?"

"Oh my god. How could I forget? Whatever happened to the gas mask?"

"I took it to a meeting."

He shook his head. "I'll watch the stove."

She sat down at the computer. Were they going to go there? She didn't think she could handle a conversation about fracking. She clicked through couple of news websites. What the hell was she doing?

Chapter 30

Tuesday, October 30

The dishes from their midnight dinner lay stacked next to them, and their bodies lay in a twist of limbs on the deep old couch. Amalia stirred first. She went to the window and crossed her arms in front of her chest. She put her hands on the glass that faced the library across the street, looked across the room for her clothes and boots. "It's passed. It's all quiet. I'm going for a walk."

"It's the middle of the night," Mark said from the couch.

"I'll call Sandra then. It's daytime in Italy." She looked for her t-shirt in the kitchen.

"You're calling Italy? He sat up. "What are you doing? You can't Skype, I'm not dressed!" He ducked into the kitchen with the blanket for his clothes.

"We always Skype. And you are dressed, dressed in a blanket." The system dialed and within a moment, Sandra picked up.

"Oh my god, how are you doing? It looks awful."

"We're fine, we survived. The worst of it seems to be past us now."

"Thank god."

"We have power."

"We?"

"I have company."

"Oh?"

"It's Mark, he's my—he's in the other room now."

"All right. Is the water bad? I mean, how far did it come?"

"I can't tell. It's still dark out."

"You should see the footage, Amalia. CNN is broadcasting cars floating around lower Manhattan, and half of the Jersey Shore washed away."

"Fires in Queens. Transformers blowing."

"And the campaign! Obama and Romney are going to be up to their eyeballs in responding to this. I don't know how the election is even going to happen."

"I forgot about the election."

"Amalia! You're living in the middle of it. Have you even looked at the papers today?"

"No, it's the middle of the night."

"Do you have any idea of the extent of this thing?"

"What do you mean? I know it's still going on north of us," Amalia said.

"Bloody hell, Amalia. You're in the middle of a fucking Superstorm that's got half the country wrapped up."

"Ok, ok, calm down."

"I'm amazed you're even able to call me."

"Why?"

"Because nobody has any frigging power there!"

"Hang on." She went into the kitchen. "Mark. It's bad out there from what Sandra's saying."

"We can't do anything about it now." He stood at the fridge with a glass of milk. "I'll have to issue a statement for work in the morning."

"Do you want to say hi?"

"Do I have to?"

"No, but, it would be nice. She is my best friend."

"I thought Jen was your best friend."

"Jen's my best New York friend. Sandra is my best Pennsylvania friend. She's still on the call. And Great Aunt Joan is her great aunt. Sandra's great aunt."

"Oh!" He stepped back and grabbed his shirt from the counter, buttoned it back on. "She's with Aunt Joan? In Italy?"

"That's how I got this place, remember?"

"You know, I can hear everything you're saying," Sandra said.

Amalia went back to the laptop while Mark buttoned. "We kind of got together," she said to Sandra on the webcam. "Fooled around all night. But we didn't, you know."

"No Baby Erenwines," Sandra said.

"I can hear everything you're saying, you know," Mark said. He came into the camera's view, his hair wetted down in the kitchen sink, which left drops of water scattered on the shoulders of his shirt. "Hi."

"Hi. Nice to meet you. Amalia, are your parents ok?"

"I don't know yet," Amalia said. "I'll call them in the morning. It's still early here. And he—his parents."

"My parents are not alive." He put his arm around Amalia. "We're fine." He kissed her on the cheek and retired to the kitchen with the pile of midnight kedgeree dishes from the floor. Amalia chatted longer, and heard him clean the pots and dishes in the background.

"He's a doll," Sandra said.

"He's great."

"I can hear you!" He said from the kitchen, over the water.

"Listen, about this apartment business. I am so sorry. Aunt Joan is going to contest it."

"She doesn't have to. Not for me."

"Not for you, for her! She doesn't want to lose it."

"Oh."

"You found a place? Is he moving with you?"

"Helping me move. He doesn't live here."

"A long-distance romance. Not the best start. You need to make a decision. Be in the same place, or don't do it."

"And you would know?"

"Listen to me, Amalia. I know a few things about romance. Distance does not make the heart grow fonder. It makes it grow more restless. And that does not a strong relationship make."

"So how's it going over there?"

"The canals flooded again, in sympathy with you over there."

"We could learn a thing or two from Venice."

"Come! Come with him. Be here. If the whole world is flooding, why not be in Venice? Be here where we know how to do good floods."

"You make it sound like a party."

"Why not?"

"I don't think global warming is a party, exactly. Maybe more like a wake."

"Good grief, you're depressing."

"I couldn't have made this move without you."

"Do me a favor? Make a decision about Mark. Be in the same place. If you're in the same place, everything can flow. If you're not, you're in for years of heartache."

Amalia said goodbye to Mark by daylight, amidst a wet, windlashed neighborhood with residents out on the streets. The Upper West Side had fared well enough. Branches down, windows intact, signage ripped. And familiar sights: pedestrians on the sidewalk with paper coffee cups, shoppers with plastic bags.

"I'll see you back up here, ok?" Mark pulled her into a hug. They stood in front of the Starbucks at 81st and Broadway, a block from her apartment. It was open, and coffee flowed for storm-shocked Upper-West-Siders.

"I hate to think of what's going on in the rest of the city, but it's way worse thinking of you in the middle of it."

"I have to issue comments. I need to get my stuff from the hotel, assuming the hotel is still standing."

"I told you, use my laptop. Work from here."

"My work's in my briefcase. I prepared some statements already and they're all on paper. I would have set this up differently, but—I didn't realize I would be working remotely this week."

She nodded, and bit her lip. "Come back. And when you do, I want to know why they're sending you those messages."

"It'll be ok."

She nodded again. "Ok."

"Try Jen again?"

"I don't think my texts are going through."

"Listen. If you don't hear from me, don't worry. The cell signals are wonky, the lines are clogged, and I can't even get through to the hotel." He put his hand over her heart. "You feel this?"

Amalia waited, hoped he would turn around, but he did not. He never did—not in the week or two they'd known each other. Such a short time and yet she felt affected. Aroused and affected. And in love?

She felt lost all of a sudden, and looked up and around. Shoppers with folding trolley carts on wheels came in and out of Zabar's down the street. She'd go there. Maybe find herself a housewarming thing or two. She didn't own pots, pans, or anything else. Only the bed mattress Mark helped her buy on the weekend. But first, coffee, Starbucks, behind her. She was short of words, short of temper, short of patience for this storm, this change. Wanted it to be over, to have passed, and all of them recovered. They needed to move on.

She felt a little uplift in the Starbucks. Caffeine contact high? Or the happy music? Locals spoke in loud voices of the storm like it was an illness, and its symptoms were to be categorized: painful, howling, hollow, still.

The music shifted to an oldie. The words of the song came at her along with its rhythm. "Love is a Battlefield." "No, it's not," she said to the barista.

Chapter 31

On the walk back downtown, Mark mused over how much she had changed him. He didn't know what to make of it. And had she changed him? Or had he changed her? Had neither of them changed at all? He made himself dizzy with it.

Mark took Broadway, still damp. The sky was clear overhead except for wisps of fast white clouds that moved north, the tail end of the hurricane. The air was warm and brisk and bit his cheeks. Low pressure turned to high.

A tall crane, hundreds of feet tall, stood snapped at the neck with its head hung over the street, south of Central Park. He was near the place he'd first run into Amalia; he saw the crosswalk where they'd collided, then looked up at the crane. Not good. An engineering emergency if there ever was one. He'd have to issue his own company's statement soon, before noon, before panic became widespread. And then he could go back to her. Volume expressed as sound, he'd said. Now, it was streetscapes that outlined an aftershock. He felt around for something he could work into his remarks.

The view changed before he got to his hotel; pedestrians appeared shell-shocked, and buildings stood dark and battered. No cars, save some emergency vehicles. Then, one cab. Awnings down, signage ripped from supports. Bags in trees, tree branches snapped.

He had farther to go, and he tried to calculate the elevation above sea level while he walked. Would the hotel have flooded? It was not in an evacuation zone. He turned down West 28th Street onto a pocket of light; powered buildings in the middle of a blackout zone. Vendors stood outside and assessed the damage. One of them had a take-out coffee. Where had he got take-out from, in this powered-down part of the city? And why did the block have power when the others did not? He went into the hotel where he found there was power, but no working phone line.

Mark went up by elevator—powered—to the 5th floor. The comments. He'd have to flesh them out and revise them according to the reports of the day, but he wasn't on site—would have to rely on other people's accounts. He called Samantha at headquarters. No answer. He tried Simon's cell, and George in engineering. Nothing. He had the trailer number for the site he'd visited on Friday; Mary wouldn't be there now. He dialed, and there was—no answer.

What to do? He pulled out his pre-prepared comments, drafted on paper while he'd flown back from Wales. Heathrow to JFK, midair storm mitigation comments, a guess of current circumstances at best. He felt clarity now in the air, post-storm.

Volume expressed as sound.

He wrote up the press release for Atlantia Actuaris on his laptop and uploaded the message to the company's CMS platform online that way. He sat back, reread the copy, and pressed Publish. The statement was live. Unverified, and live.

He'd get back to her place. He'd be with her. So tired, up all night. He lay down on the bed. Comfy. Bed. Eyes. Closed.

Chapter 32

Amalia spent the afternoon in a slow trudge around the Upper West Side's nodes and edges. She clung to them, walked on streets still soaked and weather-beaten. Central Park was closed, and so was the Hudson River access. She'd heard the trees took it hard. Felt for them.

People were more alert to one another's presence. They made eye contact; they nodded and they spoke to each other. She missed Mark. Pushed the feeling out and tried to connect to what was going on in the city around her. Maybe he was right. What could they do?

By four, she had the thought to return home in case Mark came. She shuttered the city-storm images in her mind's eye, determined to record and to not forget, and went back to wait. She unpacked her plastic bag from Zabar's and laid out her things: plates and a couple of pans.

He didn't call. And he didn't come. She stayed awake until nine, online, still powered up. She checked the news, sent out *I'm ok* emails, tried to get a signal to call her parents. But she was too tired to wait, and she walked the perimeter of Great Aunt Joan's apartment, touched every wall, turned off the lights, and fell asleep on the couch in the t-shirt and jeans she'd worn the day before. Amalia drifted toward sleep, and into a dream that began as normally as any day at work.

She knew she was dreaming: alert within it. Went out the office door and floated down the four flights to the street. Headed out across Broadway when the traffic was clear and ducked into Central Park. She walked some distance and over a bridge before she felt a tug in her legs, and stopped. To the side of the path was a large, mature stand of trees. She went into the grove below the bridge and looked up at one tree in particular, with vertical striations of grooves in the bark that held small shadow lines in the morning dream-light.

She inhaled the dry fall air, sweet with aging leaves, and put her hands on the trunk of the large oak. She looked down at her feet, then up into the limbs that reached over her head. The wind brushed through the dry leaves and through her hair. "What do you know?"

"Ask a more specific question," she heard back. She looked around and saw she was alone in the park.

"What is the right thing to do for our environmental center project?"

"What do you want to know?" She heard it in her own voice, in her head, out loud, she wasn't sure.

"Am I crazy?" She thought it, her lips still; the words formed in clear sound in the dream. "I can have this conversation out loud or in my head."

"How should we power the environmental center, if it goes ahead?" She asked it in her thoughts.

"Do what harms the earth the least. Think back to how the power is formed, as well as how it is used." And then she heard: "Use Math."

"What do you mean, 'Use Math?'"

"Math is like electricity. It is like water. It is a gentle current that can be used in many ways. Use math to find the path you wish to travel in this journey."

"I need something more specific."

"Choose a power method. If it uses more power in its consumption than in its manufacture, that is one measure. Then think about how it makes you feel. You, Amalia. Not anyone else. You are the decision maker in your dreams. You make a decision based on how you feel. Rate the way each power source makes you feel from one to one hundred. Average the numbers to find the center. Above this number is an acceptable choice based on feeling. Below this number is a compromised choice based on feeling. It is not a good or bad choice. It is a felt choice. But it is derived by math, and not emotion, in the end. Heart feelings radiate math.

"Don't beat yourself, Amalia." Again, she heard it in her own voice. "Be gentle. Be spherically open to possibility. Be agile and be lean. Move fast. This is not the time for sluggishness. Listen, and make decisive moves. Don't linger where you feel it is crowding your heart with sorrow. Be open to moving fast at times, slow at others. Now is a fast time for you, Amalia. Be fully in your work. You don't have to split your mind. It is grandly full of reach and stretching possibilities. Expand your vision of how your mind can help you at this time. It is not only able to be linear."

Later, when she awoke from the dream, she remembered it.

Chapter 33

Wednesday, October 31

Amalia stood and bent forward at the waist; her first yoga session in over a week. She looked up from the stretch to the kitchen, where the dishes Mark had washed lay drained and dry in the rack. Let it go, she told herself. If he comes back, he comes back. If he doesn't, he doesn't. She didn't control him. Couldn't. Didn't want to.

Hungry. She straightened up and went into the kitchen. Inspired by the midnight kedgeree, she thought she'd try to replicate her mother's dal and rice. She lit the gas flame to heat the water, and while it boiled she picked over the lentils, put them to the side of the sink to drain. Tipped the remains of yesterday's kedgeree into a bowl, then cooked onions and tomatoes simmered in turmeric and ghee. Lentils went into the pot of boiling water. She added the oniony base to the lentils, let it all become soft and melded.

Amalia looked out the window onto Amsterdam Avenue. Quiet out there, again. She turned off the gas, stirred the pot, and poured the dal-rice-kedgeree into a single bowl, took it out onto the fire escape. In her new and centered calm, she sat cross-legged and ate, without haste, and her eyes wandered down the block. She saw Mark cross Amsterdam, a large brown paper-wrapped bundle in his arms. She didn't wave, but sat, watched, stayed in that centered place, and waited until she heard the buzzer before she stirred.

He brought roses from the Flower District. "I'm sorry. I crashed out and fell asleep."

She wanted to burst out with "I love you too, Mark," but it wasn't what came out. She took the brown paper bundle and unwrapped it on the kitchen counter. "These are gorgeous. Thank you. The stores were open down there?" The calm stayed with her.

"Only on our block. Cash only. All the credit card machines were down. I got you this too." He gave her a newspaper-wrapped package, heavy.

"The hotel still has no phone?"

"No phone, no internet. They have power. It's pretty dark down there, everything below 34th Street."

"Except the Flower District? Amazing, isn't it. Some have power; some have no power. It seems so random." She opened the newspaper package. "Oh! A vase! Thank you."

"How about uptown? Your new place?"

"I don't know, but I have a key, so we could still move my stuff, if we can get there. I'd like to. It's the end of the month. I'm supposed to be out today. Not that anyone's keeping track, after the hurricane."

He climbed through the kitchen window and out to the fire escape, looked up Amsterdam. "We could catch a cab."

Amalia came up behind him and climbed out the window to stand next to him on the fire escape. "I'll miss this view," she said. The old library across the street would remain. "Cab it one way, bus back? I heard the buses started up again last night. And they're free for now!"

"All right, maybe we can get this mattress on the roof of a cab."

Three hours later, they stood in front of Amalia's new apartment with the plastic-clad mattress leaned up on the side of the wall outside, in front of the trash bins.

Titian emerged out the front door, and eyed Mark. "Who's he?"

"My fiancé."

Chapter 34

Between Mark, Amalia and her new landlord, the three managed to scoot the mattress up the four flights of stairs, with audible grunts at the corners where the stairs turned. Once at the apartment, Mark slid the mattress across the floor and palmed the landlord a twenty; Titian nodded.

"What was that? The guy language," Amalia said.

"I gave him a tip," Mark said.

"You did? Why?"

"Why did you tell him I was your fiancé?"

"Goodwill, I guess? Because I don't want him to think twice about you being here?"

"Exactly." He turned to the mattress. "Now, where do you want this thing? And why are there onions all over the apartment?"

They went into the bedroom and she waved to the corners. "It's small. Oh no!" She went to the back windows. Looked like the tree behind her apartment had lost a major limb in the storm. "So sad." She picked up the onion halves and put them in the kitchen sink. "They absorb the paint smell. Or so he said."

"It's not bad—kind of spicy." Mark slid the mattress into the bedroom and laid it flat on the floor.

"I was so worried yesterday." She stood between the two

rooms, watched him sit on the mattress on the floor. "You didn't come back." She sat next to him on the bed, arms crossed. Looked up at him.

"Did you think I wasn't going to come back?" He didn't regret falling asleep. The sleep had done him good.

"I don't know. I couldn't reach you." Amalia rolled off the bed and down the few inches to the wood floor, into a crouch. Arms forward while she stretched out her back, close to the floor. "I couldn't reach Jen. I couldn't even call my parents."

"But you got the most awesome pots and pans I've ever seen."

Amalia stretched out into a long push-up and then raised her butt into the air, feet shifted forward; yoga, he assumed. She stood up with a clap of her hands. "We need to lighten this place." She smiled, and in the center of the room next to the plastic shopping bag, turned to look at him and extended her arms in the direction of the farthest walls. "It's home. I want to get some candles. Might help lighten it up. You know? But we need to get my stuff up here first." She walked over to the doorway and stood in its frame, foot on the jamb.

"I'm sure they'd make an exception for the storm."

"I'd just as soon get out of there. I love Aunt Joan and all, but I'm ready for my own place."

They took the bus back to her old apartment. Amalia stood in its center and circled, raised a flattened palm to each wall from where she stood. Mark waited by the door next to her boxes with a large shopping bag filled with some of Joan's towels and blankets.

"Thank you, apartment," she said. Outside, small trick-or-treaters carried plastic shopping bags up the street. "Sweet. I heard they canceled Hallowe'en in New Jersey on account of the storm damage. Postponed it, anyway." They loaded boxes up on the curbside. Her worm box sat on top of the boxes, the new roses laid on top of the worms. "Think we can do it in one?"

"I think so." He waved his hand for a cab headed their way and it pulled over on their side in front of the pub downstairs. They had the cab loaded within minutes, and Amalia sat on Mark's lap in the front seat next to the driver, roses in her arms.

"Hold on," said the driver. "Let's follow the bus route. It's clear. You guys ok? Flooded out?"

"No, moving."

"Good luck to you. You married?"

"Yes," Mark said.

Amalia turned to look at him, then back at the driver. "How did you fare during the storm?"

"I was in Queens," the driver said. "Not so good. Some of our cabs took a hit."

"Could you go by the river? I'd like to see it," she said. "I need to see it." Mark's arms tightened around her waist while they sailed uptown through intersections, no traffic, all the way. They paid the cabbie extra to haul a few boxes with them, and with Titian's help, they were done. "I never would have thought to ask him," Amalia said.

"If you don't ask, how will you know?" They stood in the new apartment surrounded by boxes, her suitcases, and the worms. "Where does this go?" He held the compost box.

"I guess next to the kitchen? It's so tiny in here it almost doesn't matter."

"The kitchen is the living room. Here?" He opened a cupboard and slid the worm box inside. The doors didn't close all the way.

"You know, since I might be doing more cooking, I might need that cupboard space."

"Oh really?"

"Mmm hmm. I'm inspired."

"Good! I'm as hungry as a horse."

"I'm not offering to cook now, exactly. I don't even have groceries."

He pulled her in and kissed the back of her neck. "I am hungry. Like, for food."

"Maybe someone's delivering. I don't know the lay of the land up here. Let's go out?" She picked up her keys and wallet and led him out of the apartment. They walked up the new-to-her stretch of upper Amsterdam, back on Broadway, where she bought a set of red tin coffee mugs and an espresso pot, and he bought her bed sheets. "Thank you for the coffee supplies, Nadel," she said. "And thank you, Mark, for the bed sheets. The most critical of apartment ingredients."

"I don't like the thought of you being indebted to an ex-boyfriend." They ate at a taqueria in the neighborhood she said she knew from her work nearby. "That place have candles?" He pointed across the street. They went there and found a dozen colored pillar candles and a little statue of Mary.

"I don't know how I feel about Mary," she said. "I'm kind of mad at her. Because of Rose, in the subway."

"Ok, no Mary." He put the statue back. They walked at a brisk pace in the fall air. "You'd never know a hurricane hit this city," he said. "Downtown, you would." Upstairs, and in Amalia's new home, they shed their shopping bags and jackets on the mattress, kicked off their shoes, and went back into the living room.

"Shall I light the candles?" She pulled the candles out of the package. She lit the first candle. Her hands shook. She lit the second candle and placed the two on the windowsill in the living room and one on the kitchen counter next to him. "More?" She lit two more, and placed them on the bedroom windowsills. A fifth, she placed in the bathroom. She lit three more, and placed them at each of the small apartment's thresholds: front door, bathroom, bedroom. "That's enough." She looked around the apartment, bright with the new warm glow of candles, and disarranged with boxes.

Amalia's building super had done a beautiful job with the colors, and the candles brought the paint job to life. "Something else." She picked up the bunch of roses from the counter and laid them on the floor in the middle. She sat down on the floor and fingered the edge of the plastic wrap on the roses.

He wasn't sure what came next, but she seemed to have a good deal of focus. "How do I say this?" She reached out a hand. "Sit down." He did, and she looked at him, held his hands across the roses, squeezed and let go.

"I thought this was about the apartment."

"No. It's the work stuff. Mark, I love you." She smiled. "But I can't even bring myself to talk about it out loud anymore. You know—the work stuff."

"I work for a mining company. You have—thoughts about that."

"It's not a mining company, Mark, it's a fracking company. I have strong feelings about fracking. And I have strong feelings about you. I can't reconcile what you do with how I feel about you."

He sat back. "Do you want me to leave my job?"

"I want you—I want us—to understand it, and make it better."

"You want to make my job better?" He picked up the bunch of roses from the floor, spun them so the plastic wrap crinkled.

"No, not really. I want to make the industry better. The petroleum industry. The fossil fuel industry. The alternative energy supply industries."

"That's a whole lot of industry. Billions—trillions of dollars of investment, and every country on earth involved in one way or another."

"You asked me what I want. That's what I want."

"Maybe we should start smaller."

"Ok." She took the roses from him and put them on the floor next to them, and held his hands. "Start smaller."

He nodded.

"Ok, how do we start smaller? I mean, in your—process."

He thought. "I guess, we take a deep breath and we ask the Creator to guide us."

"Creator, as in God?"

"Creator, as in Creator."

She nodded. She inhaled, continued to hold his hands, and closed her eyes. "I trust you, Mark."

"I trust you too, Amalia." She took another breath, and so did he.

"Mark." She squeezed his hands. "Breathing. Our breathing together." She put a palm on his chest, and he did the same. He felt the rise and fall of their breath. She started to shake, a little. "Sorry."

He held her hand with his other. "I thought I was having heart palpitations."

"No, just me." She closed her eyes again, aware of his hand on her chest and her hand on his. "I have this image in my mind."

"What?"

"We're doing some work together. Amazing, beautiful work. Not like anything we imagine."

"What does it look like?"

She was quiet. "Close your eyes."

He felt a fluid current, a sensation that surprised and warmed him.

"I see us out on a platform together, surveying something. Like at the water's edge, or at sea, I can't tell." She nodded, eyes closed.

"I feel that."

"I see us in yellow and red hardhats."

"Like from a company?"

"They're not the same."

"So not from a company."

"Not from one company."

"I see wires, cables, like big cables transferring information. Kind of like the old telegraph cables that ran under the sea, but not. We're cutting them. Dismantling them."

"Is there power?"

"There doesn't seem to be a lack of it."

"Can you tell how it's generated?"

"It's a multifunctional platform of sorts. It seems like hybrid power, with backups built in."

"Is it being delivered? Are we at its source?"

"No, we're above the source."

"The source is below the water?"

"Maybe. I can't tell."

"Sounds like undersea drilling."

"No, I don't sense drilling."

"Geysers?"

"Maybe."

"Tidal?"

"No, I don't think so."

"I know what it is," he said, and dropped his hand to his lap.

She opened her eyes. "I lost it. Sorry."

"Hydrothermal vents. At the sea floor. Capturing a natural source of heat energy."

"That could have been it. Amazing."

"We got that together."

"You saw it too?"

"Pretty much, not in the same way. More or less. Your descriptions were good. They helped me lock in. I felt it."

"Like a current. Makes me think—what are we capable of?" She perched on the edge of the bed and held out her hands. He sat next to her on the bed, sideways, the shopping bags at the center of the bed. She started to giggle. "I don't think I can do this anymore." She suppressed a laugh that came out like a cough. "It's not you. It's—I'm happy."

"Maybe we're done."

"We're done. For now, done. Maybe more later?" She took his hand and kissed his fingers. "Thank you." Amalia went to the bedroom window and looked out. "Do you think anyone can see in?"

"They'd have to be standing on the fire escape to look in. I wouldn't worry about it. No one can see. We can get you blinds tomorrow."

"No, I know." She grabbed a craft knife from the packing stuff and used it to open a box from the bottom of the stack. Turned around to show him a light blue silk length of fabric. "I never wear this." She put it on the floor and began to cut it at its middle with the knife.

"No! I mean, you can't cut that, can you?"

"I need curtains. And this is pretty. And I never wear it. Stand back! I wield my trusty X-ACTO." She waved the knife in the air and continued to slice the fabric in half.

"I feel like I witnessed a murder."

"Oh please."

"It's so beautiful. And I never got to see you in it."

"Another time. Another sari. Give me a hand, Romeo?"

"What do you want me to do?"

"Open the top sash of the windows and stick this in, close it up tight."

"Wow, you're—"

"What would you do?"

"I know. Wait here." He ran downstairs to the main floor. The building super answered. "Got dowels?" He was back at her apartment in minutes. "Look!" He had a hammer and nails, and two long dowels. "From your super."

"You're too much."

He nailed the dowels up in place over each window. "Do you have needle and thread?"

"Somewhere, yes." She dug in one of the boxes. They stitched it together, without pins, and Mark held the seams in place while Amalia sewed the channel in place, open at both ends to receive the dowels. Mark slipped each silk curtain over the dowel and hung them back up over the windows. The fabric hung in a flat panel over each window, one with a decorative border at the bottom, the other without.

"They're gorgeous, Amalia." He shook his head. "I wish I'd seen it on you first."

She drew the curtains closed and pulled Mark to the mattress edge. "Finally." They rocked in sync and stopped when their foreheads touched. "I see you, there," she said, with her eyes closed.

"Amalia." His hands moved up her back and he slipped his fingers inside her bra strap and found the clasp, and she inhaled.

It felt different than before. Maybe it was because they were there, where they were. She helped him out of his shirt and they rocked back and forth, bare-chested, at the edge of the bed, until they fell over backwards.

He stroked her skin up and down until she shivered. They were so—opposite. She made room for him, watched him undress. She moved back and forth on him they came at the same time, rolled through orgasmic waves that merged with each other's. He closed his eyes on blue light that shifted fast to orange.

Mark lay with Amalia across his chest, both too tired to move. After an hour, one of them shifted and they turned to lie next to each other, his arm draped over her hips as they spooned in the bed under sodium-filtered city light that flowed through the silk sari curtains.

By mid-evening he got up, checked his cell messages. It was the same. "I will take you to court over this." Mark looked over at Amalia who lay in a half-awake doze in the bed. What to tell her?

"What you got?" She sat up.

"A message."

"A Message message, or just a message?"

"It might be a clue to who's on my back. This time it was a voice mail."

"Simon? She stood up next to the bed, naked but for the surreal light that came through the curtains. "I thought you said—"

"Too obvious. And I didn't recognize the man's voice. Why wouldn't he have said something while we were in Wales?"

"Someone you met some other time, on a site?" She whipped a long sweater from a box around her shoulders. "You can trace it back, can't you? Find out who that email was from before, who this voice message is from now?"

"If it's not Simon, it's someone." He kissed her on the lips. "I'll figure it out. Please don't worry." Felt a new boldness. Mark was prepared to let the whole thing go.

Chapter 35

Thursday, November 1

Amalia awoke to blue light in the room, an effect of sunlight in a direct stream through the panels of sari fabric that hung from her east-facing bedroom windows. She rolled over to find Mark and saw he'd already got up—and rolled farther over, to see him perched atop a moving box in her living room. He sat with a sketchbook, and was in a zone of—no, a trance of—of such great depth that even when she stood up and walked up to him, he didn't shift from his work on the page. "Something interesting there?"

He looked up. "Amalia." A big smile. "Good morning." He put the sketchbook aside and stood to kiss her, without the haste of the previous night. "You're yummy. I need something to eat, though. Real food. I didn't want to wake you, but now you're up."

"Groceries? Or find somewhere open for breakfast? It looked like everything was open when we walked up Amsterdam yesterday." Amalia picked up her phone to check messages. "Still nothing from Jen." She tried to place a call to her, but still got no answer. "Not going through. Again." She banged her phone on the edge of the kitchenette countertop. "She can't have gone out of town. She'd need a boat to get out an upper window of her house."

"Ok, ok. Maybe she's not getting the messages. They're not going through. You want to go and find out how she's doing?"

"I don't know how we'd get there, if the subways are still flooded."

"But the buses are running."

She waved the phone in the air. "Yes. I'd feel better. We could bring her back here."

They mapped it on her phone with a strange and modified city map made available for the public that showed a good chunk of New York City either submerged or disconnected on transit, affected by the full moon superstorm. By MTA estimates in the post-hurricane conditions, it would be at least three and a half hours to get to Brooklyn, on four different buses, without traffic delays or detours. "Let's do it." She jumped into yesterday's clothes.

"No fares." The driver pointed to the coin slot. "It's free."

"Oh, thanks." Mark walked to the back of the bus and Amalia followed. "I didn't have a MetroCard," he said. "Mine is empty."

"And it didn't matter. They're not charging right now. I could have paid for you."

"You have a life here." He looked glum. "With Jen, and your work people, the guy in Queens."

"Who I'm not dating."

"And you owe money to your ex."

She closed her eyes and thought of how they made love the night before—her and Mark—but each time she tried, Nadel was in the vision, not Mark. Go, Nadel. He was spoiling her time with Mark.

"Was it a physical thing?" Mark looked morose and sat next to her. "Last night—was that—mechanics?"

"Why would you say that? It was this—delicious euphoria." A large matron sat opposite them, her glance a ping-pong rally back and forth between him and Amalia. No privacy. "Do you want me to pay him back?"

"No, I want to pay him back."

"I'm not going to switch my debt from him to you. I'm supposed to pay him back soon, this was temporary." She looked at the time on her phone: three hours and twenty minutes to go on this bus route journey. She pulled a notebook and pen from her tikka backpack and opened it on her lap. "I owe him this much," she said. "And I'm getting paid this much, today, direct-deposited in my account. Next month, this much again. I'll pay him off in—two or three months. Maybe three or four."

He gave the numbers a sidelong look. "That could kill us."

"Why are you being so dramatic?"

"He's there, Amalia, I feel him."

"When? Last night?"

"All week, actually. I thought it was the other guy, but it's him."

"You're very sensitive."

He nodded, miserable.

She looked out the side window of the bus. They'd been better off in the apartment, shut off from the world. The bus passed a street that seemed normal on its exterior. He took the book and pen from her and turned to the next blank page. He began to write and continued for several blocks. She looked away and tried to avoid the eyes of the matron across the aisle from her. The matron; the Mother, she thought. Where was Mother Earth in all of this?

Mark finished his note, closed the book, put the pen onto the cover and gave it to her.

"Do you want me to read it?"

"I do. You decide." He coughed. "You decide when to read it."

"We have a long trip." She looked at him and unzipped her backpack again, slipped the book and pen inside. "Thank you." She put the bag between her feet and rested sideways on his shoulder. He put his arm around her, picked up a strand of her hair and twisted it in his fingers until they got to 59th and Lexington and had to get up to switch buses.

She opened the book, the backpack on her lap like a table in front of her on the bus, and held the pen beneath the pages Mark had written.

He looked out the window next to him.

I really want to make this work between us, but there's something unspoken between us, and I can't figure it out. Maybe it's this storm, maybe it's my brother, or your ex.

She let out a long breath and looked at him watch the city pass by. "Mark."

He kept his eyes on the landscape. "Keep reading."

I know you don't support what I do, no matter what you say in your more visionary states. I do believe in what I'm doing, and I don't think I'm hurting anyone, or anything. Science is a process of discovery. We make trials and errors and we make mistakes sometimes, but it's a revelatory process. Much like art.

She sank deeper into receipt and pressed her knees into the row in front of her, so that her feet came off the ground.

I know why you didn't ask me for the money, and it hurts to see it.

"I barely knew you then." She put a hand to her mouth and continued to read and he looked out the window.

By the time they got to the third bus at Queens Plaza, she'd finished and had to walk fast to keep up with him. "This place is crazy, Mark."

"Is it normally like this?" People walked in all directions with boxes of doughnuts, bundled up blankets, cell phones out. A lot of them looked dejected and some of them stood still, aimless.

"I don't know. I don't think so." She looked around the going in and out of the subway.

"These lineups are unreal."

"Should we try the subway? Maybe some lines are running now."

"It looks too crazy. Our bus was busy, but how are we even going to get on the next one? It's a madhouse." He steered her, then let her take the lead. "I'm lost," he said. She found their way to the bus stop and they stood in line. He put his arms around her in a full bear hug while they waited, and she leaned her cheek on his jacket and felt his hands below her backpack, on her back and over her wool jacket, steady.

Chapter 36

Mark snapped into a conscious awareness after the bus door gasped shut behind them at Fulton Mall in Brooklyn. She'd said something when they sat together in her apartment. She had a sense of the modulations of the earth. What did she mean? She had a piece of this for him—something in her heart would show him the way.

"Mark." She grabbed his hand on the curb. "It looks like it got wet," she said.

"Saturated is more like it," he said. "Can we walk from here?"

She looked around. "I can find the way from here." The streets were battered, bent signs, broken tree limbs, downed wires. "This is bad. Way worse than we got it." They walked in the middle of the road; he hoped to avoid loose branches overhead. "We must be getting close; I can smell the Gowanus Canal." They walked further, streets strewn with leaves, branches, and debris. Wood, garbage. "She's on Warren between Nevins and Bond. I stayed there last week, actually."

"On the ground floor?"

"They call it a garden apartment."

"A Gowanus apartment."

"She went upstairs, though, to her neighbors. They were on the roof."

"What? Why?"

"Shooting a video. I was up there once, for a party. They had vegetables."

"At the party?"

"No, growing on the roof. In pots."

They rounded a corner at Baltic. "Oh no." A man perched on a fire hydrant and watched two other men pull out a sodden mattress and a broken bed frame from a lower level apartment. They piled it next to mounds of damaged housewares. "We must have gone past it already. This doesn't look familiar."

"I hope she's way out of this." Mark looked up ahead at the debris-strewn street. He pulled her back. "The smell. This isn't good." He pressed a hand into his nose in an attempt to block the acrid sewage smell from entry.

She covered her face with her palm. "Further." Pulled him the other way and they walked along Bond Street.

The warehouses were hit hard, and the storm surge waterline above their heads marked the brick walls they passed, metal panels ripped off their fence posts. They walked in silence, stepped over shattered lumber and scattered plastic shards. A few people milled about; others hauled. Everything from sheetrock to stacks of old vinyl records was piled up on the sidewalks.

Sludgy brown water, thick, gushed in spurts from a green plastic hose into the street from a ground floor studio workshop. The man with the hose nodded at their approach. "Okay." It was neither a question, nor a statement.

"We're ok. We're looking for a friend."

"Who's your friend?"

"Jen Savin. She lives on Warren."

"Never heard of her. Warren's better than here. You want to go back that way, out of Red Hook," he waved a hand, then adjusted the pipe. A generator vibrated beyond it, out of sight.

"Need a hand?" Mark asked, watched the man adjust the line.

"It's downstairs, actually. I need to go down but I don't want to leave this. Can you stay here for a sec? While I go down to check the pump?"

Mark nodded and stepped away from Amalia and toward the man, extended a hand. "I'm Mark."

The man raised his gloved hands in the air. "No way you want to touch this. Nigel," he said, and disappeared into the workshop.

"What is this? Smells foul," Amalia said.

"I'd call it chemical soup by the looks of this place."

"What, the Gowanus?"

He nodded. "It's a Superfund site."

"I heard that. Dumping for years."

A maroon van approached and threatened to spray the brown glop from the plastic pipe onto their legs. Amalia stood back and Mark grabbed the wet pipe. He redirected it sideways to bring along the gutter next to the curb.

"Going back into the sewer now."

"Where else would you have it go?" He put it down and wiped his hands on his jeans.

"I don't know, I'm just saying." She pulled out her phone. "It's past lunchtime. We're not going to find anything to eat here."

"And I don't think I want to eat the fruit we brought, not without washing my hands first."

She tried Jen again. "It's me, Amalia, we're in your neighborhood, call me." She left a text as well.

Looking for you, pls call or text, A xo

"No luck," she said to Mark.

Nigel emerged from the building with a roll of black plastic trash bags and a gallon of drinking water in a white jug. "Thanks, man. You want some?" He held out the jug.

"For my hands." Nigel poured clear water over Mark's hands.

"Where's your friend, then?"

"I don't know," Amalia said. "She hasn't been answering her phone."

"Maybe it floated away," Nigel said, and moved his hands in a dance, his voice a singsong.

Chapter 37

Amalia stood at the edge of the Gowanus Canal and looked across at the still brown water. "Jen said the neighbors used to hear gunshots at night."

"Seriously?"

Amalia nodded. "Seems calm to me."

"Does anything live in here?"

"I remember hearing about something, fish or something. Maybe a manatee? I can't remember."

"A manatee?"

"No, really." She laughed. "I think it was a manatee."

"Little Manatee, you didn't choose a very nice home."

"No, it's good." She turned to him with her hands in her pockets, and wanted to touch him, but didn't want it—the brown goo—anywhere near. "We need to get you back to a hot shower. And a laundromat. Come on. Let's go find Jen." She walked back the way Nigel pointed until they found Warren and turned up the street.

"This is pretty," he said. "Sad for the trees that lost their branches."

Amalia went up to the row house on Warren and knocked on Jen's ground floor front door. She peered in the windows. "It's dark in there."

"I assume she lost power," Mark said. "The whole block seems to be out."

"All of Brooklyn is out, by the looks of it." She ran up the front steps of the house and banged on the front door to upstairs. "Jen! Paige!"

"Who's Paige?"

"Her roommate. Neal! Steve!" She yelled up to the roof. "Anyone there?"

"How come I never heard of Paige?"

She came back down the steps and sat down on the second to last tread, and he sat next to her, on the fourth step, so their feet lined up on the pavement. "Paige. The one with the Pussy Riot t-shirt."

He shook his head. "This does not ring any bells. The Pussy Riot shirt, however, I cannot forget. Etched in my mind forever."

"Maybe I never told you her name."

"And they're a couple?"

"They were. Jen is dating Suky. I think." She turned and looked at him. You're ok with that? I mean, it doesn't offend your Catholic sensibilities?"

"Sorry? What's wrong with being Catholic?"

"You haven't been acting very Catholic with me," she said, and whapped him on the leg with the back of her hand.

"True."

She went to look in Jen's window again. "I kind of wish I could—oh my god, Mark!"

"What?" He jumped up.

"Check it out." There on the coffee table, through the window, Jen's cell phone signaled with its red message light on and off, on and off.

Chapter 38

Mark stood with his back to the black wrought iron gate at Jen's Warren Street brownstone.

Amalia pulled out the notebook from her backpack and sat back down on the step. "Two notes I guess, one for each door."

Jen & Paige. We came to find you. Come to new apartment anytime. Call me. Amalia. PS Your cell is inside.

She held it up. "Ok?"

"Do you think you should put your address and phone number?"

"I don't want to, no. Not to hang up outside here." She flipped through the notebook. Focused in, his words read aloud.

"I need to know you're ok with my job. It's great to share a vision with you—I just don't know how to get it off the ground."

How come she hadn't got it? He leaned on the wrought iron gate in front of the house. "I'm in love with you," he said.

"You're not mad at me."

"No. Why would you think so?"

She let the book slide off her lap to the step below.

He reached to grab it, and broke a near fall on the step with his hand. "Ow." He wrapped the other hand around his wrist and twisted it around.

"Please sit." She took the book from him. "I so want to hold your hands. But there is no way I'm going to with that Gowanus muck on them. I'm sorry."

"I'll wash them."

"I read this and I thought you were mad at me."

"Amalia, how could you think I am mad at you? I don't want to be at odds with you. I don't know how to get there."

She turned up the corners of her mouth in a small smile. "We should go. Eat, wash, get out of here. Not in that order." She scribbled a second note, ripped the pages from the book and went up to Neal and Steve's front door and tucked one note into the mail slot, then came back down and slipped the other note for Jen and Paige under their door mat so that it stuck out.

Chapter 39

They left Brooklyn on foot. At their current rate, they'd make it to the other side of the Brooklyn Bridge in two hours. Talk about a snail's pace. She held back and he turned to look at her where she stood. So handsome, he was. How lucky, she was.

They walked through unlit streets, gray by daylight, around fallen trees, along leaf-strewn sidewalks and over heaved paving stone sidewalks, away from downed power lines, and past yellow police tape. People milled around, generators and chainsaws riled up the sound of the neighborhood, and cars attempted to pass through the streets.

They crossed the East River and the breeze across the Brooklyn Bridge revitalized them both. They stopped half way across to eat the fruit they'd brought; Mark used his sleeves to try to hold the fruit. "Let me," she said. "This is easier. Although it's fun watching you try."

She looked across and down to the area below, where the bridge met the shore and Pier 17 stuck out into the water, its lettering looming large over the shattered structure below.

"Doesn't look good," he said. A man with a camera on a tripod stood at the edge of the bridge, focused outward and down the edge of Manhattan. "You think he's a tourist?"

"Journalist, more like."

"What's going on down there?" He pointed to a shattered wooden pier below them.

"I don't know, why don't you ask the journalist?" Looked to her like the storm—or the storm surge—had hit it hard. "He looks so sad."

"It's not a funeral. It's a—a coastline." Mark turned her by her jacket to him, and she looked down where his hand had touched the fabric. "Sorry. Gowanussy. I'll wash properly."

Amalia looked out at the water and the structure beyond, arms crossed. "It's terrible. Crushing." She wanted to open up to it somehow, to him, to the city, but—too hard. She leaned back and then forward on her feet, and then all the way forward to touch her toes, and the bridge deck, then wrapped her arms around her calves and softened her back into the fold. She looked back along the length of the Brooklyn Bridge, upside down.

"Someday, this coast isn't going to look like this."

"It already doesn't." She spoke from the upside down bend, aware of the sensation she was suspended by the hips over the East River. She felt free in it, but didn't want to lose their balance in conversation.

"I know it looks like destruction now. But it won't look even like this. It'll look—natural. Normal. People will be used to it."

"I don't know if I like where this is going." She unfolded herself and stretched out her legs to the side, shook her ankles loose, looked out across the bridge to the coastal edge of Manhattan. "Mannahatta." She'd heard it was called that by the native village populations who'd inhabited the space before colonialism. Before, during. Where was the Mannahatta spirit now? She wondered what the old ways would say about this hurricane and its impact, but didn't want to ask Mark what he thought. Too much—too much what? Too much potential for confrontation.

"I don't mean people are going to adjust right away. It could take decades for people to pull back." He looked down and followed her sight line. "Centuries for the coast to settle."

"Settle from what, exactly?" Maybe he was open to the conversation, after all.

"Water level rise."

She nodded. "And—and this water level rise. I have thoughts about it. As I am certain you do." She shook out her legs.

"I take a long view. A millennial view."

She turned and looked at him, his shoulders framed by the chords of the bridge behind him. "Ok, smart guy. Lay it on me."

He shook his head. "Not now. No. There's too much fight in you now."

"There is not."

"I'm not walking into a trap again with you."

"It's not a trap, I have no trap. I'm not—I'm not playing games with you. I want to know what you think." She did. She could hold down the anger. "About—" she bobbed her head up and down and tried to get the words to flow. "About sea levels."

"You mean about global warming. Climate change." He took a step back. "I'll be happy to talk about it with you when I don't feel like you're going to jump down my throat."

"Fossil fuels." The man with the camera turned to them.

"If we weren't burning up so much fossil fuel, the earth wouldn't be warming, the poles wouldn't be melting, and these storms wouldn't be forming over the warming oceans. That's it in a nutshell." He turned back to the view and fiddled with his tripod, moved it a few inches closer to them.

Mark did not respond but stepped forward. "What is that, down there? If you don't mind my interruption."

"South Street Seaport. You from here?"

"I—I'm here on business. She lives here."

"But I'm not from here."

The man nodded. "Fossil fuels." He turned back to his equipment.

Amalia and Mark walked along the remainder of the bridge deck and onto land, down the blocks-long sidewalk, fenced from traffic on both sides. At the end of the bridge they turned onto Centre Street, open to the city that spread before them.

They found an uptown bus and took it, watched lower Manhattan pass by, dark, wet, in recovery. Food vendors ran extension cords across the sidewalks. People walked in a congenial, stunned silence, congregated around building entrances, cell phone chargers gathered at working power sources. "Mark! We need to come back here to help."

"What could we do?"

"You could—like those guys we passed—measuring flood levels as far up as they went on the buildings."

"They were from the US Geological Society. I'm in private industry."

They got off and walked over to Mark's hotel, which Amalia had not seen in more than a week. Amalia lit up at the flowers across from the hotel. "It's bright here. I thought nobody south of 34th Street had power. Or 39th?"

"Never lost power, here."

"Must be the flower power. This place is amazing!" They walked in and out of floral shops from 6th Avenue to 7th and back on the other side of the street. "I am in heaven. This is New York? This was here all along? I had no idea." They went into a shop and bought more roses, pink ones this time, and he asked the vendor to put them in a vase.

"They sell them next door."

"I don't need anything fancy. An old one of yours. It's for my hotel room."

"Let me see." The man disappeared in the back and Amalia looked around the long, narrow floral shop. "I wonder what that is." She pointed to an old black and white photo behind the counter.

The vendor reemerged with a tall vase, elegant.

"What is this?"

"Mexican Revolution," he said. "The revolution of 1910."

"Are those your relatives?" She pointed to the mustachioed men in the faded photo.

"Maybe the boss' relatives. Not mine."

"What was it about?"

He nodded and looked back at the photo. "Land reform. You know Pancho Villa?"

"The name rings a bell. I'm not sure."

"You know Zapata?"

"Like Zapatista, sure," Mark said.

"Yes, exactly. The Zapatistas began as followers of Zapata."

He flashed a bright smile and handed the flowers to her while Mark paid, and then gave her the vase wrapped in a plastic bag.

"How were you during the storm?"

"We had power, mostly," he said. "But no phone, no internet. The credit card machines are down. We're very happy for cash payments, now. Customers aren't coming, everyone thinks we're not open."

Mark gave him back the change. "You keep it."

"No, sir."

"No, I insist."

"And what do all those questions about the Mexican Revolution have to do with anything?" Mark asked her outside the store. "Just interested in history?"

"Don't know, it just came to me. I wonder if there's a connection to us."

"What kind of connection?"

She followed him into the hotel elevator across the street and carried the heavy brown paper bundle of flowers in her arms like a bouquet on display, rather than a wrapped package. The doors closed and she took a step toward Mark, kissed him, hands-free. "I'm sorry I was cranky before."

He kissed her back. "It's ok. It's a cranky kind of day."

"I do love you, you know."

"I know," he said. "I love you too."

"We'll figure this out."

He nodded. "Easy."

"I wish you weren't so Gowanussy now," she said. They kissed again and then realized the elevator hadn't moved.

He pressed the button up to the 5th floor; fiddled with his door card and let them in, and stepped out of his shoes, jeans, jacket and shirt, kicked off his shorts and socks, and went without a word into the bathroom where he began to run a very hot, full blast stream of water.

Amalia closed the hotel room door behind them. She saw housekeeping had turned down the bed and left a tray with candles and matches on the pillow, a nice courtesy.

"You don't mind, do you?" He called through the open bathroom door and steam poured out of the room. "I couldn't stand it anymore. And I don't think you could, either."

"No, you're good. Get clean." She put the flowers and vase bag down next to her backpack on the side table. "These need water."

"Be my guest."

"I don't have anything to trim the ends with."

"There's a Swiss army knife in my bag, the work bag. The one by the window. Side pocket."

He allowed her in. Into the work bag. "Ok."

She put the bag on the bed and unzipped the side pockets, felt around until she got the knife. Her hand rested on the large zippered compartments at the center, and she withdrew her hand after a moment and put the bag back on the floor.

Amalia took the candle tray from the bed and set it on the side next to the brown paper bundle. She lit the candles.

She opened the flowers on the bed and they fell wide, splayed. She laid each stem in her palm one by one, cut each end with the knife upwards toward her. She stripped off some of the lower leaves and arranged them in the vase, and set it on the side while she wrapped the trimmings and rolled the paper up. She wiped the knife on her jeans and left it on the side to wash, then got up to feed the roses a drink from the bathroom sink.

Chapter 40

Mark let his shoulders drop in the shower where hot water and steam washed away the last of the Gowanus muck.

"Knock, knock," she said into the deep steam of the bathroom. "I like this flower arranging. It's a good habit. If I ever abandon architecture, I will throw myself into flowers."

"This steam can't be good for them." He stuck his head out. "But wow, how gorgeous." He came out of the shower, wet.

"You," she said. She put the vase on the bathroom counter. A heavy scent of rose essence hung on the droplets of steam. He wrapped her arms around his bare, wet skin and she tilted her head up to kiss him, but he shifted his weight and lifted her to the bathroom counter so she was between the roses and the sink, on the cold marble counter and wrapped against his warm, naked body.

She undid her bra and let it fall and he trailed kisses along her shoulder. He moved to unbutton her jeans and she unzipped them, slid off the counter to slip off her pants and socks to the floor. "Help me back up." He lifted her around her waist, back up to the counter, and the cool marble was a shock to her bare skin. She pulled her coat out of the sink and dropped it to the floor, wrapped her legs around Mark, met him at his waist. He led her into the shower and the hot spray covered them both.

"It's the umbrella. The Mexican Revolution is under the umbrella with us. That's why it's important." She rested her hands on his chest and the water came down over his head and shoulders, splashed onto her.

"What umbrella?" He turned them around so she was below the shower.

She rolled her neck in the stream of warm water. "You remember when we were at the museum last weekend and you asked me what I thought about the land, and art, and American art?"

"Yes." He reached for soap.

"The umbrella. I feel like we're all under this big umbrella together on the continent. And the revolution—there's something there, to understand, about where we are all at now, here."

"And that is—what? Turn." He turned her around so her back was to him.

"Maybe it will come to me in a dream."

"I like those dreams of yours," he said. "Visionary." He soaped her back, moved his hands to the front.

"Illusory is more like it. They don't always make sense to me."

"Hush."

"You're working tomorrow?" Amalia lay next to him in his hotel bed.

"I should look at the train schedule." Mark kissed her on the top of the head and got out of bed, pulled the duvet off and around him like a cape. He went to his work bag and unzipped the large central compartment and pulled out his laptop. "Nothing yet on New Jersey Transit. And not on Amtrak either." He closed his email fast, didn't want her to see Anwen had written. Checked his phone. Once and for all, he'd delete those National Weather Service updates. "Done. No more National Weather Service."

"Don't you need it?"

"If I need it, I'll look it up. I do not need to be reminded several times a day."

"What time is it?"

"About three."

"Check later? Or stay in the city. The trains will be up and running soon."

"I don't know, the lines were hit hard. They even had boats on train lines." Heart pounded. Should he tell her about the message from Anwen?

"I saw." She sat up. "You know what the guy said? The photographer. On the Brooklyn Bridge."

He turned off his phone and laptop and turned around. What had she seen? "Boats on train lines. Fossil fuels. I know. I heard." It wasn't about Anwen.

"Do you think—and I know this is your work and all—but do you, Mark, as a concerned human, think fossil fuels are related to Hurricane Sandy?"

"Amalia, if I knew I'd be the smartest guy around." He wrapped the duvet around him and extended his legs in a stretch across the floor. He was in the clear. Heart slowed.

"So you don't?"

"I don't think anybody knows. Show me someone who thinks they know and I'll show you a fearful, arrogant bastard who thinks they know better than—than—" He needed to calm down. She'd think there was something to hide, if he got insistent.

"But what about the statistics? The science?" She pulled the blanket and sheet tighter to her chest.

"Science is what I do. And I know all about it. It's—manipulation of data to support a theory. There's nothing objective about it."

"Are you saying you manipulate data?"

"Sometimes, yes."

"How do we get something fixed to measure off then? How do we create policies based on unfixed measurements?"

"We go for the middle. Take a lot of samples and look for patterns. Find averages. Seek order."

"And that's where the subjectivity comes in? How those edges get defined?"

"Something like that, yes." They were on another tangent; he could relax.

She nodded. "What do you feel, though? If you had to put a feeling to the numbers."

"I told you. I don't know."

"You don't know what you feel, or you feel uncertain?"

"The latter." She'd pegged it.

"Me too." She got up and wrapped the blanket around her and went to the window and looked out at 28th Street. "Quiet out there now."

"They start early, yes. You can hear them. You remember when you slept here last weekend—no, two weekends ago—and we woke up early on Monday? All the street noise?"

"I loved that."

"You did? You barely gave me a look when we said goodbye."

"I looked down the street after you," she said, "but you didn't turn around. Maybe you did. There was something blocking the way between us, some construction."

Chapter 41

"I feel sleepy with you today," Amalia said. They'd gone north of 39th, in search of an open restaurant where they could sit and relax, eat, not think. She held his hands on top of the table over the laminated menus, in a window seat at Lindy's. "Nice to lie in bed with you."

"You can say it out loud, you know."

"What?"

"Nice to make love with you."

She smiled. What could she say to that?

"Are you supposed to go to work tomorrow? I thought you said something earlier," Mark said.

"I was, but Betsy and Max and Sharon still haven't been able to get in, so they emailed us to stay home."

"I know who Betsy is. What about the others?"

"Max is Betsy's business partner. Sharon is the HR Manager."

"You have an HR Manager for such a small firm?"

"It used to be a lot bigger, before the recession. I guess they all stuck it out together. She does more than HR. Bookkeeping, marketing, all that kind of stuff. She built a new website for the company."

"Made herself useful."

Amalia nodded. "I like her. I talked to her about the Atlantia

Actuaris investment. You know, the environmental center. I told you about it. When we were at Mildred's."

"Vague recollections of running around a parking lot—"

"Oh god. But she knew what she was doing, didn't she? She knocked the edges off us."

He let go of her hands and pulled out a menu. "The center. Tell me." He looked down at the menu.

"It's one of the projects I'm working on. The funding went south and the firm introduced the client to someone from Atlantia Actuaris. Atlantia ended up underwriting the project."

"Mmm hmm."

"So Atlantia Actuaris was going to make us all rich and famous, but here's the thing. It's an environmental center."

"And..."

She sighed. "Gas isn't green." She opened her hands.

"Someone was ok with it, if it got so far."

"A lot of people were ok with it."

"But not you."

"No. It's not green, and it's hypocritical to say it is."

"I'm sorry, but you're wrong there." He sat forward and twiddled the paper straw wrapper. "It's—" he paused. "I don't want to lecture you."

"So don't."

"Amalia. This is important. It's a fundamental divide in our relationship."

"Fine." She sat back. "Bring it on. I'm ready."

"Gas has fewer carbon emissions than coal or oil."

"Not hard."

"So you agree?"

"No—I mean, coal and oil are high in emissions, so it would be hard to go higher."

"Ok." He put down the paper straw wrapper. "Fewer carbon emissions—a good thing for the short-term climatic bubble we find ourselves in."

"Short-term bubble? It's monumental, Mark. You make global warming sound like an anomaly."

"It is an anomaly."

"A human-made anomaly."

"If you like," he said. "It's different from a historic norm. But there are larger forces at play than those of humankind."

"Of which we know very little."

"We know about geologic-scale aeonic shifts."

"Aeonic."

"Gas helps us now because it reduces the bubble effect."

"I wish you would stop calling it that. It's the Greenhouse Effect."

"If you like."

"I don't like! I don't like any of it, Mark. I wish we weren't in this situation in the first place."

"Which situation?"

"Of—of—the ice caps melting and the sea levels rising and temperatures rising and millions of people around the world at risk of death and displacement!"

"Ok, I can see that."

"Mark! You are so exasperating!"

"I asked, 'which situation.' Not trying to be exasperating." He pushed back and waved for the waitress. "Eggs. Scrambled. With bacon."

"Same. No bacon, no toast," Amalia said. "Ok, so not exactly the same."

"You. So contrary," Mark said. "Ok." He leaned in toward the center of the table, hands clasped. "This environmental center at work. Didn't you get in trouble over it or something?"

"I did. I had started to do some research on energy options for the center, and Betsy distributed it at a board meeting. But it wasn't done."

"So..."

"I was still figuring it out. Honestly, I'm still figuring it out."

"I'd like to see it."

"You know, one of our projects is near my new apartment. I could show you."

"I'd like that." He sighed. "I am at sea. It's been a weird week."

"Because you haven't gone home?"

"Partly. I'm—happy about being with you," Mark said. "Disturbed about work. Uprooted from home. And in the middle of this Sandy chaos. And this. This—environmental crisis we seem to be in."

"You mean about his fossil fuel comment? And the hurricane?"

"No, I mean you and me."

"We did ok. Where we were, in the storm."

"That's not what I—" He took a deep breath and looked up at the ceiling. "You're right. I can't believe we came out as well as we did."

"The dividing line between north and south is unbelievable," Amalia said. "The power line."

"There are the pockets, too. Like, my hotel has power, even though the blocks around it don't. Jen's place had water come up, but her stuff looks dry."

"Betsy said they kept power in New Jersey even when most of the rest of their town lost it. Her email said they have guests staying who don't have power."

"Makes sense."

"How's your place in Philadelphia?"

"I don't know. I've been here. Tim is away. And it's Quakertown, actually, not in Philadelphia. Outside. The neighbor said the house is fine. I mean, I haven't seen it for myself." The waitress brought their dishes over. "Great. Thanks. That was fast." He looked up, smiled, picked up his fork and began to eat. "I'm starving."

"I'd like to see it. With you. I'd like to—if you're inviting, I'd like to come."

"Of course, I already did." He ate fast, and sipped water in between bites.

"Mark." She poked around the food on her plate. "How do we figure out everything we're trying to figure out?"

They walked north after their meal. At 60th Street, she checked her phone again. "Nothing. We might as well." She indicated the front door of her office.

"Wait." He pulled her back. "This is where I first saw you. Here." He tapped the spot with his foot and pulled her hand, tugged her toward him.

She looked up and down the block. "This is it. Our starting point, even though we didn't know it at the time." She slid her arms into his open jacket and over his checkered shirt, and hugged him up the back. "I'm lucky. Lucky we saw each other at the Hungarian Pastry Shop. And after."

"I'm the lucky one," he said. He bent his head down and they kissed between the two subway entrances.

They pulled apart. Like lovers. Oh wait, they were lovers. She smiled.

"What?"

"Nothing." She unlocked the front door and took him up the elevator. "Funny, it looks like a light is on back there," she said. "At least we kept power. Hello?"

"Hello!" Voices floated out from the back of the office.

In the conference room, around the table, were Jen, Paige, Neal and Steve.

"What are you guys doing here? We went to Brooklyn to look for you!" She held Mark's hand and took in the four of them, papers spread on the table, last week's old roses pushed to the side, limp but still pretty.

Jen jumped up. "Oh my god." She hugged Amalia, who let go of Mark's hand.

"Are you ok? I was so worried. I went to your apartment but you weren't there. You left your phone at home."

"I lost it, actually."

"No, it's at your house," said Mark. "We saw it on the table through the window."

"You're kidding me." Jen let go of Amalia. "You must be Mark."

"I am indeed Mark." He took a little bow and extended his hand to shake hers.

"No way, you get a hug." She gave him a strong-armed hug, stepped back and smiled at him. "Nice to meet you, Mark." Jen extended her open arms around the two of them at once in a wide embrace.

"What are you all doing, sleeping here?"

"We're having a campaign meeting," said Neal. "The election is less than a week away. We have to rally. People here are getting off track."

Amalia looked at Mark. "Obama."

"I figured, from the looks of the stuff on the table."

"We're phoning. Reminding people to vote."

"You're—doing this? Running a volunteer campaign from our office?"

"Kind of."

"Do Betsy and Max know?"

"I haven't seen them," Jen said. "We talked, though. Betsy said it was ok to stay here for a few days."

"Jen, can I talk to you? In Meeting 2?" She led Jen away from the table and down the hall. "You're sleeping here?"

Jen nodded.

"Where's Suky? Can't you stay with her?"

"She's still in LA."

"Oh god, Jen. Come to my place at least."

"And stay with you and Mark? I don't think so."

"I'm going to Philadelphia this weekend. Probably. Crash at my place. You'll be doing me a favor. You can keep my worms company."

Jen nodded. "Yes. I say yes." She hugged Amalia. "Thank you, friend. So what's up with Mark?"

"I don't know." She tapped the table where she perched, and scratched off bits of glue from last Friday's model-making session.

"I can see he's crazy about you."

"He is. And I'm crazy about him."

"You got past the kissing, I assume."

"We did." She smiled. "It's all good."

"Thank god. Any more of you moping around the office about Mark and I'd have to jump off a bridge or something."

"I wasn't like that."

"You were so like that! Did you ask him about the geothermal stuff? The geology atlases?" She nodded her head over to the site model on the side table.

"No. I started to. It's—complicated, Jen. I don't want it to be complicated."

"What do you want?"

"I want to be in love."

"And are you?"

"Yes, totally."

"Do you think he knows?"

"Of course! We tell each other all the time."

"He said he's in love with you? Oh boy. Listen. You have to get it out of your head that people are only one way. Let the politics go."

"It's not the politics, Jen. It's the fracking."

"The fucking fracking again. This is killing you, Amalia. Seriously. You almost lost your job over this, and now you're going to throw away Mark over it too."

"I didn't say that."

"I'm getting that vibe from you, though. I know you, Amalia. You might—put your foot in your mouth."

"I have already. A few times."

"Thank god he already fell for you."

"He works for Atlantia."

"Seriously hope you are joking."

"But so what? It's important. I'm so over not speaking my mind."

"So I see." Jen's mouth twisted in a grimace that Amalia could not decipher.

"Do you think it can work?"

"It's up to you to decide to make it work. Then yes, you can. If you meet in the middle."

"I can't. I can't compromise."

"Won't."

"I don't think this is about choosing sides. It's about following a new vision."

"Ok." Jen's face relaxed. "So he works for Atlantia Actuaris. So what? You're bigger than that, and so's he. You could find another track. One that's not about meeting in the middle."

"It's there. I already felt it. We—sat together. Meditated, kind of."

"Go that way, then. Let go of the feeling that you're compromising, and jump into something else."

Amalia got off the table and walked to the site model, squatted down to look at the farmhouse foundation section. "How do I—how do you—be flexible when you're trying to stick to your principles?"

"I already said, stop looking at it as compromising."

"Fine. What would you do?"

"I don't have this issue that you do, Amalia. With the gas industry. I'm ok with it."

"You're ok with the effects of fracking?"

"No, but I trust there will be enough government oversight to protect people in the long run."

"Not likely. Not yet. And it's not just people. It's land, waterways, air quality. All life. Everything."

"There you go again. You're making this too big."

"But it is big. That's the whole point."

"You said you're meditating together? Sounds serious."

"More serious than sex?"

"Way more! My point is, he's not going to throw this all away, and neither are you. Meditate your way through it."

Chapter 42

Mark stood at the window and looked out at the compressors in the rear yard. Amalia scooped up the roses and took them away for disposal. "They're getting depressing," she said.

He crossed his arms and listened to the chatter of her friends, which slid between election probabilities and storm damage elsewhere. He felt parallel to the group; not disconnected—different. Maybe it was a Brooklyn thing. Maybe it was a gay thing. Or an Obama thing. That was it. The Obama thing.

He felt sidelined in the conversation because they thought they knew who he was, based on a few comments about his political leanings. Which were fluid—they might have his vote. Not likely, but possible. He watched a pigeon land on the roof and peck at leaf debris, no doubt cast off from trees not far from here that he could not see. Philadelphia had rooftops with compressors, too, and pigeons and homeless pregnant people. He shuddered.

"Ok?" Amalia came up behind him from the kitchen. She wrapped her arms around him and he turned away from the window and into her hug. "What's on your mind?"

"You," he said, and kissed the top of her head. "And the fact I might have to go to Iceland for work next week."

"No! Take me."

"I could, if you could get the time off work."

"I'm kidding. There's no way."

"No way what, the time off or the trip?"

"Both. I need to be here when the office is up and running. We're way behind on work now, we've lost almost a week."

"And so has everyone else in the city. It's not like a week is going to matter in the long run. Or maybe it does matter, who am I to say. I don't know anymore." He hugged Amalia tighter. "At least come to Philadelphia this weekend."

"I will if—you tell me what you were thinking about. When you were looking out the window."

"What." He pulled her away and looked at her. "I was thinking about sightseeing in Iceland with you."

"You so were not. Such a bad liar! He's such a bad liar," she said to Jen who came in with Paige and coffee for the table.

"You should move here," Paige said.

"I—we—haven't talked about it." He wrapped his arms tighter around Amalia. His stomach leapt and he shifted off the windowsill. "We should let these guys get back to work, don't you think?" He smiled and hoped his discomfort didn't show. "It was great to meet you all."

"It was great to meet you too, Mark." Jen gave him a big hug and whispered in his ear. "Be good to each other."

Jen turned to hug Amalia. "Thank you for looking for me," she said.

"And me," Amalia said. "One day all those text messages will come through. Here." She wrote her new address on a piece of paper. "You can take the bus or the subway might be running again, I don't know. You'll have to check." She looked at Mark. "You're going back to Philadelphia tomorrow?"

"Probably, yes," Mark said. "It would be great if you could come to Philadelphia," he said to Amalia. "After work, if you're working, and after my work, I can pick you up at the train station."

"And Jen. Why don't you meet her here tomorrow and give

her your keys? You know she'll be here, whether or not you guys have work."

"We could work, actually, even without the rest of the office. We could get our model done. I wanted to ask you about that. We need to get some geothermal information specific to the area. Diagrams."

"Why don't you ask one of the installers, then?"

"Sounds easy."

"It is—they probably have it as part of their promotional material."

"I never thought of that." She went to her computer, which had power, and fired up faster than she expected. "There's a lot of messages, here. Oh! Mildred wrote. A few days ago." She scrolled down. "She wrote a whole lot of times."

Dear Amalia,

I write this note to you from British Columbia where I am waiting for the East Coast storm to pass. As my church is closed for a month, I decided to make a trip out West to visit my homeland. My congregants are faring well in my absence, and since I have been temporarily relieved of my duties, there is very little I can do in ministry for them at this time.

But that is not why I am writing to you.

Amalia turned off the screen. "This. It's private."

"But I read it. At least, as much as you would let me read."

"It's for me."

"She's right," he said. "I am in love with you."

Amalia turned around and stood up, pushed the chair away. "Come on." She pulled Mark up. "I'm—I don't want to be here anymore."

"You didn't check if Betsy wrote."

"It doesn't matter. I'll come back tomorrow. I want to work on the site model. If Betsy's here, she's here. If she's not, she's not. Come," she said. She pulled him by the hand away from her desk to the end of the hall by the elevator and drew him into a kiss.

He kissed her in return, pressed her into the wall next to the elevator, his arm wrapped around her waist, hand on her back, and—

The building's fire alarm set off, a mechanical scream that vibrated down the walls and floor and—

"Oh my god, what's going on?" Jen ran toward them. The sound of the siren careened through the space, bounced off walls and desks.

"I pressed the fire signal button," Amalia said.

"How did you do that? You'd have to press hard."

"It must have been my knuckle," Mark said.

"Can you turn it off?" Neal came down the hallway.

Jen grabbed the office phone at reception opposite the elevator. "I'm calling it in."

"I'm sorry!" Mark raised his voice over the alarm.

"This is too much. I need to get out of here until they turn it off," Steve said.

"No! Not the elevator," Paige said. "You're not supposed to use the elevator in case of fire."

"There's no fire! It was us. It's ok," Amalia said.

"It's ok," said Jen. "You just pressed the button. How did you do that? That button doesn't even stick out." The six of them got into the elevator and went down to the main floor, and the whole building rattled with the fire alarm. And on the street were dozens and dozens of other people who left the building, and the building next door.

"One alarm must have gone off in both buildings," Amalia said.

"This is total overkill," Neal said. "Didn't you call it in?"

"I did, and they said someone else had already called." Jen stood back and looked up, then over her shoulder to see the firefighters deploy from the trucks with haste and push into the two buildings' entrances, loaded with gear.

"Clear the area." The police blasted commands through a megaphone.

Mark wrapped his arms around Amalia when she shivered.

"Look." Steve pointed up. A thin stream of smoke emerged from a shaft between the two buildings.

Chapter 43

Amalia stood outside her little office next to the taller one adjacent to it. Looked up at the old façade. She felt protective of it; didn't want it to come to harm. It was historically significant, Betsy had told her. Designed by the same architect who did the Dakota, where John Lennon was shot. It meant something, the connection. She said a little prayer to Durga for the building, and for good measure, threw out a comment to Mary as well. It couldn't hurt to be on the safe side. She followed Jen on the walk uptown, walked hand in hand with Mark.

"It's your last night together," Jen said.

"Don't worry. You can't sleep in the office with the smell of smoke coming out the ducts." She tried Betsy again on her cell.

"He said it was lucky. That the sprinklers went off when they did. Duct fires can spread quickly."

"Betsy's line's still dead," Amalia said. She called directory assistance. "Grohman. Maxwell Grohman." She spelled it for the operator and waited for the connection. "There's no one picking up. It's not even going to voice mail." She hung up. "Sharon. But I have no idea where she lives."

"I know she takes Metro North in. Sharon Andler." Again, directory assistance placed the call.

"Hello, this is Sharon." She picked up on the first ring.

"Sharon, it's Amalia. There was a fire. At work."

"Oh dear god."

"Everyone is ok. But the sprinklers went off upstairs. It was a duct fire."

"Where are you now?"

"Walking north, away from the smoke."

"There's smoke? Outside?"

"It spread. It started in a duct. I guess it was coming out the top. I'm not sure. It's under control now. There's the smell. The smoke didn't get into our office at all, I don't think. But there's water pouring from the ceiling tiles. They said the sprinklers malfunctioned and went off in more zones than they should have."

"Have you tried Betsy and Max?"

"Betsy, yes, I've been leaving messages for her. Max, I tried, but I wasn't able to get through."

"Max is away. He drove south because it's so bad on Long Island. I'll reach out to Betsy, and call me back if you hear from her. We're lucky to get through this week, the phones have been very spotty."

"How are you doing, Sharon? Up there?"

"I have a nice toasty fire, and me and my cat are enjoying it very nicely. Lots of firewood."

"No power?"

"No, no power. I'm charging my cell phone in my car."

"We got you on a land line, though?"

"I know, it's strange. The phone is fine. The internet is fine. I have to conserve the phone battery. And my laptop battery. I can charge at my neighbor's house."

"They have power?"

"Across the street, yes."

"How odd." Amalia covered the phone and said to Jen and Mark, "She has no power, but across the street they do."

"Is she running extension cords?"

"Are you running an extension cord across the street? From their house to your house?"

"No. but I could, I suppose. I have a long one. What about you, Amalia?"

"I have power. I never lost it in my old place, and I moved to my new place, and it has power too. Jen's coming to stay."

"Betsy told me Jen was staying in the office for now."

"Yes. Until the sprinklers."

"Don't worry about a thing. I'll call Betsy. She was planning on going in tomorrow. I can call the tenants. I can't get there, though. There's a tree blocking my driveway, I can't pull out my car, and my train line's not back in service. It's fine. The neighbors are banding together." They signed off with a promise to stay connected, regardless of their ability to reach Max or Betsy.

"This is such a weird time," Amalia said. "Never realized how dependent we are on all of these systems until now."

"We need a new system," Jen said.

"An upgrade," Mark said.

"No, something—different."

Mark shook his head. "We're not getting to different anytime soon. Upgrades will get us there more smoothly."

"I don't know," Amalia said. "There might be room for both." They approached 81st Street and Amalia took out her set of keys. "I'm glad I kept these," she said. "We'll get the extra bedding and then go up to the new place." She opened the front door and let them in. "Hello, old apartment building," she said. They went up the elevator and to Great Aunt Joan's apartment. A shiny new lockset was installed in the door. "Uh-oh." She tried the lock but it had been changed.

"Now what?"

"We can always sleep in the lobby downstairs here if we need to."

"Very funny."

"No really, what now? We don't have extra bedding for Jen."

"Sleep in my bed," Amalia said.

"Very kind of you, but I don't think I'm into that."

"No," Amalia said, and pushed the down button on the elevator. "You sleep there and I'll go back to Mark's hotel. If it's ok with you," she said to Mark.

"You're the one who's been bed-hopping for two weeks."

"One more night won't kill me."

"Where is it?"

"28th."

"But there's no power down there."

"The hotel has power. No phone or internet, but power."

Jen shook her head. "It's so random." They stepped into the elevator and went down. "If you're ok with it, yes."

"So—do we go uptown? Or downtown? I'm getting confused. I don't need anything from home." She gave Jen the keys. "You have the address. The apartment door sticks a little; you have to pull it toward you when you turn the key. And the intercom doesn't let you hear who it is. Can you spray some water into the worm bin on Saturday?"

"You're not coming back tomorrow? Before you go to Philadelphia? Don't you want a change of clothes?"

"I guess." She looked at Mark. "What are we going to be doing this weekend?"

"I thought we might hike. If you like that kind of thing."

"I would love to go hiking. I'll need different shoes. And my Gore-Tex."

"I could bring them," Jen said. "Down to the office. Tomorrow morning."

Amalia pulled out her notebook from her backpack and ripped out a piece of paper. "There's a note for you at your apartment, by the way," she said. "On this notepaper." She wrote a short list for Jen and gave it to her. "It's all unpacked in the closet. Meet me at nine tomorrow morning? At the coffee shop downstairs, though. We can go up to the office to look but I don't want to wait there."

They said goodbye to Jen and caught the bus downtown to Chelsea. Amalia leaned her head on Mark's shoulder most of the way down, eyes open; she felt dizzy with the disjunctions of the day. They shifted off the bus and shuffled down the street to his hotel. “It feels like my apartment, not a hotel.” he said. “Like we each have our own apartment here.”

“It’s not the best week to see the city in an ideal light.”

“I don’t know about that. It is kind of ideal. It’s stripped down. Bare. A lot of it is broken down, doesn’t work. But the people are—emerging. There is a spirit of connectedness here. I never knew.”

Chapter 44

Mark's hotel room was easy to pick up, to pack up; it hadn't been home for long. "This needs to be cleaned." He picked up the open Swiss Army knife and took it to the bathroom.

"Sorry. I got distracted." Amalia smiled and looked into the room. "When did you make the bed?"

"I always make the bed."

"But we—wait. Did we make the bed at my place? We sent Jen there."

"I made the bed."

"You made my bed?"

"I did. I always do." He washed the knife in the bathroom, tucked it back into his work bag. He sat at the computer and fired up the NJ Transit website. "Lo and behold! We have a train."

She came over. "Wow, yes. *Northeast Corridor running on alternate schedule as of November 2.*"

"I guess we're taking the train."

"And me with you? I mean—I could go with you in the morning." Amalia pulled out her phone and notebook. "Oh, messages have all arrived. From you. From Tuesday. From Jen from Tuesday and Wednesday. All at once." She put the phone down and lay back on the bed, kicked off her shoes to the side, lay back with the notebook.

Mark looked over his shoulder; she was distracted. Her focus warmed him; smart and sexy all in one. Lucky guy. He pulled up the last emails. Something else from George. The specifier didn't get the concrete mix right on the casing. Next email. Anwen, again, this time with a picture of Matilda the cat. He deleted it. Thought better of it, dug it back out of the trash, left it in his inbox. He ought to write her, although he had no idea what to say. Nothing from his mystery man.

The words in the man's threat held no power over Mark. He'd found something deeper to focus on, that made him happier, and the happiness rose to block out the fears he'd ever had about everything else.

Chapter 45

Friday, November 2

Amalia packed up her library novel into her backpack, Mark zipped his laptop into his work bag and she followed him down onto the platform. Three train rides—NJ Transit, SEPTA and the light rail to Doylestown, Pennsylvania—and her head spun.

They walked out to the Park and Ride where Mark steered her to his car, a small, tidy European car with rounded edges.

"How do you fit?"

"Barely. Not my choice of car."

"Your parents?"

"No. I bought it with Helene."

He drove them into Quakertown via strip malls and he dropped her off at his house, showed her where to find the tea, the bathroom. "Here's the key. Go for a walk or something. I'll be back before six," he said. "Go into town if you want something to eat. I'm sorry there's not more here now." He kissed her goodbye, and left her at the door, her hiking boots kicked off, jacket still on. She closed the door and stood in the living room to watch him drive away.

She turned and faced the living room, wide and dark in the early afternoon. The house was cold. Mark had turned down the heat before he left. He must not have been back since before his trip to Wales.

She found the kitchen, a dark-paneled room with a blast of daylight that shone in the sliding glass patio doors. A pile of unopened mail sat on the counter, and a round wooden table was positioned beneath a basket light. There seemed to be wall-to-wall carpeting through the whole house except here, where it turned to rusty colored linoleum.

He must have inherited his parents' decorating. No. He said he grew up in New Hampshire and moved here for work. She sat at the table and stared out the back windows to the deck and grass beyond, into the neighbor's yard. She looked at the stack of paper on the table, felt pulled to look at it, and then censored herself.

She pulled off the top paper: a utility bill from September. Beneath that, a stack of photos and receipts. A coupon for a local car wash. She looked at the fine print; it had expired October 31st. She put the stack of photos and receipts back. I can't do this. One photo stuck out the edge of the stack and she slid it out.

It was a small square, a color photo of a woman. A tall, long-haired woman, dark hair, a flowered, sleeveless dress. She looked strong, at least in the picture. Amalia couldn't tell. She flipped it over; it was marked in blue ballpoint pen.

me, 1984, pregnant with Mark

She looked at the photo again. The woman had her hand on her belly. Amalia slipped the photo back into the stack of receipts and put the coupon and bill back on top. There were other photos. But not now, she couldn't—cross it.

She peeked into the main floor bathroom, a long and mirror-tiled powder room. She could go upstairs later. For now, she needed to get out. She shoved her feet back into her hiking boots and tied them, zipped up her rain jacket, brought only her wallet and cell phone, and left her backpack with the bag of clothes she'd picked up from Jen at the coffee shop downstairs from work. She locked the door as he'd shown her before. Pocketed his keys and held them in her hand inside her jacket, and warmed the metal against her fingers.

The walk was treacherous where the sidewalk was nonexistent and she had to traipse along the edge of the highway and in the grassy front yards of businesses along the way into town. She passed from Mark's part of town and into the older homes, old stores. Pretty. She found the deli where he'd said it was.

She looked at the menu board, ordered. She stood back and took in the store. It looked the same as in Manhattan; the candy bars at the counter were the same, the water for sale in the fridge was the same. So why did she feel so ill at ease? The cook passed her food across the deli display case. She took it to the checkout to pay, and stood in line behind two lip-locked teens. "You're next," she said, and tapped one of them on the shoulder. She took her food in a shopping bag, walked past similar duplex houses of a similar age, 1970s-style. The hurricane had taken a toll on some of the roof shingles and cladding, and the trees were beat up. Back to the house. She glanced at the downed branches, wondered why he didn't live at the prettier end of town, the historic end.

Amalia ate her lunch in silence at the kitchen table, and afterwards, she went upstairs to look around. She lay down on his bed, she thought it was his; it was the tidier of the two rooms. The bed was covered in an old patchwork quilt she felt was very much his. She rolled over and traced the edges of the fabric patches with her finger. One of the patterns looked familiar. She sat up and grasped the quilt, pulled it off the bed and ran downstairs to the kitchen.

Her heart pounded and she pulled the old photo from the stack on the kitchen table. There, in the photo, was the same fabric she held in her hand, that of the floral patterned dress worn by his mom. She sat there with the quilt in her lap, the photo in her hand, and she stared out the back window, blank of thoughts, until her cell phone rang in her pocket some time later. She saw Betsy's name on the display. "Betsy?"

"Amalia. You saw the office. Can you get here in the next hour?"

"I'm sorry. I can't. I'm not able to get there."

"Amalia—are you ok? I mean, do you have power, you're all right?"

"I'm fine, Betsy. I'll be there Monday."

They hung up, and Amalia looked down. She still held the photo of Mark's mother in the floral dress. "I'm lost," she said to the walls. She went to her backpack and took out the plastic bag of weekend clothes Jen had put together for her and went upstairs with them, laid them on top of the dresser in Mark's bedroom.

She sat on the edge of the bed and felt the rough wool blanket that had lain beneath the quilt. There was nothing up on the walls, except wood paneling. An alarm clock sat next to the bed on the side table. She stood up and went to the closet.

What was she expecting, a cascade of—she wasn't sure what—sports equipment, skeletons? The door felt heavy in her hand and she looked in, pulled a long cotton string to turn on the closet ceiling light.

He had pressed shirts lined up on hangers, baskets of folded clothes on the side. A few suits, a ski jacket. Above, folded blue jeans. A pair of ski boots on the closet floor. She turned off the light and pushed the door closed. She stood at the bedroom window and looked out on the backyard. Fingered the photo in her hand, and went back downstairs.

She left the photo on the edge of the counter next to the stack of bills, no longer self-conscious. Her connection to the quilt left her with a sense of urgency to dig deeper into the bedrock of the house.

She found the basement door and crept downstairs. A bare light bulb hung from a corner section of the basement ceiling, and she pulled its cord. The space was illuminated by the incandescent glow and her eyes rested on a large, white deep freezer. She went to it, and lifted the heavy lid. A blast of cold air met her in the face. She looked in. Meats, categorized by animal and body part, were bagged in clear plastic, dated and stacked like they were ready for grocery store checkout. Did he hunt? If he did, he hadn't mentioned it.

If he hunted, he must have guns in the house. She closed the freezer and looked around the basement. Stacks of boxes lined one wall, and she recognized Mark's mother's handwriting on the ends of some of them. On the other side of the basement, fishing gear lined up and hooked into a peg board on the wall, hip waders fallen to the side, below a bright orange jacket on the wall. She looked at the label inside the jacket: xl. Mark's? Timmy's? So he fished, and maybe hunted.

She continued through the basement and found no sign of firearms, so she turned off the light and went upstairs. She sat on the couch in the living room. After a few minutes she got a chill and went to the kitchen for his patchwork quilt. She wrapped it around her, tied her lunch remains up in the plastic bag they'd come in, and put the photo of his mom back into the stack of receipts on the kitchen table.

Amalia went back to the couch and looked out the window. How close was it to six, when he said he'd be home? She pulled her cell phone from her jacket pocket and sat back down, stretched out her legs. Across from her was a floor to ceiling bookcase around the fireplace, dark wood, as wide as the room up to the door to the kitchen. From across the room she could see the shapes of the books where they rose and fell like the skyline of a city, but what they told her, she couldn't yet see. She stood up and scanned the rows.

They appeared to be books of his parents' travels and studies. She pulled some out at random. Mythology. Put them back, pulled out more. Landed on an orange 3-ring binder with a handwritten label: *Abenaki Quilts.*

She took it off the shelf and when she settled back on the couch with it, loose papers fell out.

Quilts. Patches; photocopies of quilts. Annotations in colored pencil, and field notes, interviews. Some photographs. She flipped through the binder. It was categorized: natural images; historic images; settlement images.

There was more. Children's images, bits of poetry. It was a mess; no, a jumble. It made sense to the person who'd assembled it. The handwriting matched that on the boxes in the basement, and on the back of the photo.

At the back, letters of inquiry to publishing houses. She looked through them. Most were dated 2008, some earlier. It was an unfinished book project.

She put the book back. It was too much. "Mark. Come home." She looked up at the sky, almost dusk. He must have left work. She went upstairs and spread his quilt back over the wool blanket on the bed the way she'd found it.

She pulled her toothbrush from the stack of clothes Jen had packed for her and found the upstairs bathroom, as mirror-paneled as the powder room below. She looked around while she brushed her teeth, and opened the medicine cabinet. But this yielded nothing of interest. He must have brought everything with him.

She was hungry. It was almost six, and they had made no plans for dinner. Her lunch had worn off. She went downstairs, turned the lights off behind her.

The kitchen felt empty and cold. The sunlight had passed over the glass patio doors some time ago, which left the room to face the evening exposed without curtains. She opened the cupboards, all of them, and stood back.

They were packed with dry goods, and one cabinet was filled with mismatched glass jars, labeled in Mark's mother's handwriting. She pulled a jar out and opened it. The lid came off with years of encrusted allspice ground into the threaded cap. She sniffed it and it was still good. She took another, and another, and lined them up on the counter in front of her until she had every old jam jar of spices and herbs open in front of her, their scents gentle and faded with age.

She found a bottle of cooking oil in a cupboard near the stove, and a large frying pan down the side. But what to cook? She opened the freezer compartment of the fridge and rooted around until she found something recognizable, this time some white fish, lettered in Mark's handwriting, August 2012. She found a plate in another cupboard and peeled the plastic wrap off the fish, laid it across the plate, and defrosted it in the microwave.

The spices she chose were random, selected for their potency in the moment rather than any logic to seasoning. By the time he got home, the house smelled of cardamom and her eyes burned with chilies, the fish was cooked and she'd made rice tossed with the baby green peas she found in the freezer, scented with cumin. She stood at the back door, zoned out on the outlines of trees in the backyard.

The door in the front slammed shut. "I'm back," Mark called out from the front hall.

"I knew you left a while ago, I felt it." she said. "But you still managed to surprise me." Her heart raced in spite of expectation.

"What smells so great?" he asked.

"I made something. I hope you don't mind." She took him by the hand and led him into the kitchen.

He stopped in the doorway. "What did you do?"

"What do you mean?"

"It's different in here. Something has changed." He put his bag down and went to the table and sat. He looked around the space. "You've been busy. The house feels different."

"Different how?" she asked. "I didn't mean to stir anything up."

"You've attended to the corners. I can feel it."

Chapter 46

"I can't tell what's going on unless you tell me." He pulled into the two story brick parking garage on Race Street at nine in the evening and locked the wheel with a large red club. Better to be safe than sorry. He didn't want her to think he was paranoid, but he wasn't going to hide it.

They walked out and he steered her into Orianna Street. It glowed in evening lamplight with shadows cast across the cobblestone path. Wanted to show her the passage. "Every city has its time," he said.

"Time in history?"

"Time of day. The time it springs to life."

"I can't imagine that kind of patchwork is consistent across a whole city," she said. "Places change block by block." Amalia hurried to keep up with him. "Listen, Mark." She held his arm and he slowed down. In the distance, horseshoe beats on pavement drew closer, steady and slow. They stood in the long walkway, the sound framed by old brick walls and new wooden garage doors. When the horse passed, he heard the hiss of rubber wheels peel off the pavement. Laughter floated up from the carriage. Tourists.

"Thank you," he said, and pulled her toward him. He felt her resist, a little. "Ok?" He let go. She stepped back into the lamplight, and leaned on the wooden doors behind her.

"What do you think of the right to bear arms?" Her eyes were dark.

"Ah—," he crossed his arms. "I thought this would be a romantic passageway to walk through."

"It's lovely. It's—also provocative."

"The right to bear arms." He'd better take this one slowly. "You've chosen the right place to ask the question," he said. "We're a stone's throw from the signing of both the Declaration of Independence and the Constitution."

"I'm not concerned about the past. Only where we are now."

"It's a theoretical question, but—"

"Do you have a gun in the house, Mark?" He heard her voice tremble with the question.

"No. Why?" The passageway was silent around them.

"Because." She stopped.

"It's the bear thing isn't it," he said. It'd be over in a moment. Just needed to humor her.

"What bear thing?"

"Last week when I was on site and someone might have shot a bear. That's what's got you spooked."

"I'm not spooked."

"Something's got under your skin. Can we walk?" He started to take a step away and reached his hand out to her, but she stayed put, framed by the wooden doors and lit from the side by the electric lights.

"I looked around your house."

"And?" His heart started to pound, without warning. "There's nothing there. I've bared it all. I can't hide anything from you." He stood, one arm extended to her.

"The freezer. In the basement."

"Is full of frozen meat from New Hampshire."

"And someone used a gun to bring it down."

"Probably, yes, unless they decided to use their bow and arrow."

"Come on, don't joke."

"I'm not."

"So you don't hunt?"

"No, regrettably." Is that all this was?

"Regrettably because—why?" Her hands shifted to her hips.

Mark! Don't walk into this one. "If you're going to eat meat, it's good to know how it is—procured."

"Procured? I can't believe you said that."

"Amalia, I'm not up for a fight now. Can we walk?" He pulled his jacket around himself.

"It's not that I want to fight," she said, "I want to get clear. I want to know where you stand."

"I'm feeling fight," he said. No! Don't engage like that.

"So about the bear," she said. "What happened then, back on the frack site?" She took a step toward him and the light fell behind her, which cast a dark shadow on her face.

"I had a meeting. After the trip to Wales, on one of the sites. They wanted to go over the safety plan before the hurricane."

"I remember."

"I—I wasn't feeling so well. I went for a walk around the edge, past the work site."

"They let you walk around?"

"Of course."

"Ok."

"I stopped when I heard something, and it was a family of deer in the woods. I watched them, and then shots were fired. I backed up. If someone was there they must have seen me. But the bullets went past me, Amalia, I felt them. Two of them. Two shots. They said later there had been a bear on site, that maybe someone had tried to shoot it."

"Were they aiming at you?"

He looked at her dead on in the dark light of the alley. "I never thought of that."

She frowned, and began to walk down the passageway toward the next street.

"Amalia. I thought they were spinning me out of the company."

"Why."

"They hustled me back to the Pennsylvania site with no reason—there was no need for me to be there. Felt like busywork—like they were looking for a reason to keep me out of the office."

"Why wouldn't they fire you? Or at least, talk to you?"

"I don't know. I'm valuable to them. They say I have a way of—engaging—of talking about—of making the earth's song make sense to people."

"Mark." She looked at him and turned him by his jacket sleeve to her. "You're not hearing the earth's song. You're killing it." Amalia paused for a breath. "What do you want, Mark?"

"I want to do this with you," he said. "To figure out how to—get powered in a healthy way, and how to stay powered, for many, many generations." He stopped in the alley. "Why, what do you want?"

"I—I want to know we trust each other enough to do what it is you say you want. Without sabotaging each other in the process. Without undercutting. Just—moving it forward. It's not enough to screw around and hope it all works out for the best."

He shook his head. "You don't get it, do you. You're so stuck in your 'I'm right' that you don't see any of it. You don't see that what we're doing is powering the country. Empowering people." He pulled away from her and walked up the block. "I can't do this, Amalia. I'm not doing this anymore." His back to her, he walked fast and turned left at the tall, stony façade of the United States Mint.

Chapter 47

After moments of shock in which she stood frozen, Amalia turned up the street to face the building that loomed ahead. Where was Mark? She saw him a block ahead and she dashed up the street, swerved into the center line of the road to avoid a knot of pedestrians. She caught up to Mark and grabbed his sleeve, and ran full force into him when he stopped and turned to face her. "I'm sorry."

"Enough of sorry." He flicked her arms off him in one motion, continued to walk, and rubbed his arm where she'd smacked into him.

"I'll listen," she said.

"I don't have anything to say," he said. He walked fast, and she had to trot to keep up next to him.

"Ok. Don't say anything. Stay. Stop." She grabbed the back of his jacket.

"Let go of me."

"Let. Him. Go," a deep voice said. A broad-shouldered man in a flannel jacket stood on the sidewalk next to her, so close she could feel his hot breath.

She was afraid to look up, the man on one side of her and Mark on the other. Hemmed in. Energy squeezed. Personal space obliterated. She looked up at the man, his pale eyes so light she could almost see through them, his dark pupils that made him appear like a cat, predatory.

"Hey man, it's ok. Back off," Mark said.

"If she's bugging you, you don't need to take it, buddy," the man said. His voice and size bore down on Amalia. Holy shit. This was screwed up.

"We're fine. Leave us alone," she said, without a glance up. She slipped her hand into Mark's and squeezed.

Mark pulled her away from the man. "Keep walking. He's crazy. Don't turn around."

"Been there, man," the fellow said. "Don't stand for it." His voice carried down the street.

She walked with Mark's hand gripped tight and quickened her step.

"Don't run," Mark said.

"Ok."

They walked at an even pace, didn't talk, didn't turn. Held hands, tight, and passed by two more intersections.

"Is he gone?"

Mark looked around. "He's a block behind us."

"Should we call someone?"

"No. Why?"

"He's—very—threatening."

"He's fine."

"He's threatening to me. I didn't do anything and he bore down on me."

"You—" He stopped and let go.

She grabbed his hand back. "Keep walking," she said, and turned to look behind them. "Your guardian angel is following us." They turned and lost themselves in a group of tourists gathered around the Independence Visitors' Center, closed, but lit for photos.

"He's gone." Mark let go of her hand. "Are you ok?"

"Don't ever leave me alone like that again. What if he'd come after me in the alley?"

"But he didn't," said Mark.

"He might have," she said. Her voice shook. She tried to take a breath in.

"Hey." He put his hand behind her neck and stroked it, a little too hard.

Her body began to shake, and she hoped he couldn't tell. She needed to breathe. Under his hand, her neck tightened. She wanted to breathe. She shook harder all over and she couldn't help it, her muscles gave away her outer calm. She pulled away from his hand and bent forward, gasped for a breath, and she hid her face in her hands and hoped he would go away. The harder she tried, the harder it was to draw oxygen from the air between her fingers.

"Is she ok?" A woman standing nearby approached. "Do you need a doctor?"

"She's fine. Lover's quarrel," he said. "We're fine." He bobbed down and put a hand on her back.

"I want to go home," she said. She looked up and knew she must look frightful, tear-stained, but she didn't care. He had one hand on her back and another on her knee. She straightened up and wiped tears from her cheeks. Breath came in.

"Do you want me to go and get the car?"

"No, don't leave me." He put his arm around her shoulders and she shook it off. "You're too heavy on me," she said. She reached for his hand and held it for the silent walk back to the car. Voices floated up from the side street into the passageway. She closed her eyes and held out hope they would find a way to bridge the gap between them.

Chapter 48

Mark drove them back to the house in Quakertown, not much before midnight. At home, he parked, went in first, and held the door open for her. He flipped on every light in the house, jacked up the heat and lit a fire in the fireplace. She went upstairs for the quilt and blanket from his bed, and they curled up against the couch with the living room curtains drawn, the fire bright, and all the lights on around them.

After she'd fallen asleep, Mark said a short prayer to the statue of Mary that stood atop the mantle shelf over the fire. He fell asleep next to her there, on the floor, on the rug, in front of the fire, under the quilt.

Chapter 49

Saturday, November 3

Amalia woke first and saw the flames had burned down to coals. Light and heat blasted around them and she slipped out from the warm nest to the kitchen, pulled the glass doors apart and stepped barefoot onto the back deck. A light Pennsylvania mist rose off the lawn and morning sun shone through.

It was chilly, early, but the air refreshed her skin after the warmth of the house. She felt turned inside out. New. Needed to let go of angry. She gave the old haunting to the morning, sent it to the trees.

She turned when she heard the door slide open behind her, looked through the veil of her hair, loose around her shoulders. She must have been out there for a while, because Mark had already been up and made coffee, which he brought outside, hot.

"Here," he said. She rested the cup on the deck railing and kissed him. "I'll be right back." He returned a moment later with the quilt. "Who were you talking to before I came out?"

"I wasn't."

"I saw you from the kitchen."

"I was—talking to myself."

"I thought maybe my mother," he said.

She nodded, because it was easier. And then, she said, "Nadel. But I wasn't saying—I was thinking."

"I saw your lips moving."

"And you're a lip reader now?" She took a sip of coffee. Didn't want to get into a scrap with him so early. She put the coffee down and took the quilt from the deck railing and lifted it between two spread arms, flipped it around like a cape, and whipped it around her shoulders. "We all have demons," she said.

"Come here, Dracula," he said, and dug his way into the quilt with her.

She squealed when he tickled her armpits under the quilt and a little flock of birds at the bottom of the garden took off at the sound, which made her laugh more.

She let him burrow his head into her chest beneath the quilt and held him there against her clothes, the same she'd worn the night before and had never taken off. His breath was warm through the fabric of her t-shirt and felt heavy there.

"I need air," he said, and popped his head out of the quilt. He turned inside it so he was in front of her and she wrapped them both in it from behind. Mark stuck a hand out for his coffee and sipped it while she held him in the quilt. "It's cold out here," he said. "We're going to need to layer for the trail today."

"I have my layers. Jen found everything in my apartment."

"And we'll need to take lots of food. Water."

"I saw some stuff in the basement. Outdoors stuff. Fishing?"

"My dad's. We could take it. You want to fish the Delaware Gap?"

"Could, I guess. It's been a long time. I've forgotten how."

"Actually, me too." He peeled out of the quilt and tiptoed barefoot over the dew-soaked deck to the grass below and out to the edge of the yard by the fence. He pulled up a large aluminum bucket of water from the ground and dumped it out. He picked up a lid from the other side of the yard. "Hurricane took this across the yard."

"What's that for?"

"It's an ash bucket," he said. "We used to use it to scoop out the ash from the fireplace in New Hampshire. I emptied it out a while ago and left it here, but I'll do it before we go today."

"What do you do with it—the ash?"

"I put it on the compost," he said.

"Is it good for the compost?"

"I have no idea, but that's what I do."

"My worms would die," she said.

"Maybe, maybe not," he said. "Maybe your worms will have to meet my compost heap."

"Oh, really? Maybe your ash bucket would like to come to New York and become my new compost bucket," she said.

They packed and layered within a half hour for the hike. She sat in the passenger seat surrounded by water bottles and maps, and checked their bearings on her cell phone. The drive up to the Delaware Water Gap was cheerful, and he'd brought some music from the house that she rotated through while he drove. She took off her hiking boots and rested her stocking feet on the dashboard, off to one side, toes on the glass.

She sat back and ran her fingers through her hair, then reached for her backpack behind his seat. She took out a hair-elastic and bundled her hair into it in a pile on top of her head, put on some lip gloss, blank of thought.

He merged onto I-80 East. "This goes across the country, you know. California to New Jersey."

They left the car locked with a note that detailed their whereabouts and return time. "I always do," Mark said. He took her deep into the forest along the Appalachian Trail from the parking lot. There were branches down from the hurricane, but the trail they found was passable, and they looked for walking sticks.

"What do you think this one is?" She held up a stick.

Mark fingered the bark. "Copper birch."

"There's another one." She gave him the taller of the two sticks and they used them to propel along the muddy trail.

"This is incredible," Amalia said. "Like you can feel the forest breathe."

"I can think in here," Mark said. "Or not think. I'm more myself here. When I'm in a forest, on the Appalachian Trail, wherever, I feel like my body is part of it."

"I feel it in my body. Mark, that's it. I feel all of it in my body."

"I don't understand. What?"

"When I hear what you are doing in your work, or what companies like yours are doing—I feel it in my body, I internalize it."

"No one's trying to hurt you."

"I'm telling you how I feel, down to my mitochondria. In my bone marrow. In my soul." She looked at him. "Surely you get that." She extended a hand and pulled him up the hill.

They walked through the woods, double-wide on the trail, and when they met another hiker on the path their hands stayed clasped as they stood to the side. When the hiker had passed, they embraced in slow motion, and listened to murmurs of the forest life around them.

"I'll take your pack?" He put it on his shoulder and took a bottle of water from his pack, tucked his stick under his arm while he took a small sip.

She stretched, calves, shins, quads; twisted side to side. "I guess I don't get much exercise these days," she said.

"You walk a lot."

"I do, but I don't stretch much anymore. I used to do yoga religiously."

"Religious yoga," he said.

"It's a thing." she said. "But that's not what I meant." She rolled her neck, stretched her arms in front and behind. "Can I have some?" She took a long swig from his water bottle and let out a satisfied "aaah" when she pulled the bottle from her lips, and opened her eyes wide to the filtered light around them. "I had a roommate in architecture school in Vancouver who was studying to be a yoga teacher. I learned it all from her." She took the backpacks and sticks and held the two poles while he stretched out his shoulders and back. "You don't feel it in your legs?"

"No, not so much. Just here." He stretched the middle of his upper back. It's hard to get to, you know? It's like it's not one muscle group."

She rubbed him between the shoulder blades and the backpacks and sticks she'd been holding slipped forward and fell to the ground. "Oops."

"No, don't stop. Leave them. That gets it. Hits the spot."

She let the packs lie there on the ground, and put one hand on his right shoulder and used her other forearm and elbow to dig deeper between his shoulder blades.

"Holy cow, that's deep," he said, and leaned over.

She rubbed the area over with her palm and the fabric of his jacket numbed her skin.

"Do that again. The strong thing."

"That was my elbow."

"Do that." He leaned into his cupped hand, propped up on his knee. She went in circles on his back, and he let out grunts and whimpers when the muscles moved beneath her elbow." I feel it on the front, all the way through." He took a deep breath.

She picked up the two backpacks and assessed the mud. "It hasn't rained, this is old mud, kind of dry."

"The trail took a hit," he said, "but it's not as bad as it could have been. Up north, though, I wonder."

"The hurricane went more out to sea, didn't it?"

"Last year, the White Mountains got hammered by Hurricane Irene."

"Is that where you live? I mean, lived?"

"It's where we hike, me and Timmy." He stretched out his back and bent forward to touch his knees.

"Can you touch your toes?"

"No way," he said. "But I can reach farther since you did the elbow thing." She put a hand on his back when he stood up.

"Are you ok?"

"Something's different." He pounded his chest with his fist and coughed.

"I feel like I need to burp—but I don't. I can't get it out." They walked deeper in, and stopped for lunch on a log to the side of the trail, then turned around. The crowds were sparse, not crowds at all, but a few intrepid souls out to do their section of the Appalachian Trail.

"Have you done the whole thing? The whole trail."

"I have not," he said. "I would love to."

"I wish I could give you that," she said.

"What, the time to do the whole Appalachian Trail? You'd have to come with me."

"You think we could do it? Months on the trail?"

"If we didn't kill each other," he said.

She shook her head. "I'm done fighting with you. That doesn't mean I agree with you. Far from it." She stopped and stretched her calves against a rock on the downhill. "You know when we sat together? In my apartment?"

"With the candles."

"Yes. More of that. I want more of that."

"I want more of this," he said, "Less apartment. More woods."

"Both. I agree. But less fighting."

"I don't think we can meet in the middle, though. That doesn't work either," he said.

She began to walk again, plunged her stick into the mud, and pushed off rocks when she came to them. "It's because we're missing out on something else. It's not either-or. On the energy front. It's not renewable or non-renewable, like you said. it's not fracking or not-fracking. Everybody's missing out on the bigger picture."

"Which is—"

"We need to create a manageable, long-term power grid, to supply the way people live. Without damage to the environment."

"You sound like me talking."

"I never said otherwise. I never didn't want that. Double negatives." She shook her head. "You know what I mean."

"You're saying we wanted the same thing all along?"

"Your company has a different way of—procuring, to use your word—than I think is sustainable, and different margins of tolerability of the environmental impacts."

"You're glossing. What are you trying to say?"

She walked faster on the downhill, and her stick flew behind her with every step. She began to hop from rock to rock, down the trail. "We agree on this," she said. "Energy must be supplied."

"Yes." He kept pace beside her, his stick below his arm.

"How much, to whom, where it's delivered, when—we more or less agree on that. Maybe not on the how much. That's debatable. But everyone should have equal access. Maybe not at every time of day equally, but every person should have the access."

"Yes."

"Ok, so we start there. Without prejudging the what of it—the materiality of it—we agree on the baseline of delivery."

"I think so."

"And that suggests a grid."

"Which we have."

"Which a lot of people think they need to opt out of."

"Not a lot of people."

"Ok, some people. Some people live off the grid, and I bet more would if they could, easily."

"And is that a good thing, to you?"

"No, it's inefficient. It's good to have a backup, but with so many people on the planet—All for one, and one for all."

"I never knew what that phrase meant," he said.

"Isn't it from *The Three Musketeers?* One for all, all for one. All for one, one for all. It means, we're in this together."

"Ok. Sounds like 'Mitakuye Oyasin.'"

"Which is what?"

"It means 'All My Relations.'"

"In Abenaki?"

"No, in Lakota. It's kind of been—appropriated."

"What if—imagine—if the grid was universal. A universal web of energy delivery that transcended country boundaries."

"Never going to happen."

"No. Don't say that. Imagine it."

"I can't see it."

"Maybe not now. And don't think of the how of it. Imagine that it is that way."

"I sometimes imagine making tea. When I'm writing a speech. I did that in Wales. And I've been thinking about it for Iceland, for the geothermal project we are getting going."

"Making tea."

"I imagine a regular person turning on their stove, whatever kind of stove it is, with whatever kind of fuel source they have, and I imagine their kettle, their actual kettle, what it's made of, and the water, and how they got the water in the first place, and then they make tea." He was out of breath. "Can we slow down?"

"No, I'm good," she said, and flew across the mud.

"Ok." He picked up his pace again. "The tea. You have to heat the water, you enjoy the tea. It's universal."

"So we start with that. Enjoyment. It's enjoyment of something—universal enjoyment of something that is dependent upon energy supply."

He stopped for a drink of water. "About this power thing," he said in between gulps of water, "you can't be saying, everyone gets the same power supply, evenly, across the world. That doesn't take into account regional variations in culture, demand, topography, you name it."

"I'm not. I'm saying—everyone makes tea. How do they make it? Differently. But everybody does it."

"And they need to continue to do it."

"And so do their children, and their children, and their children."

"I can't see how the tea metaphor gets us anywhere," he said.

"It's your metaphor, not mine. You said you use it when you think up speeches."

"I do. But it's more to get people to connect with an appreciation of their energy supply."

"So that's what I'm saying, too." She took the new bottle of water from him and took a swig. "Appreciate it."

"Are you saying people here don't appreciate their energy supply?"

"They take it for granted. Definitely. The way we take clean water for granted here. You know, Betsy—my boss—said they had some chemical in their drinking water in her town last year. Tetrachloroethylene."

"Dry cleaning fluid. New Jersey? That stuff's an endocrine disruptor," he said.

"Like the methylene chloride in the frack fluid—remember? I talked about that at Mildred's thing."

They hiked out, another hour or so, to the parking lot. The sun had gone down but the sky remained bright. Three hikers passed overhead on the ridge over the parking lot, and trudged in sync, silhouetted against the forest behind them.

"They look like part of the trail," she said.

"That's what we'd look like, if we did the whole thing."

"You think they were up there during the hurricane?"

"I doubt it. In the Whites during Irene they pulled everyone off the mountains."

"You included?"

"Me included."

The drive back was quiet, no radio or CDs. She pointed out landmarks and he commented on the ones he'd visited, and told her a history of Interstate 80.

Once back in Quakertown, they drove up the street and pulled into the parking pad in front of his house. Three of the neighbors stood outside on the lawn and Mark's front door was open.

"Mark." She sat forward and grabbed the dashboard in front of her and the car lurched to a stop in the driveway.

He opened the car door, left it open behind him and ran from the car to the house.

Amalia followed, and heard the neighbors before she heard Mark.

"It was contained," the man said. "They broke down the front door."

"We called 911 when we saw the flames through the window," another said. "We didn't know how to reach you."

Amalia walked into the living room. The book wall and rug were charred, the remains of the family quilt not recognizable. The flames had come as far as the couch and burned the side of it. Streaks of dark brown smoke and soot streamed up the walls to the second floor and into the hallway outside the kitchen. The smell was the worst; the dank, wet soot gave her an immediate headache, and she had to press her face into her sleeve to filter it.

Mark stood in the middle of it and his muddy hiking boots picked up ash and fiber. She could see his jaw tense and unlock, tense and unlock, and he said nothing, turned in a circle, over and over and over again.

"It's my fault," he said.

"They said it started in the fireplace," the man said. "A hot coal exploded out onto the rug, or something. But no one saw it in time. Chief said it burned for ages."

"I didn't put out the fire before we left. I didn't make the bed."

Amalia looked into the kitchen and saw the ash bucket still by the inside of the back doors. She picked it up and brought it into the living room.

"We're not going to need that now."

"The Chief said to give a call if you show up," the woman said. "They left a few hours ago."

"Thanks." Mark crossed his arms and turned his back to the window.

"We've been coming back every so often to see if you're back."

"We left all the doors and windows open to try to air it out," the man said.

"Thank you everyone."

They checked into the hotel off the highway for the night. "Don't sit," she said. "You're too muddy, too ashen." She pulled him into the bathroom and they undressed. She turned on the hot water in the shower and opened the paper-wrapped sliver of soap on the bathroom counter. She held the shower curtain open for him, but he didn't move, so she put her arm on his arm. "Come here," she said, and she wrapped her naked body around his, and they leaned on the counter while the room filled with steam around them.

The shaking stopped and he tried to find her mouth with his but she pushed him off and led him into the shower where she soaped his back in circles, until he bent forward and leaned his hands on his knees and cried. She turned off the water and led him out, and held the curtain for him.

She wrapped him in white hotel towels but he was too tall for her to dry all over, so she pushed his shoulders down to indicate he should sit on the edge of the toilet, and he did. She dried his hair with the hand towel and dabbed his ears and neck, pressed the top of his head into her chest between her breasts. His breath had evened and become smooth, and she noticed its raspiness had gone.

He lifted his head and watched her fold the wet towels and put them one by one on the laminate countertop.

"It's gone," he said. "The burping feeling that wouldn't come out."

"Maybe you needed a good cry."

He stood up and for a moment she thought he was going to kiss her but he pitched forward to the door, pulled back the bed sheets, and flopped down. She followed and pulled the sheet and blanket over him, and shower droplets soaked into the sheets when she leaned over him.

She climbed in from one side and slid in between the cool

white sheets and lay flat on her back, spread her wet hair in a fan on the pillow. She shivered, and she didn't touch him when she lay down. He slid closer and rolled so he was on his back next to her, and they touched at points along the sides of their bodies, and together where her skin was still wet.

"I need to call Timmy. I'm going to have to tell him."

"It's not like the house was lost. Most of it is fine."

"But it's his anchor. And our parents' things."

She put her hand on his chest and felt his heart beat.

"Ok, it's my anchor too."

"You want to see him?"

"I do. He's in East Stroudsberg."

"We could drive. My parents are north of there—Scranton."

"It'd take a while."

"There's time. I could call in sick on Monday."

She scooted herself forward and pressed herself small into his body, pulled her knees up into her chest, and he wrapped himself around her, warm. She felt a hum that made her think they were surrounded by song.

"Do you feel it?"

"I feel it," he said. "The hum. It's in me."

"It's beautiful." She curled her head into his chest and he pulled a strand of her hair between her fingers, and smoothed it out, over and over again.

He started to shift.

"Stay. There's no rush."

Chapter 50

Sunday, November 4

Mark sat across from Timmy at the Friendly's Restaurant in East Stroudsberg, Pennsylvania.

"How'd the midterm exam go?"

"Good. I'll know next week." Timmy pushed his bacon around the plate, so it caught drips of maple syrup, and the crisp edges of the meat scraped the ceramic surface.

"What are you studying?" Amalia leaned forward, her shoulders hunched.

"Biology. Mostly. And some other stuff."

This was painful. He must hate her. Timmy had only heard of her last night.

"You know what I like? I like veterinary medicine," Timmy stabbed the bacon with his fork and held it up. Syrup dripped to the plate.

"Timmy."

"Stop. It's Tim."

"Tim." Mark coughed. "It's going to take some time for me to get used to it."

"Get used to it, then."

"No. you can't do this, Tim." Mark wiped his mouth and threw the napkin down on the table next to his plate.

"I'm not doing anything. You're the one who showed up and said you wanted to meet."

"Can you give us a minute, Amalia?"

She gave Mark a look he couldn't discern and slid out of the booth and walked to the back of the diner.

"Tim." He looked over his shoulder to make sure Amalia was out of earshot. "She's my girlfriend. You could try being nicer."

Tim sat back. "I don't need you and your girlfriend checking up on me. I've got my own life here now. Why did you come here? You already told me about the fire on the phone."

"I thought it would help."

"Help you, maybe."

Mark shrugged. "Maybe."

Tim sat back and took a sip from his mug.

"When did you start drinking coffee?"

"Last week," Tim said.

"You like it?"

"Tastes like dirt." He laughed. "I don't know how you can drink the stuff."

"Keeps me going, I guess," Mark said.

"I brought some stuff for you to take back to the house—stuff it turns out I don't need," Tim said. "There's no room in my apartment now."

"I don't know about the house. What's going to happen. They're sending an engineer next week to look at the bearing wall."

"And you're staying in a hotel for now?"

"We are."

"We."

"She came out for the weekend."

Tim nodded, and his mouth twisted into a smile.

"What?"

"Nothing." He picked up the bacon with his fingers and crunched down on it. "I'm seeing someone. She's out in the car."

"What? Why didn't you bring her in?"

"I told her to wait until I saw what kind of mood you were in." He picked up his phone and typed in a quick message. "You're safe," he said to Mark.

"Amalia can come back? You're going to be civil?"

"Civil! I'm always civil, big brother."

Mark stood up and went to the back of the restaurant to find Amalia, who sat on a brick hearth in front of a false fireplace. "I'm sorry."

"Don't be. It must be hard for him." She slid off the chairs.

"Come back. He has a surprise for us. A girlfriend."

"Did you know?"

"Just found out." He held out a hand to her. "I am so glad you are here."

They sat down a moment before Tim's girlfriend approached the table. Short and dark-haired, her light brown eyes glowed against caramel skin, offset by a bright silver nose ring. She carried a bright red backpack with a heart drawn on the front of it.

"Meet Candace," Tim said, and stood up.

Oh god. Little brother was in love.

The young woman beamed. "Sorry I'm late," she said. "I was at the library."

"It's ok, I told them," Tim said.

"Oh." She smiled and looked up at Mark from underneath her eyelashes. "I'm nervous," she said.

"Don't be." Amalia shook her head. "We won't bite."

"It's kind of like meeting his parents."

She settled into the booth next to Tim, who put his arm behind her across the back of the seat.

"Do you go to school together?"

She looked up at Tim. "You didn't tell him?"

"We—uh. We live together. And we work together at the café."

"I thought you said your new roommate was Conrad."

"Candog. I call her Candog."

"Because I don't like Candi," she said. "So," Candace said. "What about you two? How long have you been together?"

"Uh—since the fall." Mark squeezed Amalia's hand, but she let go of his hand beneath the table and took a sip of her coffee. She waved down a busboy across the aisle for more coffee.

"I heard about your parents," said Candace. "I'm sorry."

Mark nodded. "Thanks."

"He still cries at night, in his sleep, sometimes," Candace said.

Tim shook his head.

"You do. There's no shame." Candace slid down his shoulder.

"You're lucky to have each other," Amalia said.

"They're so young," Mark said.

"Where are your parents?"

"In Nairobi."

"You're from there?"

"Me? No, I'm from here. They're missionaries."

"They're—missionaries?"

"Do they know about you two—living together?"

"They know I have a new roommate called Tammy."

"Tammy and Conrad."

Tim twisted out a smile for Candace. "We're getting married."

"No. Way."

Amalia looked at Mark and put a hand on his knee below the table.

He tried to take a long, slow breath. Told himself to inhale. To exhale. He felt for Amalia's hand beneath the table.

"I'm pregnant," Candace said.

Amalia squeezed his fingers, hard.

"Ow! I mean, wow!"

"We're great," Tim said. "Never been happier." He ran his fingers through Candace's hair.

"I guess there's nothing to discuss, then," Mark said. "Except, school, and work, and how you're going to support yourselves. How you're going to support another life when you're not in a position to support each other." He'd never had the talk with him.

He'd always thought Mom and Dad had done that. Should he have given him condoms? "Did you use condoms?"

"Mark!" Amalia pinched his hand.

"Can we steer this conversation back to the point at hand? We're going to be parents, and we're getting married. We'd like your blessing," Tim said. "And we're hoping, you can pass on the family rings to us."

"Our blessing? And the rings?" Mark sat back. "I don't know what to say. You're your own person. I don't—have any control."

"Mark." Amalia pulled their hands to the seat of the bench between them, and gave him a look. He didn't know what that look meant. Was he in trouble? "Give them your blessing," she said. "It's the right thing to do."

"I can't bless something I know nothing about. Am I happy for you? Yes, I guess so. You seem like a nice person, Candi. I mean Candace. But how are you going to do this? I can't support you all, you know."

"We worked it out. We're going to take turns finishing semesters and taking care of the baby."

"And keep working at the café."

"I might get something else. Another job on the side."

"I assemble props for the theater too," she said.

"You can't do that when you're pregnant," Mark said.

"Of course she can," said Amalia. "She'll be very safe. You'll be safe."

"Absolutely." Candace nodded.

"It's great," Amalia said. "You're young, but—it's happened, you're in love, you want to be together, and you've got a plan."

"And—you're going to have a baby. I'm going to be an uncle." Mark blinked. "My baby brother is going to be a father."

Amalia reached over the counter for Candace's hand and held it between her two. "Congratulations."

It wasn't congratulations. It wasn't right.

"Thank you, Amalia," Candace said.

"Mark?"

"I don't know. It's a lot, all at once. I'm still getting used to the idea."

"As long as you're getting used to it, that's good enough for us," Candace said.

The waitress came to the table with the check. "All done?" She waved to the busboy who began to clear their table. "It's our busy time, sorry."

"Where are you guys going now? We came all this way."

"Back to the library, later. We can hang out."

"We're going to Amalia's parents later, for dinner. It's closer than we've been, so we figured we would."

"We can't leave them now," Amalia said. "Not after coming so far to see them."

"We can come," Candace said. "We can. She looked at Tim. "It's family."

They drove north from East Stroudsberg in a convoy of their two cars and arrived at Amalia's parents' house in Scranton, early for dinner.

"*Romney/Ryan!* Nice," Mark said. "How come you never told me?" He pointed to the Republican party election sign on the lawn in front of the two-family house.

"I never knew," she said. "It was Obama last time." She got out of the car and pulled the Romney sign out of the grass, and carried it with her to the front door.

"When you called from the diner did you tell them about Candi and Tim coming too?"

"I did. I told them everything," she said.

The door opened before she could knock, and her parents stood there with smiles and open arms. "Welcome!"

"What's this?" Amalia held up the Republican party sign she'd pulled out of the grass.

"Your father had a change of heart."

"This is Mark, Mom. Dad. Mark, meet my parents, crazy politicos of West Scranton." She propped the lawn sign up in the modern front hall where they stood.

"Not really," she said. "We don't vote here." She fake-whispered behind her hand. "We're Canadian."

Tim and Candace came up the walk hand-in-hand. "And this is Mark's brother Tim, and his fiancée Candi."

"Pleased to meet you," Amalia's dad said. He shook Tim's hand. "I'm Joseph. Congratulations on the baby, son." He didn't shake Mark's hand. Amalia straightened the election sign where it had fallen.

Her mom hugged Candace. "I'm Soumya. You can call me Sou. Now." She took Amalia and Mark by the hands. "Come and tell me all about the new apartment."

Chapter 51

Dinner was warm and congenial, and the Romney/Ryan sign was forgotten fast, but the congratulations of Candace and Tim were not. Amalia cleared the plates from the dinner table, leftover scrapings piled onto the top plate. Candace got to her feet to help her carry the glasses into the kitchen. "Thanks," Amalia said. "You don't need to do that. You must be feeling tired."

"No, I'm fine." She hesitated. "It comes in waves actually."

"You didn't eat much."

"Hunger comes in waves, too."

Amalia nodded. "I wouldn't know."

"Do you think you guys will—you know—"

"Way too soon." Amalia shook her head. "I mean, I didn't mean to suggest—"

Candace shook her head. "No, it's ok. It is soon. You're right." She sat down and tears pooled in her eyes.

"Oh." Amalia wiped her hands on a dish towel and came over to her, put a hand on her back and sat close so their knees touched. "Do you want this?"

"The baby?"

Amalia nodded, then Candace sat down and started to cry. Amalia pulled her into a hug and smoothed her hair. Sobs emerged from Candace's chest, and soon the two of them were in tears together.

Mark came in with the plastic bag of the quilt remains. "Oh."

"It's ok." Amalia pulled away from Candace, wiped tears from her face.

Her mother followed Mark into the room. "He's got the quilt."

Mark brought it to the table and Amalia took it from him, pulled out the remains of the charred quilt and showed her mother.

"Bring it to the light," her mother said. "Put it on newspaper." She brought a section from the recycling bin and spread the paper across the kitchen table. "Here," she said. She gave the bag to Candace to hold and then pulled the quilt out, and wispy black fibers rained out of the bag. She unfolded each section, and with every movement more of the fabric fell apart. "This is gone. This part is ok." Her hand hovered over the quilt like a metal detector.

"That part was under the couch," Amalia said. "It must have been protected. Only part of the couch burned."

"And the books too?"

"Their parents' books."

"I wish I'd seen them," Candace said.

"We can cut out these sections. We're going to have to be ruthless with it," her mother said.

"There's so little to save, it's worth hacking into it. I know how much it would mean to Tim," Candace said with a hand on her belly.

"I can bind the edges while you're all still here," her mom said. "But we're going to have to make the cuts now. The boys should see it first and decide."

Amalia went back into the living room. "Tim? We're ready." Her dad stood up and put a hand on Tim's back and the two walked into the kitchen.

"We can save this and this. Maybe this."

"Maybe ten percent of it."

"I say do it," Mark said.

"You want to do the cutting?" Her mom handed Mark the sewing shears. "Along here, this side of the seam."

He took the scissors from her and held them for a moment, open, over the fabric. Amalia looked at him and knew he was saying a prayer, in his own way. She saw something then—and knew—that he wasn't Catholic, not anymore, although he probably didn't realize. The scissors made a smooth slice through the fabric on contact.

"Like a hot knife through butter," Mark said. He continued to cut until he reached the interior corner of the good section.

"Now come at it from this side," her mom said.

He walked around the corner of the table and cut in, and severed the threads from the charred section of quilt.

When he met the first cut, her mom slid her hands underneath it and lifted the good section.

"Beautiful."

"You, now," he said to Tim.

Tim moved over to the other corner of the quilt. "Come here," he said to Candace. "Together."

She put his hand over his and they cut into the fabric together.

"This one might need a rounded edge," her mom said. "Turn it here."

They turned the scissors in a semi-circle to save the most fabric they could. When they got to the end, her mom lifted the panel and held it to the kitchen light above.

"It looks translucent," Tim said.

"Like stained glass," Candace said. "I wonder why this corner was worn more."

"That's the side Tim used to snuggle up with when he lay down," Mark said. "It's worn out from him."

"I used to like the fuzzy patch in the corner."

"Wasn't that from your old teddy bear?"

He fingered the fabric. "It would be nice to have this for the baby."

"Then this is the best piece for you," her mom said. "It might need some additional backing to strengthen it."

"Can you bind it on a curve?"

"There's a few things I can do. Appliqué it onto another piece, snip the binding inside to make it round the corner. It depends what you want to do with it."

"A baby blanket would be nice."

"It might not stand up well to a baby as it is. We can stitch it onto something stronger and make this a panel on it."

"That's the backing?"

"Backing and binding. And new batting. I have it all upstairs in Amalia's old bedroom."

"And the rest of it?" Tim looked at the blackened quilt. "It's still damp here."

"Doesn't smell great."

"We can hand wash these good parts but I'd do it after the fabric has been stabilized. What do you want to do with the rest?"

Tim looked at Mark and raised an eyebrow. Mark nodded.

Amalia looked back and forth between the two brothers. They spoke to each other in glances she didn't understand. "What?"

"Mount Willard," Mark said, and Tim smiled.

"Time for a break," her dad said. "Come, all of you." He put on Stevie Wonder in the living room, turned up the volume, and danced back into the kitchen, and sang along out of tune. "What? It's a good song," he said. "I just called to say I love you!"

"You are so corny," her mom said, and patted him on the hip.

"I just called to say I love you!"

"Dad." Amalia looked at him down her nose.

"You're going to need glasses if you keep up your sneering," he said. "It's for your mom. She likes it. I can't be embarrassing you, surely."

"I'm not embarrassed for me, but for you," she said. "Letting it all hang out."

"You should try it sometime, Amalia. It feels good." He danced with her mom in a mock tango across the floor, which left her in giggles at the kitchen counter.

"Take her dancing," her dad said to Mark.

"We met dancing," Candace said. "In the café."

"There you go," he said. "And now they have a baby on the way."

Her mom shook her head and clicked her tongue at him.

"Oh, come on. Don't tell me you guys haven't—," Tim said.

"All right then! How about that quilt?" Amalia grabbed Mark's hand, and led him up to the sewing room. He closed the door behind them.

"My old room," she said.

Stevie Wonder's voice wound its way up the staircase, filled the hallway outside, and the sound glided under the door.

"Come on." He pulled her into a hug and slid his arms down her sides.

"I just called to say I love you."

"You are as corny as the rest of my family," she said.

They circled in the center of the room, surrounded by her mom's fabrics and button boxes. "This room isn't mine anymore," she said. "I moved almost everything."

"You don't have a lot there," he said. "We only moved a car's worth."

"I have some boxes of books in the garage here," she said. "I was waiting—to see if I was going to stay there, in New York." She pulled him tight to her and held him so that her arms pointed up his back toward his shoulder blades.

"He's playing it again," Mark said. The song wound its way into the room again.

"Move in with me." It came out before she could censor its jump from thought to speech.

"What?"

She'd lost control of her senses. She pulled back, and slid her hands lower to the back of his belt. He fell forward on her and they landed on her old bed. "I said, move in with me." She'd said it, hadn't she.

"You two in there?" Her mom knocked on the door and came in. "I'm not used to knocking on my sewing room door," she said. The song blasted into the room behind her. Mark sat up, Amalia behind him. "Sorry! You were kissing."

"No we weren't."

"You can kiss, I don't mind."

"We weren't."

"I have some good backing fabric in here. There's blue and there's yellow. See which one you like better, Mark." She pulled out a large flat bin from beneath Amalia's old bed. "We could bring it downstairs."

"I'll carry it," he said.

Her mom piled him up with the bin, and a box of embroidery thread. "Take this," she said to Amalia, and handed her the bindings, rolled in a wicker basket.

"Are you knitting? I see yarn in here," she said.

"I'm trying to finish a baby outfit for Amalia's cousin Ritu's shower," she said to Mark. "Babies on the brain. I have babies on the brain."

Amalia looked at Mark and shook her head. Don't respond, she implored with a look. There was no way they were going down the grandkid path with her baby crazy mother. No!

Downstairs, Stevie Wonder was on his third or fourth round of the same song, thanks to her dad, egged on by Tim and Candace who spun around the kitchen in their own dance.

"Can't be good for the baby," Mark said, back in the room.

"Come on big brother. You're jealous."

"Not jealous," he said.

"I just called, to say, I love you!" Tim sang out loud, and spun Candace in front of the stove.

"They're all crazy," Amalia said. "My crazy family and your crazy family." She shook her head.

Chapter 52

"You can sleep here, Mark." Amalia's dad pointed to the couch in the study.

"Ok. And—Amalia?"

"She'll sleep in her old room, of course. Your brother and his fiancée can sleep in the guest bedroom upstairs."

"Mr. Erenwine."

"Please. Call me Joseph. Joe."

Mark sat down on the couch next to the pile of blanket and pillow Joseph had set down.

"What is it, son?" Joseph sat down next to him.

"What if—I mean, would you—"

"What is it?"

"I have thought—" No.

"Spit it out. It can't be any bigger than your brother knocking up his girlfriend." He turned to Mark. "Unless that's what you're—"

"No." Mark shook his head. "Although—no." He took a deep breath. "Amalia asked me to move in with her."

"Oh!"

"And I haven't answered yet."

"I see."

"She'd be horrified to know I mentioned it to you."

"Agreed. We shouldn't tell her."

"Ok—"

"Unless you want to. Do you want to? Move in with her?"

"Um. It's quick. We just met."

"Listen, son, when you know, you know."

"I would have thought—"

"Please. I'm a modern man."

Mark shifted up the couch. "I guess what I'm trying to say, is, in light of possibly moving in together, and my brother and his girlfriend sharing a room, would it be—possible—for Amalia and I to do the same? Share a room here? But don't tell her I asked."

Joseph nodded. "The beds."

"Oh."

"That's the only reason."

"I see."

"Your brother could sleep here if you would prefer. And Candace could sleep in Amalia's room."

"No." Mark shook his head. "I get it. Musical beds."

"Something like that."

Mark stood up and Joseph put his hand on his shoulder. "Welcome to the family, son." They walked out to the living room together. Amalia sat in front of the gas fireplace. Mark sat down in front of her. Her mother was in the middle of a quiz.

"And how did you meet?"

"We ran into each other," Amalia said. "And then we ended up speaking on a panel together."

"The one about natural gas." Joseph Erenwine sat down. "Very good. That's important."

"We have strong thoughts about it," Mark said.

"Amalia always did know how to express herself," her mom said.

"'Express' doesn't quite sum it up," Mark said.

Amalia shook her head. "We were in disagreement about fracking. You know—hydraulic fracturing?"

"I know it well," Joseph said. We're running a study now."

Mark watched Amalia and Joseph. Wondered if her dad was someone he could talk to. Wasn't sure—decided to play it safe and listen. "We're doing chemical testing of some of the components of the fluid. It's an independently funded study."

"No such thing," Tim said. "It's never independent. Someone's always behind it."

"In our case, that's the university. I'm at the University of Scranton."

"I'm at the University of Pennsylvania in East Stroudsberg—we are," Tim said, "me and Candace, and I'm sure they must have corporate backing," Tim said.

"We have donors."

"See?"

"It's about as independent as it can be, and still have donors. The money comes from somewhere."

"How are you handling it? The conflict," Amalia said.

"Transparency in the process. That's always the mantra. Repeatable, transparent results, publicly available."

"My parents would have liked you," Mark said. "They were all about clear communication."

"What did they do?"

"They were anthropologists."

"You grew up in New Hampshire?"

"We did. Moultonborough."

"And how did you boys end up in Pennsylvania?"

"We moved to Quakertown after our parents passed."

"Did you know someone there?"

"No," Mark said. He turned around to Amalia. "I haven't told you all of this." No time like the present. "I needed to get a job, a better paying job, after Mom and Dad died. Tim was still in school. He had two years left until graduation."

"And he didn't want to move me."

"But my teaching job at the college wasn't going to cut it. Geology. I'd only just started. Part-time. And things weren't going so well with Helene either. The move was the last straw for her."

"I had no idea," Amalia said.

"So there was a job in Philadelphia, but I couldn't dump Timmy in a big city and be away for work all day and night."

"He liked the library," Tim said. "In Quakertown."

"Really? There are worse ways to pick a town, I suppose," her mom said.

"The library reminded me of the one in Moultonborough. We saw it driving down on one of our trips. I figured, if I can keep the locale kind of similar—well, maybe the rest would fall into place."

"Good theory."

"How'd that work?"

"I don't know, what do you think, Tim?"

"I think." He took a long breath and closed his eyes. "I think I was fortunate to have you, bro." He opened his eyes and looked at Mark. His eyes welled up, a sudden spring. "I don't know how I would have got through it without you." He wiped the stream of tears from his face.

"Hey." Mark got up and inserted himself on the couch between Tim and Candace. "I've got you." He held his brother's head in his hands, kissed him on the forehead and held him close.

"Well." Soumya stood up and put her hands on her hips, eyes on the brothers. "I'll make tea."

Candace scrambled to come after her. "I'll help."

Amalia followed, her dad stoked the fake-fire, and Tim and Mark stayed in a tight scrim on the couch until Mark released his brother.

"I never had a brother," Joseph said. "You boys are very lucky to have each other."

Tim roughed up Mark's hair and wiped his face on his sleeve. "I wonder what Mom and Dad would say now."

"Dad would have kicked your ass back home."

"Mom would have said she should have an abortion."

"Dad wouldn't have."

"Whatever happens," Joseph said, "we're here if you need us." He reached over from the fire and patted Tim on the shin.

"Thanks." Tim nodded.

"Amalia asked me to move in with her," Mark said.

"No way!" Tim looked back at Joseph.

"He knows."

"This is nuts! Go bro!"

"I didn't say yes. Or no. I haven't said anything yet."

Chapter 53

The kettle shrieked and blocked out the sound of men's voices from the living room. "What are they whispering about in there?"

"I don't know. They seem to have their own secret language," Amalia said.

"Yes, what was the mountain comment earlier? Mount Something. Mount Someone," her mom said.

"I have no idea."

Her mother arranged the teacups on a tray and stood next to the kettle. "He seems very nice, Amalia. They both do."

"We're lucky," Candace said. "I feel lucky."

Amalia pressed the palms of her hands into the countertop, and raised herself up on her toes. "I asked him to move in with me."

"Oh! Amalia. That's new." Her mother poured milk into a little ceramic jug and sat it next to the sugar and cups. Amalia could never be sure what was going on in her mother's mind.

"New? Complete and total understatement. It's awesome!" Candace punched her on the arm. "So when's it going to be?"

"He hasn't answered yet."

"It seems early. I know how hard it was for you after you and Nadel split up."

"That's in the past," Amalia said. "Kind of. I owe him money. Something I have to figure out."

"You will, honey, you always do."

"I'm thinking of taking on another job, to earn some extra money. Something with color. Displays or something. Staging. I'd have to make a website, I guess. I don't know how you start getting clients for that sort of thing."

"We could use you. The professional theater in Scranton."

"Really? Would I have to be here often—for meetings?"

"No, half the stuff is built out of town and shipped in parts."

"I like it." She kissed Candace on the cheek. "Thanks, sweetie. You're a life saver."

"Let's go in," she said. "Do you think they're done whispering?"

Amalia pushed the swinging door and held it open for her mother with the tray, and Candace behind her.

"Amalia has some news," her mom said. "The stage set design news," she said. "The other thing—that's your business."

"What other thing?"

"That they're moving in together," Candace said.

"I—Amalia." Mark came to her in the doorway where she stood, paralyzed.

Oh god. How embarrassing. She'd screwed it up. "I'm sorry." She winced.

He put a hand on her waist and she relaxed a little. "I say yes." He kissed her on the lips and gave her a little electric shock.

"Bravo!" Her dad clapped.

Chapter 54

Monday, November 5

Mark rolled over on the floor and into the bed frame legs next to him. Not the welcome he expected.

"Good morning." Amalia leaned over the bed down next to him. "I was going to check the train schedule for Philadelphia to New York."

"No. Come here." He pulled her down into the warm nest of blankets. "How'd you sleep?"

"Well, but strange dreams."

"There's a train at seven, which we're not going to make. Then they're every hour or so, but I have no idea now since the hurricane."

"I left a message for Betsy that I wouldn't be in until tomorrow, that I needed to take another personal day."

"She was okay with you missing work?"

"She didn't reply to my text message."

He sat up. "You don't want to piss off Boss Lady, now. Give her a call. You know as well as me that messages haven't been going through since the storm."

They went down to the kitchen and found Amalia's mom in the middle of breakfast preparations. Her father was out in the yard and she saw him put the Romney/Ryan sign back on the lawn. Candace and Tim sat at the table with cups of tea.

"We're heading out to get back for morning classes," Tim said.

"I'm off today," Mark said. "Amalia is taking a day off."

"We're not open yet," Amalia said. "The boss said the office should be back up and running by Wednesday."

"Election day tomorrow," her mom said. "Where do you boys vote?"

"Quakertown. We're registered there," Mark said.

"Actually, I registered in East Stroudsburg," Tim said. "It was more convenient."

Joseph came in and washed his hands. "We can take the sign down after the election tomorrow."

"I can't believe it's already tomorrow. The hurricane threw everyone off."

"Don't you have an Obama sign, Mom?"

"I do. It's in my car window. I can broadcast more widely that way."

"We decided to split up the territory instead of fighting over lawn space," her dad said.

They packed up, rolled up bedding, dug out Amalia's book boxes from the garage, and stood out on the street next to the Romney/Ryan sign. Joseph closed the trunk of Mark's car which hid Amalia's book boxes beneath the shaded glass, and came around to give a round of hugs.

"Don't forget this," her mom said. She came out with a glass dish of food. "Put it in your freezer," she said to Mark.

Amalia shook her head. "I don't know why you're giving it to him and not to me."

"You have to eat with him, honey. It's incentive. I put the chicken tikka masala recipe on a card on top." She handed Mark the bag.

They all said goodbye to Tim and Candace, with promises to meet up soon, halfway. "We could come to you," Amalia said. "My parents are here. And I'll call you about the theater."

"The director is never in early, or I'd have you come by now to meet him. It's really close."

"Could we swing by to take a look before we get on the highway?"

"We have time," Mark said.

They said goodbye to Amalia's parents and left in the same convoy of cars they arrived in the day before, this time with Mark behind Tim. They pulled up in front of Candace's theater, a small outfit in a large warehouse structure on Cherry Street. He parked across the street in a bakery parking lot.

Candace knocked on the side door. "The custodian is here. I don't have a key."

The door opened and a small woman beckoned them into the darkened space. The back of the theater was a tangle of concrete block walls painted white, old black laminate countertops with bright bulbs above cracked mirrors, and heavy red canvas drapes that concealed costume racks whose dark rubber wheels peeked out from beneath the hems.

"Our workspace is in here," she said. "It's small." They walked down a hall with naked bulbs that hung from the ceiling, walls plastered with years of taped-up show posters, all signed by the actors.

"It feels so—tight. All the layers of the theater family are piled up here in this hallway."

"It's congested. We could do with opening it up. The director says he'd love to rearrange the rooms in here."

Candace opened the door into the small workshop, a double height space with racks up the walls and a cable arrangement that hung from the ceiling. Dimensional lumber and bolts of fabric lined the walls on one side, and disassembled parts of stage sets were stacked in a jumble on the other. "We assemble the props in here. It's part wood shop, part textile shop." She pointed into another room off to the side. "We paint in here," she said, "when we spray. It's ventilated."

"Works for you?"

"It's the only thing that works in here at all. They got a grant for the ventilation system a few years ago. I was in high school, used to volunteer here. I remember it before. It was awful, you felt dizzy when the paints and solvents were being used."

"Thank goodness for the system, then. And better products."

"What do you mean?"

"Low VOC products."

"I've never heard of them."

"Seriously? Less stinky paint. It's formulated differently. Low in volatile organic compounds."

"They're better?"

"They're supposed to be better," Amalia said. "But to be honest, they give me a headache too, and I find it hard to breathe when I'm near them. I felt better with the old fashioned formulas."

"They put minerals in paint now," Mark said. "Mineral based coatings."

"Those aren't new. But they're good. Better. Formulated in a different way," Amalia said.

"I could suggest a change," Candace said.

"You know, you ought to wear a proper NIOSH mask when you're pregnant. Regardless of what you use. Don't want the fumes to get into the placenta."

"Can't they get in through the skin? Find out, ok? We'll look into it too. It's important," Mark said.

Candace nodded. "I could still do the textiles and wood assembly, even without the painting."

"We'll figure it out with you."

"The theater should be doing that."

"They don't know. We haven't told them."

"Ah."

"I don't want it to get out. To my parents."

"They're going to find out eventually."

Before they hit the highway from Scranton to Quakertown, they pulled over for gas. "You did all the driving yesterday,"

Amalia said. "Want me to take a turn?" They swapped seats and she adjusted the leg and mirror positions to fit her smaller frame, tilted the rearview mirror so she could see the view behind.

"How much time did you spend here?"

"A few years of high school. Then I was back in Canada for university."

"We have time, you know, if you want to go off the highway. I can get you lined up with the train from Doylestown early tomorrow morning."

"And you're off today because of the house."

He pulled out the map book in the passenger side and handed it to her. "Want to pick a new route?"

"No. we're doing this one Amalia-style, on radar. My radar."

She pulled out of the gas station lot and fiddled with the radio until she found a station that played a classical piece she recognized, piano, and drove, then turned right at the next opportunity.

Mark pulled out his phone and checked messages while Amalia wound their way out, and later off an exit ramp into a small town with a drive-through donut shop.

"It's pretty, but it's not quite what I had in mind for exploring," she said. She looked across at him. "What? You look concerned."

"Nothing. Just work."

"Put that away."

"I can't, I'm working from home today."

"No day off?"

"Officially yes, but when stuff comes up I still have to deal with it."

She nodded. "Would a donut help?" She pulled into the drive-through and ordered him a donut and a tea for herself, and drove back out to the highway. "Maybe we need the map after all. Meandering here leads to more of same."

He didn't reply, still caught up with his work. Needed to focus on the stream of messages that had come in.

"Mark? Where should we go? Exploring?"

He exhaled. "You want to explore the area? Turn left at the next exit."

The radio announcer commented, ". . . D-minor, Anna Tomowa-Sintow, Soprano. . ." She didn't catch the rest.

"This is pretty," she said.

"The music or the landscape?"

"Both. They flow well together." The violins rose.

"I recognize this, did you hear what they said it is?"

"No, something about a soprano. Turn up here, where the light flashes."

"Taking me on a back roads tour." She looked over at him, still focused on the messages in his lap. "You all right?"

"I might be making a big mistake bringing you here."

"Where are we going?"

"Half a mile down, we're going to turn left at the T."

"Are we going to one of your sites?"

He typed a message. The soprano echoed the chorus on the radio.

"We are. We're going to one of your sites," she said. Her foot pressed a little harder on the gas, and took them up beyond the side road speed limit.

What should he do? He had the information in his palm, and Amalia on his left, in the driver's seat. The weave of voices on the radio made it hard for him to think, buffered him from what he needed to see. But he listened, and found the pace of the music soothed him.

It was an injustice, he felt, to keep her out of the loop. And yet there were proprietary concerns. How to handle this, how much to tell her. He would tell her what she needed to know. What he'd put in a press release. Earlier than the public would hear it.

"There was a leak."

She looked over at him.

"Ok. What kind of leak."

He listened to the spacing between the words of the chorus, a deep male voice interspersed with the women in the group. "Both kinds. Information and chemical."

"Ok." She frowned. "Are you supposed to be telling me this?"

"I can't not tell you. I don't know how not to tell you." The men's and women's voices of the chorus bounced back and forth and their voices overtook the orchestra in the background. Their voices. "I have to be honest with you." The drums in the piece boomed over him and he moved to turn the radio down, but when he reached for the volume, the music paused in a moment of silence, and he withdrew his hand. "Turn left here." He pointed to the T-junction. "Go another mile. I'll tell you."

The music rose again in a symphony of voices and instruments. "I recognize this piece," she said. "I can't place it."

"Something happened here before I went to Wales. There was a well casing leak."

"Ok."

A single male voice sang out, backed by deep wind instruments.

"I can't tell you more. We're testing, and it's contained."

"Are people affected? Their water? Their animals?"

"I don't know. Possibly. Maybe. That's why we're testing."

"How did it happen?"

"Unusual soil conditions, extreme hydrostatic pressure. A subcontractor under the gun to meet a deadline."

"Surely there are more checks and balances in place, to prevent that?"

"We're looking into it."

"What does this have to do with you?"

Was she giving him a way out? Another male voice sprang out in the radio's song, and echoed the first. "I'm spinning it."

"What?"

"They want me to spin it. For the media. Before it leaks."

"But you said it already has."

"They think I had something to do with it, that I leaked it when I was in Wales."

"Oh?"

"To you."

"Excuse me? How do they know about me?"

"They don't. But they saw our emails. I left one open—in Wales—they said." His voice trailed, overtaken by a female voice that spun out of the operatic play.

"I need to turn this off," she said.

"No. Please." He put a hand over hers on the radio. "It's good. It's—helping me." They listened to the soprano voice, soft, and drove down the road. "Slow down," he said. "There's no rush." He needed more time to think of what to say when he got there. Amalia's foot stayed steady on the pedal. The violins kicked up again in the music, the voices died away, then chimed in. "This is it," he said. The music softened and he spoke. "I'm going to have to quit," he said. He shook his head.

She shook her head. "When we sat together in my apartment, in our apartment—and we closed our eyes with it, it was very clear that you and I have some work to do with energy issues, from within. Not by quitting."

"I'm not quitting to walk away from the issues. Or for you. And I'm not even sure I'm quitting. I—I need more freedom to express myself, not be bound by the company."

The music, soft in the background, soothed him. He could do this. He fell silent, then realized they'd missed the turn. "We missed it. Can you spin it? We need to turn around." He looked over his shoulder. "It's at the farmhouse back there. I was distracted."

She let a car pass from behind and pulled into a driveway up ahead, turned, and went back the way they came.

Backtracking. There was something to it. "You remember when you talked about the umbrella? Over the continent. Canada, Panama, Bolivia. And we got these emails from Mildred."

"You got them too? The Defend Our Coast emails?"

"And another one, about the War of 1812."

"I didn't get that one."

"Check. I'll bet you did."

"Ok."

He was concerned about her lack of reaction. Where was the fiery Amalia? Maybe she suppressed it while driving. "The umbrella. The Americas."

"Yes."

There it was. Some acknowledgement. He went on. "What we're doing has impacts beyond our borders. Beyond state borders and beyond national borders."

Amalia nodded. "Here?" She pointed to the farmhouse.

"Yes, turn right opposite the farm. Dirt road. The car might not like it but we'll be ok."

The music pattered between male and female voices and violins, and soothed him. "We need to take a more global approach to this," he said.

"Agreed. I had a dream."

"Another one?"

She nodded. "Last night. The plates, the tectonic plates, all the microcontinents—were held together by concrete."

He frowned. "People poured the concrete?"

"Yes."

"To hold the plates together?"

"Yes. Last night."

He nodded. "I see. And you think this means—"

"We're at risk of overfracturing, globally. To the point we're going to be patching seismic joints in the long run."

"Really? I don't think that's a concern," Mark said. "I've never heard anyone say so."

"It was a long term vision."

"Millennial?"

"Something like that. There was something else."

"What else?"

"There was gas—methane or something, I don't know what. It escaped. More of it than we could bear."

"So—"

"It goes back to your protocol."

"Ok."

"We need a global approach to fracturing the lithosphere, so we don't have to do a patch job later. The protocol needs to address it."

"Here?" She pulled the car to a stop at the end of the dirt road and in front of a blockade.

"I'll call ahead," he said. "They're not expecting you." He pulled up the site number on his phone. "Mary? It's Mark Stone from the Philadelphia office. Yes. I'm here. I have my wife with me."

"You liar."

"Do you want to go on site or not?"

She drove into the gravel parking lot and pulled up next to the shuttle bus, where the driver napped behind the wheel, his paper spread across his chest.

"How come you have a shuttle bus here?"

"We're trying to be environmentally friendly," he said.

"You have got to be kidding me."

"He was the first one I told about the shots fired in the woods," he said. "Come into the office trailer with me. I don't know what's going to happen after. Mary works there, she's very nice, you might sit with her while I meet with the others. I can't bring you into the meeting. I'll be in the next trailer."

"Fair enough." She turned off the ignition and the music stopped on a soft vocal note. "Nice piece," she said. "I wish I could remember what it was."

"Amalia." He stood next to the car and looked at her over the roof of it as she got out. "I love you."

"I know. Do what you think is best."

Chapter 55

Mary poured Amalia a cup of old coffee in a Styrofoam cup, artificial creamer stirred in, and they sat, Mary on her computer, quiet. Amalia stared out the trailer window to what she supposed were water containers, trees beyond them. "You ever email with Mark while he was away?"

Mary nodded. "Typing," she said.

Ok, so maybe scapegoating Mary as the culprit on Mark's back would not fly. Amalia shifted and pulled out her phone to look at the time and messages. "Do you know about the War of 1812?"

Mary shook her head. "Still typing," she said.

"You're very busy." Amalia sipped her coffee, good in spite of the mix of ingredients. She put it down. "Where do you get this water from?"

Mary stopped. "Our water is fine." She waved a hand. "I fill it up in the bathroom."

"May I use the restroom?"

"Be my guest." She went back to typing.

Amalia tiptoed back to the toilet so as to not disturb Mary. She pushed open the door and saw a large wheelchair accessible room. How would a wheelchair even get into the trailer? Maybe they built ramps. She stood in the center of the room and pushed the door closed. Behind the door stood a water dispenser and a row of large, clear plastic water bottles, drinking water shipped in. Thank god. No way would she want to drink coffee made from contaminated frack wastewater.

Amalia went back to the chair opposite Mary and sat down, looked out the window, fiddled with the coffee cup.

Mary looked up. "How long have you been married?"

"What?"

"You and Mark. I didn't know he was married."

She nodded. "Not long. Less than a year."

"Congratulations." She went back to typing.

This wouldn't work, Amalia thought. She couldn't be part of lies. She'd rather not be there at all. "I'm going to go back to the car," she said.

"Ok, be my guest. Don't wander, they don't like it."

"No problem. Tell Mark, will you?"

"Will do."

Amalia went back to the car, looked out at the denuded and hardscrabble landscape, got back into the car. Cast a glance across at a row of shipping containers, all bright and shiny and with Atlantia Actuaris on the sides. Blinked. Fuzzy. Closed her eyes. Thought back to what she'd read of methylene chloride. Was that what she sensed?

She put the key in the ignition to turn the radio back on, engine silent. She must have missed ten minutes—and the same piece of music still played on. The voices.

Her stomach did a flip. What had happened to her outrage? She'd become all mushy in the middle since she met Mark, not fired up. She'd forgotten her activist heart. If she ever had one. She turned up the volume on the radio opera and listened, closed her eyes to the site around her, and let her mind drift with the music. She was done. Over it. Opened her eyes. She drove out the dirt road and in the rearview mirror she saw Mark open the door of the second trailer and run down the steps after her.

Her phone began to ring in her pocket and she knew it was Mark, but she ignored it, and drove away from the site. What she didn't expect was to be chased—by a little shuttle bus. In her rearview mirror, she could see Mark up at the front of the bus. Her phone rang again.

She pulled over before the main road. The shuttle bus pulled up around her and in front so that it blocked her forward motion. She turned off the ignition.

Mark got off and she saw him wave a hand to the driver, and he came toward her. The bus pulled off the road in a three point turn into the bushes, and turned to point back toward the site. The driver waited.

Mark knocked on the driver's side glass. Her hands froze on the wheel, locked in place. He spoke through the glass. "Let me in."

"I can't do this anymore. Pretend." She turned her head to look out the window and saw his fingers pressed into the edge of the door where the bottom of the window met the metal. She reached down and clicked the door unlock button.

He opened the driver's side door and bobbed down next to her, so her head was above his. "Amalia."

Her throat was tense, and she couldn't speak.

"Why did you fly away?"

She shook her head. "I'm getting confused. I'm dizzy. This place—makes me crazy." She'd seen—or felt—something off the containers, or was it the land? Some kind of dense air—an unhealthy aura? It wasn't pleasant.

"Let's go then. Can I get in?"

She nodded. "Do you need to go back?"

"No, I didn't take anything in with me. Just a bunch of unfinished thoughts."

"Get in, then."

"I'd be more comfortable if I drove. You look pretty shaken," he said.

She unbuckled her seatbelt without a word and got out of the car, and when he helped her out to her feet, he caught her in a hug and she began to shake in spasms. "I need to get as far away from here as possible." He helped her in on her side. She buckled in, and once he seemed satisfied she was not going to run away, he moved the barricade, waved to the shuttle bus driver, and got into the driver's side. When he turned the ignition on, the radio came on, and the same piece of opera played on, and on, and on, the chorus of male and female voices interwoven in song. "You're missing work," she said. She cleared her throat. "Won't they want to know the rest of what you had to say?"

He shook his head and was silent.

She leaned back on the headrest and looked out the side window at the Pennsylvania farm landscapes roll past. Some of the farms had new copper cupolas atop the barns; new horse fencing. Just as often, she'd see a farm that was dilapidated and with two by fours that held up a sagging porch. Had one sold out, the other not? She shook her head and listened to the music. The male sang to the female, the female to the male, and the bounce back and forth gave her a headache.

"...and that was Mozart's Requiem in D-Minor, completed by Franz Xaver Süssmayr and starring Anna Tomowa-Sintow on soprano, conducted by Herbert von Karajan, recorded live and brought to you without interruption for almost a full hour of glory," the announcer said.

They drove in silence and listened to the applause of the audience fade in the radio background like raindrops, percussive, and a few miles further down the road, they turned back onto the highway.

Chapter 56

He took her to the old wooden playground in Quakertown. "Library," he said. "The one Tim was talking about." He pointed across the street.

"This is good," Amalia said. "I like this playground." She got out of the car.

He extended a hand to her and helped her across the muddy field to the playground, quiet during school hours. They held hands around the wooden structure and walked through. He felt the old carvings of initials and hearts in the wood, smoothed over time. Loves that might have lasted, or might have faded. "I gave my notice," he said.

"Ok."

"Don't. Don't say 'ok'."

"It's ok. I have nothing more to say." She kicked at the bottom of a vertical piece of wood that supported a playhouse roof.

"I'm not leaving the industry."

"All right."

"I'm going to consult."

"To the industry?"

"Yes." He nodded. "With your help."

She shook her head. "You don't want my help."

"I do. I need it." Was this a dream or a nightmare? Maybe he got to choose. He turned and he was on the other side of the structure, away from her.

"This place has been good to you." She spoke from the opposite corner of the playground.

"It's home," he said. "Has been home."

"Do you miss New Hampshire?"

"I do. And we need to go there." He turned around and leaned on the wooden railing to face her.

"Oh?"

"The quilt. Mount Willard."

"You and Tim."

He shook his head. "No. You and me. Tim won't go, it's too far for Candace now."

"We're going to New Hampshire?"

"If you'll come. Next weekend?" He looked at her, tilted his head, but didn't reach out to touch.

"Maybe. Let's get you to New York first."

"They didn't even want two weeks' notice." He took a deep breath. "We came to terms." He turned and looked out again toward the library. "They did want me out," he said. "And it's a blessing. I can speak my conscience now. I'm not beholden to any company. I'm free," he said. "Free as a bird."

"And what would you say, given this new freedom?"

Chapter 57

Tuesday, November 6

Amalia took the train back to Manhattan—a slow journey, punctuated by a view that shocked her. In the Meadowlands, outside of New York City, were thousands of large, dead fish, stranded in the trenches on either side of the train tracks. Victims of the storm surge and fall.

At 59th Street, she emerged from her last rail connection and shielded her eyes from the brightness of daylight. Stopped in at the Starbucks for coffee, then headed up to check on the state of her water-logged office.

She heard it all before the elevator door opened: male voices over the cacophony of demolition sounds. The dull rip-thud of water-damaged sheetrock. An electric screwdriver in reverse. "Is Betsy here?" She stepped into the space with the tray of coffee in front of her. She looked left, toward the conference area, and saw the table top propped up on the window wall; to the right, in the glass-fronted offices, filing cabinets pulled back from the partition walls, desks on end.

"Amalia!" Jen's voice came from the other side, near their desks, and a moment later she popped her head around the corner. She came over and gave her a hug, dusty from head to toe. She sported a dust mask around her neck, cute but ineffective.

"What are they doing?"

"Partitions and carpet. They said the rest is ok. Except the desks, they were made of MDF and swelled up."

"Where's Betsy? Did Max and Sharon make it in?"

"Betsy's not in yet, still voting in New Jersey, and Max is MIA. Sharon's train is running but a tree's still blocking her driveway. She came in yesterday."

"And today?"

"Staying home to vote. Said she didn't want to take her chances." A man walked past them to the elevator with heavy chunks of sheetrock boards.

"Something happened. While I was away."

"I know that look," Jen said. "What is it?"

"Mark's moving in."

Jen's eyebrows shot up. "In, as in, with you?"

Amalia nodded.

"Wow! I mean, that's kind of fast isn't it? You just met."

Amalia nodded again. "I know." She bit her lip.

"So how did it happen?" The man came back from the elevator empty handed and went back down the hall past them.

"It kind of popped out. From my mouth. I was under the influence. Of music. And family."

Jen gave her a sideways look, and turned to jump back from another man with a load of sheetrock.

"It felt right."

"And does it still?"

"It does." She smiled, and pushed her hands into her jeans pockets. "It does."

"What happened with Paige? Is she moving out? I didn't like to ask."

"We—reconnected. We're figuring it out."

"After the storm?"

"After the campaign. So yes, after the storm."

"You bonded over Obama?"

"We realized what we had in common was—worth something.

We didn't want to let it go. But we're figuring it out. It was good to have space to myself. It's been a supercharged time."

"The storm?"

"No! The campaign. Why do you keep mentioning the storm?"

"It kind of redefined me, somehow. I feel changed. Or ready to change. I'm not sure which." She watched the workers stack water-soaked desktops at the elevator. "You know, it took me six hours to get here from his place this morning. But it's faster from Philadelphia, and if you take Amtrak instead of NJ Transit."

"And why wouldn't you?"

"Cost."

"Doesn't seem to be a concern to him, Mr. Oil Man."

"He's in natural gas, Jen."

"Same difference."

Amalia sighed. "He's a geologist."

"You're hard up for this guy."

"There was a fire. On the weekend. At his house. We stayed in a hotel." She looked up at Jen. "We hiked the Delaware Water Gap. And I met his brother."

"You have lost me. Drink that coffee before Betsy comes back, she's in no mood for moping."

Chapter 58

Mark stood on the front step of the house in Quakertown and extended a hand to the insurance company's engineer. "Mark Stone." He showed the woman around the house and took care to let her make notes without interruption. She measured the exposed beam, then went back to her car for a crowbar.

"Hold this." She handed him her clipboard and equipment and pulled off the metal framing behind the bookcase to expose the wood stud framing. "Went right through," she said. "The main beam had a slow burn all day," she said, "and it's borderline. The old books were like kindling, kept it going. I can calculate the depth that's still acceptable, but I can tell you from experience it doesn't look good. The vertical supports are shot. You shouldn't even be in here. You have somewhere else to stay?"

"I do."

"It's going to need to be rebuilt," she said, "at least this portion. You're the homeowner?"

"Yes."

"Might be more valuable as a tear-down at this point," she said. "For you or someone else to rebuild."

"But it doesn't look bad from the outside."

"It's the core," she said. "The core of the structure is shot. I'm not saying you couldn't save a good portion of it, but this all needs to come down. The foundations looked good to me. It depends what you want to do, what your long term plans are." She put down the crowbar and took her clipboard back from Mark and jotted a note. "I'll make a recommendation for a complete replacement."

"I don't want that."

"It's better for you. You don't have to. But the adjuster can process a higher claim amount for you if we do it this way."

"Is that legitimate?"

"Totally. The structure is shot. You can reuse the foundation. That's the story."

He nodded. "So stuff like the fact that the bathtub and cabinets are ok—that doesn't mean much?"

"Not if the structure is unsafe, no. And the cabinets had smoke damage. I can't imagine you'd want to go to the trouble to save the bathtub, but that's up to you."

"All right. Where do I sign?"

"Nothing to sign. I'll submit this report, and the adjuster will follow up. I need your current address—where you're staying."

He frowned. Oh god. He didn't remember their new address. "Give me a minute?" He called Amalia but it went to voice mail. "Ok. I'll give you my brother's address."

"Fine. It's easier if you're in state."

"Is it a problem if I'm out of state?"

"Not that I know of." She smiled. "Planning a trip?"

"Planning a move, more like it."

"Mr. Stone, I wish you luck." She shook his hand and left with her crowbar in one hand and clipboard and equipment cradled in the other arm.

He walked upstairs, uncertain of the stability of the structure around him, and began to move his things to the car.

"I'm arriving tomorrow," he said. "Wednesday. That's ok?"

"Ah, yes," Amalia said. "Why the rush?"

"My house was written off by the engineer, and is about to be condemned by the town. And the hotel is not the same without you."

"Oh, Mark. I'm sorry. Does the landlord know?"

He laughed, then stopped. "Didn't I tell you? I own it. I bought it with the money from my parents. And there's a lot of stuff. My parents' stuff."

"You're bringing your parents' stuff to my apartment? I don't think there's room. Mark, we need to talk about this." She paused for breath but he could hear panic in her voice. "Can you put your parents' stuff in storage? For a month or two? Until we decide what to do with it all?"

"I guess so."

"There's no room for the freezer," she said.

"Yes there is. In your living room. It's empty."

"Oh, Mark. No."

"And then there's the furniture. I have the bed sets from Tim's and my rooms. And the kitchen table and chairs, which are covered in soot."

"Uh huh." She took a breath. "It's just stuff," she said. "This stuff doesn't make us. Betsy and Max don't need this stuff to be good architects. They're still architects without it."

Chapter 59

Amalia stood in line with her third take-out coffee of the day and moved around the public school, in line to vote. PS 9 was a zoo, a polite zoo, but busy. She tried to recall the last time she'd voted in a US federal election. She'd been in Vancouver and had voted early, by mail. Her first time had been in Scranton, before architecture school in BC.

And now. She made her way into the building, did the soft shoe shuffle with the other Upper West Side voters. It wasn't her neighborhood anymore. She could have gone anywhere in the state, Governor Cuomo said they could move around because of the storm. Could have voted on 157th Street, or near work. So why had she come to this place? Nostalgia for Aunt Joan's?

An old man stood a few heads in front of her. His motions were slow, but the rest of the line moved at his pace. She noticed his hand shook on his cane with each step.

She checked in with a poll worker once inside and waited her turn. A sea of white voting boxes on blue metal frames sat perched on the old linoleum floor. The old man voted and turned around toward her; his cane dropped from his hand when he wiped his eyes.

"Sir! Are you ok?" She took a step out of line. "Do you need help?" She picked up his cane and put it in his hand. He grasped it, and her hand covered his.

"There's nothing you can do." He shook his head. "I meant to vote for Romney." A big tear escaped. "But I saw it wrong. I cast the vote and realized after. Obama."

"Oh. I'm sorry."

"What do you know. What are you, a Democrat? Look at all these people. Every one of them a Democrat." He waved his cane and lost his balance.

"Wait." She took a deep breath and he steadied himself on his cane.

"You're up, miss," the poll clerk said.

"Please let someone else go ahead. I'll be a minute." She squeezed his hand over the cane and took another deep breath. "You believe he was the right person for you to vote for?"

"I'm a lifelong Republican. I wouldn't have had it any other way."

She nodded and closed her eyes. "Would it help—if I did it for you?"

He shook his head. "You wouldn't."

"We need to vote our conscience." She took another deep breath. "Sir, have a good day." She turned and stood back in line, stared straight ahead, and did not watch him leave the building. She walked up to the white voting box and stood, legs wide between the metal frame. Another deep breath. And she voted.

Chapter 60

Mark was focused on outcome when he went to the seniors' center to vote. Surprised when he heard a woman call his name. It was the aide at the front desk. He recognized the woman from Tim's Quakertown high school, a guidance counselor who'd helped him with the transition. He forgot her name—

"Maisy," she said. "From the high school."

"Maisy." He nodded.

"This way, Mark." She pointed him past the front desk into the room set up with temporary polling booths.

He wondered about Maisy. She seemed to have two or three jobs at once, and this was a new one to him. She had a kind heart, and her support had meant a lot to Tim in the transition years, as he called them in his mind. He wished he could do something for her.

He waited his turn and when the poll clerk called him up, he went behind the blue curtains of the polling booth and looked down at his feet on the floral carpet. He shifted his posture, stood up straighter, and raised his hands over his head in a tall stretch over the top of the booth. He bent down to the voting tablet and made his electoral votes. He stood back, satisfied, and when he turned to exit the curtained poll, he felt his phone vibrate in his pocket.

Amalia. He took it out.

It's not too late! Vote Green!

It's too late,

he wrote back.

I voted for Obama.

You did not. Can't believe it.

Liked what Jen and friends were saying.

Calling you!

He walked past the front desk and waved goodbye to Maisy and his phone rang. He stepped outside past the thin line of voters that filtered in.

"I cannot believe you voted for Obama. I was sure you were going to go down the Romney path."

"Not Johnson?"

"No, I never felt it. I could tell you had doubts."

"Not doubts about him—doubts about the impact of the election."

"Listen, our office is a mess here, can I call you later, love?"

By eight, the polls had closed on the East Coast, and the center and West still cast votes for president, vice president, a few governors, attorneys-general, senators, school boards and referenda. It was a big day for the country, the day they saw how aligned they really were. He turned off the radio in the kitchen and went down to the basement, notepad and pen in hand. The smoke smell was less down there, easier to be there than upstairs.

He stood in front of the deep freeze in his basement, and considered the stability of the wall overhead. The trailer he'd rented in the afternoon had a wide opening, and the freezer should fit. He took out his dad's tape measure and jotted down the freezer's dimensions on the notepad he'd brought down. How big was Amalia's front door? And the narrow staircase? The angled door into her apartment? He'd eyeballed it when they brought the mattress in last week at under three feet, and he'd tested it with his arm length. It wasn't going to fit. He sat on the basement steps and thought for a moment, then went outside and drove the few blocks back to the seniors' center where he'd voted.

"Hi, Maisy."

"Voting's closed, Mark. Did you forget something?"

"No. I have a deep freezer. And a lot of good meat. I'm moving. Could you use it?"

Maisy's brow furrowed. "You'll need to ask the management company. They handle that kind of thing."

"I need to know now. I'm leaving in the morning."

"How much meat?"

"A freezer's worth. A family friend hunted it in New Hampshire. It's good, venison."

"There's no doubt these people could use it. I don't want to say no to you, but I can't say yes, either."

"Is it a little yes?"

She laughed. "I wish it could be." She looked away and her eyes unfocused for a moment. "It could be. I could take it. I bring food in for them every week. You know, for the ones who have no family. I cook it up in the back."

"Could you?"

"You'd have to get it here. I could park it in the back."

"You're perfect." He kissed her on the cheek. He drove back home and hummed to himself. He could leave the bedroom set. Maybe bring the kitchen table and chairs? He should go over it with Amalia. She'd care, or maybe she wouldn't. He wasn't sure.

Once home, he found the 2x6s they'd moved the freezer into the house on, then emptied the freezer and brought it up on the 2x6s out the basement doors. It was light in spite of its bulk. He could almost walk it there if he had a dolly, then laughed to himself at what a sight that would be. He moved the 2x6s to the back of the trailer and slid the freezer in, and then went back and piled the meat up onto the passenger seat and floor where it slid around in its packages.

So strange. He hoped no one stopped him. He started the car and then thought better of it, went back inside and searched for the rings. In the bottom of his bedroom closet, in a box. Pocketed the bunch of them; wasn't sure what do with which one, but at least he could give two of them to Tim.

Satisfied, he drove back to the seniors' center and found Maisy at the front desk, with the poll workers on their way out the door.

"Do they count the votes here or somewhere else?"

"They take them out. They're almost done, then you can move the freezer in through there."

"The meat's thawing in the front seat."

"Oh dear. Ok." She came out from behind the desk. "Bring it. You can move in while they move out."

He juggled with the lumber, freezer, meat, poll clerks and dismantled voting booths to get the assembly in place in the back of the facility where she showed him. They brought the meat into the freezer and he gave away a few packages to the poll workers, surprised and pleased, and it made him happy to share the food around. He thought of his mother, and the food she brought every year to the Pow Wow.

Amalia's mom's chicken tikka masala sat on the floor of the car. She'd packed it in a freezer bag with ice packs, and it would stay cold for a few more hours, but he didn't want to eat it without Amalia.

He drove to the trailer rental facility, dropped off the hitch in the overnight drop area, and went back to the hotel. He emptied the hotel room of his few belongings, checked out, and moved his book boxes and two suitcases from behind the reception desk to the rear and passenger seats of his car, then rested the frozen tikka masala on top. He blasted the radio to whatever came on, hit the highway for New York City, and conducted and hummed Vivaldi while he drove.

He felt lighter without the food and the furniture. A good move. Those people running the seniors' center could have hunted for their own fresh meat. "What a thought," he said aloud over the music. He shook his head. Why not? They should have fresh meat. They could grow vegetables, so why not provide for themselves entirely? It could be a work program for young people. He wondered what Amalia would make of the idea.

The drive was dark, and he tuned in and out of election results and music. He thought to call Amalia first, but he wanted to surprise her at how unburdened he was. She'd be pleased. She couldn't have wanted a deep freeze in her living room. Their living room.

He felt the arc of his transition: suburban to urban, inland to sea. It came to him in both the shift of biogeography outside the car, and the change in the air that came into the car. He took the Lincoln Tunnel in, open through the whole ordeal of the storm, he'd heard, one of the only island crossings to have been unaffected by the hurricane. He made it in two hours flat, and peeled off at the 157th Street exit. He pulled over and called her.

"I'm here," he said.

"I'm here," she said. "I'm out with Jen. Where are you exactly?"

"In Manhattan. Near the apartment. I'm off the highway."

"What?" He heard her cover the phone, muffled voices in the background. "You came early."

"I have a surprise."

"Ok!" More muffled voices. "Ah, I'm on the Upper West Side still. We had dinner down here. Can you wait about half an hour? Or come here? We're in a pub watching the election results come in."

"I'll wait," he said. "Is it ok?"

"It's great. I'm glad you're here. Meet you at the apartment in half an hour."

He drove down, parked in front and hoped a bus wouldn't come up behind him. He listened to the election results while he waited. Almost eleven. Still no call. It had gone back and forth all evening, had swung between Romney and Obama, and the fringes not mentioned even once on the radio. No surprise.

Chapter 61

"I'll be fine," Jen said. "It's slow getting back. The power's on. Go be with him. Go!" They hugged goodbye at the subway entrance and went their separate ways, uptown and downtown.

Amalia stood on the crowded evening train, Columbia University students on and off, intermingled with shift workers at the beginning and end of their hours. She jumped off at her stop, no their stop, she corrected, and ran to their apartment. By the time she reached him at his car, she was breathless and cold.

"Hi!"

He got out of the car and met her on the sidewalk with a kiss. "You didn't have to run. I'm fine."

"I didn't want to miss any more of the election results! How fast can we do this?" She opened the front door and propped it open with a book box from the passenger seat, and peeked toward Titian's curtained window. "We're on our own."

"Let's do it, then, as fast as we can."

She ran up the four flights and unlocked the front door, her first time back in the apartment in days. "Apartment! It's happening. Now." She turned on the radio to the election results, and ran back downstairs with the apartment door propped open. "Where's the freezer? I thought you rented a trailer."

"Surprise!" He stacked boxes on the sidewalk. "No freezer. No bed. No furniture."

"Wow. I mean, good, I guess. Are you ok with that?"

"Totally. Let's get this upstairs." He carried two boxes at a time in his longer arms, she one at a time, and they left her radio on while they hauled up and down. They were done by eleven. Exhausted.

"Leave the car where it is?"

"We might get a ticket."

"Fine. I'm too beat to figure it out."

She pulled out two bottles of beer from the fridge and opened them both, passed him one, still breathless. "We did it!" They clinked bottles and she closed and locked the door behind them, kicked off her shoes and lay flat on the living room floor, surrounded by boxes, bottle of beer next to her where she lay.

"Come in here." He looked out the window, and saw the moon come up before him, late; three quarters full. A welcome sight to him. He flicked on the light and closed the curtains, and raised the radio volume. They sat on the bed cross legged, giddy from the move and the election. "Listen," he said.

"Kiss me first," she said.

He kissed her. "I'm beat." Sipped his beer.

She smiled, took a swig and leaned on the other wall where the mattress met the corner, and listened to NPR make its call for Obama's win.

Chapter 62

Wednesday, November 7

Amalia was late.

"It's 9:55," Betsy said. "What did you do, sleep in?"

"I'm sorry." Amalia felt herself blush and she cast a sideways look at Jen whose head was bent over files.

"No time like the present to catch up," Betsy said. "Now. You have power?"

"Yes."

"Heat?"

"Yes."

"Hot water?"

Amalia nodded.

"And your train line is running?"

"Yes."

"So—tomorrow, no excuses for being an hour late."

"Yes. I'm sorry." Something was wrong. Amalia needed to be more in alignment with work; she wanted to be more in alignment with Mark. She felt more true to herself, though, and that gave her confidence.

"We're picking up the pieces on all the projects here," Betsy said. I'd like you to follow up with this list of consultants on the environmental center and condo, and also on the hotel. I've reached out to all the clients. Set up meetings for this Friday for all consultants on each project, separately."

"Ok."

"And Amalia. See how they're doing with their own storm recovery. Anyone not in a functional office since the hurricane can work here before and after the meeting on Friday."

"Where?" Amalia looked around the new, one-room office space.

"Conference table. Which should arrive with the second van load. Jen, have them put it in the middle of the space."

Jen looked up from filing. "Yes, Betsy." She smiled.

Amalia gave Jen a look. What was that?

"I'm going out for office supplies," Betsy said, and left Jen and Amalia alone in the new office, door ajar to the shared warehouse floor.

"She's pretty tightly wound today," Amalia said.

Jen shook her head. "You need to try harder, Amalia. She's not going to put up with this, you know. You were already on probation." She turned back to the files. "Are you still on probation?"

"I voted for Romney. I didn't tell you last night," Amalia said. She flipped open the project directories Betsy had left in her hand. She scanned each list. "Wait. Did she mean, set up separate meetings with each consultant? Or set up separate meetings on each project?" Jen's head was in the files. "Jen?"

Amalia bit her lip. Come on, it wasn't complicated. Some of the consultants were the same. She found a pad of paper and a pen and jotted a bubble diagram of the job relationships, and figured they could have three meetings, grouped to suit the different gatherings of consultants. Seemed logical.

"Are we using our cell phones?"

"Yes. No landlines hooked up yet."

Amalia called Sunil's cell phone first. Get the hardest one out of the way first. She needed to let him know about moving to his neighborhood. And about Mark.

He picked up on the first ring.

"Amalia! I recognized your number."

"Sunil. I've been meaning to call you. But now—"

"Listen. I've been thinking."

Oh no. No.

"I might have been a little hasty the other week. I had a lot on my mind."

She swallowed. "Sunil? I'm at work. I'm calling about a meeting."

"Oh." She heard his voice fall flat.

Darnit, she didn't have a way with words with this guy. "Can you come in on Friday to meet about the center and the condo? Two consecutive meetings."

"Who will be there?"

"Me, Jen, Betsy. Suky, maybe Simon from Atlantia if he's in town." The great reunion. It turned out she hadn't killed the deal with Atlantia Actuaris, after all. "Betsy also offered to have you use our new office that day if yours isn't operational. We relocated after the storm. We're in Chelsea now."

"Generous of her. I am not operational here," he said. "My office in Brooklyn is still out of power."

"How are your parents?"

"My dad's in hospital, he had a heart attack during the storm."

"Oh god, I'm sorry."

"My mom's ok. Their house is fine."

"I wish your dad well, ok?" The next call was easier. "I'll be there," Suky said. "Email me a confirmation."

"Will do."

"Is Jen going to be there?"

"Um, yes."

"Did she tell you what she did?"

"What?" Amalia frowned. Maybe it wasn't the easier call.

Amalia turned to Jen after they hung up. "What did you do?"

"Nothing."

"Did you hurt her feelings?"

Jen shook her head. "I broke up with her because she said she was going to vote for Romney."

"Jen!" Amalia shook her head. "I can't believe you would do something so shallow."

"Look at you, Miss-Embrace-Everybody. You don't have it all figured out. Some of us don't compromise."

"I never—" Amalia stepped back. "Going for a walk." She picked up her backpack and jacket and headed for the door.

Outside, she remembered Mark's hotel a block away. His old hotel. She found her way through the weave of fresh floral displays on the sidewalk. The blooms, still varied in their late fall color, lifted her mood.

She thought about the craziness of the past few days, and on a whim pulled out the phone number of the theater director in Scranton that Candace had passed along. Nothing to lose. Everything to gain. She already had her sketches scanned from when she'd tried to set up an Etsy shop, a misguided effort due to her underestimate of how much work would be involved. She could email him her drawings today.

He answered on the fifth ring, and she imagined him in the passages behind the stage, or in one of the dressing rooms.

"This is Amalia Erenwine, friend of Candace—" She'd never learned Candace's last name. "Candace suggested I speak with you about set design."

"Good. The proposals are due this Friday at four. Did she give you the renovation details?"

"No, I'm sorry? I was calling about the stage sets—the woodwork? The drapery?"

"Yes, good. We have a Request for Proposals out for an architect for the theater renovation."

"I see. My firm would be happy to submit a proposal," she said, and hoped it was true. "Could you please email me the RFP?" She spelled out her work email address.

"Yes. We have several firms submitting. But we always like a personal connection. Candace mentioned you are her sister-in-law."

"Ah. We would be pleased to submit. Friday at four."

"Nothing digital, though," he said. "I'm afraid I'm very old fashioned. Paper only."

She took a breath, and looked over some Scotch thistles in front of one of the shops. "We can do it," she said. "We'll do it." She walked back past the thistles to the roses, and inhaled red, orange and white, soft scents. They made her chest expand. Asked their price; more than she wanted to spend out of her own pocket. She put them back and snapped a picture with her phone instead, and smiled on her way out of the shop.

What had she got herself into? Mark's old hotel was up and across the street, and she had a moment of nostalgia for what was only a week ago. She wound back to the office and wondered if Mark was in one of the nearby coffee shops. Later. Connect later.

She buzzed downstairs for Jen to let her back up, and the intercom released with a click. Up the new elevator, she got off at the fifth floor and turned left into the new office. "Jen," she said. "I have something. A job."

"You're leaving?"

"No." She shook her head. "A job for the firm. How do I tell Betsy and Max?"

"She'll be open to it. We were rolling around ideas for new projects this morning."

"You were?"

"She's putting me in charge of a small one. With her oversight."

"Oh." They had a secret relationship without her? "The RFP is due Friday, by mail, to Scranton."

"By courier?"

"I guess. So it could go out overnight tomorrow."

"One day for the RFP—and you haven't gone over it with Betsy or Max."

"Betsy. Max doesn't seem to be present in any decisions this week."

"It's a renovation of a big old theater in Scranton. They want to redo the mess of corridors in the back. Maybe more."

"Oh. Congratulations. How did you find it?"

"No congratulations. We don't have the job. I don't even know how to present it, or get the proposal ready by tomorrow."

"It's not right." Jen went to the window. "Something's wrong with this. I feel like we have our priorities backwards."

"How so? You think we should be back on the environmental center and the condo uptown? Don't we still need to get back in touch with those clients?"

"No—shouldn't we be doing something like, say, I don't know, providing housing for people in Red Hook? Or on Staten Island? They got wiped out after the hurricane. We got off so lightly by comparison. And there's the water thing, too."

"What do you mean? What water thing?"

"How come nobody's talking about the water's edge?"

"I'm sure they are."

"No, what I'm hearing is they want to rebuild at the water's edge."

"Oh. That would be bad. I'm sure they're not."

"Amalia, just because to you and me it makes no sense, doesn't mean it's not happening. People love their waterfront communities. They're invested in them. And they're rebuilding them."

"Already?"

"Already talking about it. And the government should be talking about buying up the land."

"You think people would go for that?"

"Maybe, maybe not. The government could clear the area through the process of eminent domain. Good for the collective, and all."

"I don't think it would fly. It would be like a mandatory draft. But for land—" Amalia's thoughts flew to Mildred's meeting, to

Sunny and Amreeta and the gas mask. "So—you think we should say something about it?"

"I don't know. It seems like architects should be more—activist-like. More proactive. Less passive. Less like sheep following developers and city planners. More assertive."

"Architects are assertive."

"Architects. No. Architects are assertive of ego—not of common need."

"I don't think that's true."

"You might not be like that," Jen said. "But others are. You see the good in everyone."

"No I don't."

"It's not a bad thing. It's not—realistic."

"I see the bad, I do. We went over all this with the gas industry talk."

"Which is still hanging, by the way."

"Meaning?"

"Meaning, have you changed your tune?"

"No, why would I? I still think they have destructive practices."

"Amalia. You're in bed with the other side."

She shook her head. "It's not like that. He quit."

"You were sleeping together before he quit. And what's he going to do, go and work for an environmental nonprofit? I don't think so."

"No, he wants to consult to the industry."

"So he's staying—in the industry. And I'm asking, how do you feel about it?"

"I thought we were talking about the water's edge. And rebuilding."

"It's all tied together, Amalia. Building, rebuilding, powering—it's the same. So tell me. How do you feel about Mark continuing to work in the gas industry? In the fracking industry?"

"I—" Amalia's stomach did a flip. "Can we get back to the proposal at hand?"

Jen shook her head. "You're punting," she said.

Amalia and Jen unpacked boxes for an hour, turned music on over the computer speakers, watched the sky turn to bright and even white cloud above the buildings. Nor'easter on the way. She and Mark would be home together before the next storm hit.

"So what does happen at Betsy's house? Who takes care of the kids?"

"I don't think her husband is working now," Amalia said. "Didn't she join Max in the last couple of years?"

"No, she used to work for him in the same firm before kids and then he went out on his own started this up," Jen said.

"Without her."

"I don't know."

"Didn't you stay at their house once?"

"It was very happy."

"And? Who was with the kids?"

"Ben was taking the kids to school and picking them up and buying water filters."

"Ah-ha."

"Ah-ha nothing. I'm sure they have it all figured out," Amalia said.

"You mean, you hope they do, because if they do, you might."

Amalia looked at the blank white sky outside, above the old warehouse buildings across the street, and her eyes went fuzzy. Nice. Pre-storm softness.

"She wants me to stay late tonight."

"And you said—"

"I said yes, of course. But this would've been our first proper dinner at home together," Amalia said. "I was hoping to cook."

"What were you planning to make?"

"I have no idea. What does one make for one's first shacking up dinner?"

"I don't know, chocolate dipped strawberries?"

"Betsy said it's okay if he comes over here."

"Romantic," Jen said. "I'll be finding somewhere else to spend the evening, thank you."

"You're not going to help me with this thing?"

"I'll stay for a while. I have to study tonight." Jen picked up the paper copy of the RFP and spread out the pages. "Let's wire this thing before Betsy calls back."

"When's your next exam?"

"In a week. Paige thinks I should push through them. And she's right. So I rescheduled so I can get through faster."

"I don't know. I don't want to fail any of the sections."

"Everybody fails sections."

"No, they don't. Nadel—my ex—he didn't."

"Nadel is Mr. Perfect, then, isn't he."

"No, he was focused. I'm not going to do it until I can get through them all on the first try. I'll—study more."

"All right, you heard it here. Ms. Amalia Erenwine on the night of her shacking up dinner announces she will pass all Architecture Registration Exam sections on the first try. Why don't you throw in the green building certification exam while you're at it?"

"I might."

"And what is Mark going to do while you do all of this, now he's unemployed?"

"He's not unemployed. He is starting a new company."

"Whatever. Company, unemployed. He has time on his hands. My point is, you're busy. Forget this theater job. It's out-of-state on top of it all. Are you going to make site visits to Pennsylvania?" Jen looked away.

"I voted for Romney."

"What?"

"I voted my conscience. There was an old man in line ahead of me and he wanted to vote for Romney, but he voted for Obama by accident."

"And you believed him."

"What?"

"How do you know he was telling the truth?"

"He had tears in his eyes."

"Tears can be faked."

"For a vote?"

"I'm just saying."

"You are too much." Amalia wadded up the paper bag from her lunches and threw it at Jen's head.

"All right." Jen dodged the ball of paper. "If we're getting all confessy here, I should tell you what I did. I nominated a new candidate before the election. I wrote it in."

"So who did you vote for?"

"Obama, of course."

"Ok, so who did you nominate?"

"The other Obama: Michelle."

Chapter 63

Mark's doodling took him deeper into his center, far from the coffee shop environs where he sat. He was surprised by the intrusion of the server. "Working on something interesting?" She smiled down at Mark. He covered his brow with his palm extended to shield his work. Needed to propel the work forward. "What are you doing?"

"I'm starting a company. This is for the website." He shook his head and then sat back, took a sip of the coffee she'd put in front of him. "Excuse me. I need to focus."

She nodded and went to another table. Noticed the long curl of her red hair that escaped from the elastic thing on the top of her head. It must have a name. Amalia would know what it was called. It reminded him of Anwen, and of Amalia, in the same moment.

WALES.

He wrote it in big letters on the top of the page, above his name. He did feel a resonance with the country, even if he hadn't got off to the best start with its womenfolk. He wondered how Simon made out over there, then hoped Simon had made out with care and respect, and not with Anwen. Her words hung in the periphery: if you're going to come over here and lead us on, you owe us something in return. He hadn't responded to her email, didn't know what to say. He was sorry. Maybe that was what he ought to say.

He tried to draft a brief message to her in his sketchbook, which resulted in a doodle rather than a coherent sentence. Decided to go with the doodle; a figure eight on the left side of the page next to *WALES*. He added,

Papua New Guinea?

at the bottom, and then put the pen down.

Who was it? He presumed it was the same individual who had left the emails, texts and voice mail messages. So far, he'd decided to ignore it as a prank. After all, his name and contact information were public, and he was in a hot-seat job. But with Amalia and him so—connected at the hip—it seemed responsible to get clear on it all, to be rid of the pest.

Maybe it was a figment of his imagination. He wrote,

unknown

on the center of the next page. Someone after the company? After the infrastructure? After the country? No. Why would they target him for that, so exclusively, and so specifically? Turned to another page. Who else had anything on him, any concern at all? Helene came to mind. Was she missing him? Did she want something? Was she—pregnant? Oh, god. No, she would have just told him.

Thought about the women in his life. There was Mary from the site. Amalia had thought Mary was crushing on him, but he doubted it. Still, he turned to a new page and wrote,

Mary

at its center. What about her? She was more sibling-like than anything, even though he didn't know her well. Sweet. Was she looking out for him, warning him?

Warning him about what? He'd decided not to confront Simon about the messages, but he was an obvious source of it all. Did Simon question Mark on some level? Was he suspicious about Anwen? And—Mark was still unsure—had Simon seen the message from Amalia, in the site trailer in Wales? He couldn't recall if he'd closed out of it or not.

This was all easier with Amalia, and it was she who he wanted to keep in his focus, not Anwen. In the very middle of the page, in large letters, he wrote,

AMALIA

and drew a large circle around her name.

Went back to the note for Anwen, half drafted in his sketchbook.

I am truly sorry to have misled you. I meant no harm. You are a vivacious woman and I am sure you will match up with someone who will be the right fit for you.

It wasn't right, but it would do. He typed it on his laptop and sent it to her. Mark waved for the red-tressed server. "I'll take my food to go when it's ready," he said, and when it was, he left and walked toward the Hudson River.

The clerk at his old hotel had said there was park access over there, but he was darned if he could see how, through the solid blocks of brick apartment buildings. The river was somewhere ahead. After a few streets of twists and turns, he noticed a heavy black trestle bridge that crossed above the street. Cars and trucks passed below. A well-dressed couple emerged from a metal staircase at the bottom of it; intrigued, he went up the way they'd come down.

He stood on the deck of the trestle bridge and looked up and down its length, shocked at the artistic play of new construction and vegetation along its length. It looked like a playground. A grown-up playground. Tourists strolled along the wood deck and stopped for photos. He didn't know which way to go, both directions offered more than he could digest. He turned left, and followed the bright white spot of sun that shone through cloud.

Was this the park the hotel guy had told him about? He saw a man squat at the garden bed on the side, and saw he wore an official-looking hooded sweatshirt over another long-sleeved hoodie. "Are you—do you—?" He stopped, and the man looked up.

His bearded face was round, and dark eyes peered out from behind pale skin hidden by his darker facial hair. "Hi!" The man sat back on his heels and wiped his forehead with his arm, which left a streak of dirt across his face. "Can I help you?"

"Where am I exactly?"

"Twenty-fourth. The next staircase is there." He pointed. "Unfortunately, the elevators still aren't working since the hurricane. Power should be back soon, I hope."

"Too bad."

"Our utilities are all underground." A man approached on a three-wheeled bicycle with a Parks Department logo on a rear container. He turned and watched the person cycle away and read *Highline* something on the back of the bike.

He walked farther until he came to a covered area with chairs and he sat down and ate his lunch, watched people walk by, backlit by the brightness of the cloudy sky. When he was done, he bundled his trash and pulled out his sketchbook, and began, once again, to write.

The linear park reminded him of an elevated train line. Might it have been that? An inhabited, occupied rail line. Occupied. He rolled the word around on his tongue. Occupy.

Occupy Sandy,

he wrote, and thought of Mildred's last email about the activist group that formed after the hurricane. No, he crossed out his words. The group didn't have anything to do with him. If Occupy Wall Street had nothing to do with him, why would Occupy Sandy? They were protesters, weren't they? Protesting what...the weather? Climate change? Power generation? The Keystone XL Pipeline? He wrote,

Keystone XL

on the paper. Ok, sort of more to do with him.

He frowned at what he'd written and scribbled out, though, and circled the crossed out *Occupy Sandy*. Was there something there? Maybe he could ask Jen, or her neighbors—they seemed like they might be up on all that. If he asked Mildred she'd get too excited. Not going to ask Amalia. Too hot.

No. Stop. If there was something too hot to discuss with Amalia, then that was a sign he should talk to her about it. He took a deep breath through his nose and held it in his lungs, then let it all out through the mouth.

What did he want? If he didn't look through anyone else's lens. No more corporate side-taking. Only him, Mark. He sat back, tapped the pen on the page, then shoved everything into his bag, closed it up, and continued to walk south. When he emerged from the covered walkway to the open trestle, he felt the snowflakes on his cheeks before he saw them, and looked up to the white sky.

Mark walked until he was slowed by sleet in his face. He buzzed the intercom at Amalia's office. "It's me, can I come up? I'm freezing." He stomped his feet and gave a last look at the slick wet street before he went inside and up to the fifth floor.

"Mark? We couldn't make out who it was." Amalia pulled his icy hood off his head and unzipped the coat, pulled up to his nose.

"It's turning to snow now," he said. "It's getting pretty."

"Till the dogs come out." Jen said.

"Yuck." He unwrapped the scarf from his neck. "How's it going here?"

"Good, we're well into this proposal. But Mark, I have to work late, I'm sorry. You can stay."

"Good job prospect here," Jen said. "I hope we get this."

"What is it?" Mark walked over to the conference table.

"No! You're still dripping. Stand there." Amalia pointed to the middle of the room. "It's the theater in Scranton, Pennsylvania, the one Candace works at. Turns out it's a huge job."

"Oh good. We need to find out about that for her, don't we. The placenta thing." He rubbed his hands together and warmed his nose.

"What placenta thing?" Jen looked up at him, then at Amalia.

"We said we'd look into whether the VOCs in the paint cross the placenta," Mark said.

"You sound like you know about babies," Jen said, and looked back and forth between the two.

He looked out the window from the center of the room. "How about I go dry myself off with paper towels in the bathroom? I'll work here while you plug on with your deadline." He backed out of the office and found the bathroom down the hall, dried himself off as best he could with the paper hand towels. Did he know about babies? Not really, but he was about to be an uncle, in—in how long? Had they even asked when Candace was due? And what about that—were they going to get married? Was he supposed to do something—pay for their wedding?

He went back to the office and took in Amalia's absorption in her work, and Jen's out-loud mutters over something on the computer screen. Women at work. Didn't want to interrupt. He took out his sketchbook and pen—the green one—and sat on the floor by the window. With no chairs, the place had a sense of motion, fluid. Like a train station.

He was soon absorbed in work of his own, an intricate doodle that appeared to him to be in a form somewhat like a Maori warrior tattoo, but more Celtic. Kind of Pacific Northwest. It wasn't bad. He flipped the page to a blank sheet. Now—needed to turn it into a logo. No. What he needed was to dig out his old contacts list and make some cold calls. Not to doodle. He continued to swirl the pen, and pulled out the blue one too, so the green and blue ink mixed on the page in an intricate twist of lines that meant little, but that pleased him.

He followed the ruled lines of the page with his pen, and ended in an arrowhead that pointed to the next page, and the next. He stared at the blank sheet and wrote a large question mark in the center of it, then in lines that radiated from the center, he drew empty bubbles. He was without organized thought. For the first time in a long time. He looked up over his head and leaned back on the wall so his sight lined up with the sky outside, and he felt the whiteness of snow fall as if it were on his own face, without glass between him and what existed outside.

He looked back down at his sketchbook. *Anwen,* he'd written before. Did she want to hit him up for jobs, for her men, as she called them? Worse—had he forgotten what had happened that night, and was she—no. Maybe there was a simpler explanation. She could be on the side of a competitor.

He felt a jitter inside, and wrote,

Samantha.

But the voice had been a man's. No matter. Maybe she was working with someone. Back to George. What could George want? Mark had been so tired that night at the hotel, when he'd thought George was the source. They'd both been suspicious of Mark. He thought back to his recent interactions in PR. There was the woman at Mildred's meeting. The one with the sister in the Northern Tier, with the headaches.

His silence was interrupted by the buzzer, and he jumped up to answer it. Could not locate the intercom, sat back down. Jen let the caller up, and a couple of minutes later two delivery men arrived with six heavy desk surfaces for Amalia's new office.

"We're behind," the one man said. "Jammed out there with the storm."

"It's ok," Amalia said. "We're working late." She signed for the delivery and once she'd closed the door behind the gentlemen, she stretched from side to side. "I wish we had the chairs already. I'm getting stiff working like this."

"I need to get going. I have a few hours of studying ahead of me tonight. You ok finishing up?"

"I will be. Maybe Mark can help?"

"If I can." How he would help, he had no idea. But he nodded, and hoped he came across as agreeable.

Jen got up and stretched. "All right, you love birds," she said. "Wish me luck."

"You'll do great. You have a week left to study."

"I meant, navigating my way home in this snowstorm. And

you shouldn't stay late, either, proposal or no. Betsy will understand. You don't want to get stuck."

"Fine, fine. Thank you. We'll be fine." Amalia smiled, and Mark wondered if she was trying to get rid of Jen. He couldn't figure them out. On again off again friends. Still, he liked Jen, and he'd hoped to ask her about the anarchic Occupy movements. But when? This might be his best chance.

"Jen. I want to ask you something," he said. Didn't matter what Amalia thought.

"Mmm hmm?" She wrapped her scarf around her neck, half focused on him, half focused on the door.

"What do you think of the Occupy Sandy movement?

"Really?" Jen pushed the scarf from her mouth. "I can tell you, if I wasn't here, I'd be there."

"The Reverend Mildred's been emailing," Mark said. "I was curious."

"I don't know anything about a Reverend Mildred. But Occupy Sandy's doing amazing work that nobody else is," Jen said. "Do you know they started an online wedding registry so people can donate goods no matter where they are?"

"I saw that," he said. "So you think it's a legitimate political movement?"

"I don't think the Occupy movement has a political center," she said. "It's more free-form. Heart-centered."

"No, I don't think that's true," Amalia said. "They're very anti-capitalist. Doesn't that count as a political stance?"

"I don't see how you can be anti-capitalist in this day and age," Mark said. "Not in this country."

"Maybe not in any country," Amalia said. "But maybe it's not a movement about capitalism. Maybe it's a movement about something else. Like being earth-centered."

"There isn't a 'them,'" Jen said. "It's a bunch of people all around the continent—and farther—who work from a different value set. Polarizing it into capitalist versus anti-capitalist misses the beat. It's not what it's about. At least not the way I see it."

"Maybe you're right," Amalia said. "Still, I don't see how we can support what they do when we're here working late on a deadline for a proposal to design a bourgeois theater complex in another state."

"We can support," Jen said. "We can send them stuff from our bourgeois bank accounts through the wedding registries. It's not for the Occupiers. It's for the residents of the communities. The Occupiers are organizing the flow of goods."

"The flow of goods. And services," Mark said. "Capitalist."

"All right, maybe, but it's small scale. Micro-capitalism.

"Is it micro-capitalism if it's using Amazon and UPS?"

"Whatever. I have to get going so I can study. Make a donation online. God knows people could use it. Ok kids, I have to go." Jen ducked out to the elevator and closed the door behind her.

He sank deeper into a new doodle, and this one incorporated what began to look like a map, a coastline, a river—he wasn't sure. It began to resemble one of the treasure maps he and his brother had made as kids. Looked up at Amalia, who was again deep in her work.

What had happened to those maps, all those years ago? Someone had kept them, or tossed them, but not him. Perhaps his mom, keeper of the treasure. He continued to doodle, and the line took a swerve around the bottom of the page and up again, and connected at the top. It looked sort of continental.

"Did you ever get that email from Mildred? The one about the war between Canada and the States?"

"Maybe. I have so many messages waiting for me since before the storm—I haven't got to them yet."

He wrote,

War, Canada, US

on the side of the doodle. He frowned, and flipped back to the page with the question mark in the middle of it. He scribbled out the mark and wrote,

Resources

at the center, then stared at it, wondered what to write next. Crossed it out, and wrote,

Water.

No. Scribbled it out and tried,

Energy.

He started a fresh page and traced the pale blue lines, then crossed them to form a grid, then filled the boxes in with littler lines, and continued to fill in the space like a Landsat map over farmland. Halfway through, he stopped and turned, pulled himself up on the windowsill, and looked out. It was getting stronger out there. "Do you need me to help?"

"I don't know what I'd get you to do. Unless you'd like to resize and crop images—"

"I'm good at that. At least, I could be." He walked to where she stood at the computer by the window. Amalia had a photo of a large building complex up on the screen. "Wow, you guys did that?"

"Max did it. Here—you set up at this computer next to me and crop the images in this file to match this template," she said. "I don't know why they didn't have this done already."

"Maybe they never needed them before."

"I guess. I'm not clear on how they used to work, he and Betsy. He had a firm and then she joined him, but they had worked together at a bigger firm before she had kids."

"They're partners?"

"Business partners. She's married to Ben."

He clicked through images Amalia had set him up with, at the computer next to hers. "I was thinking about marriage, actually," he said, then stopped. "Came out wrong. I was thinking about Tim and Candace. Getting married." He twisted his mouth, hoped she wasn't looking at him, and stole a glance up—and she did, indeed, stare at him. "Them getting married. I wonder if Mildred would do it. Marry them."

"Maybe." She looked away.

He worked on a few images, and saved them to the server location she'd shown him. He felt flushed. "This is all for the Pennsylvania job?"

She worked fast; he wasn't used to her focus. He wondered how they'd manage to find time and space for their thoughts, in such a small apartment. The office was bigger, by a hair—but—

"I'm done," she said. "I can finish the ones you haven't done yet." She came over to his computer and put her hand on his lower back. "Thanks," she said, and kissed him on the cheek.

"Are you allowed to do that?"

"What, kiss you on the cheek?"

"In your office."

"Who's here to see?"

"I don't know—them?" He waved toward the window and to the lit studios across the street, at eye level with them, where curtains billowed from open windows to the snowstorm outside.

"It's New York. People don't care. They avert their eyes. Or they look. Either way, it doesn't matter."

"You're so private," he said.

"Around other people. Not—I'm not worried about the people ogling us from the other side of the street. Because you know what? They aren't ogling us."

"I can't believe I live here." He closed the last of the images on the screen. "Amongst the oglers."

"No oglers, Mark Stone." She smiled and went back to her computer. "I'll call Betsy and let her know I'm done, then we can go out and celebrate your arrival."

Chapter 64

Amalia stood in the elevator and wrapped her scarf over her head and around her neck, and tucked the ends into her coat. "At least I'll be warm. I hope the buses are still running."

"Do they ever shut down?"

"During the hurricane they did. I don't know about tonight."

"Hard to believe we were in the middle of a hurricane what—a week ago?"

"Week and a half." She stomped her feet to get warm. "Remember what the guy on the bridge said about the hurricane? And climate change? Fossil fuels?"

"Amalia—citizen science is not necessarily good science."

"Ok." There would be another opportunity. "We're resilient New Yorkers," she said, and linked her arm with his on the way out of the elevator. "We'll brave the weather. We'll get home."

"I don't think I'm a New Yorker yet," he said. "Isn't there some sort of test I have to pass first?"

She opened the office door to the snowy bluster outside, "Welcome home, Mark." She pulled the scarf over her breath. "Let's get the subway, might be less windy down there." They walked fast to the 1/9 line, and walked with care down the slick steps to the train level.

"I need a new card," he said.

"You should get one, get a monthly pass."

"I will." He purchased a monthly pass from the machine and held it up. "Ok, now I'm a New Yorker." They went through the turnstile and huddled with other cold commuters who waited for the train that did not appear to be delayed. "Amazing," he said. "I would have expected it to be backed up down here."

They squeezed onto the next train, standing room only for the moment, and Amalia held onto the lapels of his jacket while he held onto the strap over her head. "Hey, this is our first commute home together!"

"You are correct." He kissed the top of her head.

"We're straphangers. That's what we're called. Straphangers. Commuters who hang onto the subway straps." She pointed to his handhold.

"You're hanging onto me, so you're a coat hanger."

"Ha, ha, very funny." She rested her head on his chest, felt for warmth through the wet fabric of his coat.

"I've gone through every lead I can think of," Mark said.

"I thought you said you weren't concerned. That PR wasn't concerned."

"I don't want it to hang over us. There's more for us—and I don't want this in the way."

"Things change. Maybe now you're not with Atlantia, they'll let up on you." She pressed her cheek into his cool chest. "We'll need to warm up when we get in," she said.

"I thought about dinner. Your mom's chicken is in the freezer."

"Ah! Of course. We can make rice and peas with it." She looked up.

"That would be great. And I picked up a little something on my walk," he said. "A small contribution to dinner. What are you smiling about, smiley?"

"Nothing. I can't stop." Her tummy leapt when she said it.

"It's ok, I know. Me too."

They stood all the way back uptown, silent and bright,

bumped by commuters on and off the train. When they emerged from the station they were enveloped in whiteness, tinged with the orange of the city's sodium lights that beamed down through the snow.

"We got here before the dogs did!" He extended his arms to the flattened landscape, featureless except for lampposts and the suggestion of building façades set back from the street.

They stopped across the street from their apartment building. "Did you move your car last night?"

"No, I fell asleep. Oh no."

"It's not there."

They looked at each other and she laughed. "Holy cow! Your first day in the city you got towed. I can't believe we didn't even notice it was missing this morning."

"Maybe it wasn't." He shook his head. "I needed to get rid of that thing. It wasn't me."

"I hate to break it to you, but it's sitting in a pound now waiting for you to pick it up."

"How do you get a car out of the pound?"

"I can guarantee you this is not the night to pick it up." She pulled him by the hand across the street and stopped in the middle of Amsterdam Avenue. "This is beautiful." She turned her face to the sky.

"I don't even remember if it was here this morning. I'll need to get it back before we go to New Hampshire this weekend." Mark watched, turned his gaze between the apartment building and the cemetery, then back to her. "This is amazing. You can't even see the curbs."

"The snowplows must've been by earlier. I can feel the road down there beneath the snow." She checked the mailbox and they went upstairs to the fourth floor. "I never got the keys made for you. I'm sorry."

"No problem. Tomorrow. Upstairs." They peeled off their cold layers stiff with ice and snow and hung the range of wet garments around the bathroom.

"It's so hot in here." Amalia said, and opened the windows while Mark bent in front of the oven to turn it on for the chicken.

He opened the air vent next to the kitchen counter. "About to get hotter. There an exhaust fan here?" He walked into the bedroom and opened one of the windows. "We need to ventilate the gas." The sound of a radio in the distance streamed in, staccato of classical music across silence of the snow.

"No, this window is the ventilation."

"Is that legal, I mean to code, to not have a fan for a gas stove?"

"I don't know. Maybe because it's an old building it got grandfathered in."

"They don't teach you in school?"

"They don't teach you New York City building code in Vancouver, no."

"Got it. Isn't it kind of universal, though?"

"There is an international code, but New York City has its own, too." She rinsed the rice in the sink while she spoke. "Did they teach you regulations in grad school?"

"What, geology regulations? States of matter, properties of geophysics?"

"I don't know. How did you learn what guidelines govern the natural gas industry?"

"On the job."

"Same here."

He put the chicken in the oven. "This is going to take a while, from frozen." He padded in his socks to his bag and pulled out a long paper bag. "The treat." He slid a bottle of wine out of the sleeve. "I figured, a nice bottle of wine."

"Perfect." She kissed him and she took the bottle. "It would be nice to have something other than the tin mugs for it."

"Ah." He turned to his bag. "The second part of the surprise." He pulled out a white tissue-wrapped package and held it out.

"No. You bought wine glasses? You need to let me buy something." She took the package and unwrapped it. "These are gorgeous, Mark." The glass was fine, flecked with colored fragments suspended in the thicker rim of the glass. "I've never seen anything like this." She set the two wine glasses on the counter top and watched him pull a new corkscrew from his bag. "You thought of everything." She poured the rice and peas into the saucepan while he uncorked the wine.

She rinsed the new goblets in the sink and he poured, they clinked, he backed up to the bedroom and he pulled her along.

"My mind is a blank and this snowstorm has soothed my soul. I want to lie with you in our warm bed."

She smiled. "You are a romantic." She looked over her shoulder at the pot on its medium heat. "We could lower the heat on the saucepan, I guess."

"That's the spirit."

She went back into the kitchen and fiddled with the stove. "How are we going to take this out? We don't have oven mitts." She brought her glass of wine back to the bedroom. "The music's loud through the bedroom windows."

"We could use a towel. For the chicken." They clinked glasses. "I would like to propose a toast," he said, and held his glass up to hers. "I would like to propose we get married, when my brother and Candace do, and we move ahead with all the love in our hearts we feel is there, fully expressed, together."

She sat up on the edge of the bed, and held her glass by the stem. Oh holy mother of god. "Mark." He'd proposed to her and she was unprepared. She felt calm, and a little ripple of butterflies in her belly was all that put her on guard. She took a deep breath and the butterflies leapt up to her throat.

"It's soon, I know."

"It's not that."

"I should have given you some indication—"

"No."

"I didn't know it was going to come out like that. I mean, I did, but I didn't think it through."

"So you don't want to get married?" Now the butterflies flittered.

"I want to get married. To you. With you. More than anything." He held his glass in midair, and she wondered if the toast was complete, or if there was more.

"But—now?"

He sat back, and looked like he might spill the wine on Great Aunt Joan's old quilt, but he righted the glass.

"We are on our own time," she said. We're not on anybody else's time. I love you, Mark," she said. "You excite me, and you perplex me, and—I can see us spending the rest of our lives together."

"But—"

"But nothing. I'm not saying yes or no." She stopped and took a deep breath, and looked away for a moment to the silk sari curtains that blew in and out over the hot radiator air. "I'm feeling yes. Mark, I'm feeling a yes."

He sat forward on the bed, the wine glass in his hand. "And?"

"It's not a yes for this moment—I don't want to get married because your brother is." She put her glass down in her lap. "What I mean is, we need to talk about stuff before we get married." The music from outside shifted, her awareness of it peripheral, but it soothed her.

"Did you know before I asked you?"

She looked up at the paper lantern that now hung from the center of the ceiling—the one he'd bought for her after their dinner out—and shook her head. "No. But I knew I wanted to live with you."

He took her glass after the toast and put them both on the floor, then pulled her into a brief kiss and a long hug. The radio announcer's voice outside gave way to piano music, then a woman's voice carried through the snow and into the room in song.

"We're being serenaded," she said.

"Do you know what that is? He sat away from her and listened.

"I know it—what is it?"

"My mother's favorite piece."

"Which was what?"

"The Ave Maria. Schubert. She played it whenever she was sad, or happy, or whatever. It was like her anthem. You'd have thought it had been written for her."

"I guess she would be either happy or sad for us now, then." Amalia lay back and listened to the song come in with the snow from beyond the curtains.

Chapter 65

Thursday, November 8

"Stand clear of the closing doors, please," said the recorded voice over the subway's public address system. Mark took the train downtown, a slushy trip, but manageable in spite of the storm. Parked himself at Moda, the only open café he knew of near Amalia's new office, a narrow slot on West 27th populated with Fashion Institute students.

Opened his laptop to the image he'd worked on the day before, a picture of a woman in a cape who swooped down from the sky with a baby and a fishing rod. Across the sky were the airplane cloud letters

S y b i l i s h e r a

Sybilishera is here!

Below the image was a website address and an international phone number. The woman's cape swooped up behind her, framed by a tall tree on the right and a cluster of buildings on the left, and beneath her wove a river and a roadway, entwined with a bridge.

"What've you got there?"

He was startled at Amalia's voice. "Hi!" He turned the screen to her. "What do you think?"

"I have no idea what this is."

"I made it."

"What do you mean?" She unwound the scarf from around her head and neck and draped it with her coat on the back of the empty chair opposite him. "You drew it?" She peered at the pencil sketch, scanned to the computer. "Kind of looks like me," she said.

"I had to model it on someone. I'm not so good to be able to draw from memory."

"What's with the fishing rod?"

"Feed the masses—"

"And the baby?"

"—while nurturing?"

"And the international phone number?"

"I registered it. It's the number for my new business."

"All right. And the banner? This is her name? I don't even know how to pronounce it."

"It's an idea." He turned the screen back to face him. "I'm playing with doodles."

"And what about the energy protocol idea?"

"Maybe she can be the carrier of it—the messenger."

"I thought you were thinking of something more United Nations–like."

"I don't know how to do that. I know how to do this."

"Interesting." She sat down. "Did you get the car back?"

"I did. Took all morning to track it down, but it's parked in a lot near the apartment now."

She widened her eyes then went back to the counter to order. "Did you eat already?"

"I did. But coffee sounds good." He looked up at the red-tressed woman behind the counter and smiled. "Like this?" He turned the screen to face her from across the narrow space.

"Wow, it's kind of—she looks like Wonder Woman," the server said. "Except less curvy."

"Hey! That's based on me."

"All right, I can put in curves."

"No, no. I like her. I'm joking. Why did you draw a woman? Why not a man? Or both?"

"Maybe I will. This is what came to me first."

"And how does this relate to the new company? Are you proposing we fish our way out of the energy crisis?"

"No, I'm—blending ideas. Thinking of what the guys I used to work with would relate to. It's a graphic novel. About energy and power." The woman with red hair came back and put two coffees in front of them, and he moved them away from the edge of his computer.

"And this character, this—Sybilishera—," Amalia pronounced the name with a slow roll through the syllables. "She's the—the—mascot?"

"Spokesperson. She delivers messages."

Amalia picked up the cream jug from the table and poured it into her coffee, and stirred the darkness with white. "Look," she said.

"What? The swirl?"

"No, the color. It's the exact color of you and me." She extended her arm and held it over the cup. "Our skin color is like this."

"You think if we have children they'll have the same skin color as us?"

"I don't know. Probably. But there are recessive genes, too, they could be darker or lighter. But that's not what I was thinking of."

"Ok, what?"

"What color is Sybili—whatever her name is—what color are you going to render her skin?"

"If I do."

"Meaning?"

"I thought I might keep it in gray tones. And color the river. I don't know. I'm not much of an artist."

"You drew this."

"I drew this because I used to read a lot of comics and mythology when I was younger. It's kind of all in my head. My world."

"When did you do this? Didn't you say you were drawing from me?"

"The hair, and the forehead and cheeks. I kind of did it while you were asleep this morning. The face part."

"Is that creepy?"

"No, it's—kind of beautiful."

"I wasn't drawing you with this in mind. I was waiting for you to wake up, and I grabbed my sketchbook and started doodling. And I doodled you."

"Can I see?" She flipped ahead a few pages. "And this is the final?" She looked at the pencil sketch that matched what they'd looked at on the screen.

"I took a picture of it and emailed it to myself.'

"Clever. I've done that." She turned the notepad on its side.

"What are you doing?"

"Imagining this in different formats. If you turn it on its side, it looks like she's flying into something. Right side up, like she's flying between something."

The server approached with Amalia's meal and held it up. "Italian Sushi for the Italian Wonder Woman." She placed it on the table and Mark put his laptop away.

"Thanks." Amalia smiled. "I'm not Italian, though."

"You're not? I could have sworn."

She shook her head. "Are you?"

"No, why would you think I was?"

"Why would you think I am?"

"I don't know." The woman walked away.

"She was just asking."

"I can't stand it when people assume they know who I am simply by looking at me," she said. "Don't you?"

"No, it's never bothered me." He put the notepad away and sipped his coffee, black. "Do you remember when we met? I mean, when we took the bus to Mildred's and we sat on the side of the road?"

"Yes of course. I was wearing Paige's Pussy Riot t-shirt and pants."

"Those were her pants too?"

"They were indeed."

"You were changing at Paige's house?"

"I stayed over. With Jen."

"With—with Jen?"

"We didn't sleep together if that's what you mean."

"Are you—interested in women?"

"I'm interested in you."

"That doesn't quite answer my question."

"Ok, there are some women I find attractive. But I'm interested in you. I'm more interested in men. Surely you've had a look at a guy every now and then, Mark? Yes?"

"Maybe, yes, but not in a—"

She shook her head. "It's all this pigeonholing. We have to stop pigeonholing people. It's causing too much grief. People are who they are. Regardless of what they look like or who they're interested in." She shook her head. "These assumptions, these polarizations—they drive us—they drive our decisions—they affect too much of how we relate to each other—but they're not helpful. They're not truthful." She pulled her notebook from her bag. "I have my own sketchbook."

"The architect and her tools," he said.

"You have to stop calling me that. I'm not an architect yet."

"You are to me. And, you will be. You and Jen are doing those licensing exams."

"Yes." She began to draw the contours of his cheek and jawline, top of head, neck and shoulders, then shaded with his pencil. "But it's one big exam. One big, fat exam. With lots of parts."

"Sounds painful."

"I hope not," she said, and drew the waist and trousers of the character. "Hey, how did you decide what to draw me wearing in your sketch?"

He smiled. "It's the Pussy Riot t-shirt and pants you wore the day we went to the fracking panel."

"Ah! Cool." She drew the rest of the Mark character and left him barefoot, with a big belt buckle cinching his waist, pants and checkered dress shirt. She handed him the pad.

"Why barefoot?"

"I don't know." Amalia took a mouthful of prosciutto and arugula, then spoke fast with her mouth still full. "No, I do know. Because you feel with your feet; when you walk, when you feel the soil. The ground."

"I like it. May I?" He took out his phone and snapped a picture.

"This is goofy," she said. "I don't think this is how you're supposed to start a company."

He laughed. "I know! It's fun, though. I did make some calls this morning. I called my old professors, brainstormed some ideas with them. We were pretty close. They helped me a lot when—after—," the sentence hung in the air. "And some industry people, too."

"And?"

"I told the industry people I'd be willing to consult on their PR issues. But only if they let me have full reign over the content."

"What did they say?"

"Uh, they laughed at me."

"Oh. I'm sorry Mark."

"No, it's ok. I was being optimistic."

"Now, this is optimistic." She waved her fork at her notebook. "All our doodling."

"This is good. There's a seed here. Something to do with communicating a message to a large number of people, in an entertaining fun way."

"And what's the message?"

"You know, you kind of said it a minute ago. Not pigeonholing. Being open to the conversation, all of its sides."

"And these two characters—"

"That look like you and me—"

"Are open to the conversation."

"Sounds like we need a Mildred in there."

He laughed. "Could be. Did you see her last email? She said the power's sketchy in the Rockaways."

"No, she's there, now? She gets around. What's she doing there, making people run laps?"

"They have enough on their plates without running laps. But you know, some of the Marathoners ran all the boroughs last week to offer support. After the Marathon was canceled from the storm damage. Maybe that's what took her there."

"Jen thinks we should be volunteering there. Or anywhere. But we've been so busy with work. Is that what Mildred's message was about?"

"A pipeline," he said. "Natural gas. There's a proposal to run a gas pipeline through the Rockaways."

"Really? Did you know about it?"

"I'd read about it. But not this effort she's involved with."

"Which is what?"

"To block it."

"Oh. And what do you think?"

"Honestly? It's silly. It's a line extension. It's not a big deal."

"Maybe not to you. But they got hit hard by the hurricane there. Surely they—whoever they is—wouldn't want to put a pipeline in an area of risk, that's hurricane prone? Wouldn't there be a chance of explosion?"

"I agree, it's worth looking at. But I wouldn't start out assuming it's bad."

She nodded. "You know, before I met you I would have. Assumed it's bad."

"And now?"

"And now—it could be bad, or it might not be. I'd have to research it. I'd look for precedents. Like in architecture, we look for precedents."

"I see."

"You know, our heroes could do it. They could fly around looking at ocean edge precedents, in cartoon format."

"Could be good. Keep going."

"I have to finish eating—I have to get back to work. Sorry, I only have a short lunch break today." She ate a few more bites of food. "I should take this with me." She looked around for their server.

"Use this." He pulled a glass container from his bag.

Chapter 66

"I thought some more about it," Amalia said. They'd worked through the afternoon in their separate spaces, and he picked her up after work. "You could have Mildred flying in holding an egg timer or standing on the bridge." She pulled her coat around her against the wind.

"But it wouldn't be Mildred. Somebody else," Mark said.

"Someone fairy godmotherish."

"You know, if you read her messages, you'd see she's not so much of a fairy godmother. She's getting involved with causes for the sake of getting involved—but she's not looking at the science." He pulled out his Metrocard and they walked down the slushy subway station steps.

"Mark. She's passionate. She has an opinion. And she does look at the science. She listens. Better than a lot of other people. She couldn't have got the panel up and running otherwise."

"And we would not have met."

"We'd already met."

"True, but you wouldn't talk to me. And how could I have ever found you again?"

"I don't know, I suppose you could stake out the spots we'd seen each other. I know! You could poster. Put up Sybilishera with a 'have you seen this woman' note."

"I wouldn't have got to this without you, Amalia."

"What, the poster?"

"No, the—whole thing. I'd still be in my job." He pushed through the turnstile to the train platform.

"And now you're working from a café in Manhattan."

"Never would have predicted that a few weeks ago. But good timing." He paused, looked at her, looked away. "I got an email today. There's a class action suit. It's a group with a Pennsylvania address and they said they're representing homeowners, but it seems to be connected with an out-of-state group as well."

"And—does this affect you?"

"I might be asked to testify."

"Oh, Mark. I'm sorry."

"Why? I'd welcome the chance to speak the truth."

"They'd let you?"

"I'd be under oath."

"But aren't there laws to protect companies—patent laws, privacy laws, that sort of thing?"

"They've got the legal team working on it."

"Maybe you should, too, Mark. I mean, ask a lawyer. Before you go spouting truths the company might have protection against sharing."

The train pulled up. "It doesn't seem right. If there's evidence of some wrongdoing, it should be shared."

"Even if you were part of covering it up?"

"I wasn't."

"But you might be seen that way. You were their PR man."

"Recently. I was back of house for a couple of years."

"I still think you should talk to a lawyer. My dad said the patent thing around chemicals and companies is tight."

"Maybe I could talk to him?"

She squeezed through the crowd onto the train to find a strap to hang onto. "He's a chemist, not a lawyer."

"He'd get the issues."

"He's on the research side of things. Not involved with the field. But you could talk to him."

He lowered his head. "Let's can the class action talk on the train."

She nodded. "So what are we going to have for dinner?"

"We'll have to get creative. And figure out what to do with all the boxes."

"Any luck with the shelves?"

"No, I never got to it. I was too busy getting the car out, and then working with Sybilishera," Mark said.

"You know, her name looks like 'Sybil is Hera.'"

"Female oracle as societal warrior." He nodded.

"So that's what you meant it to be? How'd you land there?"

"My parents used to feed us mythology books. And we absorbed all we could from them. I guess it had to come out sometime."

At home over the stove, Amalia stirred the rice pasta in its pot and listened to Latin pop radio waft down the air shaft, the music punctuated by Mark's laughter on his phone in the other room.

"Sybilishera," she said to the boiling water, and added some herbs, chopped basil Mark had found at a market.

"Sybil is Hera." She turned to face the boxes in the room, slotted spoon in hand. Who was Hera? Mark said she was related to Zeus. And who was Sybil? Or was it Sibil? She played with the letters in her mind as she twirled the long noodles on the spoon.

What were they doing? She still had a job. He was doodling around looking for some way to make sense of his work. And were they getting married? Or did they want only to do this big ecological mystery project together? She frowned, and added handfuls of spinach to the pot, stirred. The music outside the air shaft reached a crescendo and she put down the spoon, turned down the heat, and went to open the window.

Chapter 67

Friday, November 9

"Amalia's going to meet us at ten for coffee," Mark said. "She's tied up in a meeting right now." He hugged Mildred hello and greeted her companion Bert with a handshake. Bert filled the door of Moda.

"Working girl," Bert said.

"Woman, Bert, woman. She's a woman." Mildred turned to Mark. "How is she? And how are you?"

"Great, actually. We moved in together."

"You approve? I mean, being a minister and all." He felt himself redden.

"Mark. I hail from the great province of British Columbia where we recognize the sanctity of common law relations as equivalent to marriage."

"Like Amalia." He smiled.

"Amalia was born in Vancouver, was she not? I was born in the States. Georgetown, Maine."

"Daughter of a rum runner, she is," Bert said.

"Now, now, stop telling stories." Mildred swatted him. "My father had to relocate us after Prohibition ended."

"And where are you from, Bert?" Big Beard Bert.

"What she said." He looked around the café. "I thought there was no power in Manhattan." Maybe he was a modern-day rum runner, too. What did they trade?

"South of 39th Street."

"But we're south of 39th Street."

"This area is a tiny anomaly in the power grid," Mark said. "The Fashion Institute, Amalia's new office. My old hotel."

"And this café."

"Yes, this is my new temporary office." He led them to his table and smiled at the redheaded waitress, now on shift. "Have you been staying nearby?"

"We've been in the Rockaways. Rockaway Beach. And staying at JKF Airport. Near the airport. We flew in from Vancouver and got stalled with all there is to help out with down here. I picked up Bert on my journey home during the hurricane. When the Church was closed."

"She didn't exactly pick me up. We knew each other before," he said.

"I chained myself to a tree for Bert," Mildred said. "In the olden days, in Clayoquot Sound."

"I got your email about volunteering out there for Occupy Sandy." And still didn't know what to make of it. He took the three menus from the server when she returned. "Four, please."

"It's a mess," Bert said.

"It's in recovery, Bert," said Mildred. "We met a most remarkable family. Our taxi driver took us to his neighborhood when I insisted."

"They need help?"

"They said it was the seawater," she said. "It mixed with the insulation on the electrical wires and caught fire."

"And set a whole neighborhood on fire," Bert said. "Breezy Point. It's too close to the water. Living too close to the water."

"The old mother wouldn't leave. She said, 'I came from the water, I go back to the water.' Or something like that." Mildred looked wistful at the thought. "They said they lived on the water in Iraq. It was ok until Saddam drained the marshes."

"So they were better with the water? On the water," Mark said.

"They said they knew how to live with it," Bert said. "It was a way of life that met their needs. They lived in one area, they knew it. It supported them. They took care of it."

"What did you do? What can you do?"

"We couldn't find them when we went back," Bert said. "We ended up volunteering for YANA—You Are Not Alone. They were organized."

"What they really need, Mark, is, they need to not have this natural gas pipeline go through," Mildred said. She peered at him and straightened up, her attention now focused on him, mood shifted.

That was the Amalia look. "Uh, I don't know what you want me to do about it," he said.

"I'm not asking you to, but since you mention it—what is happening with your job? Are you here now? Commuting to Philadelphia?"

"I quit." The redheaded waitress came back with a fourth menu.

"Want to wait for the fourth in your party?"

"We'll order now. If you're hungry," Mark said to Mildred and Bert.

"Fine by me," Bert said, and Mildred nodded. Mark couldn't figure them out. They shared little grins and head bobs.

"So you quit? Why?"

Mildred was on the in, and she was impartial, or used to be. He wasn't so sure about this Bert character. He looked like a retired biker hippie gone soft. "There's a court case. But that's not why I quit."

Bert sat forward with a furrowed brow, and Mark sat back. "Intel?"

"Bert. This is not the CIA." Mildred slapped him. "Or FBI. Or whatever."

"CSIS might be interested. We have cross border issues with energy, you know."

Mark laughed and spat out a spray of water. "It's not like that. It's a discrete well casing that leaked on a site in Pennsylvania—no impact to speak of."

"Oh?" Mildred cocked her head to one side. Where in Pennsylvania?"

"Between Philadelphia and Scranton." He told her the name of the place, dismissed it as trivia she'd forget. Seemed to satisfy her.

"What are you doing now, then?"

"Consulting to the industry, actually. I'm working on my marketing now."

"Good, good, very important," Bert said. "I'm self-employed too, you know. Lavender."

"Lavender? Like the flower?"

"Flower, essence, herb, you name it."

"Import, export?"

"Cultivation, sales."

"You should sell here," Mark said. "Do you?"

"Just in BC."

"Oh, you're Canadian too?"

"American actually. But I live there now."

"What took you up there?"

Bert looked around the restaurant. "The war. The war, you know. The Vietnam War."

"Oh. Oh! I see." He nodded. "My grandparents were conscientious objectors. But they didn't have the border issues since they were under treaty rights to go back and forth. My grandma is still in Quebec."

"So you're Canadian, too."

"It's distant. Amalia's more Canadian than I am."

"This is my first time back," Bert said. "Born and raised in Arcata. Arcata, California."

"Didn't they clear you guys?"

"The pardon. Still makes me nervous."

"Amalia should be here soon. I'll order for her."

"You know what she likes?"

"No, she texted me." He held up his phone.

Mildred nodded. "You two are doing well."

Mark went to the counter to order. A moment to think. Who was this Bert guy? Mildred must have picked him up when she was back in Canada during Hurricane Sandy. They had a history. Mark went back to the table. "So you're not going to export to us?"

"Tariffs. Can't do it."

"Lavender tariffs?"

"Cedar industry tariffs. We export resources to you and we get slapped in the face."

"But lavender?"

"It's the principle of the thing. I don't support the exportation of Canadian goods to the US."

"I see. So I guess you don't support the Keystone pipeline then?"

"Mark is a petroleum geologist, Bert. He understands the issues all around." She looked at him. "And you agree Keystone is a bad idea. It's too risky."

Mark frowned. Why did he feel like this was a set up, and where was Amalia? "I don't, actually. It's a legitimate path to North American power independence." That was what he would have said a week ago, when employed by Atlantia Actuaris.

Amalia arrived fifteen minutes later and showered them all with hugs and kisses, spread her joy. He took her bag, held her hand, sat down next to her. He was the luckiest guy in the world. He smiled to himself, and sat back to listen to Amalia's version of their moving-in story.

"—and then we danced around the kitchen to Stevie Wonder, and it popped out."

"And you said yes."

"Pretty much, yes, not right away, but that night."

"I kind of panicked the next day, though," Amalia said.

"Really? I thought you were fine."

"On the frack site? I freaked out."

"You went to a site? To a fracking site?"

"I took Amalia to one of our hydraulic fracturing sites on the way back to my place in Quakertown. The one I told you about."

"And?"

"Mark had a meeting. We drove in and he said to go into the first trailer with Mary the receptionist while he did his thing. So I went into the first trailer and hung out with Mary."

"And what's there to do there while you're waiting?"

"I don't know, drink coffee, use the toilet, that's about it. She's not talkative. I left. And I kind of freaked out and took off."

"The shuttle bus driver drove like hell to catch up to you."

"Thank goodness." She smiled. "I'm sorry. I did panic. Not anymore."

"Because he quit?"

"No. I saw something. Some—I can't really say. I don't know what I saw. Honestly, I don't know what to think anymore."

"About this case? Tough one," Bert said.

"You told them?"

Mark shook his head. "Not much."

"Is there evidence against the company?" Bert's brow furrowed, voice deep.

"I think it's there, actually. In Mary's trailer." Mark wasn't sure how much to say.

"What would it be? This evidence?" Bert peered at Mark.

"Notes from the neighbors. Anecdotal stuff that would get thrown out. Stuff that wouldn't make it to headquarters."

Bert nodded. "Are you implicated? I mean, is that why you quit?"

"Bert." Mildred's tone was sharp.

"I'm not implicated in anything. And it's not why I quit."

"But you did say you might have to testify,' Amalia said.

"I don't know how to testify."

"You should tell them," Mildred said. "Just like that."

"You need to get your hands on those files," Bert said.

"Maybe. I'll bet they've been shredded by now."

"They do that? Isn't that illegal?" Bert laid his palms flat on the table.

"No, I don't think so. It's letters. It's nothing official. Mary likes to stay on top of the recycling."

They finished their coffee and snacks, chatted about Bert's impression of the city. "Neighborly" was his primary take away from the experience so far. "Lots of city birds."

"Pigeons, Bert, they're pigeons."

When they finished, Bert offered to buy another round of sweet treats. "To celebrate your cohabitation," he said.

"There's something else to celebrate," Mark said. He looked at Amalia.

"Yes."

"Oh! She's pregnant!" Bert clapped.

"No. We're engaged."

"You two. How marvelous," said Mildred. She clasped their hands together on the table. "I knew it." She kissed each of them on the cheek. "You are a wonderful couple. Many blessings to you both." She pulled back and covered her mouth with her hands, then clasped them together. "You two are like children to me."

They walked Mildred and Bert back out to their car, parked in a lot a block away. "You staying down here? Or heading back?" Mark held the door open for Mildred.

"I got my permit. My Operating Permit to run the church. It's waiting to be picked up in Binghamton this afternoon. We're going to zip back and get it, drive through Pennsylvania on the way." Mildred pressed into Mark's shoulder and whispered in his ear. "What did you do with my foil package?"

Chapter 68

The horizon ahead was treed with one interruption: a regular, mechanical and unmovable structure that punctuated the view. "A cell phone tree!" Amalia and Mark passed the Cross Bronx Expressway en route to New Hampshire.

"Clear signals all the way," Mark said.

Amalia settled back in, careful not to put her feet up on the dash. Mark needed to be able to sell the car. "Nice of Max to let me off early."

"Does he think you're Jewish? Let you off early on a Friday for Shabbat?"

"Maybe. I don't know. Sephardic? I've been asked before. I'll enjoy Shabbat with you now."

"You want to drive? We could trade." He peeled off on 684 toward Brewster. The leaves were glorious and red on either side of the highway in the four o'clock light.

"Is that a reservoir? On the left. New York City drinking water?"

"I think it comes from down the Croton Aqueduct on the other side," Mark said.

"The drinking water doesn't come from an aquifer?"

"There is an aquifer, below New York City. The Magothy Aquifer. But I don't believe it supplies the water."

"So that reservoir there must be a supply source. I like knowing where it all comes from. How it connects." They passed a *Deer Crossing Next Two Miles* sign. "Watch out, don't want a repeat of the bus incident."

"No, indeed, we do not. But I'm used to it. Driving at twilight with wildlife." They passed a bridge. "*Greenwich, Connecticut*. And now we're back in New York State. That was a little spur. You know this area?"

"Not at all."

"Then you sit back and enjoy the colors." They passed Mount Kisco. "Amazing formations here, check out the striations in the rock."

"It looks like you could eat it—like ice cream layer cake."

"Bit crunchy. Check this out." He opened his palm and flashed it to the open valley view in front of them.

"Oh, wow. What are those pyramids on the hill?"

"IBM? A research center." They drove through the area and out 84 East to Danbury.

"What do you think of eminent domain? As an idea. I've been meaning to ask you. Jen and I were talking about it."

"The government seizing land for a higher cause? Not a fan."

"But for the coastline? Instead of rebuilding?"

"How would they? It's built up with vacation homes from Maine to Florida."

"Not only vacation homes. Living communities. Full time people."

"Never going to happen. Too expensive. Look, if private insurers won't touch it, why should the government? Too much risk."

"There's another approach—a non-governmental approach. You could call it land-based. You know that *ArcNews* magazine you read on the bus back from Mildred's? That's all about an interdisciplinary approach called Geodesign. Geography, geology and urban design, landscape architecture, architecture, all planned together through digital mapping technology like GIS."

"Environmental design. I can get behind that."

"Exactly. It's not only about who owns the land or insures the property—it's about the ecological intent behind the design. It takes a bioregional approach."

She pointed to an exit sign ahead. They parked at Danbury Fair in Connecticut. "I don't mind driving. I don't think there's any deer along such a busy stretch of highway. Can't imagine. And you can enjoy the leaf colors."

"Stop in Brattleboro, Vermont, then. We can switch back there. And there's a bookstore I want to show you."

"Done." No more eminent domain talk, she thought. Needed to let it go, flow more in the direction of this Geodesign, environmental design. She drove them through Connecticut and Massachusetts to Vermont, a smooth and quiet ride.

He was disoriented in Brattleboro. "It was here, I swear."

"When were you last there?"

"With my parents—a few years ago." He looked up the block of the old mill town, busy with fall leaf peeping visitors. "Back in a sec, meet me in that café?"

She went into the café and down the back to the view of the river, and the mountains beyond, red in early evening light. A spectacular spot. Train line below. He'd said the area got hit hard during Hurricane Irene. Rebuilt after the washout, she guessed. She turned when she sensed him come in behind her, and there he was at the counter. "Beautiful here," she said.

"There was a fire. The old Brooks Building burned since I was last here."

"So no bookstore?"

"The guy in the bike shop said the Book Cellar got water damage from the sprinklers."

"Sprinklers save lives, you know."

"They do."

"There will be another bookstore. I promise."

"He said they have another one—Bartleby's Books—it's in Wilmington. I wish we'd stopped on the way over." She tugged him back to the car. Soon they were back on the road and across the river into New Hampshire. Buildings for sale in Hinsdale, a historic town. "I always think of crossing the bridge between Vermont and New Hampshire as coming home. But not just home, like to family roots. But—geologically."

"Like you emerged from here?"

"I've always felt New Hampshire held stable ground for the rest of the Northeast. You know?"

"We could buy land here. Lots of lots for sale. What's with the *Live Free or Die* on the New Hampshire license plates? I don't get it."

"Throwback to the British, I guess. But the spirit lives on, here, and now."

He steered onto 119 past an old community center and town hall in Millstream. "Hydro power here."

"Looks like it hasn't changed in a hundred years," she said, and pointed to the old dam and mill building. "What river is this?"

"Ashuelot."

"Good name."

"There are good names in New Hampshire."

"Abenaki names?"

"Some of them, yes, indeed."

"*Pisgah*," she said, when they passed Pisgah State Park. He turned them onto Route 10 through Winchester.

"Farmland and quarries."

"*Monadnock*," she said. "Another good place name."

"Also a geologic feature." He turned off at the Applebee's in Keane. "I need to take a break. Getting dark, hard on my eyes."

"Your tired, old eyes." She smiled, and then smiled at the thought of being old together. Dinner was quick, and they were back in the car. "You want to pull over for the night? There's a Holiday Inn there," she said.

"I don't think I want to drive all the way to Crawford Notch in the dark," he said. "I don't know what kind of damage they got up here after Hurricane Sandy, but I remember roads were washed out after Hurricane Irene."

"So—stay here?"

"I can do better than this," he said. "I have something special for you."

She dozed through the next counties of New Hampshire, lulled by dinner and a warm car, and opened her eyes in Concord. "*Merrimack River*," she read, the sign illuminated by car headlights. Beyond Concord, open bonfires lit backyard farmland. The glow of yellows overtook the reds of the tree leaves in the evening light. "Laconia, 20 miles. They must not say very much there," she said.

"Why do you say that?"

"They're Laconic. Get it?"

"My dad was from Laconia."

"Oh. Sorry." She looked out the window. "What about your mom?"

"Quebec. East of Montréal. Near Lac-Mégantic," He took Exit 23 East.

"*Winnipesaukee!*"

"We're close."

"To where?"

"To—where I grew up. And we need to watch out for that." He pointed to a *Moose Crossing* sign. The windshield blurred over with rain and Mark switched on the wipers.

She made out a lit sign with moveable letters: "*Guns! Ammo! Knives!*" Her senses stirred at a familiar scent. "Smells like wood smoke here," she said. "Even through the closed windows."

"Smells like home." The power lines on the right side of the road glistened in the wet, dark sky, red from the brake lights of cars ahead. "It'll open up after the taverns." They drove past a Harley Davidson Motorcycles. "We're close, now."

"*POW-MIA Highway*," she read. "*Meredith!* This is pretty. The town of Meredith." It was lit up with Christmas lights, already.

"Center Harbor, then Moultonborough, where I grew up."

"We're going there?"

"Through there to Crawford Notch. But in the morning. I thought we could stay here."

"Where, exactly?"

He turned into the parking lot of the Moultonborough Public Library, a long, low building, white, and lit up on the outside at night.

"We're staying here?"

"No, I wanted you to see it."

"Because of the Quakertown library?"

He nodded, but did not turn off the car ignition. "A bit farther to go. But wait." He opened the glove compartment and pulled out something reflective. "Wear this."

She opened it up—and unfolded two reflective vests, like highway workers wore. "Why?"

"It's hunting season. And the land we're going to isn't posted."

"Mark?"

"Put it on. Trust me." He pulled out of the library parking lot and drove out and off the main road, and the wheels soon hit a gravel road.

"This is where you grew up?" She looked up at the trees, more tall than heavy, and down ahead. "It's very dark. But pretty."

He pulled up in front of an old white farmhouse set back from the dirt road. There was a For Rent sign on the front lawn. "Somebody's mowed the front lawn." He turned off the ignition. "Stay there for a sec, ok?"

"Not moving a muscle unless you tell me it's ok. I don't want to get shot."

"You're not going to get shot." He went to the front door and looked in, tried the door, then disappeared around the back. He didn't return for several minutes, during which time her heart began to beat fast, soothed by the sound of rainfall. "As I suspected," he said when he returned. "Our old couch is still in the living room. Nobody's been here since we moved out."

"This is your first time back? I thought you said you guys were in the White Mountains during Hurricane Irene."

"We were. But we didn't want to come back here. And these are the Ossipees, not the Whites. I'll take you to the Whites tomorrow."

"Ossipees." The sound of the name soothed her.

He came around and opened the door for her. "I know this place like the back of my hand. Lived here more than twenty years."

He took her up a long and brush-covered trail, through the woods. Her feet sank into the mud. "There's old growth forest up here. Used to be, anyway." He turned on a flashlight and shone it behind him, for her.

"You happened to have a flashlight in your bag?"

"Watch your step. Old cellar holes here." He shone the light over the foundations of a long-gone building. They walked in the rain, to a wooden shack. He tried the door. "We never locked it." It opened with a hard push. "Hang on." He struck a match.

"You had matches in there too? You are a boy scout." She crossed her arms against the cold. The cabin was dark and dry; she was happy to have not been mistaken for a deer by a local hunter.

He lit a propane lamp that hung from the center truss of the little cabin and she squinted to let her eyes adjust. A modern woodstove sat in the middle of the space, piped up to the ceiling. The ceiling, open, built of wide wood boards, had an old 1970s style chandelier hung from its peak. Two long and old couches, an antique coffee table. She looked along the edge. "Ew." Two mice, long dead, bodies stuck out of traps.

"You like it?" He stuffed wood into the stove, lit it and stood back from the glow. He took the mouse traps outside. She heard him release them with a snap, and he came back in with the empty traps.

She felt the warmth already. "I like it. I have no idea where we are, but yes, I like it. But to stay here?"

"We can warm up here." He poked the fire. "Sleep on the

couch?" He pulled back an old quilt, mouse-eaten. "We could push the couches together."

"I don't know, Mark." She shouldn't be a princess. "The Holiday Inn looked good." Oh, but she was such a princess.

"All right, how about this. I wanted you to see where I grew up—and we can stay here, warm up. The rain's letting up, we could try to make the drive to Crawford Notch tonight. We're way beyond the Holiday Inn, now."

"Doesn't sound safe. You were concerned about the roads before. It'll be fine. We can stay here."

"Are you sure? Nobody knows about this place. We'll be fine here."

"All right, Mark. I trust you." They moved the couches together, turned off the propane light, and slept by the warmth of the wood stove under the old quilt. Later, the rain stopped. She heard the sound of mice in the fall leaves outside. Still dark out. Then, cries—loon cries? Dog cries? They yapped and interrupted, around the little house. How near? How far?

"Coyotes," Mark said. "It's ok."

Chapter 69

Saturday, November 10

On a country road lined with low stacked stone walls, Mark pulled the car off to the side in front of the figure of a woman, a sculpture in white. "Niobe," he said. "They put her back up." The morning sky shifted out of peach and into blue-gray, uncertain of its weather direction.

"She fell down?"

"Yes—a sculptor lived there. This fell down ages ago." He peered at the plaque below the statue. "From what I remember of my old mythology books, she got around. Lots of children. But grief was part of it too—the loss of her children, her mourning." He started the ignition. "We'll stop in at EM Heath first and get some groceries for the next couple of days."

"I need some shampoo, too. You think they have it there? I mean, at the Highland Center?"

"Yes, but you can always get something and bring it up." They got their groceries and coffees and walked out to the covered wooden walkway around the old shops in Center Harbor. "I want to look into Keepsake Quilting," he said. "For old times' sake. Mom always used to go in." They walked out toward Bayswater Books.

"I forgot my shampoo. Meet you back here?"

Mark went on his own into Keepsake Quilting; a man alone in a woman's world. Not today, it turned out. Several men browsed inside, unaccompanied, and none sat outside on the chairs.

What was he on the lookout for? Fabric to put into a new quilt, to merge with the old one? He walked around the store in a daze, looked but didn't touch, drank in the colors.

He knew what it was. Not fabric. He sought a remembrance.

Chapter 70

She kissed him and went back into the grocery store, found the toiletries aisle. Scanned the shelves, shampoo. Shampoo. There it was. Next to the—pregnancy tests. Aha. She took the shampoo off the shelf, then picked up a pregnancy test and weighed them in her hands. No need. Surely, no need. She put the box back and took the shampoo to the counter, paid, and went out to the walkway.

She saw the quilt store up ahead, couldn't see if it was open yet, but Mark wasn't outside, so he must have gone in. She needed a minute. Pregnancy test? She stopped at Bayswater Books where a woman set up a display outside. "Are you open yet?"

"Yes, please, go on inside. Welcome."

Amalia went in. She needed another minute, and this was a good place for it: mostly new books inside, a warm feel to the place, all packed in. Straight ahead, a shelf of used books. She went to it and pulled the first one her eye landed on: a Maeve Binchy novel. How wonderful it would be to have Maeve to distract her, to take her mind off it all. She waved to the woman outside, paid for the book, and went to meet Mark at the quilting store.

He came out before she came in to find him, with a small plastic bag tied with a cloth ribbon. "I got something. To add to the old section of the quilt we were able to save. Think we could work with it?" He untied the ribbon and pulled out a small, folded piece of cotton fabric. Yellows and blues. It would tie the parts together.

She ran a finger over it. "It's lovely, Mark."

They drove up to Crawford Notch the slow way, the way he'd said they had to go during Hurricane Irene when the roads were washed out. Pretty, leafy, reds and golds. Her mind was elsewhere, and she took out the Maeve Binchy to read while he drove. When he turned off the highway at the Highland Center, she was lost among an Irish love story, recollections of the Irish Hunger Memorial, and the mountains of New Hampshire. Peaks ringed the center and she felt it like a hug. A gentle, geologic hug.

"We're here, Amalia."

She followed him into the new lodge, rustic modern architecture, worth a look in more detail when her head was in it. She leaned on the front desk next to him, fingered the maps held down on the counter. Hikers came in and out and the front desk staff attended to them all.

"Hi, how can I help you folks?"

"Stone," Mark said. "Checking in."

She followed him up to the room, a bunk bed room like he'd said, and they had it to themselves, a family room. "I need to get my head still, can we sit before we hike?"

He steered her out and down the hall into a library with wicker rocking chairs that faced a view of the mountains, and leather recliners on the other side of a big wooden table spread with books and games. He took her to the window. "Saco Lake," he said.

"Saco."

"And Mount Willard is around the corner. Easiest hike for the best view, if you ask me."

"And that's where we're going?"

"Yes. It's where our parents took us when we were little. Before we started on the 4000 footers."

She sat back in the chair and rocked, closed her eyes, thought of Maeve and the loves she created in Ireland. And in her dozy state, she reached for Mark's hand.

"You ok there?"

"I'm enjoying the feeling of being relaxed so much I might have to sit here all day."

He got up to stand at the window. "Willard." He pointed out the window. "It's where we scattered our parents' ashes. At the top."

"So it's like a gravesite hike?"

"No, it's way more—I don't know—expansive. You have to see. The ashes aren't there anymore."

"How do you know?"

"It's ash. It's lightweight. Blows away, composts in."

She frowned.

"What?"

"Are you even allowed to? It sounds like people would breathe it in."

"I don't think so. Not where we scattered them. But you know, we're all breathing the same air people have breathed for millennia. I heard a study on the radio that said we're all breathing particulate of William Shakespeare's air. The air that went in and out of his lungs is the same air that goes in and out of ours. Molecularly speaking, we're made of the same stuff he was."

"You're not helping. You're not making a good case for me getting out of this comfy chair and interacting with the world! I don't want to breathe William Shakespeare and your parents in the same breath while huffing and puffing up a mountain. How high is it?"

"What do you need, coffee? Let's go get coffee." He pulled her up out of the recliner and away from the mountain view, and dragged her downstairs to the lobby. "This might help." They passed the gift shop of the Highland Center and he picked up two cute toy birds, fuzzy like teddy bears, and squeezed them. They each squawked in their own bird-specific tones. "Audubon fundraiser."

"Love it." She picked one up. "Maybe one of these will help." She snuggled one of the birds. "You help me get up Mount Willard?"

"Come on, dining hall's this way." he said. "Let's see if they've got any coffee for you."

They passed the front desk, surrounded on two sides by hikers who sought directions. "It's not the usual hotel crowd." She caught up. "Some of these folks look seriously rugged."

"Some of these folks have come straight off the Appalachian Trail," he said. "Been hiking for months."

She laughed. "I can't imagine any of them would need an Audubon bird to help them get up Mount Willard."

They got coffee. "Let's start easy, shall we? Saco Lake. It's flat and close and beautiful. And I want to see it since it reopened."

"It was closed?"

"From Hurricane Irene." He took her across the highway by hand and they found the entrance to the lake trail, clockwise. "Newer growth."

She hiked behind him and the ground was soft, the new trees close. Around the lake. Past boulders, over logs. Slippery; had to watch her step. Said hello to other hikers, with children.

"You ok? You've been quiet this morning," he said.

She followed him up the trail to Elephant's Head, and met other hikers and some with kids on the trail. She chatted with the parents at the top of the rock while they corralled young children back from the cliff edge. And somehow, she pulled out of the funk. Maybe it was the parents. Or the exercise. Or Saco Lake. Hard to stay stuck in a mood in that place.

They went back for lunch and stood in the lineup for the dining hall. "You know, they have a building tour here. I did it before but you might like it. You can look into the GARN."

"What's the GARN?" She enunciated the long vowel sound while she filled a thick white ceramic cup with coffee.

"Big kiln, basically. Heats the whole complex with wood. All the buildings get heated from the one source. And it's clean burning."

"Wood is clean burning?"

"Not usually, but if you contain the emissions it is." He lifted the lid on the chili and helped himself to a large portion.

"And you want to get up Willard today. And we take the quilt ashes?"

"I should call Tim before we do."

She followed Mark to the tables in the dining hall. The high ceiling and natural light made the room glow, and she relaxed in the room. Families and individual hikers spread out across the wooden tables and chairs, trail maps spread and food consumed. "It's like a big family." They chose a seat next to a couple of young men with scruffy beards. "Hi." The two looked up and went back to their meals.

"Welcome to the Appalachian Mountain Club!" Mark lifted his coffee mug to Amalia's and they toasted.

"I'm liking it so far," she said, and smiled at the two men who contemplated their food. "It's my first time," she said to the one next to her.

He turned, and his blue eyes twinkled. "I'm on my fourth month," he said.

"Wow. Where did you come from?"

"Alabama. Georgia. We skipped the middle. Going to go across to Madison Hut and end at Pinkham."

"You going out in those?" The man pointed to Amalia's light hiking boots. "Get geared up downstairs. They loan out boots."

"It's a good idea," Mark said. "We can go after breakfast. You can borrow lots of other gear, too. Jackets, poles."

"Poles?"

"For hiking."

"Oh." She felt at sea in the new environment. "You know, I did hike a lot in BC. In Canada."

"Oh?" The man next to her nodded. "Cool."

"But we never used poles."

Mark laughed and stood up. "I'm going to step out and call Tim before he goes on shift, ok? I don't want to miss him. You be ok for five minutes?" He smiled, kissed her on the top of her head, and went out the side door to the front of the lodge. She could see him under the deep eaves of the roof, on his phone.

"He's a good guy," the man next to her said. "You been together long?"

"Since—," she stopped. "Since the perfect amount of time."

"Sweet. I'm Jason," he said. "This is my brother Jonny. So where do you and he come from?"

"New York," she said. "More or less. And other places before that."

"We're going back to New York after this trip. We've got work to do." Jonny laughed. "He's a stockbroker."

"Seriously?"

Jason nodded. "I'm taking a few months off."

"I never would have guessed," Amalia said. "And what about you, Jonny?"

"I don't know what I'm doing. I dropped out of law school and hit the hills."

"He's disillusioned."

"Environmental justice is not to be had in this land. And the best way to get it is to take to the hills."

"Or so you think, now," said Jason.

"You're in environmental law?"

"I'm not in any kind of law. They teach you all kinds. But that's what I wanted to do."

"And it wasn't all glory and glee like he thought it was going to be."

Jonny shrugged. "I'm happier in the mountains."

Amalia turned to him. "No." She put a hand on his arm. "Don't. I mean, hike, yes. Do that. But get back in there. The world needs people like you."

"Like me, how so?"

"Who care enough to—hike for four months. And put the

passion for the earth into a law career." She looked up at Mark, on his cell phone, through the window.

"You going to marry him?"

"I think so, yes." She smiled.

"Too bad," Jonny said. He stood up and picked up his tray. "You're a gem." He winked and walked away, which left Jason the stockbroker at the table with Amalia.

"He's fine," said Jason. "He's broken. Broken hearted. His girlfriend left him at the altar, more or less. That's the part he didn't tell you."

"Oh. I'm sorry to hear."

"You're good. With most people he grunts and walks away." He laughed and stood up with his food tray. "We're here one night then we go onto Madison. You going to the huts?"

"I don't know—I'll have to ask Mark. He's the hiking cheerleader here."

Jason laughed. "Have a good hike, wherever you go." He followed the way his brother had gone out, tray in hand, and Mark came back moments later to her alone at the table.

"I had an idea," Mark said. "I ran it by Tim and left Mildred a message."

Chapter 71

Mark watched Amalia run back and forth along the concrete hallway in the basement of the Highland Center, in the new-to-her boots on loan from the L.L. Bean Room. His cell phone buzzed and he ran upstairs for a better connection, took the steps two at a time to the carpeted corridor of the lodge and answered the call when he reached the lounge. "Hey. You got my message?"

"She said yes! She wants to take the slot tomorrow," Tim said.

Mark sat down in one of the armchairs in the lounge after the call and looked left to the Audubon birds and right to the view of the mountains out the window. There would be more quilts. Generations of quilts. The thought made him feel small, like a little bird in a murmuration of birds that shimmered across a very, very large sky.

Chapter 72

Amalia untied the laces of the borrowed hiking boots where she sat on the bench. Mark stood, framed by the door to the equipment room.

"All set. They said yes. Everyone said yes."

"They're getting married tomorrow? It's hard to believe. Mildred's back up at her church?"

He nodded. "I wanted to spend more time up here with you. It's a lot of driving for a short trip."

"It's all good. I have boots. And I have poles." She turned to the AMC staffer. "Am I good?"

"You're good," the woman said.

"Let's hit the hills, then," she said to Mark, and lead the way back up the stairs, to the front of the lodge, and out to the trailhead.

"This was an apple orchard, see?" Mark pointed to the grove of trees to their right, interspersed with brush and saplings.

"Before—was it a farm?"

"I guess so. This was cultivated. And there was an old lodge here too, that burned down."

They walked on the trail from the foot of Mount Willard, and the autumn flame-colored forest closed in around them.

"I'm glad of these," she said, and waved the hiking poles.

"I thought you might be. Can get muddy up here this time of year."

"Not for you though?" Her words were clipped, and she stopped to catch her breath.

"I like my legs."

"I like my legs too," she said. "But I'm thankful for the help."

"You want to take a breather?"

"I'm going to need a lot of them. If this slope is any. Indication. Of what's ahead." She leaned the poles on a tree and unzipped her backpack, took a swig of water. "I need chocolate."

"Already!"

"For me. It's essential," she said, in between sips of water.

"I happen to have some, but let's save it for farther up."

"Oh! You're going to hold out on me. So not fair." She put the water bottle away and pulled herself up the hill by the poles, the wet rocks underfoot. "Beautiful. The trees. The light. The color of the leaves turning."

"Filtered light. Fall leaves."

"Yes."

"We used to come up here every year," he said. "This was like our starter hike before we'd go to the huts and Mount Washington."

"This. Was. Your. Starter."

Part way up, he stopped at Centennial Pool. "Here, we have chocolate." He smiled and broke off a piece, handed it to her.

"Let's get this thing done, shall we?" She swung the pack on to her back, grabbed the hiking poles and strode out of the clearing and back onto the trail, uphill.

By the time they reached the top of Mount Willard, Amalia was tired and exhilarated. She pulled herself up the last few steps to where the soil beneath her feet turned to solid mountaintop rock, dropped her backpack and poles, and pushed forward in the chill air to see the view wrap around and beyond. "Oh my gosh.

We are so high up. I had no idea we'd climbed so high. We were all ensconced in trees. And now this." She opened her arms to the panoramic ring of distant mountaintops around the valley.

Mark smiled and took the plastic bag from his backpack once again and slid the charred quilt fragments out and laid them on the rock. He passed a piece of chocolate to Amalia and took a swig of water before he ate his own. He looked out, and Amalia found the will to stem the flow of her own chatter so that she matched his mood, quiet.

"I came here with you to say goodbye to my old life," he said. "And to welcome my new one." He lifted the quilt fragments up to the air and the wind blew some strands away. Amalia wasn't certain if he was talking to her or to the quilt, to the mountain or to his parents.

He left the quilt under a scrubby pine, pinned down by a loose rock. Most of it had brushed or blown away halfway up the mountain and here at the top. He came back and held hands with Amalia for a moment, but then turned, and headed back down the mountain without comment.

She ran back to the cliff's edge to grab her bag. She shoved her water bottle in, and picked up her poles. She caught up after fifty paces. "Hey. What's the rush?"

"I want to get down in time for happy hour."

"Seriously?"

"They have beer and wine starting at five. In the lounge. We're late."

She took long steps to keep up, her poles to the sides, no help now. "We came all this way to leave quilt ashes and you dragged me up a mountain and now you want to rush back for happy hour?"

He kept on ahead. He appeared to intuit the footfall ratio of boots to rocks, steps to slush. "I'm done."

"With what?" She tried not to slip.

"Done clinging to the past."

Chapter 73

Mark sat down across from Amalia at the metal patio table with a Tuckerman Ravine beer popped open, clinked her glass of red wine. It had been an odd hike, not gone as planned. His grandmother's engagement ring stayed tucked in his jacket pocket, secure for the time being.

He watched her face, soft and bright in the evening light. Her eyes darted from one mountain peak to another, captivated. "I'm going to check in with Tim," he said, and left the table to call. His cell phone flashed with a text message.

I know what you're up to, who you're working with.

It came from an unknown number.

Samantha had said reports were filed by site neighbors. What did that have to do with George's subcontractor concerns? And what did that have to do with this message? He decided to ignore it. To not let it spoil his night. Deleted the strange message, called Tim. Confirmed plans, returned to Amalia.

Chapter 74

Sunday, November 11

Mark drove them out Crawford Notch in the morning, cool and colorful with fall leaves, crisp and even in smell. Veteran's Day, Remembrance Day. "If we push through instead of staying here for lunch, we can go rock climbing in the Gunks." As good a tribute to strength as any, he thought.

"Fine. I'm in your good hands. Don't let me fall."

He drove them down through the Lakes District again, and pulled onto a side road. "I can't come here without this." He turned the car down an access road to the left.

"Bearcamp."

Mark parked the car in the gravel lot in front of a still lake, ringed not by houses but by trees, gold and green and bare. She sat in the passenger seat of the car and watched him strip down to naked, every last bit of clothing on the narrow sand beach. He waded in toward a boulder that protruded from the water, then at thigh-deep, he dove in.

She got out of the car and stood next to his clothes. "You are crazy! What if someone sees?"

"Who's to see? It's great. I've never dunked in November before."

"You must be freezing." She picked up his jeans.

"It's good. Come on in!"

"No way."

He floated on his back and looked up at the high gray cloud. "I saw a sundog here once. Floating on my back like this." Closed his eyes on the image. A silky smooth water bob. Then, way too cold. He flipped over to tread water.

Amalia lifted her arms to the sky in a radiant and reverent pose.

"Are you praying to the sky?"

"It is like a prayer," she said. "It's part of the Sun Salutation—part of that rotation of poses."

"A prayer to the sky?"

"To the sky, the sun, the earth." With the sparkle off the water, that prayer of hers was magnified. "The rotation."

He flipped over and swam then waded back to the shore, kissed her cold and wet, and shook off the water. Wet limbs into dry clothes, and they were back on the road.

Chapter 75

"*Pemigewasset.*" Amalia entertained herself with place names on the drive back. Her cell phone buzzed with a message, but the signal was so spotty that she was not able to retrieve it. They passed *Wind Farm Yes!* and *Wind Farm No!* signs in New Hampshire, an artesian well digging hydrofracturing pickup truck in Vermont. In Massachusetts she slept, and in Connecticut, she was back to place names.

"*Poquonock. Mattatuck.*"

When they got to the Shawangunks in New York, they met up with a local rock climbing group that Mark knew and the instructor gave Amalia a quick lesson. "Put your foot here. Hand over hand here. Land here." She found her way up the slope while the instructor belayed the ropes to hold her taut, safe. She was glad it was not Mark.

"Hey, you know belaying?" She heard them below. "When she does her second pitch, you belay her."

The pull of the rock against her fingers felt impossible, and her arms shook from the force of the counterweight of the rock versus her body. She'd never felt so tiny, not even at the top of Willard. Only her and the rock, and an instructor she trusted, and—Mark. Down below. She lost her focus for a moment and her foot slipped, which sent her several feet and she crashed her right shoulder into the rock. Ow.

"Steady. You're ok," the instructor said. The ropes stayed taut. He knew what he was doing. He'd protected her from a fall. She took a deep breath and looked down. Mark and the instructor were only twenty feet below, but it was twenty feet more than she felt comfortable with.

"Hand over hand. Land there," The instructor said.

Once in Binghamton, Mark ran around to the passenger door and opened it for Amalia, who emerged with her right arm in a makeshift sling.

They followed Mildred to the main sanctuary and all stood in silence at the door. Amalia followed behind, and took in the entire scene. Mildred had set roses up along the sides of the room near the front, and candles, lit. She'd invited witnesses, too. Frankie from the fracking panel, and Bert, Mildred's big guy from BC. So strange, this expansion of family. Amalia felt groggy from the painkiller, but happy—content.

"We'll seat everyone in the front, then we'll start. I invited some guests to fill out the crowd, I hope you don't mind."

"Sweet," Amalia said. She felt butterflies in her stomach at the thought. Kind of wished it was her. But. It wasn't their day. Another day. Another month. Another year?

He seemed to read her mind. "We could too, you know. Too. Today. Together. Be married. Here. By Mildred."

She nodded. Her eyes blurred and she wasn't sure if it was the pain of the fall or a side effect of the medication, but a tear fell and she brushed it away. "Eloping? That's what it would be."

"You hurt yourself?" Mildred reached out a hand, warm. "I can do some Reiki if you like."

"I don't know."

"I have something else." Mildred leaned in. "Just the thing. Just between you and me. It's—," she moved closer and dropped her voice, "pot."

Amalia sat in the front row of the main sanctuary of Mercy Church, her joy at the current celebration a block to any discomfort she felt from the fall. A block—or more like, an eraser.

"We are gathered here today in the presence of our Creator to witness the marriage of Timothy Randolph Stone and Candace Ernesta Pilliwee. Friends, this union is a special one, all the more sacred because we are holding in our circle the potential of the growing family of Timothy and Candace." She paused.

Candace took her vows from the stage next to her. "Tim. I love you with all my heart. You came into my life that day last June and changed me forever. Little did I know that we'd be getting married within the year. I promise I will always listen to you, cherish you and be your best friend."

Tim straightened up and took his paper from the stage next to him. He reached for Candace's hand and held it while his other hand held the paper. His hands shook. "Um." He stifled a cry, and squeezed her hand, then let it go. He wiped a tear.

"I'm sorry. I'm emotional." He looked at Mark. "I wish Mom and Dad were here."

"I know. Me too."

Tim started to cry harder and big tears rolled down his face. Candace gave him a hug. Mark held them both in a big embrace.

"I'm here for you, bro."

They stood like that for a long moment, and Amalia sat on her own. She wiped a tear from her cheek, turned to look at the row of guests Mildred had invited. They looked familiar from the fracking panel discussion; must be church regulars. Not a dry eye in the house.

Mark stepped back and sat back down next to Amalia, held her hand again, and held it tight.

Tim held his vows. "Candace. I love you with all my heart. I love the growing family we are making together. I love your spark and spirit, and I will do everything in my power to let that flourish in our life together." He paused. "I promise to cherish you in sickness and in health, in poorness and wealth. I promise to listen and to honor and to provide, to be your best friend and to give you everything you need and want and more. I am so excited to be starting our new life together as husband and wife." He smiled. "Thank you, Candace."

"Oh!" She pulled him close for a hug, which turned into a kiss. "I love you, too," she said. They were in tears again and Mildred stepped forward.

"Do you have rings to exchange?'

"We do." They each took one out of a pocket and slid them on the other's left ring finger.

Amalia tried to get a closer look. They looked pretty nice, keepers. She wondered if Mark had helped out.

Oh god, they couldn't get married then, they didn't have rings. She looked at Mark who was caught up in the reverie of his little brother's marriage.

"By the power vested in me by the Universal Life Church, I now pronounce you man and wife."

"'Married' is fine, Mildred," Tim said.

"Ok, by the power vested in me by the Universal Life Church, I now pronounce you married. You may kiss—"

Amalia stood at the back of the parking lot and faced the old carriage house behind the church. "What should I do?" She spoke to the trees in front of her. No reply.

"What do you want to do?" Mark's voice came up behind her; she saw his reflection in the glass of the carriage house. "Come back in." She followed him back into the kitchen. Mark flicked on the light and they sat opposite each other at the cafeteria table beneath the flicker of the bare fluorescent light tube. He reached for her free hand.

She held her right forearm in the sling beneath the table, bent at the elbow. It ached, a dull pain. "Mark, don't you find it kind of ironic we're having this conversation here, now? In Mildred's church?" She pulled her left hand back from his and cradled the elbow in the sling.

"It's the kitchen, technically." He reached across the table. "I need to tell you. Something kind of happened with Anwen in Wales. She slept over. But I didn't—we didn't—I couldn't—" His voice trailed off.

"Mark. We weren't together then. It's ok. I got all wrapped up in Nadel, too. I'm sorry about that." She shifted the arm in the sling. "There is something, though. Something came up at work on Friday. Radon."

"Radon? As in the gas?"

She nodded. "What do you think of radon?"

"I don't—I don't have a personal opinion of radon. It's a naturally occurring radioactive gas. Colorless and odorless. Comes out in basements, that sort of thing."

"It's one of the major sources of lung cancer."

"Where are you going with this?"

"You know my grandfather has lung cancer. Mesothelioma."

"I remember you said. How did he—was he a factory worker?"

"No, he worked as an accountant for the railways in India. But his office looked onto an asbestos mining site. He said if they'd had air conditioning he might not have got it—wouldn't have had to keep the windows open."

"That's crazy."

"I know. He's not at all focused on the fact that if he hadn't been working next to an asbestos mine, for Christ's sake, that he wouldn't have got sick. Makes me so mad. He's in India, in Kolkata, in a hospice there. My parents are putting up his costs. My point is, Mark, that his illness came via industry. And the hydrofracturing process used in your natural gas industry releases radon into the air, and that can cause illness too."

"Any ground disruption can do that."

"The work you're doing is having a toxic effect. On a lot of levels. And I felt it when my grandfather got sick and nobody believed me."

"First of all, I'm not hydrofracturing anything myself. I'm consulting to companies that do it, and I'm there to help them get around problems like this. Second of all, I'm sorry about your grandfather, but his mesothelioma has nothing to do with what I'm doing."

"So you acknowledge there are problems. At least we can agree on that?"

"I'm not sure we agree on the nature of the problems," Mark said, "but I'd say, there are areas for improvement with oversight."

"Because..."

"Because industry should be regulated. Any industry. All industries." He squared his shoulders.

"Because people are getting hurt by the industrial process. People, animals, water, land—" The fluorescent light flickered overhead.

"And what's in there?" He pointed up at the light tube. "Those aren't healthy, either."

"No, they're not, but that's not the point."

"I'm sorry, why is that not the point? You're talking about what's toxic in our environment. I'm pointing out something in our immediate vicinity that is, and you're dismissing it. I think you're making my line of work out to be something you can't handle, because you don't want to get married."

"I do want to get married."

"Tell me one reason why."

"Mark. Don't go all harsh on me."

"Really, I want to hear. Why do you want to marry me?"

"Because I love you and I want to be with you."

"I think you want to change me."

"I do not. I want you to open up and see what's happening in the world."

"Amalia. I see. I see plenty well. I see there are billions of people and more emerging, and we have not figured out how to feed and clothe them all, let alone how to deliver clean energy to all of them. I'm working on this. This is my passion. You're talking about undercutting an industry that's in service to billions of people. I don't agree with that. We need to make a plan for the future, not pull the rug out from underneath it."

She frowned. "I don't get where you're going with this."

"I agree, natural gas is complicated. So is oil, so is coal. But solar's expensive to produce, and—"

"It's getting less expensive to produce."

"And it uses some toxic chemicals, too."

"Don't dump on an emerging technology. It's being worked out."

"I could say the same for natural gas. And in fact, why don't I. I'll use your exact words: it's an emerging technology that's being worked out."

"Being worked out at a huge cost, with irreparable damage."

"It's not irreparable."

"Why? Because you take the millennial perspective?"

"Yes."

"That's not good enough for me, Mark! I want our children to have a clean home on this earth. And I'd like to live long enough to see our children's children not have to solve the problems we're creating for them. Mark, this isn't a seven generations thing. It's more like a two generations thing. Our children are going to be going to engineering school to figure out how to clean up after us."

"Maybe not engineering."

"What?"

"They might do something else."

"Whatever. They'll be writing sonatas and concertos expressing their earthly angst over all we've left them."

"What are we talking about, kids?" Mildred popped her head in, a plastic bag in her hands.

"We're out of alignment because he refuses to see his industry is screwing up the environment," Amalia said.

"Not true. Not fair. I see everything you're saying, but without the—the—"

"Now, Mark, Amalia, hang on. There are professional differences and there are personal differences. But surely, this is a factual matter? That statistics could solve?"

"If the statistics were available, we would have a ball," Amalia said, and sat up; her shoulder hurt but she decided to ignore it. "How much drinking water is being used in the hydrofracturing process, in gallons? In the US? In the past year? Projected for the next year? How much water and air is being poisoned by spills or leaks or—and you know all about this: well casing failures?"

"It's not quantifiable. And the natural gas industry isn't to blame."

"See? He's slippery. When you think he's going to agree with you, he gets out of it."

"Amalia. this is your husband-to-be. He's on your side. Maybe see that for a moment. He's not out to get you." Mildred paused. "Let's take a break from this and shift gears. Think about—think about Christmas. How do you see yourselves this Christmas?"

"You're assuming it's an important holiday to us."

"Is it?"

They looked at each other. "Yeah."

"Your first Christmas together. Not so far in the future. One day. It's something we can all visualize."

"I'm not quite ready to let go of the other thing."

"Don't let it go, then. Ask it to wait for a minute. Bring this other thing in next to it. Christmas. A family holiday. How do you see it? This one coming up."

"I'd like to see Tim and Candace, but I suppose we don't have to spend the actual day with them," he said.

"I go to my parents' house. But they went on vacation once while I was away at school."

"So you've had experiences with and without family. And you could consider a new tradition."

"It would be nice to go somewhere. The two of us."

"Before babies. Christmas without children."

"I never had children. I'm not the one to advise you. But I love you both and I want to see you happy, so I'm pushing you to find the good bits between you."

"We love you too, Mildred," he said.

Amalia nodded.

"You have career aspirations," Mildred said. "Listen to each other, write it down. Write down your goals and share them with each other. It's not so polarized as you two see it. It's not about the 'I'm right and you're wrong.' There's a nuance. I know you both see that. The gray in the middle is rich. Lots of tones to explore there. Let the edges go. Stop clinging to your sides. Don't let fear get in the way."

"I'm not afraid."

"I think you are," Mark said.

"Of what?"

"I think you're afraid of not living up to some environmentalist ideal you've set up for yourself. That you'll be letting yourself down if you agree for a moment that—that—natural gas is a viable transition fuel."

"You. It's not. It's not being treated like a transition fuel! It's being treated like an end in itself. Like there's no Plan B for when it all runs out. What are we going to do, go and frack Mars when it runs out here?"

He shook his head. "I. Believe. It is. A transition fuel. I'll write it into the comic. That's the whole point of it. To engage these debates in a more relaxed forum."

"You're writing a comic book?"

"We are."

"You are too?"

"We're kind of doing it together."

Mildred smiled. "So you do have a way out of this. You're drawing your way out."

"Something's happening, but I don't know where it's going, to be honest."

"Maybe it's this place. We're fine when we're not in the crucible."

"Meaning?"

"You remember in high school science class the crucible they set up over the Bunsen burner? Did you do that?"

"I remember somebody fried a spider in it once."

"We're the spider. We've got to climb out of the crucible."

"Crucible or no, I can't pull you two out. But you can agree to help each other find a way out. You've got the brains. You've got the passion. But you—," Mildred said, and pointed at Amalia, "you have got to cool it."

"What? Why me?"

"Because you're the hot head here."

"You can't call her that, you're a minister!"

"You'd be surprised what I can call people. All the more excuse to call it like I see it. It's myself in you that I see. It takes one to know one. And kids. If you're writing a comic, I'd like you to put this in it. Our church membership voted in favor of divestment from fossil fuels. Like you said, Amalia. We're finding other alternative energies to support us—the solar people are installing next week."

"You are? That's wonderful! Mildred's right you know. We need to focus on the good stuff."

Mark shook his head. "Natural gas is a transition fuel. Like I said. This is a perfect example."

"You know I don't think this sling is making me feel any better. Help me take it off?" She rotated both of her shoulders. "I needed to move it."

"I'll do my best to never lead you into getting banged up again. I promise." He held her hands, both of them, and looked her in the eyes. "Amalia Erenwine, will you marry me tonight?"

Her tummy did a flip and the butterflies raced. She returned his gaze, focused. The medicine must have worn off; she had clarity back between her eyes, all through her body.

"I do intend for—us to—have rings. In fact," he pulled out a little box from his pocket, "I have this for you. I meant to give it to you on the top of Mount Willard. It was my mother's."

"What about for you?"

"I have my grandfather's ring." He pulled out another. "Candace has my grandmother's ring. And Tim has my dad's."

"Oh." She ran a finger over the rings, one at a time. "Why didn't you—give it to me on the top of Willard?"

"I thought you would say no."

"That's why you ran down the mountain?"

"Kids," Mildred said. "Amalia had forgotten she was there in the kitchen with them. "Before we do this thing—" Mildred sat down opposite Mark, next to Amalia. She pressed her palms into the flat table and Amalia put her own hands over top.

"Mildred? Are you ok? You're shaking."

Mildred pulled her hands from Amalia's and brought out the plastic bag she'd come in with, and took out three manila file folders.

"Recognize these, Mark?"

"No. Are they yours?"

"No, Mark, they're yours." She pushed them across the table to him. "Don't ask me how they came to be in my bag. But if they help, use them."

He flipped open the first folder and handed the other two to Amalia. She opened the top one of the two in her pile.

"These are medical receipts." She looked up at Mildred. "Are they yours?" She looked down again. "They have a Pennsylvania doctor's office address on them. Not yours?"

"These are handwritten notes from—" He flipped through. "Where did you get this? Did you go door to door? Collecting testimony?"

"You could say I went door to door."

"Have a look at this." He passed his folder to Amalia and pulled the third one back from her, opened it. "Mildred. This is from Atlantia Actuaris."

"It's evidence. Yes it is. Use it if you find it helpful."

He shook his head. "How did you—"

"No matter, no mind."

"I do mind. I can't use documents I procured through some unknown means. Did you subpoena these through the church?"

"Can you do that?" She frowned. "I never thought of that."

"Mark, this is serious evidence if it's true," Amalia said. "The medical testimony seems to go back to the—wait—when did the wells go in?"

"2010."

She looked through. "It's about that time."

"And the symptoms increased last summer." She looked down. "A seven-year-old." She winced. "Mark. You really need to talk to a lawyer."

"No. No lawyers," Mildred said.

"But this is his career on the line, Mildred. Look," she said to Mark. "Unless she tells you how she got these, I wouldn't read a word of it. It's too risky. Mildred. What are you up to?"

"I'd think you would want to read it," Mildred said. "I went through a lot to get you this. It cost me."

"You paid for it?"

"No. I paid no one. I simply paid a visit to Mary in the site office and we had a chat."

"And she handed these over to you? Like that?"

"Not in so many words."

"What did you do?"

"Bert and I took a drive. On our way back up here, before we had to pick up the new permit. I had a map. I went where Mark said the site was. I put your description together with the map. And I knocked on the site trailer door, and she thought I was the cleaning lady, and when security caught Bert wandering around the site, she went out, and I got the files."

"Mildred," Amalia said. She shook her head. "What about Bert?"

"He said he was photographing birds."

"And they bought it?"

"Seemed to."

"Does she know you have them? The files?"

"She will Monday morning when you call the company to tell them you have them in your possession, Mark."

"And why would I do that?"

"Because they were in an easily accessible place where you could have had your own work stashed, and you grabbed them by accident when you left the work site."

"So you want me to lie? I'm looking for the truth."

"Fine. So tell them the truth. Tell them a little old lady came and collected evidence that is rightfully public information."

"Medical bills are private."

"Whatever."

"No, she's right. I could call them and tell them. I could say Mildred got these files—somehow—and I want to return them. I could do the right thing."

"No," Mildred said. "You need to use the information. Not return the information."

"But that would be wrong!"

"Aaah! Youth is wasted on the young!" She stood up.

"We could have a look and make a copy of the information. And then return it tomorrow," Amalia said. "You'd do both. Read and return."

"Like a library book."

"Exactly."

"And what am I supposed to do with this information?"

"I don't know, put it in your comic book." Mildred walked to the door. "I didn't do this for nothing. Make use of it somehow." She went down the hall. "I have something for you too, Amalia."

"Mark. What are we going to do?"

"We're not going to let this throw us off tonight. If we want to be married, then let's be married."

"Yes. I say yes." She smiled wide and the butterflies subsided and rose. She took Mark's hands across the table.

"You don't want to have your parents here?"

"Yours aren't here."

"True, but—"

"We'll have a big party at my parents'. They'll want to invite the cousins. And the neighbors. And Dad's colleagues from the university. Maybe we could even visit my grandfather in Kolkata and have a party in the hospice. That's for them. This is for us."

Mercy Church seemed to expand to fill the second wedding of the day. Frankie pushed play on the CD player, which let out Vivaldi's *The Four Seasons*. It had seemed the best choice of the music available in the office, and Amalia stood tall, linked arms with Bert, and walked up the makeshift aisle of folding chairs, lined with the witnesses, Frankie, Tim and Candace. Amalia rocked back and forth on her feet, found the inner chord that linked her to the earth's core, and to the center of the universe, wherever that was.

Mark stood at the stage next to Mildred, and when she reached them, Bert kissed her on the hand and sat down. She stood opposite Mark. They took each other's hands, and Mildred began.

"We are gathered here today in the presence of the Creator to witness the divine union of Mark Stone and Amalia Erenwine. Do you have middle names?"

"Redd. My mother's maiden name."

"Sengupta."

"All right. Mark Redd Stone and Amalia Sengupta Erenwine. This marriage is a well-forged union, one built on shared insights and a bright connection. We support you in your marriage, Amalia, Mark. Do you have vows you would like to share?"

"I do." Mark squeezed Amalia's hands. "I haven't prepared anything. I'll speak from the heart." He looked at her, his eyes bright. "Amalia. the first time I saw you, you took my breath away. I couldn't think straight. The second time we met, I knew I'd been bitten by love in a way that made my head spin. And the third time we met was on our way up here, to Mildred's. It's here that we let our differences all come out, but it's also here we come together to find a common path together." He paused. "I see us having a full life together with children, and grandchildren. Careers may come and go, but we support each other through it all. We're riding a wave of creative collaboration, and it's one I hope continues through our lives together. I promise to do everything I can to keep that flame between us burning bright." He squeezed her hands again and she took a deep breath in. "I love you, Amalia Erenwine, and I'm so thrilled to be your partner in life." He leaned back on his heels, pulled her toward him and she landed with both palms on his chest.

"It's my turn." She smiled, gave him a little kiss, and stood back, held his hands. She looked out at the room and back at Mark. "It's us. We're eloping. I don't know what to say."

"Say how you feel about him," Mildred said.

"I love you with all my heart, body and soul."

"Say something about your future together," Mildred said.

"I—see us growing a family together. I see us building a house together and growing old in the house, patching the roof when we need, rebuilding the steps before our grandchildren come to visit. I see us looking at a shelf of books we've created, comics, environmental blueprints for living. I see us staying up late over drawings and maps, a candle on the side of the table, cups of tea leaving water marks on our work. I see us—sleeping—lying next to each other, resting, refreshing. I see us growing old together, caring for one another." She looked up at Mildred. "That's what I see."

"Does anyone have anything else to add? Either of you? Any of you?"

Candace called out, "Welcome to the family!"

"Do you have rings to exchange?"

"We do." They each took the other's out of their back pockets and slipped them on; the rings were large and fit with room to spare; needed to be tightened. They held each other's hands, and Mark spun the wedding band around Amalia's finger.

"By the power vested in me by the Universal Life Church, I pronounce you married. You. May. Kiss."

Chapter 76

Monday, November 12

Back in Manhattan's historic Hamilton Heights, the newlyweds toasted their nuptials with morning espresso. "For you, Mrs. Stone," he said, and handed her coffee in one of the red camping mugs.

"Didn't I tell you? I'm keeping my name." She stood at the kitchen counter, had dressed in a hurry for work, hair left loose around her shoulders. Amalia's favorite Norah Jones CD played on her computer.

"Of course you are. Maybe I'll change mine."

"In that case, good morning, Mr. Erenwine."

"Technically, of course, we still have to go to City Hall at lunch."

"And we will. I could bring Jen! She could bring Paige."

"You think—they might get married?"

"Them? No way. Jen's taking it slow. She said so."

"I don't know, Jen's got wedding bells twinkling in her eyes."

"Seriously, Mark?" She swigged the espresso and put her mug in the kitchen sink. "I'm already late for work. What about you, what did you decide?"

"I'm going to call Atlantia Actuaris," Mark said.

"And confront them about the files?" Amalia wrapped herself in her wool jacket and scarf.

He nodded. "I'll do it from here. Don't want that conversation overheard by anyone."

"You want me to stay with you?" She jiggled her apartment keys. "You need these," she said, and tossed them to him.

Mark caught the keys and shook his head. "No. You go. You've got an important day ahead."

"How do you know?"

"My spidey senses tell me."

"All right, Spiderman—I've got to get going so I don't miss my 8:30 meeting." Amalia gave him a quick kiss goodbye and she left.

His wife. He smiled, looked around the apartment. Their apartment. Mark made a second pot of espresso, looked out the air shaft window. Powered on his phone. "*You have something of mine.*" He read the email message aloud from his phone. Anonymous. Could he trace the ID? It seemed more urgent to do so now, now he was married. Marrying. They still had to do the paperwork.

Told himself not to focus on what he didn't want. Needed to focus on what he did want. Deleted the message. Wait—could he undelete? Maybe George could trace it. Unless it was from George, in which case it would do no good.

Mark left on the CD to cover his voice, and called Atlantia. "I have something you might be interested in," he said when he got Simon and Samantha on the phone.

"Old PR notes? We can do without those," Sam said.

"We will need your full cooperation for the trial," Simon said.

"I'm going to plunge into this." He walked through the bedroom and sat on the edge of Great Aunt Joan's old quilt, looked out the window to the tree. "I have evidence the well casing leaks caused water poisoning that may have led to some serious health conditions."

There was silence on the other end of the phone, then Samantha said, "You think this evidence of yours is going to stand up in court somehow?"

"You're going rogue," Simon said. "Get it out of your head."

"You may be interested that this evidence was submitted to Atlantia Actuaris in 2010 and 2012, and was handled by Mary in the field office. It never made it to headquarters."

"No idea what you're talking about," Sam said.

"We can prove there is a relationship between the impact on the local population's health with emissions from our work. We can cite the Jacobson Effect."

"Mark," Simon said. "This is career suicide."

"I'm simply reading information that was dropped in my lap by a well-intentioned friend."

"Mark, whatever you've got there, it's of no interest to us," Sam said.

"It might be. It's from the field office."

"Not likely. Can't imagine why it'd be there on site," Simon said. "What you say Mary had."

"Mary got cut off. Shut out."

"If Mary's guilty of anything, it's of making bad coffee, and that's about the extent of her wrongdoings," Sam said.

"So you deny the existence of these files?"

"Files plural? You have more than one," Simon said. "And how did you happen to come into possession of these files?"

"I told you. A well-intentioned friend."

"Look, Mark, I don't know what they've got you smoking in New York. This is a sob story about some files we know nothing about. I suggest you ditch these supposed pieces of evidence, or you hire your own lawyer to defend you and you take this on your own."

"You're named in the class-action suit," Sam said. "So you're on the hook one way or another. Testify with us or testify on your own, but you will testify."

"Mark," Simon said, "don't do this. We can't do anything for you if you go out on your own."

"I don't know. I'm looking at some serious evidence here."

"It's hearsay. Can't be substantiated, whatever it is. And how do you know it isn't fabricated evidence? Maybe the so-called friend who passed it on is working for the other side."

"We can help you, Mark." A weak pitch from Sam.

"I'm done, I already quit." He stood up at the end of the bed.

"You're still part of this."

"I'm standing up."

"Against the industry."

"No. Guys, I'm standing up for the industry. We're better than this."

Chapter 77

Amalia stared at the email and blinked. Looked twice to be sure. "We got it!" Amalia jumped up. "We got the Pennsylvania job." There was another message from her parents, *Call Home* in the subject heading. She would, later. "We've got to call Betsy."

"She's at a meeting for a new job," Max said.

"Will she be back?"

"This afternoon." He walked over. "Congratulations. I understand you're responsible for bringing it in."

"Will you work with Betsy on it?"

"If she asks me to, I'd be delighted," Max said. "We always look at the big picture together."

When Max left the small office for the restroom, she went next to Jen at her computer. "Mark proposed. I mean, to elope. On the weekend. And we did!"

"Oh my god, you didn't!"

"Lunchtime. We're going to City Hall at lunchtime to get the license, and a civil ceremony tomorrow. Yesterday was for kicks. Come with us?"

"Oh my god. You are insane."

"I need to step out for a minute, got to call my folks. Cover for me?" She grabbed her bag, and when she fished down into it for her phone, her hand ran across the plastic bag Mildred had given her when they'd left. In it was an old t-shirt that said *Greenham Common*, and a torn sheet from a journal of Mildred's. She'd told Amalia to save the reading of it for the right moment. She held it in her hands, and from the hallway she rang her parents and read it while the phone dialed.

Consider the desire, not the need.
Consider the benefit, not the deficit.
Consider the journey, not the outcome.

"He died," her mother said. "In his sleep, in hospice."

"We tried to reach you," her father said. "The nurses were very kind."

"Mark and I—Mark and I were visiting a dear friend." She looked down at the piece of paper from Mildred's old journal. The rest would have to wait.

Mark buzzed her at one and greeted the staff with a wave. "Ready?"

"Yes." Amalia wrapped her scarf around her neck.

"Congratulations, everyone. I got Amalia's message about the project."

"Thank you, Mark. And I gather some congratulations may be in order on your end as well," Jen said. "We've heard whispers."

"She's going to meet us downtown with Paige," Amalia said.

"Since you're here, Mark—," Amalia put her bag down. "This is a copy of what we sent out on Thursday. The proposal." She pulled out the office copy of the theater book. Easier to focus on that.

"This looks great, it's a really amazing range of work you've done." Mark flipped through the book, put his bag down, and perched on a stool. "You know what I really want to see? The environmental center project."

"You are a sucker for punishment, Mark," Jen said. "I'd be pleased to show you." She waved him over. "I've got it here." She sat at a computer and clicked through to open files.

"What are you showing him?" Amalia came over. "The renderings?" Easier to let it go than to hang on.

Mark stood next to Jen and his finger followed her mouse track on the screen. "Call for worldwide ban on fracking. This is what got you in trouble?"

"That, and more." Amalia grabbed her bag. "Let's go."

"Wait." Mark stood fast at Jen's computer screen. "What do you think now?"

"I—still think—there should be less fracking. And more mindful if it happens at all." She steered him away from Jen's computer screen. "I had a weird dream a while ago. I didn't tell you about it because I didn't know what to make of it. It was about aligning the heart with the mathematics of a situation. Didn't make sense."

"And that's how you feel about a ban on fracking?"

"What I realized is—if we perceive natural gas—and fracking—are green, then we'll find evidence to substantiate the belief. But if we perceive, and believe, natural gas and fracking are not green, and they are toxic, then we'll find evidence to support that. It's a mind-game. But if we stop pushing so hard, we might find the path we want out of the woods. Solutions—solutions come when we're not pushing."

"I'm not pushing."

"I know. Do you hear, though? We've all said what we think the problems are. We can't see the answers while we're still focused on the problems."

"We have to do something else."

"Kind of. Refocus, or let our minds rest—"

"Like when we meditated."

"Exactly."

"And then—"

"And then, the answers will arise. If we focus on a new direction, it seems to me we'll get there a lot faster than if we wait until we have to find our way there." She picked up his bag on the way by her desk and pushed him toward the door. "I need to take this man away," she said to Max. "Secret mission." Pushed him out to the elevator. Her hand shook when she pressed the button.

Mark followed. "That was a lot."

Amalia pushed the down button on the elevator call panel. "Come here." She snuggled into his coat, buried her face in his chest. "My grandfather died." She took a breath.

"Oh, Amalia." He ran his fingers through her hair but it irritated her, did not soothe. "What happened?"

"He expired. So the hospice said. In his sleep." She stared at the floor numbers on the elevator panel. "I can't think. I wish I'd known. But he's been with me all day."

"You couldn't have done anything. It was out of your control." He released her from his coat. "I know what you mean. When you say he's been with you."

It was too raw for her to discuss. "What happened this morning?" She stood for balance as the elevator slowed.

"When I called Atlantia? Class action mania. They told me I'm going rogue and they can't help me. I don't know what to think." They reached the lobby and he led her out by the hand. "They denied any knowledge of the files. Said my trusted friend might have fabricated the evidence. It leaves me in an awkward position. I need to do something with it, and I can't."

"That's how I feel about my grandfather. I'm numb—I'm not feeling. It's ok, though. I know. It'll come—sadness, whatever. It'll come."

"I agree." Put a hand on her back, guided her out to the street. "We could give it all to Sibyl and Hera."

"They're twins, now?"

"It's too big a job for one person." She met his pace, step for step. "I thought of who it might be," Amalia said. "Leaving you the messages. When I read Mildred's journal." She pulled it out.

Mark flagged down a cab. "Read it to me on the way downtown?"

Unsigned marriage license in hand, Mark and Amalia walked

out for photographs with a random assortment of other newlyweds.

"I can't believe you cool cats eloped without telling me," Jen said.

"We told you, we invited you. You were there to pick up the license. We have to come back tomorrow to make it official."

"Yesterday," she said. "I meant yesterday."

"That was—impromptu. And not remotely official." Amalia hugged Mark, Jen and Paige all at once with one arm, with the unofficial marriage license in the other.

"Better give me that for safekeeping," Mark said, and took the paper from her. "Don't want our most precious possession flying across the street, now, do we?"

"We'll have to go back to City Hall tomorrow to seal the deal."

"Or we could go back to Mildred."

"Let's call her. Let her know we got the license, at least." Mark dialed from his cell. "Frankie?" Amalia watched Mark's face turn ashen, then he hung up. "That guy is weird. I don't trust him. And I have no idea why he was answering Mildred's phone."

"What did he say?"

"All he said was, 'What are you going to do about it?' To be honest, I'm more concerned about Mildred—she's got him hanging around."

"Call back. Get Mildred on the phone." Amalia sat on the steps of City Hall and took the phone from Mark. "We love you, Mildred." Mark waved to her and motioned that he wanted to make another call, so she gave him her cell while she talked to Mildred.

Chapter 78

Mark dialed Simon from Amalia's cell phone, from memory. Simon wouldn't recognize the number.

"Amalia! How are you?"

What? "How the hell did you know this is my wife's cell phone number?" Mark looked up at Amalia who sat across the steps from him, oblivious and distracted by her conversation with Mildred. The line went dead.

Chapter 79

Amalia returned to the office late after lunch, in a happy and confused state. Mark had confronted her and she'd come clean about a late night message she left for Simon after she'd retrieved her bag, and when in a moment of fuzziness she'd thought she could change him. But that was all, that was it. In the end Mark had agreed it was best left in the past.

The surprise had been what Mildred revealed. The messages—a strange amalgam of anonymous texts, emails and voice mails—had been left for Mark by a very confused and drug-addled Frankie. Mildred apologized, said he'd been the one to connect her to a source of pot once; she'd needed it to soothe her glaucoma. Said she'd meant no harm to come, none at all.

"We got it." These were Betsy's first words when Amalia and Jen walked in.

"I know!" Amalia joined in the dance.

"Where were you both?"

"Getting a marriage license! At City Hall!" Amalia extended her ringed finger for Betsy and Max to see. "I had this yesterday, actually. We had a little ceremony last night. We're going back to City Hall tomorrow for a civil ceremony."

"You two, oh my goodness, I had no idea!" Betsy hugged Jen and Amalia together. "And here I was thinking it was simply your curiosity when you asked about same sex benefits," she said to Jen.

"What? Oh. No. Not me."

"I'm with Mark, Betsy. Not Jen."

"There's a lot to celebrate here," Max said. "New marriage, new project for the office."

"You know, of course," said Betsy, "this theater complex is funded by the natural gas industry." Her words could not have fallen more flat.

"Amalia." Jen spoke with caution in her voice.

Amalia stood up tall. "Betsy. Max." She would say it with clarity this time. She thought for a moment. "Natural gas is a transition fuel. It should not be treated as anything but. We need to offer alternatives in the powering of this building. We may not be able to change the underlying financial structure on our own, but we can be way-showers of technological opportunities."

"It's too early to say," Max said. "We haven't even had a meeting with the engineers yet. We might be able to do it as a cogeneration project and keep the power on site. Reduces the energy loss in transportation. Becomes a more efficient use of fuel."

"I'll work with you on this, Amalia." Betsy said. "I agree it's up to the architecture profession to lead the change. We're the ones specifying the systems. Making recommendations to clients. It's up to us. But we need a bridge."

"And this project is the bridge?"

"I don't know," Max said. "Transitions take a long time."

"They don't have to," Betsy said. "And we don't have a long time, Max. At least, I don't. I'm not willing to put my professional career squarely in one camp without considering how we're getting to the next one. And if you're not willing to accept that, I'll—I'll go out on my own," she said.

"And I'll go with her," Jen said.

"And me." Amalia looked across the office at Max. "You'll see."

At six, the buzzer rang, and Amalia let Mark up to the fifth floor. "For you," he said, and extended a bunch of red and white roses. "Red for us, white for your grandfather."

She smiled, and held the roses up to her forehead, brought him in. "Everyone, my husband Mark."

Max shook hands, and Betsy embraced him with a big hug.

"Hang on a moment, love," she said to him. She put the roses next to her computer. "I just saw an email come in from Mildred. Can you wait while I check it?" Amalia clicked on the email. She read it aloud:

"The Legalization of Marijuana: All Welcome. Mercy Church, Saturday Panel Discussion. P.S. Marriage counseling offered by appointment. All unions welcome. Bring your running shoes."

Acknowledgements

One of my favorite things to do is to thank people for their input and involvement, and for their contribution to the flow of ideas.

I love to write to authors to tell them how much I appreciate their work, and sometimes they write back. I'm always inspired by these interactions, no matter how large or small. To that end, I'd like to thank these brilliant souls for their advice in writing this book: Porter Anderson, Jennifer S. Brown, Meg Waite Clayton, Claire Cook, Elizabeth Gilbert, Stuart Horwitz, Midge Raymond. And even though JK Rowling may not realize it, she was instrumental in helping with kid-care while I wrote my first draft. Thank you all.

On a more tangible level, I send a big round of applause and thanks to all who read and commented and helped in the day-to-day reading, writing, re-writing and reading-again of this book. Readers and commenters included Alison Bain, Derek Breen, Tom Cantillon, Cassandra Chowdhury, Dev Chowdhury, Sheila Chowdhury, Pamela Costanzo, Barb Curtis, Lori Dalvi, Deidre D'Entremont, Rita Desnoyer-Garcia, Jack Donahue, Lara Freidenfelds, Ann Frommer, Anna Ghosh, Sandy Humby (for the alchemy of roses), Devanshi Jackson, Daniel Lindenberger, Mary-Kate Nolan, Gregory Smith, Tracy Spangler, Annette van Der Feltz, Felix Wu. The folks at When Words Count writers' retreat in Vermont took special care of me while I finished the first draft of the manuscript. Many more helped in conversations and I thank you all as well.

Extra applause for my technical professionals who helped publisher ASEI Arts to assemble this product: editor Jillian Magalaner Stone, whose sensitive insights paved the way for a better book—thank you so much; Lori Dalvi, shamanic-graphic-designer extraordinaire—you're always appreciated; Paul Morgan and Finite Visual, Odyssean videographers—thank you for your craft. The wisdom imparted by Katharine Myers and Russell Fernandez in advance of publication was so helpful that I am without adequate words to convey my appreciation.

Super-duper extra applause for my husband Tom and my boys James and Chris. Without you, I would still be standing at the base of Mount Willard, waiting to write this book. Thank you for your ongoing encouragement and love.

—Maia

Bonus from the Author

Maia's Talk for Students of Architecture

March 22, 2017 | Earlier audio version previously shared on blog

Hi, I'm Maia Gilman, an Architect with a Master of Architecture from UBC's School of Architecture. I graduated in 1999. I had my own practice for a number of years (I was a sole practitioner in design for thirteen years and was a sole proprietor in my own architecture firm, Maia Gilman Architect PLLC, for seven of those years), before I decided to go back to corporate. I call it "corporate" compared to smaller scale "lean and mean" working on one's own.

I wrote a book [this book!] because I had a lot to say about a variety of topics and I felt these topics fit together; I thought the way they worked together as themes was unique, and this was something people, especially students of architecture, could learn from. To that end, I am here to tell you what I know and show you how I brought it out through the book.

How did I get to this synthesis, and what can you learn from how I got here?

I was hiking with my family in New Hampshire in 2011. As I was hiking up the mountain I had a very sudden, strong inspiration thought that I should write a love story about hydraulic fracturing. I knew about fracking but I had never written a novel, and certainly not anything that might be considered a love story. I thought, "really? That's a pretty big idea. How on earth am I going to do that?"

I spent about a year researching fracking, making notes about how I could tie this together with a love story, started putting it together with phrases, an outline, expanded the outline into narrative, and then the dialogue came super-fast. A year later I started to write. I pulled the whole thing together into a 300,000-word first draft, more than double the length of this finished novel. I spent another few years carving away at this material, finding the synthesis of the ideas I'd had in this verbal dump of a first draft.

I was fortunate along the way to have smart people help me with reading, tossing ideas back and forth, and crafting a good story. It's been a collaborative process, both with other people and also with the universe, or whatever you want to call that being-open-to-the-flow-of-ideas. I would say meditating was an important part of my process, putting an idea in my mind of what I wanted to achieve before going to sleep; sleeping; waking up and writing down the thoughts immediately upon waking. That was essential to this process. Those are all things I recommend for you as you ponder how to put design-thinking to good use in the world.

How can you bring this focus or synthesis of ideas into your architectural practice, your architectural development, your architectural career, your architectural journey?

The practice needs to be mindful; it doesn't have to be what you would call spiritual, or religious, but it does need to be mindful. That doesn't mean you have to meditate but it does mean you need to get centered, focus on your breathing, and pay attention to when you feel "on" and when you feel "off." If you feel off, don't try to accomplish the work, especially design-thinking-related work.

If you feel off, do one of two things: go outside and pump up your lungs with some good fresh air, or have a nap. I figured that out the hard way, and I'm giving you the easy way. Do those two things. It doesn't matter if you're at your desk and you have a deadline. Take five minutes. It will be worth it: by five minutes, I mean literally five minutes. You can power nap with your head on your desk for five minutes. Let yourself drift into alpha state sleep, wake up, and you're good to go. I highly recommend it.

Once you feel "on" and connected to your work, you need to translate this focus.

It's exactly what Mark is doing in *The Erenwine Agenda* when he is doodling. It's not clear where it will lead, and that's ok. The direction comes out of an expanded sense of connectedness, guided by the compass of your own intentions. It's almost like translating this metaphysical approach to the physical into a design process. You can do it on the computer, you can do it with pen and paper, you can do it with 3D modeling—sculpturally—or 3D modeling on the computer. You need to translate it. you need to get those multidimensions of metaphysical experience into the very tangible and physical building product you are learning to create. Amalia accomplishes it in *The Erenwine Agenda* when she floats through hand-sketching without forethought. You can do it on your own or in a group. If you find yourselves stuck, you probably would do well to step outside of the studio and go for a walk. Let the thoughts generalize before you jump back in.

I think this applies to all creative work, really. You need to translate the flow of energy into your creative product, otherwise you're just sitting there with amorphous ideas and you're not sharing them. That's not helpful to anyone else!

Those are my top tips, and then questions. I can answer questions about these things:

I can answer questions about mindfulness in creative work,

I can answer questions about the creative process of creating this book,

I can answer questions about architecture as a career path,

I can answer questions about being a mom in design professions (in my profession, architecture, specifically), and

I can answer broader questions about ecology and Geodesign.

I am not going to answer questions about fracking because I don't consider myself an expert on fracking, but I can point you to resources that might help.

Anyone who wants to chat after, one on one, feel free. As always I love to follow up on Twitter, Facebook, Instagram—so do send me messages—and thank you so much for having me. I really appreciate it.

Namaste.

—Maia Kumari Gilman, Spring 2017

CPSIA information can be obtained
at www.ICGtesting.com
Printed in the USA
BVOW08s1714291117
501545BV00008B/1128/P